Jane Rogers was born in London in 1952. She read English at New Hall, Cambridge, followed by a postgraduate teaching certificate at Leicester University. She has worked in comprehensive schools, further education, and as Writing Fellow at Northern College and Sheffield Polytechnic. She has paid several extended visits to Australia, where her family now live. Her television play, *Dawn and the Candidate* (Channel 4), was joint winner of the Samuel Beckett Award 1989. She lives in Lancashire with her husband and two children.

# Mr Wroe's Virgins

**JANE ROGERS**

*faber and faber*
LONDON · BOSTON

First published in 1991
by Faber and Faber Limited
3 Queen Square London WC1N 3AU
This paperback edition first published in 1992

Phototypeset by Wilmaset, Birkenhead, Wirral
Printed in Great Britain by
Cox & Wyman Ltd, Reading, Berkshire

A CIP record for this book is
available from the British Library

ISBN 0–571–16528–1

*In memory of my father*

PROFESSOR ANDREW ROGERS

'We have it in our power to begin the world over again. A situation, similar to the present, hath not happened since the days of Noah until now. The birthday of a new world is at hand.'

Tom Paine
*Common Sense*

# MARCH 1830–31

# Leah

'The Lord has instructed me to take of your number, seven virgins for comfort and succour.'

Seven? They say his wife is sickly, but seven? Judith touches my elbow, I know, I am trying not to giggle. It is so quiet, it seems no one breathes in the whole of Sanctuary. I must not laugh. I must not. Will he really? Will they let him? Who?

Once Abigail Whitehead said to me, 'Can you imagine doing it with the Prophet?' We laughed with our heads beneath our quilt work, for fear God might have overheard. He is staring us out, everyone looks down. They are still and reverent; they take it for God's will. When Abigail said it I imagined his strange back, which is like the thick shoulders of a bull. He is the ugliest man I have ever seen, but he is powerful.

Would I? People begin to clear their throats, to glance at one another. My sister Anne is looking at me. She widens her eyes. Me? I smile at her and pull a face. But she is serious; she mouths a word. 'Thomas.' Thomas. When her own child is born, she will have no time for mine. I must remove him. I have promised.

But what is she thinking? To the Prophet's house? Does she think he will take kindly to a virgin with a bastard child? Perhaps she thinks that I could hide him there, keep him secretly. It may be possible. They say the Prophet's house is vast. I watch him now. His eyes continue to move slowly over the congregation, the silence goes on and on. He sees me. I can feel the blush rising up my cheeks. He is looking at me. The congregation shifts and sighs.

3

There are girls they would be glad to give. I know some as eager to be rid of daughters as any farmer his vicious cow on market day.

You can see what he wants, how he stared at my blushing. If I did . . . If I went . . . I would be the prettiest there. They will hardly hand over the marriageable ones.

Is this what Anne means? What if he did not like me? He sits himself down, now, and we are on with the hymn singing. Thank heavens it is not now. There is till this afternoon to decide.

Is he looking? Glance quickly. Yes. He is looking at me again, now all eyes are on their hymn books. If he wanted me, I could make him do anything. Could I live that life? Surely they would not make us pray all the day. We should have fine rooms, and servants at our beck and call. The church has money. 'Comfort and succour.' Pray, how must we comfort him? I cough to save myself from laughing. We would not be prisoners. If it is anything tolerable, then I should be able to bear it. Will Judith? And the Elders and church close by: he could not maltreat us.

If I could win his favour . . . I should be in a fine position. The favour of a man who talks to God, and whom the entire church fall over themselves to obey. But I should like to know what he has done with his wife.

If I stay at home, I make my daily visit to my sister's, to see poor hidden Thomas. I am locked into my room at night and guarded, ever since my father caught me creeping in at dawn. Allowed to walk out only with my saintly insipid cousin, who would faint away at mention of my child (although his thoughts are so fixed upon matters spiritual that I doubt he has any notion of how a child is conceived). What other escape will I ever be offered? The Prophet will never guard seven as closely as my father guards one.

He is *still* looking at me. Has he noticed me before this day? I never thought of him but that once, with Abigail. If I did . . . he would be obliged to agree to Thomas. For his own preservation.

It is as neat as a row of my good plain sewing. The answer to my

4

prayers. That makes me laugh. Judith pats my back, I cannot catch my breath. Hush, I must be calm.

How it would please my father! To so far exceed his neighbours in virtue, as to give the Prophet a *pretty* daughter!

# Joanna

'The Lord has instructed me to take of your number, seven virgins for comfort and succour.'

Praise God. This is the sign the women are not forgot. My heart leaps to his words, as the instrument to the hand of the craftsman.

The joy of that moment will never leave me – nor, I think, will it be easily forgotten by any of those blessed enough to be present. God was indeed among us, He spoke to our hearts, He called us to join His glorious service. The joy within was so overpowering that I could do nothing but fall to my knees and thank Him – a thousand times – for calling His unworthy handmaiden. When I became conscious again of the world around me, I saw that a similar feverish joy had gripped the hearts of many. The sign we have waited for has come – Southcott's call to the women: the time of the women approaches. Ann Taylor was so overwhelmed by holy ecstasy that she fell in a dead trance upon the floor, and their good neighbour Brother Paine assisted her father to carry her out. A hubbub arose in the pews at the back – I could not quite see who was involved, but I do not doubt it was caused by a number of girls who, seeing the general enthusiasm, feared that they might not all find a place among the seven.

And this proved, sadly for many, to be the case. Elder Caleb announced that those who knew themselves called by the Prophet's request should attend a special meeting in Sanctuary at four in the afternoon: and when I entered Sanctuary, ten minutes before the appointed time, I saw that 'many are called, but few are chosen'.

The magnitude of the calling was proving almost too much to

bear for several young women, whose tear-stained faces testified to their tremendous love and hope of selection. One or two were so overwhelmed by the call of the spirit that their bodies were turbulent and agitated, and they had to be clasped and held secure by their loving parents. Brother and Sister Mayall, blest as they are with nine beautiful daughters, held fast to the hands of their elder two, sisters Rachel and Rebekah, while many a solemn tear of happiness and overwrought anticipation trickled down the cheeks of these two.

I felt no fear, for I knew myself chosen – I knew, from the arrow of certainty that pierced my heart as the Prophet spoke. Does a bird know when the dawn will rise? Can a woman tell when her child quickens in the womb? And when he stepped out into the gallery and gazed down upon us, I looked up fearlessly, knowing myself already dedicated heart and soul to this work. The call reached many a heart I might previously have thought unprepared for it – or even, hardened against it. How grossly we are able to under-estimate the faith and courage of our fellow creatures. Little did I think that Elizabeth Ogden, whose honour has been maligned by so many, and whose present girth gives rise to a persistent rumour concerning her chastity, would have so repented as to be eager to devote her future to His service: I praise Him that He calls the sinners and the outcasts. Nor did I guess that Ruth Brierly, who is so beloved by her widowed father that all remark upon it, might feel her heart called by God so that she could contemplate leaving the poor distraught old man, who clung to her in an embrace more like a lover's than a father's, unable to see the workings of God's greater will, for his own small human unhappiness.

The word had spread even outside members of our church, for there were several unfamiliar faces present. When the Prophet stepped into view in the gallery one of them gasped and began to sob. She had not seen him before, she did not perceive the power of the spirit within, but only the poor fleshly covering. It is a grief to consider the desperation of such creatures, who have neither home nor faith to call their own, and must resort to seeking shelter amongst strangers whom they fear. After the choosing I hastened to speak to her, in the hope of bringing her to knowledge of God's love – but she fled at such a speed that she was lost to me.

The Prophet raised his arms for silence. 'The Lord directs me to chose, His ways are closed to our eyes, blessed be the Lord. Let her name be spoken, who is chosen.' He remained still for a moment, then took up his iron staff, and pointed. At me. I knew. Chosen and blessed of the Lord, I knew.

'Joanna Bamford!' the servitor called, and I answered 'Praise the Lord!' Two of the Elders came into the congregation to lead us forth. From my new position on the dais I was able to see quite clearly those blessed women who are to be my sisters. Rachel and Rebekah were chosen, I rejoice to say, and they greeted their fate with a flood of grateful tears. Next came Dinah, the cripple; oh praise Him, for he loves and is merciful to the meek and the lame. Next Leah Robinson, the draper's daughter – and one of the fairest in our church. Next a tall veiled woman, unknown to me; I believe I have seen her father, a farmer, in Sanctuary before today. And lastly beautiful Ann Taylor, who was supported to the front by Brother Paine and his wife, but whose rational faculties gave way utterly under the solemn pressure of the moment, so that she threw herself upon Brother Paine's neck and, as he stepped back in amazement, fell upon the floor in a fit. Screaming, weeping and threshing uncontrollably, the poor girl was helped into the vestry room in inner Sanctuary, and efforts were there made to calm her. The Prophet, having conducted the choice, departed: we were blessed by the priest and asked to return in two hours for a dedication service – so gloriously swift was to be the execution of His will. As we departed the building (with many a pitying glance for those unfortunate creatures who remained unchosen, but who will, I am sure, be given their own ways to serve God) Ann Taylor's screams rang out more piercing and shrill than ever, leading me to fear greatly for her soundness of mind.

My fears were most terribly borne out by events later that evening: for while the rest of us prepared ourselves in white robes and earnest prayer, poor Ann Taylor, in a demented fit, burst out from the care of those who sought to help and protect her in Sanctuary, and flung herself under the wheels of the passing post chaise. I am told she has sustained the most terrible injuries, and lies close to death at her father's house. It is a source of overwhelming grief to all who know her; her good neighbour Paine has sent at his own expense to Stalybridge for Doctor Green, thinking he may be able to make her more comfortable than our own humble apothecary Failsworth.

The service of dedication was delayed by this tragedy, as the Prophet visited her father's house to carry thither God's forgiving love, and to urge fortitude on her grieving father. As we six waited in Sanctuary, Elder Caleb brought us the news that a seventh virgin was chosen, having been offered by her aunt and uncle when Ann's distressed state of mind became evident. And sure enough a seventh white-clad figure joined us, only minutes before the Prophet himself arrived, and the musicians struck up their glorious solemn sound.

Miraculous indeed the holiness of that moment; as the Priest blessed us and each of us in her heart offered up her most secret hopes to God. Joanna Southcott's prophecy will be fulfilled: the women shall play their part, as this material world draws into its final days – we shall play our part, in the establishment of His glorious Kingdom on earth. To this end was I born; to this day has my whole life tended. I rejoice in the hour of my calling, and in the company of my blessed sisters-in-God. After solemn prayers and the blessings of the Elders, we departed in procession for our new home.

# Hannah

My aunt and uncle have given me to a prophet.

Given – handed over – with less heartsearching than they would undergo in parting with a crust to a beggar.

It is a Christian Israelite: I have been once to their meeting place, which they call Sanctuary. The prophet is a small crazed hunchback with the manners of a bear, who foretells the end of the world. The elders of their church resemble tribesmen one might have found wandering the deserts of Palestine three thousand years ago, in full-length robes and hair and beards uncut, bedecked with outlandish jewellery. From the hands of the meanest pair of scavenging crows on earth, I pass into the care of a lunatic band of would-be ancient Jews.

I looked sick enough today for them to agree to leave me here while they went about their religious duties; on their return this evening my aunt comes pushing into my chamber (never doing me the courtesy of a knock) and demands that I come downstairs.

Down in the houseplace stands my uncle, with his back to the cold cheerless chimney, for they never light a fire on a Saturday.

'We have heard the word of God at meeting today, Hannah.' I wait in silence. 'He has called you.'

Me?

'Your aunt and I have worried over you, and prayed over you, and begged God for guidance over your future. We have asked to be shown your place in His great scheme, because a woman of your age with neither husband nor parent in this world is a trouble to herself and others.'

To you. A trouble to you. 'Yes uncle.'

'Today at Sanctuary the prophet showed us the way for you, as

God has spoken to him. The Lord has guided him to ask for the offices of seven virgins, to give him comfort and succour in his work.'

He stops and looks at me. I must try not to be insolent. I know from their expressions, and from my aunt's constant gnawing at her thumbnail through the split in her Sabbath white gloves, that this is serious. But I have no idea what they want. 'You are slow to understand God's will, Hannah. You are one of the chosen. You are one of the seven.'

'Me?'

'Yes, Hannah, you.'

'He does not know me – how could he chose me?'

'My child, beware of insolence. Your understanding of the ways of God is frail. He sees not as we see.'

My aunt chips in, her voice high and nervous. 'We offered you, Hannah. We both saw that it was God's will, and we offered you to serve Him in this way.'

'And the prophet accepted,' buts in my uncle hastily. 'Praise to the Lord.'

My silence makes them irritable.

'You are to live with the prophet, Hannah. To further his work, in accomplishing God's will.' They are both staring at me narrowly; my aunt is rigid with anxiety, neck outstretched, fists clenched against her skirts. This pair have given me to a prophet.

I start to laugh. It comes up in bubbles from the pit of my stomach. My body pops with the unfamiliar pleasure of it, I cannot stop. Through the tears unsettling my sight I see the pair of them inflate like hot-air balloons and slither unevenly across the floor to the right. My aunt whispers to my uncle, 'She will disgrace us.'

I shake my head, trying to breathe normally. I have the hiccups. 'No – no I will not.' I can imagine how their mean hearts leapt in unison at the thought of handing over my mouth to be fed and my body to be clothed. By what other means could they ever hope to be rid of me, an ill-favoured woman, entrusted into their care by my father on his deathbed, and lacking any other kin in this world? Not only will they escape any censure from their fellows, but they are also gaining, through their generous gift to the prophet, credit in their account books in the sky.

When I had conquered my laughter I placated them, agreeing that the prophet's request was indeed God's answer to our prayers. I nearly upset the applecart again by asking, 'Why virgins?' because my uncle answered, 'For purity in God's work,' and my aunt gasped, then began to choke on her own spittle, and had to run for a draught of water. My uncle stepped after her – I could almost see her, standing round the corner beckoning in her stiff awkward way – and then I heard her croak – 'She is not pure! That is why she asked, you fool. What shall we do?'

There was a silence and I moved nearer to the doorway for fear of missing his answer. But it was clear enough when it came. 'Well how is he going to find out?' No reply from my aunt. My uncle laughs. 'There is only one way. I think she is safe enough.'

My aunt coughed, or pretended to. 'For shame!'

My uncle came back into the room, still smirking to himself. 'You may pack your things. The virgins are to be given to the Prophet at Sanctuary, an hour from now. You must wear white; pack the rest in the portmanteau your father left.'

Given. Like a slave. If it is even more disagreeable than this house, surely I will be able to summon the energy and courage to run away.

It is dusk when we leave Sanctuary. Dressed in billowing white, blinded and half-choked by veils which flap against our noses and mouths in the icy wind, we lumber like cows along the rutted lane to the prophet's new mansion. He strides behind us with the proprietorial air of a farmer returning from market. One of the virgins is crippled, with short bowed legs – another has taken her arm and supports her lurching career over the uneven ground. Now the church mumbo-jumbo is over I find myself curious to see these other women. We are ushered into a huge hall and suddenly abandoned; the elders have gone, the prophet has gone, the doors are shut and seven of us stand around a large mahogany table, trapped.

The light is poor, a couple of tapers only burning at each end of the table, and a small smoky fire hissing in the great hearth. The place smells damp and unused. With no chairs to sit on, we all instinctively move in away from the dark walls. In an effort to see better, I throw back my veil. One by one the others follow suit, all except for a tall woman who remains leaning against the wall opposite me. The room is surrounded by a dark gallery at the upper level. It is chilly as the night outside. The cripple is leaning over the table, her white knuckles braced upon it: clearly standing is a greater difficulty to her than walking.

'Sister Dinah! There must be a chair.' The woman who supported her moves hesitantly towards the passage, then disappears into it. She returns almost immediately with a rush-bottomed chair, which Dinah sits upon, and begins to cry – whether with pain or relief I do not know. The chair-fetcher pats her shoulder and looks up at me. 'Welcome,' she says, as if the house is hers. 'I am Joanna. This is Dinah, Leah, Rachel, Rebekah. I think I have seen you in Sanctuary?'

Of course – they all know each other. 'Hannah Lees. Yes, I have been there once.'

She nods. 'Welcome, Sister Hannah. God has found work for us all to do.'

Her voice is as warm and soft as a dove's, and her face, of all of them, the most generous and intelligent. An unworldly woman, not beautiful, but with a saintly face – large, guileless eyes and a high forehead, accentuated by the swept back, pale brown hair above it. Her nose large and flattish, like a negro's, her lips wide.

Leah, beside her, is a different type. Younger, prettier, sharper. She has already appraised each of us, passing over me without concern, checking, testing, comparing. Her eyes are fixed now on the veiled woman against the wall. Leah is the sort of woman who looks at a woman like me and, in her heart, laughs. I have seen Leahs in the streets, in pairs, blooming from their stays like flowers on slender stems, putting their heads together to giggle.

Rachel and Rebekah are both very young, sixteen or seventeen, I should say, dark-haired and shy, holding hands. They are sisters. Dinah, the cripple, has golden hair and an old-young face: she is calm now, and nods to me when I smile at her.

Leah speaks first. 'Who is that?' The woman by the wall.

Joanna says, 'Hello Sister?' but there is no response. Rebekah and Rachel giggle nervously.

'It is not Ruth Brierly.' Leah's voice makes it clear that Ruth Brierly would not be welcome. The tall woman remains quite motionless. 'Who are you? Have you lost your tongue?' Leah moves towards her, following her own sharp question, but there is no reaction.

Joanna shakes her head. 'Sister? You are among friends, in God's own house. I pray you, put back your veil.' No movement.

'Can you not answer when you are spoken to?'

'Leah – ' Joanna's dove-voice is soothing, but Leah is not appeased.

'Answer me!' She lifts her hand to raise the woman's veil, but as she does so the woman ducks, shielding her head with her arms. Leah glances across to Joanna, to confirm a witness: she did not strike her. Joanna comes over to the crouching woman and puts a hand on her shoulder. We can see her stiffen beneath the idiot ruckles of white cloth.

'Do not be afraid. No one here will hurt you, my child. Come.' Something in the gentle tone of that soft voice unthreads me – loosens the tight constriction in my own chest and throat and sets tears swimming in my eyes. Gentleness, kindness: they have been lost for so long. The veiled woman allows Joanna to raise her up, and lift her veil.

We see Martha's face. Blue, purple, yellow; bruised and split like an old fruit that has fallen underfoot at market. No movement, no expression, she never even turns her eyes to look at Joanna – much less the rest of us. The eyes remain blank. An animal, beside itself with fear, might show such a face. Silence – then Joanna's pitying, 'Child, child – '

This time her gentle voice makes me weep in earnest. How could her soft voice remind me of Father's whispering rattle? I do not know if Martha spoke – I think not. We were taken, or sent, to the bedchambers.

# Joanna

The workmen have been at improvements to the Prophet's house
(mansion, indeed, I may call it) round about a year now. Formerly
we set this down to the important role it will play as Southern
Gatehouse, little thinking it would be God's intention to there
house seven of the women also. The greatest joy occurs always
where it is least looked for: praise His mysterious goodness.

Our church has provided great employment for builders and
workmen, since it was revealed to the Prophet that the New
Jerusalem is to be situated in the county of Lancashire, in our own
town of Ashton-under-Lyne. We do all we can to prepare for that
great day. Singular and fortunate are we to be chosen, amongst all
the noble towns and cities of the world. Though it has been
revealed formerly to others that Britain is to be the centre of His
second reign on earth (there are those indeed who argue that the
first Jerusalem was builded here), it is only to our Prophet that the
exact vicinity of the New Jerusalem has been vouchsafed. It is
fitting that it should be Ashton, for here are humble working men
and women – not bloated aristocrats or crafty politicians, but the
lowly – those He has ever chosen for His own. And here are more
of the faithful gathered, Praise Be, than in any other Israelite
centre; even Bradford now lags behind us in numbers attending
Sabbath meetings. Our building projects prosper wonderfully, the
new Sanctuary is complete and all four gatehouses are in the
process of building or extension. Only the construction of the City
Walls between them presents a difficulty: which God of His
goodness will make clear for us, when the time is right. At present
the short-sighted interests of landowners and farmers prevent
them from donating or even selling to us, the narrow strip of their

land which we require. Many are insisting that we purchase entire fields or rows of cottages for which we have no use, simply to get the length needful for building the City Wall. However, debate continues between the Elders concerning the precise construction and dimensions of the Wall; it is as well that work cannot begin before these questions are resolved.

Of the gatehouses, I have previously seen only the Eastern; a fine new building standing at some distance from other dwellings, out along the road to Mossley. To the east it faces open country and the hills; a majestic sight on a morning such as the one of my visit, for the sun arising from behind the hills cast great beams of silver light up between the black hill-top clouds, bringing one in mind of the nearness of His coming, which is already foreshadowed – as was that dawn – by the first beams and darts of light among the cloudy darkness of our lives. Besides dwelling space for Samuel Lees and his family, there is at Eastern Gate a large open hall where a goodly number, sixty or more, can with comfort gather together.

Southgate, the Prophet's house, which I now call my home, lacks a room of these dimensions: but it is as a whole better proportioned. It faces across a meadow and the canal, towards the town. It was originally I think a gentleman's house, but is now so greatly improved in its appearance that one would think it from the outside to be altogether new. The approach along a lane gives one a first sight of the new stone front complete with steps and noble Doric columns.

But I run ahead of myself. On the evening of our arrival, no more than a dark outline against the sky could be seen; and the great housebody where we were left waiting seemed almost forbidding, for there was little light and nothing to sit upon (a difficulty now most happily resolved, for I today procured from Mr Bentink the joiner a half-dozen straight-backed mahogany chairs to the table, and when I tell Sister Evans of his generosity, I hope we may have three more off her brother). The maid, Mary Quance from my Tuesday Bible class, appeared after a time to lead us up to our sleeping quarters: when my sisters in God were comfortably settled I followed Mary back down to the Prophet's study, where she left me to speak with him. He appeared tired and in poor health, and our interview was brief: he gave me charge over the others (which I had already assumed, God's guiding hand in this matter being clear to me) and informed me he must leave before dawn on a preaching mission to the northern towns.

'Are the servants advised as to the running of the house in your absence?' I enquired – for I had no idea of how we must proceed.

'Servants?' he replied in astonishment. 'I keep no servants, Sister Joanna, there is only Mary Quance and my good Samuel in the house besides ourselves. We are people of God, Sister Joanna, not keepers of servants.'

I was much ashamed of my mistaken assumptions, and begged his forgiveness, saying I could not understand how a house of such grandeur could be kept without the help of servants.

'Come, sister, I will take you round. It has not yet *been* kept, for I have not spent above half a dozen nights in it. Mary has swept it out and set the fires for us. Once you and your sisters have settled in, she will return to her mother.'

The Prophet showed me through the main rooms of the house with haste: none save the housebody were lit, and my impressions had to be gleaned by light of the Prophet's lamp. The great empty rooms seemed to yawn before us. I am thankful to say that a few days' experience of the house goes some way to dispelling the disturbing strangeness of that introductory tour, for it then seemed to me like a great cave, or an open mouth, into which I might peer (or indeed fall) but whose furthest confines I might never be able to see. Now I know it to be quite other: spacious but not vast; light and airy rather than dark; welcoming rather than forbidding. How foolish and contrary the impressions we receive when the spirit is overwrought with excitement. Just so dark, fearful and partial is our daytime eyesight now, in comparison with the glorious open vision the commencement of His reign among us shall bring. By daylight I perceive that the workmen have with great skill removed the original front wall and extended the house forwards, thereby ennobling the dimensions of the rooms, and making possible the insertion of modern sash windows.

When we had glanced into each room, the Prophet repeated the necessity of his early departure for Bolton, and handed me the keys.

'I pray that you and your sisters may devote your best energies to the comfortable arrangement and preparation of the house.'

I took the responsibility gladly, and only as I ascended the stairs did I recall the principal practical duty of a housekeeper – that of providing meals. The Prophet was closing his door as I turned back into the corridor, and was rightly impatient of my foolish questions.

'You must arrange it in the morning, Sister Joanna. There may be food in the larders. You must consult with the Elders concerning money for household expenses. I have no money; I carry no money. Good-night sister, God be with you.'

'And with thy spirit.'

He was absent for five days, during which time we laboured to make ready the house, and had the joy of working and conversing together as sisters in God. After prayers on Sunday morning Mary Quance set to work on the fires, and Sister Leah and I made a survey of the kitchens and offices. We found nothing edible there but some jars of preserves and two great cheeses, which were donated to the Prophet this week by a new convert. I despatched Rachel and Rebekah to fetch Elder Tobias, and by noon we had gathered from Sanctuary members the wherewithals to make ourselves a dinner and a supper. We have a goodly quantity of unleavened bread from Sister Benson, but I trust it will not be long before we can bake our own. There is a deep old baking oven but its door is so severely warped that it will not close, and must, I think, be renewed. Nor do we have sufficient fuel to attempt baking, yet; there is no peat or furze, and the stocks of wood and coal will last no more than a week, if this cold spell continues. The kitchen is little changed from earlier days, I fancy; there is a range, with spits in a rack above the fireplace, but no convenient method of heating water, which I had looked for. To be sure, we have a pump just outside in the yard, convenient both to the offices and to the wash-house, so the carrying of water will not be a difficulty.

Sister Leah is quick and apt for housework, seeming to guess at many tasks before I have even thought of them myself: I fear she may become a little impatient, but I had rather proceed in an orderly way than rush into error. Nor can one neglect the fact that three of our number are ill fitted for bustling household duties at present. Poor Sister Dinah can barely hobble about, and yet she is most anxious to assist. She has no skill with the needle, and I am hard put to invent tasks which may be performed sitting down; the dear girl has already peeled near a hundredweight of potatoes.

Sister Martha falls asleep wherever she stops. I have prayed with her but I fear she knows less of God's loving kindness than the squawking hens Brother Taylor brought down for us this afternoon. Tending her physical injuries and calming her fears must be our first aim: today after she had fallen asleep for the third time, broken a chamber pot and a good china serving bowl, besides dropping a basketful of coal across the drawing-room carpet, I told her to go to bed. But I fear she regards it as a punishment, and when I went to their chamber in the afternoon I found both she and Sister Dinah (whom I set to watch with her, pleased at finding a task so well suited to Sister Dinah's abilities) in a wretched state of agitation: Sister Dinah because she desires to play a more useful role, and Sister Martha simply afraid, not knowing what it is not to be working, whimpering and staring like a caged animal.

Sister Hannah is a different case; though educated and rational, she lacks faith. She is grieving for the death of her father, unsustained by such comforts as belong to members of our church; for she seems to regard death as a terrible, final separation, instead of a glorious beginning. She moves about the place in a dream, and lapses into silent immobility at the completion of each task, so that it seems a cruelty to set her to the next duty.

Sisters Rachel and Rebekah are good, helpful girls, and have run about busily. How young and innocent they are! When I led them into the drawing room both stopped in the doorway staring wide-eyed and would come no further.

'What is it?' I asked them.

Sister Rebekah indicated the fireplace. 'Is it the devil's work, Sister Joanna? Must we not keep away?'

I saw she was pointing to the mantelpiece, which is supported on the heads of two carved figures of women, most beautifully executed in white marble. They are clad in a Biblical or classical style, clearly appropriate to a climate warmer than our own. I patted her arm and praised her for her vigilance; indeed, I was at a loss myself for a moment, to think how such things might be permitted in the Lord's house. But were not our own forbears, Adam and Eve, naked and pleasing to God in Paradise?

'There is nothing wrong in the beauty of the naked female form,' I told her, 'nor in the craftsmanship which so exquisitely celebrates it. This house must feature the most skilful work our age affords, for anything less would be an offence to God: did not the wise men bring priceless gifts, of Gold, Frankincense and Myrrh? Only the best, dear Sister Rebekah, is good enough for the Lord.'

Besides the difficulty of reconciling my dear sisters' varying skills and abilities to the multitude of tasks which cry out for performance, if we are to have clothes to our backs and food on the table, there are other pressing concerns I must resolve speedily. The rainwater butt must be cleared out, I fear some bird or small creature has tumbled into it and drowned, for the water is very bad smelling. The joiner must be called back tomorrow or as soon as we may, for the new back door has come right off its hinges, and may topple and injure the first unwary soul who tries to heave it open. I can find no convenient sized tubs for washing, nor can I think who may be approached to donate such a thing. I pray God will ease Sister Dinah's anxieties; she is at me constantly to know what she must do next, and my unworthy brain is then so mithered I can give no useful directions at all. Help and direct us dear Lord; lead us in Thy path.

*

The household tasks begin to be resolved into a kind of order. The Prophet has given me a timetable into which our domestic duties may be slotted. As God established Order from Chaos, at the first; as day follows night, and summer, spring; so we now have order in our little world, making proper time for matters of the spirit and for more mundane cares. Samuel Walker, who accompanies the Prophet at all times, will rouse us soon after five-thirty, by ringing a handbell as he and the Prophet depart for Sanctuary. After ablutions and private prayer, we scatter to various domestic tasks, such as the raking of ashes and laying of fires; bringing in fuel and water; milking the cow and feeding the hens. We assemble again for household prayers and to break our fast, then down to the serious household duties of the day, heating water, washing dishes, emptying slops, making beds, sweeping and dusting, preparation of food and cooking, churning, and so on. We next come together for that interlude of the day which gives me greatest pleasure; hymns and musical practice. From the halting beginning of a few days ago we are already progressing to sweeter harmonies; the voices of Sisters Rachel and Rebekah, which have long been a source of joy in Sanctuary, are heartrendingly lovely in a duet, leading us up out of dull routine and almost into the presence of Him whose gift they are. I am in hope that, with such an example, we may one day coax joyful sound even from dumb Martha.

The larger office, which I have set aside for the sewing room, is by this time well warmed, and so our next task is sitting at our needlework; sewing garments for ourselves, besides household and sacred linens. After dinner we busy ourselves with further domestic tasks, with renewal of household goods and tending the kitchen garden, tending the fires, ordering and storage of foodstuffs, the deliveries of tradesmen (whose accounts I must oversee and settle) and with Sanctuary duties of polishing, trimming and renewal of candles, etcetera. We make a space in the late afternoon for a reading lesson for Sisters Martha, Dinah, Rachel and Rebekah, to be followed by household prayers and singing. Then we prepare and eat our tea, before scattering to the final tasks of the day, bringing in fresh water and seeing to the fires, tending to the cow and hens, cleaning up in the kitchen and washing dishes, washing of smalls, and one of us to be engaged always from seven to eight in the evening with reading to the Prophet. When each one's task is done she may devote herself to private prayer and Bible reading, or to a comfortable seat by the fireside with her needlework, and a share in a light supper.

This pattern for normal days: on the eve of the Sabbath a greater emphasis must be laid on preparation of food, cleaning, and so forth, that no work may be done on the Sabbath. Likewise on the eve and feast of the New Moon each month, and on the other occasional feast days. There must also be a day, maybe two days, set aside with regularity for the laundry of Sanctuary, household and personal linens. At present I fear our stocks are so small we must wash once a week, but as our needlework creates a greater abundance of linen and robes, I aspire to a monthly laundry, which will cause less frequent disruption. We shall bake once a week, on a Thursday, which will remove our sewing time; and I fear there may be many other routine tasks in a household of this size, of which I am yet ignorant. Interruption to our tasks will be occasioned by the Prophet's visitors, who must be received and accommodated. With God's help, however, with God's sustaining grace, we shall find our way to do His will.

Within this framework of order there are no times for contact with our previous lives. We are now dedicated to a new way, joyously renouncing our earthly ties, as do members of the old monastic orders. Sister Leah, however, has a strong and touching affection for her earthly family, and has applied to me for permission to see them. It can never be God's wish to abruptly sever the true ties of filial affection, and so I have permitted her, during the times for domestic duties, to visit them. I have been in some anxiety concerning the others on this subject for though none have expressed a desire to see their family, yet surely they may? I applied to the Prophet, and he has relieved me of this responsibility by stating that if any wish to leave the house on other than household duties, she should apply to him. Leah was, I fear, much vexed by this news, and absented herself from sewing this morning. I shall trust to her own conscience to bring her into obedience with the Prophet's desires, for she is a sweet and sensible girl.

Last night my old aunt was much in my mind, and I thought of the pleasure it would give her to hear about the Prophet (or Yaakov, as he has asked us to call him, after his given name of John) and the new life that I lead. Though I saw her in Sanctuary at Sabbath, it was not possible to exchange words; I shall, God willing, engage to visit her in the coming week.

I thank God that an order has been established, and pray for the strength of mind to keep in step with it. For inspiration and guidance I fix my mind on Mother Southcott, who never failed in her earthly work and duties, though she was called to God's work at all times of the day and night. Once indeed she committed a most grievous sin (which she freely admits, in her writings) which was to be so preoccupied with the completion of a trivial household task (she was about sweeping the floor, and then had to put the potatoes on to boil in time for dinner) that when the Spirit's voice began, and demanded that she set aside her broom and write down His words, she was impatient at His interrupting her earthly routine, and wished Him gone. I pray God I may never come to this: that I may safeguard for ever a quiet corner of my mind to Him. Dear Lord, I know there must be cooks, and sweepers, and maids of all work: but you have promised to call the women to your real work, to be missionaries and preachers, to be instrumental in the commencement of the New Age. I pray that we may not be forgotten.

*

I am ashamed, now, of my presumption. Indeed, I wonder at the source of my discontent, and think it more than likely due to the walnuts I ate the other night – for they have given me a swollen, heavy sensation, with prickling in the hands and feet. When I mentioned it, Sister Rebekah said their mother never eats walnuts, for that same reason.

I have only to look about me, to see opportunities to do His work which are offered by my sisters under this very roof. Sister Hannah is closed, curled like a winter hedgehog, repelling the merest touch of kindness. She does not pray, yet she sits, many a time, an hour together in silence, and I then feel the spirit of the Lord interceding and lifting her sorrows. Likewise He works upon the sad de-natured Martha, and has calmed her, though she is as ignorant of His love as is the dumb beast in the field.

These are your works, Lord: teach me to be content with small gains, for is not the soul of one who repents and turns to you, worth more than a thousand who never fell away? Sister Hannah is your Kingdom to conquer, Sister Martha is yours to be made captive, and I the midwife to their births into the spiritual world.

Hannah has asked me about the history of our church. It gives me pleasure to cast my mind back, for that sweep of memory retrieves many incidents and moments which enhance the value of the present, establishing it in context, like a jewel in a rich setting.

We had no leader of our own in Ashton before Prophet Wroe, but were under the leadership of the Bradford Prophet, George Turner. When Prophet Wroe first came among us he was much distrusted. Some of our number did not readily remember that He prefers the poor, that He will often choose as His mouthpiece the rejected, the humble, the despised: a carpenter's son from Nazareth; illiterate fishermen disciples; a poor farmer's daughter from Devon. How natural then that His mantle should fall upon John Wroe, the crippled woolcomber's son from Bradford. It was when I saw his public baptism in the Medlock that I myself became convinced he was of God.

Many elements combined on that day, to add weight to his claim. I dreamt, the night before, of a small dark creature – a bat, I think, although I could not be sure – which fluttered and seemed to limp in the air across a field until it reached a body of water, into which it fell and, as I thought, drowned. But this dark and disturbing creature (I had been loath to approach or touch it, its quick fluttering motion being curiously repulsive) was transformed, once submerged, into a silvery fish of great size and magnificence, which soared and leapt through the water with beautiful agility. I have no need of an interpreter to tell me that this refers to Prophet Wroe, whose unprepossessing physical appearance, hunched back and dark aspect had led many (including, shamefully, myself) to mistrust him – but that in the spiritual domain, his power and excellence are beyond all doubt. The fish indeed figures Christ, and prefigured also the transforming element of water to be used in that day's baptism.

The day was full of miracles: a hot, glorious September day, on whose clear air the joyful sounds of our musicians in procession carried so clearly that crowds of the poorer sort came out to follow us. Though they were noisy and boisterous – some of the young men, indeed, shamefully under the influence of strong ale, and inclined to offer insults to our women – yet I thank God that they were amused to follow us, for having followed, many found themselves swayed and called by His power. We crossed the Medlock at Oldham Road bridge, and spread down along the bank; some of the crowd following, some remaining on the bridge, and others fighting their way down on the opposite side, among the close-growing stunted oak trees and blackberry brambles. When the Prophet stood up on the back of a cart to speak, some of the poor lost souls on the bridge began an obscene chant, soon taken up by others of their number – the repetition of which drowned out his voice. With perfect dignity, the Prophet descended from the cart and began to wade, fully clothed, into the water. We (may God forgive us for our lack of courage) clustered fearfully together at the water's edge, uncertain if we were to follow him or no, and dreadfully afraid of the jeering mob. When he was in waist deep, the Prophet stopped and, facing the crowd, raised his arms above his head. There was a sudden increase in the clamour on the bridge, and a number of missiles flew through the air and splashed into the water around him. He did not flinch, though one fell close enough to make a splash right in his face. His immobility seemed to enrage them and then the air was thick with flying objects – pebbles, sticks, bottles – some even flung their clogs, and others joined together to heave rocks towards his head. He was soaked by the gigantic splashing on all sides but, by God's divine protection, not one of these objects so much as grazed his body. The hail ceased as suddenly as it had increased – all eager, no doubt, to see how they had hurt him – and in the silence his voice rang out.

'I praise my Maker for His protecting love. He offers you forgiveness, and the same protection from spite and danger, by the washing away of sins in this pure water. Come down and join His flock.'

Truly they were astonished by his courage, and by the miraculous protection God had provided him from their clumsy onslaught. I have heard cynics, talking of that day, say that Mr Wroe would not have had so many willing to be baptized, had not the heat of the sun and the choking dust of the crowded road driven them to seek refreshment in the water: but are not the sunshine and the dust also of God's making, do not His great designs and purposes run through all things? Within minutes the river was swarming with people. Many, in the rashness of their enthusiasm, jumped from the bridge, and I thank God none were seriously hurt. Three of our Elders waded out to assist the Prophet, and with their help he baptized and blessed one after another steadily for upwards of an hour. Elder Caleb counted one hundred and eighty-seven baptized that day, and if that is not a miracle, what can be? It was difficult, from the seething mass of bodies in the water, from the pushing and the calling, the jubilant splashing of excitable youngsters, and the rejoicing of the newly baptized, to see clearly what was happening: but God steeled my courage, and arm in arm with Ann Taylor I waded out into the water and at length found the Prophet, and received his blessing along with a good ducking in the Medlock water. I am grateful to God not only for the spiritual forgiveness and regeneration of that holy moment – a still, close moment with God, even amongst the shouting and splashing of hundreds – but also for His practical goodness in protecting us all on that day from the ill effects of the river water. For on many an occasion before and since I have seen the water run black or cloudy with waste stuffs from the mills, and glimpsed the bloated bellies of poisoned fish floating downstream in shoals. None who entered the water that day felt any other than its symbolic effects, of cleansing and purity: this again I count a miracle.

From that day on the Prophet's power increased among us: his courage and dignity are truly of God – and if any should have doubted and desired further proof, the veracity of a number of his prophecies must have provided it. His prophecies have ranged over matters great and small, and in all cases they have been accurate, either materially or spiritually. He has predicted sickness (of the Malloy family; of Reverend Beecher; of Sarah Vaughn's child), death (of Mrs Baker, Elder Joshua, the younger children of the Andrews) and recovery from sickness (of too many to name, who have joined the church as a result of his intercession with God). His foreknowledge of the weather is legendary with our farming people: he foretold the late snows last May, the high winds of the previous autumn, the perpetual wetness of the preceding spring. They come to him now for advice on when to cut their hay, when to let the sheep out on to the hills at winter's end – when best to sow, when to reap – a thousand pieces of invaluable advice are made available to them by him. He can tell the best day for a wedding or a baptism. In politics, he foretells the violent demonstrations and strikes of the machine breakers – and their suppression by masters and soldiery (the failure of the Bradford woolcombers' strike being the most recently fulfilled prophecy of this sort). He foretells also the up and down turns in the fortunes of our church, announcing *before* John Stanley made the offer to finance the new Sanctuary building (completed at a cost of £9,500) that a great gift would come to the church – and predicting at the present time a calamity and period of darkness for our church, which may arrive at the end of this year. His foresight helps us to understand God's patterns, the trials and tests of faith He must lay out for us, to prove us true.

He has also foretold great changes in the world about us; the coming of the railways being the greatest instance of this kind. Before we knew or had thought of such a thing, he described to us a great machine, smoking and creating a noise as infernal as those smoky depths from which it seemed to come; roaring on its iron way through peaceful meadows and green fields, moving at unnatural speed. He has likewise foretold the advent of a flying machine, by which men will be empowered to soar in the air like birds, and gaze down upon the tiny landscape beneath. These types of inventions I see as the last perverted and unnatural spawnings of the degenerate human imagination, before that day when His power and radiance shall obliterate all such dark shadows, and the brightness of His light shall reveal them for the toys, the nothings, that they are.

# Leah

Five days, we have been here. It feels like five weeks. The Prophet is absent and none seems to know when he will return.

As to servants; *we* are the servants! I might have expected that we must sew and cook; but to clean out fires and empty slops? To scrub floors? This must be merely temporary, until the household is properly established.

My sisters in God, as I am told to call them, set to without complaint, organized by saintly Sister Joanna. It is no surprise that she is chosen, she has been mother-henning it around the church so long now. None of them are beauties, and one – one is unspeakable.

Martha. I cannot believe that such a creature walks. It is a wild, stinking, blundering animal let loose amongst us. What has he got her for? Dinah (who has the misfortune to share her chamber) tells me she has a circle of sores around her neck, as from a chain. It is not hard to believe that whoever kept her before, kept her like a dog. Those small hill farmers live beyond any type of Christian civilization. I believe she has never seen soap or water in her life. At table the sounds of her troughing (I do not look, but the sound one cannot avoid) make my food lie queasy to my stomach. Such refinements as spoon and fork are quite unknown; food is conveyed to her mouth by the fistful. Nor does she possess the slightest notion of modesty; you may find her scratching or picking at any part of her anatomy without shame. They tumble in all together up there in the hills, brother and sister, father and daughter. She's no more virgin nor I am; that big sow's body has rutted and farrowed with the rest of the stock.

Saint Joanna hovers about her, lavishing patience and kindliness upon her, which effort is as much noticed by Martha as is the weather by a stone. The woman is half an idiot, there is nothing in her eyes. She is even too stupid to sit, unless you tell her; twice in daylight I have come across her slumped against the wall, mouth hanging open, snoring. Yesterday afternoon she came in to me where I sat sewing in the drawing room, bearing a great filthy sack over her shoulder. When I ask her what she wants she simply stares, too pig-ignorant to reply. When I question her as to the contents of the sack, she must put the filthy thing down on the carpet and peer into it.

'Take it out of here!' I shout at her. 'Look at the dirt on the carpet.' She hoists the sack – containing, I reckon, near a hundredweight of potatoes, and takes it off. A good while later, when I took the kettle to fill at the pump, I passed her standing outside the kitchen door, the sack still over her shoulder. Well, thought I, if she's too stupid to set down such a weight, let her bear it. But Saint Joanna came out, and bade her take it to the outer office. I dare say she has no other notion of potatoes than rooting them out of the earth raw with her snout, after the Irish fashion. It is an offence to the eye and the stomach, to be stalled with such a creature.

The others – save one – I know, Rachel and Rebekah Mayall, Dinah Clays the cripple. There is a small thin pasty woman from London, Hannah Lees, who barely answers when you question her. She is not of the church, for she knows none of the words to our hymns or prayers. Rachel and Rebekah may be allowed to be pretty; they have the advantage of youth, that first bloom and freshness. But anyone who has seen their mother can already see the shadow of that grossness attaching to them. I imagine the way that soft dimpling flesh will swell and bloat with passing time; as dough, left overnight by the fire, rises to near double its puffy size. They may be good for a year or two, those girls. No more.

Poor Joanna drips with saintliness, I wonder why such a woman should have a body, whose intention is to go around being the abnegation of the flesh. Her unworldliness is like a smell to warn you off.

This is what I desired, for there is certainly no competition – but I little thought I should be left alone with such companions for days on end. If only he had chosen Judith, we might at least have laughed together.

At first I was excited. Saint Joanna asked me to unpack and store the china and glasses. In the dining room there are stacks of chairs, still tied together as the carrier brought them, and boxes of Sheffield cutlery, and crates of new china. As I pulled it from its woodshavings and polished it, and stowed it away upon the shelves of the fine oak sideboard, I imagined the dining room with white damask on the table, and glasses and silverware glinting in the brilliant light of the silver candelabra. I imagined the kind of society I should meet in this room – church leaders and gentry. There is money in all this, more than I thought before. Sanctuary itself was built out of donations only two years ago; and how much more have the renovations to this house cost? Never mind the furnishings, which are all new and of the highest quality?

My daydreams are disturbed, though, when I look soberly at the other six women. They have hardly been selected to form part of a glittering social circle.

It is not difficult to get out – in that at least I was right. Saint Joanna is already so grateful for my presence (since I am more skilled and competent about the house than the other five put together) that she agrees gladly to my little expeditions 'to take clean altar-cloths to Sanctuary' or 'to collect two dozen eggs promised us of Sister Benson when I met her at the haberdashers', or even, 'to visit my parents', and does not comment on how long I am gone. So I have seen my little Thomas every day, and had an hour's chatter with Anne to keep me sane. She points out to me the wisdom of the Prophet's absenting himself at first. His apparent lack of interest in us must help to dispel those rumours about 'comfort and succour' which have arisen among the less holy members of the church (we giggled at this, till Anne's husband George called out from the workshop to know the joke).

It is true. I just hope he is not absent for too long.

Our diet of housework has given me opportunity to search the house for a suitable hiding place for my little darling – and here I have not drawn a complete blank. There are four large bed-chambers in use: one set aside for the Prophet, one shared by Rachel, Rebekah and myself, one by Joanna and Hannah, and one by Martha and Dinah. In addition, upstairs there is a dressing room adjoining the Prophet's room, a tiny servant's bedroom where one end of the corridor has been blocked off between the Prophet's room and the great hall balcony, and a large room at the back of the house which is full of old furniture. This was left in the house before the building alterations. Joanna thinks it likely the room will be fitted out for visitors, at some future date. It is the ideal place to hide Thomas, for his bed and other items would not be noticeable amongst all the other jumble.

But there are difficulties, which I had not well perceived until now. If Thomas is hidden in this room, how am I to hear him if he cries at night? The walls are thick, and the space of a corridor divides us. It is unthinkable to closet him away out of earshot – and yet to bring him within, I must confide in Rachel and Rebekah at the least.

This may be possible. They are young and biddable, and too scared almost to speak. Then my mind runs on all the complicated business of warming his feeds, the tell-tale diapers, washing and drying his clothes, keeping him silent: all possible, but requiring extreme caution, to succeed for any length of time. My first strategy must be to interest the Prophet in myself; to ease my way into his affections. He cannot be away for long, surely – natural curiosity, and whatever plans he has for us, must draw him back.

*

He is here. Suddenly there is a presence, a purpose, a centre to the house. Even though he has spent the day hidden away in his study, we are all quite conscious of him. Saint Joanna is most anxious and unsettled; at our hymn singing this morning she four times stopped us before we were properly started on the tune, and found fault with every sound we made. We are at work sewing dresses for ourselves, to the customary hideous Israelite pattern; all save dirty Martha, who is found work outside, clearing out the stable which will house the cow presented us by Farmer Benson.

As we sewed this afternoon I felt quite certain he would come in and address us; therefore I did not make my expedition to Anne's, but only slipped upstairs for two minutes to beautify my eyes with the addition of a drop of belladonna. The consequence of this was that I have had great difficulty in seeing my stitching or threading my needle this afternoon, and have given myself a headache from the effort. He has still spoken to none save Saint Joanna. Now he is here, my impatience for things to start – for this new life to properly begin – makes it almost impossible for me to sit calm and still. Early this evening he met with the Elders in the great hall, but again only Saint Joanna was requested to take them refreshments. I passed along the gallery twice, lingeringly, in the course of my duties sweeping the bedrooms; but not one of them looked up.

At supper, to my joy, Saint Joanna requested a reader. He will have one of us to read his Bible to him, every evening. I was quick to offer, and, after taking the time to tease a few curls down out of my cap, and to bite some redness into my lips, knocked on his door and entered.

The room is very bare, in strange contrast to the luxury of dining and drawing rooms. Aside from the small fire, it is lit by a single candle at either end of the long table. He sat at one end, an open Bible lay at the other. He nodded to me and indicated that I should sit before the Bible; naming chapter and verse, he then buried his head in his hands, so that I could see no more of him than the round black top of his hat. I began to read, contriving to glance at him from time to time, but he made no movement or response. I must have been reading for thirty minutes or more, and wondering whether he was asleep, when he suddenly said, 'Thank you, sister.' I stopped, but he did not look up. I sat quietly waiting to see what he would do next. His room is draughty, and the fire scarcely warms the far end, where I sat; I was shivering, in part from the cold, partly from nervousness. At last he raised his head.

'Are you still there, Sister Leah? I thank you. You may go. God bless you.' I was outside the door before I could think of any more reply than, 'Thank you sir.'

My dissatisfaction at this incident was heightened by the round-eyed timid questioning of Rachel and Rebekah, when I regained my room.

'Did the Prophet speak to you?'

'What must we do?'

'Shall we be asked to read? Only, we are very poor at it. I am sure we should be too frightened, and stumble. Did you stumble?'

He took no more notice of me than a chair.

He was absent all the following morning: it is not easy to discover where he goes. The churlish Samuel Walker accompanies him much of the time; the most sullen, ugly fellow you could hope to meet. It is he, so they say, who writes down the word of God, when it is spoken to the Prophet in the early morning. To be handy for this purpose he sleeps in the Prophet's dressing room. By day, if the Prophet is in, Samuel sits in the great hall by the outer door, keeping an eye on all who enter or leave, and stubbornly reading his Bible. He affects not to hear when one speaks to him, and appears to hold all women in the greatest contempt and loathing. Rachel and Rebekah are more terrified of him than of the Prophet himself, and will not cross the great hall when he is there alone.

In the afternoon, the Prophet was closeted in his room again, this time with Samuel; writing letters, Saint Joanna said. My offer to do the evening reading was refused by Saint Joanna, who said we must take all duties in turns, and selected Hannah. He does not eat with us: he does not even join in household prayers. As I helped her clear the dishes I asked Saint Joanna whether she did not think this odd.

'Nothing is odd, Sister Leah, though there may be much we do not understand. The Prophet has a great mission: he works to God's word. The niceties of common, everyday behaviour are not to be expected, nor must we women fall into the sin of thinking ourselves important, in this household. To be sure, it is important that we do our work, that we pray and meditate upon God's holy word, and that we use every opportunity the day offers to do Him service: but remember we are in His hands. We are outside the normal daily running of things now, we have entered His sacred household. Be prepared, Sister Leah, be ready to answer His call at any time, and do not confuse yourself with mundane expectations.'

When Hannah was returned from his room, Saint Joanna insisted upon reading to all six of us, and made us gather our chairs around the fire in the kitchen. I grant her voice is pleasant, but she reads so slowly; the solemn endless dripping of words is more gloomy than steady rainfall. Martha was instantly asleep; the others appearing to listen. Once Saint Joanna stopped and laid her hand upon my leg. 'Sister Leah, peace. Open your heart to His words and let His peace flow in.' I could not think what she was about until she paused again a little later, and again glanced at my leg, which was jerking back and forth with a quick short motion. It did not make a sound, my foot was not tapping against anything. I cannot tell why she should fuss over it. If I must hold stone still I shall burst. I have not been to see Thomas these two days, for fear of missing an opportunity with the Prophet.

'Let His peace flow in.' Peace. Peace. Pieces. Fragments, shards surround us. If she sees peace it is due to the deficiency of her own perceptions. She is blind and deaf to all, if she knows peace.

When we were at last dismissed to bed, I knew I should not sleep, and determined to slip out, once all was quiet, to visit Thomas. Anne and George will be asleep, but I can persuade her out of crossness, if I take a portion of that big cheese in the pantry – and since I had the putting away of it tonight, I am sure no one else knows how little of it is eaten. Rachel and Rebekah undress and prepare so solemnly for the night, I long to tease them. As they were undressing tonight, I said, 'Have you no young men to pine for?'

They shook their heads, watching me with big round eyes.

'None? No secret admirers? What do you think to Samuel Wrigley, who sits in the pew behind ours?' Their sheep eyes stare. 'Do you not think his leg is fine? And his dark blue eyes?'

Sometimes they giggle, but it seems they must look at one another and silently agree to do it. There is always a little pause, their laughter is always a little distant. As if the notion of laughter were unfamiliar to them.

*

Tonight is my turn to read to the Prophet again. While I read he sits with his head in his hands, staring down. What does he think? Not about me. He does not look at me; I cannot be sure he even listens. I make my voice softer; pause longer at the ends of verses, making a space to draw him in. Nothing.

I determine I will ask him some question which might force him, at the very least, to look at me, at the end: and so when he dismisses me I counter, 'Excuse me, Mr Wroe.'

'What is it?'

'Would you like me to bring you a drink of tea when we have our supper?'

He shakes his head without looking up.

'You must get very tired and thirsty, sir, working here so late at night.'

'To work for God is a source of perpetual refreshment, Sister Leah. Where do you go in the afternoons?'

He looks at me then. I try to smile, but my stomach is fluttering.

'To visit my family.'

'Not at your father's house, you do not.'

How does he know? Who has he talked to? He is staring at me so intently I am blushing now, and would given anything for that easy escape I refused at the end of my reading.

'Where do you go, Sister Leah? To visit your lover?'

'No – no. I do not have a lover.'

There is a silence while he still looks at me. I cannot tell what is in his mind. His face is almost expressionless, certainly not severe.

'Well then? Who?'

'My sister. I am very close to my sister Anne. I miss her a good deal.'

'You have six new sisters here. It is not desirable that you should absent yourself every afternoon.'

'Not every afternoon. Only now and then.'

'Today. Last night. The afternoon before. The Lord knows where you go, Sister Leah, and what you do. He sees it all. I ask you to tell me the truth, for your own sake. Do not anger God with lies.'

Has he been watching me? No one knows. Even Saint Joanna does not know how often I have been out. Who could have seen me at night?

'Sister Leah. Consider Christ's gentle forgiving love and mercy. He knows what is in your heart. Do not struggle fruitlessly against Him; own your sin and ask forgiveness for your transgression. If you truly repent, you have nothing to fear.'

He knows. He must already know. He waits, then starts again.

'Did you think you could hide your movements from the living

35

God who sees all things? My poor child, every thought in your head is known.' He smiles. A curious smile. As if – almost as if – he wished we *could* keep a secret from God. He is looking at me now. Differently.

'Sin may be the source of rejoicing, Sister Leah, if it causes true repentance, and brings the sinner back to Christ's enfolding love. How much greater the victory over Satan, when a sinner turns to Christ. A pious man gives up nothing: it is easy for him to love God. But a sinner must struggle with his soul. That is the hard-won love Christ values.'

He watches me and he smiles. He wants me to tell. But he also wants . . . I think he also wants . . . Me to be a sinner? What does he know? He is getting up, he approaches me. He puts his hand on my shoulder. I can feel the heat of it, through the stuff of my dress.

'Child. Kneel down and pray with me. Pray that He may open your heart and help you to repentence. Ask Him for His forgive-ness. He will not refuse.'

I kneel down. My skirt will be dirtied – no matter. He kneels opposite me. I close my eyes. My thoughts are swirling like leaves in the wind: what must I do? He is not angry. I think he already knows. I think he *wants* to know I have sinned. There is such a warmth – his hand, the air around him –

I must decide. God help us, Thomas, if I read him wrong. I begin to cry.

'I am sorry . . . I beg forgiveness for my sin . . .' I let the tear trickle down my cheek.

'That is right, Sister Leah. Now tell me, who is it? Who do you go to see?'

'Thomas. I go to see Thomas.'

'Thomas who?'

'My son. He is housed at my sister's.'

'Your child.' He stands. I half-open my eyes, keeping the tears flowing; he has turned away from me.

'A four-months baby. I was . . . A heartless soldier took advantage of my innocence – I was afraid.' He sits in his chair, leaning forward, watching me. Cry harder. 'I was afraid. My father would have killed me. My sister has kept the baby hidden for me. I prayed – I prayed but I could not find out what to do – ' I break off in sobs.

'A bastard child,' he says softly to himself. I throw myself forward into my skirts, so my face is against the floor, and sob heartily. After a while he comes, as I know he must do, to raise me up and help me. He does not offer me a handkerchief. I make swift use of my skirt, which is already dirtied beyond repair.

'Calm yourself, Sister Leah.' He holds my elbow but he is distanced from me. Did he think I would say something else? I am cold now. For the first time, I am afraid. I am afraid he has tricked me.

'Take this seat. Now . . .' He moves to the window and stares out. He no longer notices my presence. Help me. 'To find the happiest solution. I think it must be, to bring the child into this household.' He could be speaking to himself. 'I cannot have you traipsing about at all hours of the day and night to visit him. Nor can it be supposed that your sister is able to keep him indefinitely.'

'She is with child herself.'

He ignores me. 'To bring a fatherless child into the household of God would be an act of charity. To offer a Christian upbringing to the issue of a sinful union. An example may be made of it, at a ceremony of circumcision.' He pauses. 'But it must be presented to all, as an orphan. The church can afford no scandal.' Now he turns to me. 'You would be willing to pretend it was not yours?' Then he laughs quickly. 'Of course. It is in your own best interests. Your parents know nothing of it?'

I am shivering. My tears are dried up, but I cannot speak now, in truth. I nod.

'Very well. When you visit your sister tomorrow you may arrange for it to be left . . . not here. At Sanctuary. After dark. I shall send Sister Joanna on an errand after supper.' He continues to stare out of the window, drumming his fingers upon the frame. When at length he turns back he is impatient. 'You may go, Sister Leah. Go to your room. Pray for forgiveness; He is ever-merciful to sinners.'

When I stand the room moves a little. I have to catch at the edge of the table. He does not come to help me. 'Can I . . . Please can I go to find him, at Sanctuary?'

He is eager for me to leave now, he speaks quickly and carelessly. 'If you wish. Why not? It may be better; the child being your discovery will provide an excuse for the partiality you may show at times. Goodnight, Sister Leah.'

I find my way to the door. He wanted me. I am sure. But now . . .

Curious that the joy I should have expected to feel, at the knowledge that Thomas is to live under this roof with me, is so dulled. I have longed for it, lain awake and plotted for it – and now indeed gained it without the sacrifice of my person I thought it would be necessary to make. I should be happy.

I could not sleep that night, although there were no thoughts that kept me awake. No plots, no plans, no fears that I can name. Rather, a dullness. A kind of darkness inside myself. I am glad Thomas may come – but I would rather not be here. Anne agreed to leave him on the steps at Sanctuary main door, at eight o'clock. We amused ourselves composing a letter to attach to his clothes, and searching the Bible for a suitable motto: 'IN GOD'S LOVE AND PITY TAKE ME IN, THAT HE MAY CHERISH ME IN HIS HOUSEHOLD. FOR MY EARTHLY FATHER IS A SINNER, WHO HAS WRONGED MY POOR MOTHER. MY NAME IS THOMAS. "WHOSO SHALL RECEIVE ONE SUCH LITTLE CHILD IN MY NAME RECEIVETH ME," SAITH THE LORD. Matthew 5'

From a quarter to seven o'clock I worried, but then Saint Joanna came to me with a note, and told me the Prophet desired that I should deliver it to Elder Tobias, whom I should find in Sanctuary this evening. 'Are you content to go alone at this time of night, Sister Leah? Let me ask Sister Hannah to accompany you. I do not know why he could not send Samuel on such an errand.'

I was hard put to get her to allow me to go out alone. Mercifully, it was a clear, calm night, with the moon already up. His note to Elder Tobias I discovered to be entirely blank, when I opened it. Arriving before Anne, I hid in the opposite doorway until she had brought my darling and deposited him. She hesitated there, but I waited for her to round the corner before I came out.

Church Street was deserted, and strangely bright and peaceful in the moonlight; but they must have just finished at the mill in Henry Square, for I could hear their massed footsteps, and some calls and cries between them. It is the Irish who work down there, they live along Cavendish Street and Charles Street – I determined to wait until they were all indoors. Thomas slept, and I sat on Sanctuary steps holding him against my breast. Reunited with him at last, able to hold and keep him, I thought of not returning to

Southgate. But why should I be afraid? How could I be better off, alone, on the streets, with a child in my arms, than in the protected household of the Israelites, with a secure and wealthy roof over my son's head?

The Prophet is assailable. He is not all Godliness. There are chinks in his armour, and I have seen them. He will not be able to pretend I am not there. Or that I am merely one of the women. He must see me. Me. Leah.

When I arrived back with Thomas there was a tremendous fuss, and he was passed round from one pair of arms to another till he was peevish and exhausted. I set some milk to warm for him, but Saint Joanna seized him and carried him off, along with the note, to see the Prophet and find out what must be done. I had been thinking all day over where he should sleep, so I set about clearing a corner of the spare bedchamber, and removing my own bedding to that room. I took out the bottom drawer from the chest there, which will make a good crib for the present, and when Saint Joanna came up puzzling over where he should be placed, I was able to cut her short. I have presented it that I am but a poor sleeper and so will not suffer unduly if he cries in the night: and it must make sense to all, that he should be in a room where he will waken only one. It was getting late and she had no immediate counter-proposal, so it was arranged as I wished. I could see the reluctance with which she passed him back to me though; she seems to dote on him already.

# Hannah

Sitting in the dark. The other woman, Joanna, brings her candle when she comes in. She reads, prays, undresses by it.

'Will you pray with me, sister? Are you in trouble? Can I ease your burden?' She puts her hand on my arm.

My eyes are dry now, she does not touch me. 'Please leave me alone.'

She hesitates for a minute, then, 'I will pray for you.'

When she is in bed, and hidden by the hangings, the candle still burns. She has left it on the washstand for me. I move across and snuff it out. The pale shape of the window blooms in blackness. It is cold. I wrap my blanket around my shoulders, and resume my seat by the window.

Sitting in the dark. I sat with my father each night throughout his sickness. Now I sit on my own.

In darkness, not in candlelight. Our landlady, Lily, coming in early one morning said, 'You did not make a light? Are you not afraid, sitting by him in the darkness all night?' I was busy measuring his laudanum, sixty-five drops. I did not trouble myself to answer her.

Afraid of what? His death? A light will not stop it.

Looking out of our window at night, I see the lights in our neighbours' houses. The baker opposite puts up his shutters; but at either side of him, the small windows are uncovered, and as darkness falls one may see the flickering glow of firelight, or candle or lamp within. Sometimes a candle is set on the window-ledge. The little flimsy light against a world of darkness: what is it but an invitation? Here, it says, here I am, see my frailty, see how easy I may be extinguished. A breath of air, the touch of a finger and thumb will do it. And even if you leave me, at the last I shall put myself out, guttering and flickering to death amongst my own shapeless melted remains. As those who live out their natural life span must go at the end, spread huge with dropsy or eaten to the skeleton wick by wasting. Better to show no light, than to clutch at the false comfort of a candle.

This darkness is peaceful, quieter even than at my uncle's. I can hear Joanna's light, even breaths. Nothing, outside; it is quite still. We are well removed from any thoroughfare or neighbour, and separate even from the canal (which divides us from the town) by the length of a dark field. Night silence.

The silence of my father's nights was ripped by his cough.

While his coughing spasm lasts, every part of my being urges it to end, knows that silence at any price would be less terrible than such extremity. It is no longer a human sound, it tears out of wounded flesh, unconscious of the damage it inflicts as it erupts; no longer in any degree controlled. It brings with it, sometimes blood, sometimes bile. I wipe him, my mind and body knotted tight with willing it to end. And then when – suddenly, without the measured subsiding or throat-clearing of a waking man's cough – it ceases, on a shriek or bark or rasp of unfinished pain; then the other fear hits me; that he is really silenced. The sweating horror of that sound; the freezing fear of that silence. These two measure out the length of an interminable night. In one of his silences there are voices in the street, two men calling good-night. Out there, where darkness contains a warm bed, sleep, renewal. Here it is endurance, through the sound, to the silence; through the silence, to the sound. The darkness does not vary, the sky is black now. And now. And still. Dawn comes at forty minutes after five o'clock. When I hear the church bell toll five, I tell myself the night was quick, I only imagined it lasted so long. There is still no change, no lightening. Darkness is a substance – like a mushroom – growing with the night, spreading to fill all cracks and spaces, pressing in at eyes and ears to suffocate each living body. His retching cries are the sound of human resistance to smothering death.

He falls silent. Into the fragile quiet, the noise of a bird. One bird, coming into existence; making one note. A brief sweet sound. Silence. The note repeats. Encouraged now by its own sound, it tries another – two notes. A call, waiting to be answered. Oh thank God for the single noise that leads to the double noise that leads to the answering call and then to the repetition; the duet, the chorus, and dawn.

But while this hope is still before me, at the sound of that one little voice with its down-up call, and my unreliable eyes are still inventing me a lightening in the darkness of the sky – comes his next dreadful racking gasping cough, so prolonged and violent that I cannot believe it will not be the end. When at last it finishes, there are a half-dozen birds testing their strength outside, and a perceptible greyness at the window. But they are no use. I am already accustomed to dawn, its relief is consumed and stale. I move to the window to watch darkness sifting from the air outside, to see the still cold grey world revealed again; waiting and fearing, waiting and fearing, the recommencement of his sound. But when it comes again –

Hush. Hush. It is done. This night is quiet. Hush and listen to these light soft breaths.

*

The prophet summoned us to the dining room at midday today, to tell us (as I suspected) that we are to be domestics. The bulk of our duties are housewifely. In Sanctuary we are to be responsible for the polishing of silver and brass, the trimming and setting forth of candles, the laundering of ephods, surplices and altar linen. He also requires us for reading and singing. Neither Martha nor Dinah can read, and Rachel and Rebekah made such a flurry of 'we are afraid' and 'only to spell it out slowly' that they were also exempted. In Sanctuary and in missionary work, we are to perform a ceremonial role, and to collect the signatures of the newly converted for the church rolls. Of all the directions, I find this reference to missionary work the most disturbing, for I can imagine little more ludicrous than the sight of such an ill assorted troupe, decked out in white, processing down the street of some Pennine town to the halting sounds of our own voices, behind a long-haired bandy-legged little hunchback.

He cuts a strange figure. Everywhere he goes he carries an iron rod, for all the world like some outlandish native with a spear. He wears his hat rammed down upon his brow no matter what the company, and stares at one with such a piercing eye that one is embarrassed for him, and turns one's eyes away. His mouth is almost hidden by his long beard, so that when he opens it in speaking, and you get a sudden glimpse of that pink hole, it is obscene. His voice I grant to be fine; deep and resonant. Perhaps the depth his hunch adds to his chest has given greater space for resonance, just as a greater girth of bell makes a deeper, more sonorous note.

But for a prophet: a man of God: a leader? I am at a loss. Nor can I determine to what degree he play-acts. I am sure he is a charlatan, but, I suspect, an unknowing one. That is to say, he is a simple soul who believes (deludedly) that he is chosen of God. There is too much awkwardness and nervousness about him for an out-and-out rogue: although he is clearly clever, and used to twisting people to his will. 'Be it menial or trivial, ye do it for the Lord' – sound advice for household drudges, equal in cleverness to the economical suggestion that our reward for such labours shall be in heaven (at God's expense) rather than on earth at his own.

Anyone else but Joanna would be tired by the evening, after the routine and responsibility of the day: after a couple of unrewarding hours spent teaching Martha; after the squabble between two families waiting in the great hall to see the prophet (who is not here today, but they will not take Joanna's word for it, and insist on waiting all afternoon); after lengthy and difficult negotiations with the cobbler over footwear for the seven women, and how great a portion of the work he might see his way to donating to the cause; after cooking dinner single-handed (for Dinah is no real help); and after rescuing that dreadfully screaming baby from Leah, who insists on keeping it in her chamber but affects not to hear it when it cries of an evening. Joanna has sung it lullabies from eight till nine o'clock. After such a day anyone else but Joanna would be too tired to come in and tell me again that she wishes to share my trouble, and that God makes her heart grieve for her sorrowing sister.

'Thank you sister. I am comfortable, I prefer to sit here by the window. If I go to bed, I will not sleep.'

'You are grieving for your father?'

'I suppose so.'

'When did he die?' She sits on the end of my bed, facing me, brushing out her long straight hair as she talks.

'In the winter. He died . . . in January.'

'And your mother?'

'No. I have no mother. She died when I was a child.'

'No brothers or sisters?'

I shake my head.

'You are like me, sister.' She smiles. 'I was brought up at the house of my aunt. But God has brought us into a household of many sisters, now.'

I do not reply. Laying down the brush, she separates her hair into three parts, and begins to plait it neatly for the night.

'You lived alone with your father then.'

'Yes. I – I nursed him in his final illness.'

'What kind of man was he, sister?'

'An engraver, by trade.' I cast about for something else to say to her. 'He had great faith – not dissimilar to the beliefs of your church.'

'Then I am sure he is with God.'

There is a silence. She sits, staring at me, as if she expects an answer. I have nothing to say about God, I do not think he is anywhere but rotting in the ground.

'He was not ready to die.'

She considers this, turning over her hairbrush between her hands. 'You are not able to let him go. Why?'

She is the one who started this conversation. How I hate the smugness religion confers upon its adherents. Now I shall be lectured on how to accept death. After a while she stands up. 'May I brush your hair for you? I used to brush my aunt's, at home, before our night-time prayers.' She comes and stands beside me and begins to unpin my cap and loosen the hair. She has a gentle touch. For a while she brushes in silence.

'Did he give you your education?'

'Yes.'

'And you helped him in his work?'

'Yes.'

'You must have been very close.'
'At one time. Not at the time of his death.' Let her chew on that.
'You had an argument?'
'Not exactly. Thank you for brushing my hair, Sister Joanna. I can plait it myself.'
She arranges her clothes and kneels down beside her bed.
'Will you pray with me, Sister Hannah?'
'Thank you. No.'

Though we work hard here, we have our rest times and our privacy. There is as much food as I can eat, and a daily increasing supply of clothing. I have a sense, now, of space around me: the brittle urgency of choices with which every day seemed to present me, from my father's death up till this time, has somewhat retreated. There is a kind of calm. At my aunt's each day's crazed pattern was no one's invention but her own, each task no more than half-started before her bleating complaints cut it short. Daily at my aunt's house I faced the brick wall of that column in the Manchester Guardian: 'WANTED, by a young lady, a SITUATION as GOVERNESS in a family or ASSISTANT in a SCHOOL . . . ' Each day the wanted column gives notices of PERSONS wanted – a good plain cook, a coachman, a clerk. The only persons who must offer themselves as WANTING a position, are the educated females.

The Israelites' music is beautiful. I was reminded of going with Father to hear Haydn's Nelson Mass, and finding tears streaming down my face. My father's kindly puzzlement at my state, smiling at me indulgently, patting my arm, telling me he should bring me to the Chamber music next time, which might excite me less. (He patted my arm. Smiled at me. He was my father.)

Here in the Sanctuary greatest space is allocated to the musicians. The instrumentalists sit in the left-hand gallery, the choir in the right: opposite and facing them, stands the great organ. Their instruments are outlandish; bizarrely shaped brass and silver tubes from which perhaps our present day trumpet and french horn may be descended; goatskin-covered rounds they beat with their fingers or small hammers; chimes, bells, wind instruments with a sound so hauntingly plaintive a stone would melt to hear it – the sound of the lost world, of Eden, calling in everlasting sorrow for what is spoiled.

There are others. I cannot name them, but Joanna has told me they are built up from names and types of instruments in the Bible, and also copied from the instruments of the Jewish and Gypsy peoples. The quality of sound is extraordinary, for it has a depth and a texture to it which ravishes the hearing. As I sing with them, I am transported to their belief, into the magical world we all desire;

> Behold the wonders now appear
> Which in the Revelation stand;
> To show to man the end is near;
> And his redemption is at hand!
>
> The woman, with the Sun array'd,
> Treads down the moon beneath her feet!
> On her Jehovah's pow'r's displayed,
> She brings to man the light complete.
>
> She brings the fruit pronounced good,
> The evil fruit she casts away;
> And all who eat of this sweet food,
> Will live in one eternal day!

One of my duties is teaching Dinah to read. She will guess at each word before she properly reads it, as if the letters on the page were a sign for meaning, rather than spelling out the thing itself. Thus she is convinced that any word beginning with the letter S is evil, thanks to Satan, Serpent and Sin. It appears that the whole world is little more than a system of hieroglyphs to her; each corporeal, tangible object nothing but a signification of some more potent ulterior reality. Writing thus becomes a system of symbols signifying symbols; for as A stands for Apple, so Apple stands for Temptation and the Fall; and thus the simplest and most innocent A-word (Ant, Abacus, After) is tainted. To begin with, of course, she does not think of the innocents; when her eye falls upon the letter A she reads, first Apple, then whatever she can think of that is close; Agony, Affliction, Anger, Angel (weeping, fallen).

Over the days, I have uncovered her history. She suffers a good deal of pain in her bent legs, and also has a persistent, almost barking cough. Her household duties are consequently lightened, but she is so afraid of being thought a nuisance that she often courts exhaustion by taking on extra tasks for which she is quite unfitted. Religion is everything to her: compensates her for her pain, her physical incapacity, and the seemingly loveless life she has led. She has been an operative in one of the local cotton mills since childhood, until her ill health and deformity (caused by that work) made her unsuitable for the labour. For the past year she has remained at home, keeping house for her mother, brother and sisters. Without her precisely saying so, it is clear that they begrudged her her keep, once she was no longer a wage-earner. Her father died of the spinners' cancer, when she was very young. She sees her inclusion into the prophet's household as God's answer to her prayers. Her single fear is that the prophet may send her home, if her health deteriorates to the point where she can render no useful service.

We women whom no one wants . . .

And then I look at Martha. Indeed, she seems to haunt us all, for you will come upon her where you least expect her, standing quite still and silent. The dead crow a farmer hangs out, to frighten off the others . . .

I cannot conquer that revulsion. Joanna's kindliness reproaches me. But I do not want to touch her.

*

I am capable of performing all the duties so far assigned to me in this house; but there must surely come a time when my ignorance of the Israelite faith might present difficulties? I judged it wise to raise this subject with the prophet one night after his reading.

'Mr Wroe, I think you should know I am not a member of your faith. My aunt and uncle are members of your meeting, but I myself have never attended – '

'I know this, Sister Hannah.'

I was surprised he even knew my name.

'I – if there are spiritual duties belonging to the office of the seven virgins – I am concerned that I may be unable – '

'Such as?'

'Such as?' I repeated stupidly.

'Spiritual duties, such as?'

'I do not know, sir.'

'The duties are those I indicated the other morning. Domestic duties: together with singing in Sanctuary, reading to me, and accompanying missionary tours.'

'Missionary tours? I am ignorant of even the rudiments of your faith.'

'You are a Christian?'

I was at a loss how to answer this: there was an edge of impatience in his voice, as if he thought I had raised this trifling subject only to vex him. After a while he repeated his question.

'No sir.'

'Not a Christian. Are you a member of any faith, Sister Hannah?'

'No – no. I was – my father was – a member of Mr Brothers' congregation in London – he was hailed by some as a prophet . . .'

'Yes. I have heard of him.'

'When he was imprisoned, I left the church.'

'And have not since been seduced by any excitable Evangelical, or quivering Shaker?'

'I have lost my faith, Mr Wroe. I am content without it.'

He looked at me quietly for a bit then. His impatience had evaporated. He began to play with three quills, lifting them and replacing them alternately to make a moving row across his desk. Suddenly he asked, 'What do you desire?'

'I beg your pardon?'

'With regard to this question of faith, what do you desire to do?'

'I am not – I – nothing.'

'You do not wish to be converted?'

'It may not be as simple as that.'

'I think it may. I think it might be as simple as whitewashing a wall.'

'You are suggesting that my views are changeable?'

There was a brief silence, then he said, 'I am suggesting nothing, Sister Hannah. I merely ask what you desire me to do.'

'Nothing.'

'Good.'

'My lack of religion will not present a difficulty then?'

'Not to me. To you certainly, but not to me.' He picked up the three quills together and touched them to his lips. 'You are always free to leave, Sister Hannah. This is not a prison.'

'Do you wish me to leave?'

'Not in the least. You read well, you are tidy about the house. Naturally, when Inner Sanctum duties arise, you and Sister Martha will be excused.'

I do not know whether he instructed her to, but Joanna took up the cause of my spiritual enlightenment, and Martha and I passed a number of evenings in her company, hearing the story of the Israelite church, and of her namesake Joanna Southcott.

They believe the world will end – very soon. This was always Brothers' belief – and indeed my father's. Ironically enough, that terrible thought comes to me now as a safe old friend. My father's beliefs are still part of me, not as spiritual equipment but as the solid bricks of childhood experience.

My father and I waited for the world to end.

I was happy then. We used to pray. We were in a charmed circle, its edges formed by the writhing beasts our words held at bay: men with lions' bodies; eagles' heads with huge curved beaks on the shoulders of naked shuddering men. Candlelight and firelight trembled in that draughty room, the beasts of the apocalypse leered at us from corners. Never safer. Never never never was I safer, than kneeling on the stone floor ('Will you count your own discomfort, before the wrath of Almighty God?') which made my knees flat and bluish, pitted with indentations from the surface of the worn flags – the larger pattern of stone's pores impressed on my own – with my father rampant besides me, his loud voice conjuring and holding at bay those wicked forms which grasped after our immortal souls.

After he had shown the beasts his strength, his rage would cease. He would bow his head, and praise the Lord's name, telling me to join in. When I looked up, those walls and corners which had been blocked out by the press of gargoyle faces – were clear. Clean, empty. The demons were rammed back into the cracks from which they had sprung.

They were still there. Always there: you must never forget them, he told me. In the cracks of the material – beneath the thin crust of the earth, behind all appearances – they lurk. They can be summoned for battle, and to defeat. Or they can be ignored. You can pretend, he said, maybe for months, they are not there; but

49

unchallenged, their power grows – they feed on the droppings of sin, they bloat in the darkness like corrupted flesh. And when you are alone, defenceless, weak, they will emerge, on their pointed hooves, on their slimy bellies, slither from the shadows and come up close, testing their strength to drag you back with them, through the cracks, into the festering pit that lies behind this mask of daytime appearances. How could I not believe him?

Their power waxes and wanes, as evil flourishes or is beaten back upon the earth. When the world is as besmirched with sin as bedlam Joe in his own excrement: they are bold, they burst out. At these times you see the earth shudder – he had seen it – as if an actor standing behind a painted scene is shaking it. A hideous light, of redness, blackness, illumines the edges of all things, shows their wafer thinness.

And so I believed him too, in 1811 when the great comet blazed across our skies. The torch of Satan himself, blistering smoky orange with the fires of hell, throbbing like pain in the heavens. The ignorant people crowded into the streets to view it, crying out and pointing as if at a fairground wonder.

My father knew what the comet meant; our days were numbered. The beast walked the land, and God would let all boil in darkness till the moment that His thunderbolt should cleave the sky, His lightening set us free. My father was determined we must leave the city. We were to put a distance between ourselves and the wretched mass who screamed and whooped like children in the street, who no more knew the punishment in store for them than diseased cattle driven into the lime pit, or the gobbling flock of turkeys on Christmas eve. Many were drunk and brawled and cursed in the streets like devils themselves, more hideous in the flesh than any of the devil's own shades that danced by night on our walls.

We crossed the common in the weird red glow of the comet: it hung low in the sky, casting long black shadows from each tree and straggling bush we passed. In the twelve days before it had rained continuously, and the ground was churned to thick clay mud, which sucked at my boots so that I lost them two or three times. My father pulled me up off the muddy track and we cut across the heathland, rising steadily, till looking back we could see in the clear darkness the smudgy pall of smoke hooding that vicious city: as if it hid its face from God, who sees all things, even in the hearts of men.

When I had my breath, my father raised me up. He was laughing, his face was orange and strange in that light, I was half afraid of him.

'Not long now, my girl. Before we shall run into His arms with joy. With JOY!' He bellowed it out on the dark hill and his voice boomed and rolled around the countryside like thunder, and grasping my hand tightly in his he started to run down the hill as if the devil himself were behind us. My feet left the ground – I flew down that hill, with briars and thistles and nettles, all the plants that sting and scratch, clawing at my knees: in utter terror of crashing to the ground, not knowing how to let go his hand nor how to stay clinging on for the terrible fall which I knew must end his headlong flight through darkness, into blackness. When at last he tripped he loosed my hand – I flew forwards on my face, and slid across the sodden grass like a stone skimming water. I wet myself, and the hot urine flooded the icy cold grass beneath my thighs, so that for a terrified moment I though my body was melting and falling through a hole beneath my groin which would suck me down to the pit of hell fire.

My father stumbled across the grass towards me. He sat beside me, and clasped his arms around me. He was shaking violently.

'Do not cry. The Lord loves us, I promise you. Do not cry.'

How we made our way home: in what frame of mind we noticed, the following morning, that the comet was gone and the world not ended, I do not remember.

But demons lurk only in the corners of my childhood; now I'm a grown woman the world is flat, plain, evenly lit. Empty, both of good and evil. Like homesickness these people's faith calls me back, back to that magic circle. How my heart yearns to be surrounded again.

*

Of all the week, Sabbath is the day I prefer. There is no work upon the Sabbath, and when we are not in Sanctuary we remain in our rooms, the time given over to Bible reading and private prayer. I do not read my Bible – nor, indeed, do I pray – but the silent and inward contemplation the time affords me is a solace in itself. I take my chair at one side of the window, while Joanna sits on the opposite side, she taking advantage of the light for her reading, and I allowing my outward eye to wander over the landscape: the patched, broken ground behind the house, which must be transformed into kitchen garden during this year: the flat damp fields which lie between us and the canal, and the mill chimneys of Ashton. Towering grey clouds move in succession towards the hills in the east, and in the evening the setting sun plays gold and purple through their layers, and lights burn orange in the smoky pall over Ashton. Then I see in it the grainy softness of our aquatints, with melting smudges of coloured ink . . . Always my task, to prepare the ground and apply the aquatint; my father's to engrave the detail.

At times I am driven to take refuge in the Book. The Bible – my father's reading matter and property, and now the province of these Israelites – lies heavy on my knees. I flounder among its pages, lighting here upon the comfort and strength of Matthew, there upon the raging cruelties and genocide of Joshua. I can find no pattern or sustenance in the matter, when I read it to myself: reading aloud to the prophet is a different affair, for there seems then to be a purpose behind the words, and a poetry in their ordering which gives satisfaction to mind and tongue alike.

I was once in the habit of reading to my father. Phrases from his favourite book, Isaiah, lie close to my heart, not for their meaning, but like pebbles that a child may pick on a beach, or a jumble of talismans gathered by a superstitious old woman.

> Enter the rock, and hide thee in the dust, for fear of the
> Lord.
> As the fire devoureth the stubble, and the flame consumeth
> the chaff, so their root shall be as rottenness, and their
> blossom shall go up as dust.
> They shall roar against them like the roaring of the sea: and
> if one look unto the land, behold darkness and sorrow.
> Hear ye indeed, but understand not; and see ye indeed, but
> perceive not.

*And his heart was moved, and the heart of his people, as
the trees of the wood are moved with the wind.
For a small moment have I forsaken thee, but with great
mercies will I gather thee.
The people that walked in darkness have seen a great light;
they that dwell in the land of the shadow of death . . .
Gird yourselves and ye shall be broken in pieces. Gird
yourselves and ye shall be broken in pieces.*

Sanctuary is beautiful. Light inside is pearly; it falls directly from
heaven through skylights in the twin domes of the roof, sweet as
mother's milk. There are no windows at street level, we have no
intercourse with the world outside, save for the timeless sky.
Torches burn at the pew ends, light of hell fire reaching up to meet
sweet liquid light of heaven, and both elements caress, with a
touch here, a glint there, the rich earthly darknesses of polished
mahogany and bronze. The floor is polished oak, the air spiced
and strange with incense. Musicians lift their instruments, gold of
the sun, silver of the moon, and their sounds swell and blossom
and are ridden by the pure high notes of women's voices. Seven
candles on the altar gleam and illumine the precious casket they
call the ark, which holds the Bible and stands between them.
There is no cross here; they take it for a sign of popery and cruelty:
the sign of the antichrist. No pictures, no 'graven images' to
confuse or distract the spirit: their only symbols are Hebrew
letters, and the fair six-sided star of Judah.

Beautiful; seductive; it is no wonder his congregation are as
sheep. *Hear ye indeed, but understand not; and see ye indeed, but
perceive not.* How great a pleasure is peace and security. Might one
not easily be tempted to exchange the anxieties of independence
for such serenity?

# Joanna

Sister Leah has brought a foundling into our house: a beautiful boy child with blue eyes and a soft fuzz of golden-brown hair. He has been very well looked after, my heart goes out to that poor sad woman who was forced to leave him on Sanctuary steps. After my Bible class yesterday evening I lingered there a while, wondering whether she would return to visit the spot where she abandoned him. I prayed that she would, so that I could help her to feel His loving kindness, and clear her soul of that terrible despair which must surely have clotted it. But there was no sign of such a person. I pray He will forgive her and lead her into a better life. The child's advent into our household is a sign of great hope for us, I believe. The feeding, clothing and tending of a little one makes a very minor addition to our duties; and the rewards of innocent amusement and kindling love are considerable. The sweet shapeliness of his little form is a constant reminder of the perfection of our Lord's designs; the warm pleasure to be gained from holding and cuddling him, and watching his innocent smiles, enhances those feelings of love which all must bear their fellow creatures. In particular, I have high hopes that tending to the child's well-being will give our youngest sisters (Leah, Rachel and Rebekah) a special interest and exert that steadying influence, which the responsibility for young helplessness so frequently calls up. Signs of these good effects are already perceptible in Sister Leah, who has offered to take care of the child at night; and she (I would have said – and I stand humbled before my loving and all-knowing Father for my earlier lack of perception) the least like to be affected by maternal stirrings, of us all.

I have suggested to the Prophet that this happy event may provide instructive matter for Sanctuary congregation; not least because it shows us how joys and good effects may be the issue of sin and black despair; leading us to contemplate how God will work His designs out on a scale beyond our feeble ability to comprehend, and how contrary the final effects may be, to those initially expected. He thanked me courteously, but his sermon for this week is already determined. Perhaps he will speak of it next week.

To see Sister Leah's affection for little Thomas is quite moving. We have put his cradle in the warmth of the kitchen, for daytime use, for some of us are always about there. This morning when he began to cry she ran to comfort him and, finding him a little hot, took him out into the sewing room. She was so absorbed in thoughtful care for him that she quite forgot the oven was just then hot enough for baking, and the small pastries still without their top crusts. I am glad she did not think to bring him back into the kitchen, for it was hot. By the time I had removed the burning faggots from the oven and swept it out, then loaded the whole batch in to bake, I was drenched with sweat. I am sure Thomas would have become distressed again, in that heat.

The preparation of meats for Sabbaths and Feast days has given me some anxiety, for all must be cooked in advance, to be served cold on the day. Though my aunt and I were well content to dine on a couple of slices of cold beef on the Sabbath, it is not uncommon for some among the Elders – or even visitors from outside – to dine with the Prophet on such occasions, and more fitting fare must be provided. Sister Leah has come to my assistance, with a couple of receipts of her mother's, and once the pastries were baked we set out to try one, prior to using it for the Feast of the New Moon next Tuesday. For a stuffed goose, we took two big handfuls stale breadcrumbs, an onion chopped, two rosy apples chopped up, a cup of sweet plums, four hard-boiled eggs chopped very small, a pinch of pepper and a pinch of dark sugar. I was alarmed when she told me her mother mixes these with cream, and reminded her of the prohibition against combining milk and meat; but then she laughed and said she must have remembered amiss, for they are mixed with the juice of a lemon. Another receipt, new to us all, was brought down by Sister Benson from the farm. On her way to market she stopped off with a basket of fresh-cut lambs' tails; we first cleaned off the wool, then cut them in little bits and stewed very slow for twenty minutes. Then laid them in a deep platter, seasoned with pepper and salt, a good layer on top of sliced apples, chopp't parsley, more tails, apple and parsley, till the platter was full. Then poured in some of the broth and covered with a good paste. We cooked it one hour and twenty minutes and it was very nice cold.

I am delighted by these variations on our customary boiled meats; the flavour was remarked on by all at dinner, and Sister Leah's habitual impatience and restlessness is much soothed by the compliments her cooking has earned her. I have the highest hopes that a disposition to cherish young Thomas, and the nurturing of her native skill in housewifely arts, will help her to contentment and bring her into a closer communion with her heavenly Father.

*

The Prophet's wife and family are yet in residence in Bradford: I had forgotten this until Sister Leah questioned me concerning them. I have seen his wife, Sarah, at the baptism of their third child: a small, pale, weary-looking woman, who struggles under the yoke of ill health. She is an innocent creature, and has rendered God great service by the care with which she tended her husband, during the long illness that came upon him during 1819. His communications with God began at this time. She nursed him skilfully when his life lay in the balance, and shows commendable devotion to her three young children. Sadly, this positive and womanly attribute in her character is countered by a narrowness of spiritual vision, such that she can neither comprehend nor be grateful for the great honour of her husband's calling. She has even sought on occasion to prevent him from fulfilling God's commands (to go forth on missionary work, and once to meet with leaders of the Jewish church, to attempt a reconciliation betwixt them and Christians) by urging the importance of such trifling domestic claims as the repairing of a roof, or the indisposition of a child. Setting (as he must) God's commands above all others, the Prophet has pursued a course which has led him into bitter domestic strife. It is God's will, His trials strengthen our resolve.

Since the completion of Sanctuary here in Ashton, the Prophet has well-nigh forgone the comfortable blessings of matrimonial life: travelling first on his great mission to Turkey, then to the English Southcottian branches, and lastly to take God's word to the North. He has preached by day and received the Lord's communications by night, offering up wholeheartedly his own comfort and health, in God's service. I have heard, from Sister Wrigley, who has it from a cousin of her mother's in Bradford, that Sarah Wroe is anxious now to move to Ashton, and install herself and her children in her husband's 'great house'. Whether this shall be so I cannot tell; nor how it may suit the Prophet to have a scolding wife and three noisy children about the place. Suffice it that he has not yet made any requests concerning their accommodation. Sister Leah and the child are now in the back bedchamber, but there is attic space. The ordering of these matters is in His hands: I pray for Sarah Wroe's enlightenment, and for the spiritual nourishment of her children. I believe, and have instructed Sister Leah, this can be our only proper concern in the affair.

And indeed, that enlightenment must come: for how far can a mortal woman pursue her difference with God? She must submit to Him, and joy in giving her husband all help and wifely support in the carrying out of his arduous task. It is in part that role, of course, that we seven are to fulfil – by God's express command – to see to the ordering of the Prophet's household, which duties many would expect to see performed by a wife. But a wife has other duties to her husband, which are also ordained of God. I pray she may cease her rebellion, and follow God's desires meekly – for to this she must come in the end, will she or no.

The sad futility of Sarah Wroe's rebellion puts me in mind of Mother Southcott's tale concerning the knight and the maiden. Once a knight learned his future from the stars: it would be his fate to marry a low-born peasant girl, daughter of a man who worked his land. Fearing the shame and dishonour such a match must bring upon his house, the knight gave the peasant a fortune, £3,000, in exchange for the baby girl. Then he took her and flung her into the sea. From thence she was rescued by a kindly fisherman, who raised her to become a beautiful young maid. Again, the knight saw her: again he bought her from her keeper, again he attempted to bring about her death. The poor maiden begged him to spare her life – to which at last he agreed, on condition that she never again appear in his sight, unless it be wearing his ring – which he at that word flung far out to sea. Soon after, the wench was working in the kitchens; upon preparing and opening a fish, she found inside its belly the very ring. Wearing it, she appeared before the knight. Then at last did he fall to his knees, crying, 'Pardon fair creature, I humbly pray, for thou has a million of charms.' And then he married her, with raptures of joy and love.

It is a sweet tale – an old one I believe, from among the common people, and Mother Southcott interprets it soundly: for it truly shows the impotence of man to fight against the decrees of God, when all is already determined by Him, inside the Womb of Providence. We are His children.

The Prophet has instructed me in the role of the women of Inner Sanctum concerning punishment of sins. This was determined at the council of Elders on Tuesday. We have been provided with a table ranking misdemeanors and sins in order of severity, sever-ally with their punishments. The minor offences (such as late attendance at Sanctuary) are to be punished by dousing the head in cold water (the number of times depending on the severity of the offence) but the more severe offences are to be punished with stripes. Since a very particular method of administering the stripes is specified, I was obliged to explain in detail to the other women. I am puzzled by Sister Leah's reaction, for she seems to think it in some way wrong. I explained that the men are to be stripped and clad in a white gown. The stripes are to be administered by the women upon the naked buttocks, using the right hand. The male is to be held securely in position for his punishment by the female's left hand around his privates.

'I hope you are not serious, Sister Joanna.'

'I beg your pardon, Sister Leah? These are the duties of the women, as laid down by the last meeting of the Elders of the church. You may read for yourself – '

She took the paper from me and read it. After a moment she looked up at me. 'Do you not see any – impropriety – in the method of punishment, Sister Joanna?'

'How can it be improper if it is ordained by the Elders?'

'Because –' She sighed and glanced at Rachel and Rebekah, who were both coughing violently. I instructed Rachel to fetch a drink of water.

'Because if I may speak without offence, sister – '

'Of course, my child.'

'Because of the nakedness of the men, and the – unseemliness of the – contact – ' She did not seem able to complete her sentence.

'But sister, we are talking here of punishment ordained by God, through the Prophet. We are talking of punishment, not of nakedness. To be sure, in this case, the sinners are naked – but this represents their nakedness before God, who sees through all disguises. Nakedness shows humility and repentance, the willingness to put aside the rank and dignity which clothes may confer, and to appear as the lowest of the low. This nakedness is purely symbolic: there can be nothing unclean in it.'

Sister Leah was smiling at me; she has a full mischievous smile, very playful and pleasant to behold. 'But in the contact, sister, between the woman and the man's naked flesh – is there not a proximity to sin in that contact, which must give rise to the gravest fears for the innocence of either party?'

'I am certain there cannot be, Sister Leah. The two do not meet as man and woman, but as sinner and avenger: the man, abasing himself before God, will think of nothing but his penitence: the woman, administering punishment as an aid to repentance, must see herself as an agent of the Lord, a ministering angel, whose touch upon the man will not be as a human woman, but as an ethereal being, abstracted from the merely physical.'

'You are certain then, that in agreeing to perform these punishments, our action can in no way be deemed improper?'

'In no way – in no way, Sister Leah. I rejoice that God calls us so clearly to aid in the performance of His works. I rejoice that we are able to be His instruments.'

The system of punishments will come into force from this Sabbath, the punishments to be administered after second meeting, in the side room of the Inner Sanctum. We will perform the punishments in pairs, each pair on alternate Sabbaths, thus sharing the duties between us.

Sister Leah had one final question: 'What if a man – if the sinner – become inflamed by his punishment?'

'Inflamed, sister? To be sure it will not come to that. The stripes

59

will be neither so numerous nor so heavy as to cause permanent injury . . .'

'You misunderstand me, sister.' Poor Sister Rebekah at this point suffered a fit of coughing so severe that I sent her out into the fresh air. I hope that she and her sister will not fall ill. Sister Leah continued, 'I do not mean injury by the stripes, sister, I mean, if the effect – upon the flesh – of the chastening measures, should be opposite to that intended, and should instead produce an – enlargement – of, of appetite for sin.'

'I cannot think that these problems will materialize, my dear sister. Your anxiety for the efficacy and properness of the punishment is commendable, but I think you may set your mind at ease: I do not forsee any difficulties or dangers inherent in the exercise.' So I concluded it, for it was by then midday, and the ironing and churning still unperformed: the lamps in need of cleaning and filling, along with numerous other tasks about the house. I am pleased by Sister Leah's concern in this, however, for it has seemed at times that she may be a trifle careless where matters of the spirit are concerned. Her anxiety both for decorum and for the efficacy of the punishment strike me as most encouraging signs of her increased commitment to God's work.

And how right she is to be vigilant. Elder Tobias took me aside only this morning to speak of the need for all that passes in our household to be spotless and above reproach. 'For there are some, as I think you know, Sister Joanna, some within the church – amongst the Elders, no less – who would grasp at the chance to discredit the Prophet. One – I will not name him – but he pretends not to see the mantle of the Lord on John Wroe's shoulder. He waits for the Prophet to stumble, Sister Joanna; as we love God, we must make it our daily task to ensure His servant's name and house are pure.'

How curious, that a man who stands so close as an Elder to the Prophet chosen of God, should covet the Prophet's power – instead of rejoicing and giving thanks for that dear proximity.

*

The religious education of Sisters Hannah and Martha is my task: they stand outside the circle of Mother church, outside the band of

Israelites – and I must bring them in. Though their cases be very different – Hannah having perhaps too much education, poor Martha far too little – yet they both lack spiritual nourishment, the milk of our Mother that may sustain us through this world and into the next. Mother Southcott is my starting point for their enlightenment: what person can hear her story and lack faith, lack zealous love, both for the Prophetess herself and for the church which she has founded? And so this evening I have them both beside me, close by the fire in the kitchen. We are happier here than in the grandeur of the drawing room. The fire leaps high and casts its warm red light upon our faces and our needlework; the comfortable scents of the afternoon's baking linger yet in the air, and the only sound from outside is the gentle drumming of the rain upon the wash-house roof. I think with pleasure of the pure water gathering in our newly cleansed butt. Sister Dinah is in bed, Sisters Rachel, Rebekah and Leah choose to read and pray together in their chamber; the Prophet is in late deliberation with the Elders in Sanctuary. All is quiet, all is calm, all is peace. My two companions are earnest at their sewing, Sister Hannah working buttonholes on her white silk, Sister Martha – with slow laborious stabs – attempting a child's sampler I have pencilled out for her: GOD IS LOVE to be executed in a simple cross stitch, in the hopes that some minimal skill in the art may at length be acquired. Boney lies outstretched at our feet, his silky ears flipped forwards in his sleep, giving him a wide-awake, foxy appearance which he never has in daytime. Brother Benson, who gave him to us, has requested the loan of him tomorrow for rat-catching in his neighbour's barn. What excitement, my little Boney! You will think your doggy paradise begun! But for now – all is at peace. We sew in silence: the rain falls, the fire crackles, the dog stirs and sighs in his sleep. I may tell the life of Mother Southcott, and pray the hearts of my beloved sisters fall under her holy influence.

Mother Southcott is the founder of our faith, our Prophetess. Her early life was humble; the daughter of a poor farmer, she worked at home and then in the houses of others, as a mere domestic servant. Praise God, for He loves the meek, and these shall He raise up. His ways are not our ways, His times are not our times. Not until she was past her youthful prime, did He speak to her. In her forty-second year, on a sudden, came the glorious word of

God, calling her to do His work. I try to imagine that moment, the terror, the joy: how it fills me with longing. I have her words by heart, for the mental possession of them brings me closer to her union with God, the beauty and the sacred pain of that event –

> I was visited by day and by night. The whole Bible broke in upon me, as though Angels that were ministering spirits were sounding in my ears, that the End of all things was at hand. How hateful every appearance of evil was in my sight: how I sat drowned in tears, only to hear innocent songs, because they were not to Thy honour and Glory. How every oath went to my heart . . . All I had felt before appeared but the break of day to the rising sun, that then arose in my heart with Power.

When I imagine that Holy state, my heart beats fast, I pray that rising sun may shine for me. By virtue of God's power vested in her, Joanna Southcott accomplished miracles: the first of which was that she, who had no money, no influence, no education, gained within a few years upwards of 40,000 followers. Her message from God entered the hearts of the people; that within a short space of time, the world as we know it will come to an end. All wickedness and distress will be cast out, and a new Kingdom shall arise, ruled over by Shiloh, the second Christ. In this New Kingdom only those who truly love and dedicate their lives to God shall live. In the new Kingdom there shall be neither poverty, nor hunger, nor sickness: there shall be no injustice, but brotherhood among all mankind. And the Kingdom shall last a thousand years. Let His chosen people join the flock at the call of His Prophetess Joanna!

Sister Martha, you must not scratch yourself there, it is unlady-like. Let me see your work. What is this knot? How has this thread become so tangled, Martha? Give it to me.

The second miracle was that she had a Prophet's eyes on the future, and could penetrate its secrets, seeing even into the smallest and most humble mysteries. Through this gift she gained the love and allegiance of common people, for she knew how to save a sick cow, and when soaking rain would cause a harvest to rot on the stalk. Some say these are mere tricks, unworthy of God's notice: to be sure they are of no account in the great scale. Yet they may be enough to win the trust of an ignorant day-labourer; who, having given his trust, may readily surrender his soul. And thus by a trivial matter is a great battle won.

And the world is full of doubters, who cannot take God's word or the imminence of His Kingdom on trust, but must see proof, must touch the wounds. To these Mother Southcott extended a rope of hope to pull them up to heaven.

By day her work was among the people, preaching, writing and publishing God's word, jealously banishing the encroachments of corruption into her church, receiving and disputing with Bishops, Ministers, churchmen of all persuasions and degrees. For there will be no divisions in the faith, at the end. And by night – after these exhausting labours – by night she was the bride of God. Heavenly joy and peace beyond understanding refreshed her for the tasks ahead. How I love those passages where she speaks of God's nightly kindness, his perfection – for this love, perhaps, we all may feel one day:

> I felt myself lying as it were in heaven, in the hands
> of the LORD, and was afraid to move, fearing I
> should remove His heavenly hand, which I felt as
> perfect as ever woman felt the hand of her husband.

Her writings speak much of her doubts and fears: on these I do not dwell, for it grieves me to see so good and honest a woman, so beloved of God, able to fall away to doubt. I can only imagine that seeing the greatness of the prize if he could carry her, Satan attacked her with more than usual powers. For at times she even doubts the word of God himself, fearing it is not He but the Great Deceiver who speaks to her: begging Him, who has given her His greatest love, for proof of His identity. It is a grief to see how poorly the most virtuous human heart is able to contain and return His love.

Of the rest of her writings (which may truthfully be called God's writings, for on numerous occasions He directed her to take up her pen and simply poured the words that she should write into her ear: in her sweet simplicity she has noted twice that she made no sense of the message, for its purport was beyond her understanding, but that she wrote as she was commanded); of the rest of her writings, I am most thrilled by her remarks concerning the role of the women:

> Quench not the Spirit; despise not prophecy; for the time is come, that your women shall prophecy, your young men shall dream dreams, your old men shall see visions: for the day of the Lord is at hand.

Have not we been despised and cast down from the first? Just so low as women were cast down, shall we now be raised up high. And those of the other churches, who believe women not fit to speak and preach and pass on the word of God, but that they must sit and listen with the children (for even the Wesleyans are against women preachers now): may they hear, and mark, how God's favour is passed to women, and how He has chosen a woman for His greatest Prophet in modern times.

Sister Martha. I have unpicked that L, here is fresh thread. Now, make a start here – just here. Good.

In measure and keeping with His great love for His Prophet Joanna, God made it known to her that she was the Woman of Revelations:

> *a woman clothed with the sun, and the moon under her feet, and upon her head a crown of twelve stars; and she being with child cried, travailing in birth, and pained to be delivered.*

She was to be His bride, and mother of His son.

Now began Mother Southcott's trials in earnest. For she was sixty years of age, unmarried, and had never known a man. Yet she was with child. To you or I, this is a miracle. But to the common people it was no more than matter for ribald jokes: for obscene speculations and for the burning of wicked effigies. Her followers gathered round to shield her from the grossness of the world: but ever sensitive to the world's opinion, and ever vulnerable to the cruel doubts planted in her mind by the Arch Deceiver, she fell into a sadness, which deepended into a grief. When the time for the child's birth came and passed with no sign of her deliverance, her suffering heart broke, letting the captive spirit within escape joyful to the arms of its creator. Nay, Sister Hannah, I thank you, I am not crying. There is nothing in death to call forth tears; I rejoice in her escape from earthly trials. Now, let us put a fresh log on this fire. It will soon burn up more brightly. Good.

Many at that time were mistaken – even among Mother Southcott's closest supporters. For they made the mistake which we mortals have ever made in our dealings with God: they expected a physical manifestation. There was no physical child, though the doctors who examined her dear body allowed all the symptoms attendant upon childbearing to have existed.

The child born of Mother Southcott was a spirit, a herald of the second Kingdom, who has entered the hearts of many. Principally it animates her prophets and followers, such as Prophet Wroe – and, I pray, we women are called through him by that Spirit. Though we were cast down at her leaving us, yet we rejoice in her spiritual child, and are sustained by the truth and beauty of her writings, and by the closeness of her communion with God.

Come Sister Hannah, come Sister Martha. Set aside your sewing. Let us sing one of her own hymns, before we go to bed.

> *A woman Satan chose at first*
> *To bring on man the Fall;*
> *A woman God has chose at last,*
> *For to restore us all.*
> *As by a woman death did come,*
> *So life must come the same,*
> *And they that eat the fruit she gives*
> *May bless God's holy name!*

# Leah

By casual questioning of Saint Joanna, and the expenditure of an infinite amount of patience in listening to her replies, I have acquired a somewhat clearer notion of the Prophet's movements. He leaves the house before we even rise, and goes to Sanctuary, where he meets with the Elders for early morning worship, and to inform them of God's latest sayings. After that, as far as I can make out from Saint Joanna, he might take any one of some six or seven courses of action, for on some days he will stop in Sanctuary all morning, on discussion of church business; on other mornings he will visit the sick and dying, or conduct a circumcision; on others he will return here to receive individual petitioners, leaders from other churches, and so on and on. However, she did let slip that tomorrow he will return to Southgate by eight o'clock, since there are two young men now fully prepared for missionary work, whose knowledge and faith he must examine before revealing their destinations to them. She refused to say who they were; one I am sure will be Henry Lees, rich William Lees' younger brother, who reprimanded me for my lack of piety at the last Feast of the New Moon. I hope he is sent to Turkey. Our Sabbath morning service will be tediously lengthened: at the last departure of missionaries, we endured near two hours of well-wishing prayers and commending them to God. However, there is a benefit to all this, for not only do I now know the Prophet's movements tomorrow morning, but they also coincide with it being my turn to clear and light the fires – which excuses me our household prayers. It will be easy enough, when I have completed the chore, to slip out to Sanctuary (I may take some of our fresh candles, as a reason) at just the time when he must be ready to leave. And so I shall walk home in his company, in the fresh morning light, and perhaps win some advantage.

Thomas, I reasoned, would fit well enough into this happy plan – for he generally wakes before six, takes a feed and sleeps again another couple of hours. But this morning he is not awake. I dress myself in the darkness and feel my way down to the kitchen, which is as dark and cold as the grave. The tinder box is not where I left it in its niche above the fireplace – I feel about on the table, and then the dresser, and succeed in knocking over the tea caddy which was perched on the very edge of the lower shelf. If ever there were a group of slovenly, careless housekeepers, it is these: nothing is kept in its rightful place. There is no need for any of them to touch the tinder box, for it is invariably I who light the first candle of the day. I find it at last beside the sink, where heaven knows what splashing or spills may have damped the tinder. I can generally reckon on a light by the third attempt, but today I must strike eight times, and scrape my knuckles into the bargain, before a spark will take. Now the spill – and now the candle. I keep his milk in the oven overnight, for though the fire is dead and cold by morning, the brick of the old oven still retains its heat. Out in the pantry there will be shards of ice in the milk today; there is a freezing, bitter wind whistling under the door. Clumsy with haste I break a little bread into the lukewarm milk, and bear my bowl and light upstairs. Thomas must be woken.

He is cross and sleepy and will not feed properly. It is provoking, for I cannot remember the last time he was not wide awake and chirruping at six. By the time I am done he has spilt more than he has eaten, and is only just coming properly awake. As I lay him down to sleep again he begins to cry angrily. Thomas, sweetheart, come . . . not this morning. I am already behind-hand. But as I raise the latch his screams grow earnest. I cannot leave him like this.

And so I must take him to Rebekah – which I would rather had been avoided, for since his circumcision and the attendant distress, he has come to spend more than half his day in others' arms. First I take a light into their room; I will not have her blundering about in the dark with him. Rachel and Rebekah are not yet dressed, I lay him on her bed. His cries cease as soon as he hears her voice.

I run down to the kitchen again, to rake out the fire. Filthy, choking work: little did I imagine I would be reduced to the same status as our girl Ruth at home, in my brave new life. Not one of the others raises her voice against such menial tasks – and so I must not either. But once I have his ear the Prophet shall know how demeaning it is to his standing and the honour of the church, for the Prophet's women to be toiling like servant girls. There are four fires to clear this morning – his study, the great hall, and drawing room, besides this. Four laborious journeys out the back into the icy grey morning, where the wind whips the ash up into a whirlwind that sticks in my nose and throat. At least there is a system now for kindling and fuel, and it lies, dry and to hand, beside the kitchen range. But the hearth stones in the drawing room and in his study must be whitened after the soot is scrubbed away – already the hall clock has struck seven, and I am not half done. In the kitchen the straw and twigs blaze up swiftly, but soon dull back to a smoky hissing mass, under the weight of a couple of logs, and I must work myself into a sweat with the bellows to get them to flame. Saint Joanna will buy nothing that can be got as a donation; at home, peats would be glowing by now, but since logs are given and peat is not, our work is made the harder.

I have not lit the drawing room fire before; it is a fine-looking hob grate in steel, set in a marble chimney piece. But it will not draw; I nurse it into flame, but it dwindles and dies as soon as I stop blowing. There must be a blockage. I poke at the chimney opening, but meet no resistance. Soot falls upon the fresh-whitened hearthstone, spoiling my work. This must be done. If I do not catch him at Sanctuary this morning, when will be the next opportunity? He may not be alone again for the rest of the day, save in his study where none may enter. And tomorrow? A meeting with the Elders may take up the morning, who knows what duties the afternoon – and the day after he will probably be off on another preaching tour to some distant village. My hands are black, my nails chipped and filthy. How many more days of this must I endure? Dumbly, patiently, as if *this* were life.

'Sister Leah. Are you having difficulty?'

The last person I need. 'Sister Dinah. Are you not at morning prayers?'

'I felt a little faint. I have excused myself.'

'And you are going to lie down.' My precious time is slipping away with each slow word she utters.

'I was on my way upstairs. But I heard you sobbing, Sister Leah, and I wondered –' I am not sobbing. I wish to be done with this, but I am not sobbing. '– if I could help you?'

'I cannot – the fire will not draw.'

'Let me see.'

It takes her half an hour to cross the room. Now I am well and truly trapped, for while she peers up the chimney and remarks on the lack of a register door and wonders whether a bird may have nested there, I must watch and listen politely: instead of hurling the fire irons, down, ripping off this filthy apron and running out to wash myself. Her slow movements are like something you would crush, out of pity or disgust, if you saw it crawl across the floor.

'It *can* burn brightly, Sister Leah, for I have seen it.' So have I, Dinah, but today it will not burn at all.

'Let me try it again, while you tend your other fires, Sister Leah. No, do not worry, I think it was standing to pray on an empty stomach that caused the dizziness; it will make me feel better to be of service.'

'Thank you, Sister Dinah, you are very kind.'

'If I cannot get it to burn I will tell Sister Joanna and she must arrange for it to be swept. This opening at the top is very narrow . . .' Her slow voice trickles on as I run out of the room. It is seven-thirty by the clock: if I can be clean and out of the house in five minutes I may yet catch him before he is half-way back. Then what is my excuse for not going on to Sanctuary with my candles? I will think of something on the way. I have to break ice on top of the water-pitcher in the outer office – the cold makes my hands ache.

As I pause for a moment to slide a bunch of candles into the wide pocket of my cloak, I hear the sound which must finally ruin my plan: a sudden loud splattering of rain against the office roof. I run to the back door and look out. The heavens have opened, and freezing rain spouts down as if from a pump. I would be soaked to the skin within a minute.

The sudden sharp disappointment to my hopes, after so much haste, brings angry tears to my eyes. And now here is the day, the rest of the day to get through. I hear the women's voices raised in the morning hymn.

69

> Who can faint while such a river
> Ever flows, their thirst to assuage –
> Grace which like . . .

If he do not speak to me today: if he do not look at me today, so help me – I think I shall burst.

\*

The product of this past two weeks' hard work is now complete: we have a number of hideous, ill designed dresses. Saint Joanna tells us we must wear them all the time, not just for Sabbath; it is our 'uniform of God'. A pity God has not more taste, say I.

There are prohibitions against every aid to beauty, for we are not to insult the Lord by attempting to improve upon his handiwork. (And yet one needs only to glance at Martha, or at Hannah, to understand how vastly in need of improvement it is.) Injunctions against hair pieces and false curls do not trouble me, since no addition is needed to improve my own hair. Though it may be against the spirit of the law, I shall continue to use my belladonna – it is not against the letter, for I do not think the Prophet or Elders even know of such a thing. What gives me most cause for irritation is the prohibition concerning stays. Every item of our undergarments is detailed (is this the Prophet's work? I wonder that he has no matters of greater significance with which to occupy himself, than the enumeration of petticoats. I wonder also at the intention behind this. Does he desire us to be ugly? And if so, is this to discourage the attentions of other men? To foster modesty in us, by obliging us to lose interest in our appearances? To put a damper on his own desires? Or does he *prefer* ugly women? The wandering of his eyes seems to deny it). So the design of our stays is prescribed. We are to have no whalebone, or stiffening of any kind. A simple, wadded cotton, laced under-bodice. I tried this garment today; it fulfils the requirements absolutely, since it conceals every natural curve of the body, covering all with a generalized shapeless fatness. Am I to walk about like a pudding? I have worn myself into a temper trying to adjust the thing so that it goes in at the waist. I have complained to Saint Joanna of the discomfort, and told Rachel and Rebekah its prolonged use will ruin their figures. But my best course of action can only be to take matters into my own hands. I will wear the wretched thing on the Sabbath, and when I am likely to be inspected. The rest of the time I shall leave it off, and, now my own stays are taken from me, I shall wear a plain, unlined cotton underbodice. It will not enhance my figure, but at the very least it will not deform it.

I am making a dress, at night. A dress which is not at all allowed; from a length of brightly sprigged muslin which came like a gift, wrapped up inside the dull plain lengths we have had delivered from the draper's. How it came there, or what it is for, we do not know. Saint Joanna unrolled it, and all gathered round to exclaim forlornly at the prettiness of the colours (pale yellow, with a delicate pink and green flower). All we are allowed is plain colours. No mixtures, no patterns. And only drab, green or blue. I wanted it. I know I wanted it more than any of the others – nor had any of them the wit to take it, like it never so much. Saint Joanna murmured something about giving it to a girl in her Bible class, who has poor relations that are not Israelites: it was left lying there when we went to singing practice. So I slipped back when the others were gone, and hid it in Thomas's bedding. I have cut it out now, and last night Rebekah helped me pin it on. Sewing by candlelight makes my head ache, but I have a half-dozen extra candles (the benefit of cleaning in Sanctuary this morning) and so we shall burn them profligately. Little Rachel stares at me with her sheep eyes and says, 'But is it not forbidden?' and 'When can you wear it, Sister Leah?'

I shall find opportunity, I shall make opportunity. If I must be always dressed in ugly clothes, then life is not worth living.

Saint Joanna came out from reading to the Prophet tonight in a state of some excitement. I was in the kitchen feeding Thomas, and Rebekah and Rachel sitting with their sewing at either side of the fire.

'I have heard something strange,' she says, and sits herself at the table; then seems lost in a trance, staring into the fire and not saying a word.

'What is it?'

'Sister Joanna, tell us.'

For a long while she did not reply, almost as if she regretted having spoken, and was considering how to keep a secret. At last she said, 'The Prophet's wife is dead.'

We looked at one another. The Prophet's wife is dead.

'When did she die?'

'Was she ill?'

'What did he say? Is he distressed?'

Joanna shook her head. 'He only mentioned it as an after-thought. He told me he would be away a day or two this week, visiting the Huddersfield meeting, and settling his wife's affairs.'

'Did you ask him – '

'Did he not go to visit – ' Rebekah and I spoke at once, and fell silent together.

Joanna continued with her own train of thought. 'The comfort God provides to His chosen people is a marvellous thing. He reminded me that we should rejoice at death, for the soul is brought to a place of delights. I asked him when he heard this news, and he said she has been ailing this past six months, and that he knew of God that she could not survive long.'

'How does he know she is dead?' I asked.

'Her brother was here yesterday. I do not know . . . I did not notice him. There were so many petitioners waiting in the housebody in the afternoon . . .'

We sat silent a while, then Rachel asked, 'Will there be a great funeral?'

Saint Joanna shook her head. 'He said she is to be buried quietly, in her own parish. She was never properly of our faith. His exact words were, "God, who saw into her heart, knows her merits and her place in eternity." It was her wish, and her brother's, that she should be laid to rest in the churchyard beside their childhood home. Let us pray for her, sisters.'

We bowed our heads, and Saint Joanna prayed for the Prophet's wife, and asked God to give her a place in heaven.

'Are there are not children?' I asked.

'There are three. They stay with the brother and his wife.'

So the Prophet is rid of his entire family at one blow.

'His strength and fortitude are an example to us all. I hope he will make a sermon of this on the Sabbath: never have I seen the Lord give a man such support, such composure, in what would to many of the weaker sort, be a time of grief. Truly, He is a rock.'

The Prophet did not make a sermon of it on the Sabbath, nor is it at all widely known among church members. While Saint Joanna is impressed by his God-given fortitude, there is one fact above all that impresses me. If his wife is dead, he may take another.

Not now. Not hastily. But in time – when his bravely concealed grief is overcome, if he finds a woman to suit him, there is no reason to suppose he will not look to marrying again. A woman *inside* the faith, clearly. A woman who might make a contribution, through her skills, to increasing the comfort and standing of this house of God. A woman who might be admired for her beauty, and respected by the Elders for her position in the Prophet's favour. This makes another matter entirely, out of winning his attention.

Does Thomas count against me? I think not. Once the fact is known, and accepted – and he did accept it, easily – it is just as easily forgotten. The child is part of the household now. I am sure the Prophet does not think of him.

The question comes back again – again and again – how to secure some time alone with him; how to encourage him to more than staring at me from the opposite side of Sanctuary? A futile question at this present time, for he is off to Huddersfield today, and who knows how long the arrangement of his wife's affairs may keep him there occupied?

*

Thank God for a little excitement! Rachel and I were despatched to Ashton this morning on household errands (in itself exciting, after being incarcerated in this mausoleum since the Sabbath) and met there with one I little expected to see again. I was glad enough to be out, with a purse of eight shillings at my waist, and no sharper a companion than little Rachel, who must be taken by the elbow and dragged along the street, to save her from standing ignorantly gawping. Their mother never let them out of her sight, poor chickens, and they move abroad like lost creatures. Joanna instructed me to inform Sister Wrigley at the haberdashers, and Brother Taylor at the forge, that their goods are particularly requested for the Prophet's house: this to give them an opportunity of increasing their favour with the Lord, by choosing to donate said goods to His service. I had it in mind to add in dozen

73

small pearl fastenings to Sister Wrigley's list, for the neck of my muslin gown, which is all but finished now. I tried it on last night for Rachel and Rebekah. Little Rachel said, 'Sister Leah, will it be allowed?' but Rebekah told her to hush, and pinned the hem for me. She wanted to know when I should wear it. 'I shall find a time,' I told her; little thinking how delightfully soon that time would be!

If Wrigley as well as Taylor could be prevailed upon to make God glad, I thought I should take four shillings for my labour; and I passed the time walking into Ashton, planning how I might help Fat Wrigley to her good deed. It would be more amusing to mention it at first, and watch her anxiety mounting with my pile of goods on the counter. But this would give her a longer space to find a way out, and might also give her reason to question the (forbidden) pearl buttons. Oh, what is not forbidden? Why, only that which is dingy, colourless, ugly. All pleasures – even to the taking of snuff! – are a sin. I decided I would spring it on her at the end, when she had already reckoned my bill and was opening her greedy palm. Surprise and embarrassment, not to mention fear for her immortal soul, might propel her into sudden generosity.

We went first to the forge, since kind Brother Taylor could then be an example to Fat Wrigley. The yard was awash with nuisance from the stables, which the lad was swilling out – so we watched the smith from the other side while he finished what he was about. While we waited, Rachel revealed that she has never been at the forge before. Her mother told her it is unfit for ladies. Considering the woman is no more than the wife of a hat-maker, she gives herself extraordinary airs. When Brother Taylor came out to us, flexing his shoulder and stretching his arms in the cool air, I asked if Rachel might draw closer to see, and he threw down some straw for us to walk across. The smoky heat, and taste of his sweat in the air, is delicious. The fire irons we were come to fetch were ready, but to please Rachel he took a rod which was red in the fire and, deftly bending it, beat it into a horseshoe, before plunging it into the sizzling bucket and hanging it to cool. She was full of childish excitment, and wanted to know 'if it be not against the rules', whether she might stay to watch while I went for the sewing stuffs. Seeing a soldier dismounting and leading his horse into the yard, I was about to refuse, when I suddenly recognized him.

'Yes – yes, you may wait for me here.' I crossed to him quickly, before he came within earshot of the forge. He was watching me.

'Is it Leah? Is it you?' We both burst out laughing. 'Whatever are you dressed as?'

John Saddler, one of the officers, whom I knew when I was courting Jack. He was looking thinner, and better for it, but for the addition of a black eye and a split lip.

'You can talk!' I told him. He touched his lips and laughed again.

We were able to chat for five minutes or more, while Rachel gazed into the furnace, and Brother Taylor hammered and sweated. The company are split up, and Jack is gone – as I was told – to Devon. Only John and two other officers are kept up here to train new men.

'Why, are you thinking of running after your true love?' he asked me. When I told him I hoped never to see Jack again, he looked astonished, but said no more. Thomas has been a well-kept secret. Seeing Rachel, he noticed the similarity in our dress and returned to his first question. He was most amused at hearing we are two of Mr Wroe's famous seven virgins. Then I realized the danger of blabbing to him about my affairs. If he should start to talk about me in the camp, and the talk find its way back to Sanctuary members . . . when I was in Jack's company none of them knew my home or connections. There was nothing for it but to ask him to keep his meeting with me a secret. At this he laughed again, and asked me what it was worth.

'Please.'

'Very well, I will keep a secret.' He turned to make some adjustment to his horse's bit, so after a moment I moved on. Then he called me in a low voice, 'But shall I see you later, Leah? Tonight, maybe?'

Oh I love that moment! His eyes on me, serious, waiting: and me, after a pause, 'Why not?' with a lightness and a laugh that he catches straight from me, so that both our cheeks are suddenly flushed. He wants to turn and go about his business with the blacksmith now, but I have his eyes, he cannot move.

'Ten o'clock, at the canal bridge.' I turn on my heel quickly; I am light, I am pretty, I am on my way to Sister Wrigley's. The pearl buttons and donation cannot fail.

Nor did they. And the buttons were sewn on, for ten o'clock at the canal – and there, wearing atop my muslin a black greatcoat I found in the outer office (belonging I suspect to Samuel Walker) I met him. Having left the outer office window open half an inch, so I could get in without too much disturbance, later in the night.

Oh it is a pleasure a pleasure, to be with a man again!
'Would it be asking for trouble to take you where we could get a glass of ale?' he wanted to know, as we walked along the dark towpath, past the barges moored with their flickering lights, and the tethered munching horses.
'It would,' I told him and he laughed, and said well the path was too dirty for such a lady as I, with the mud and horseshit. So I showed him my pattens, telling him I came prepared: and he pulls out a bottle of wine from his pocket, and says, 'So do I!'
And then I teased him with wishing to ruin me, and he replied that he had only the most innocent of occupations in mind, and we both speculated on what those might be.

When I crept back into the house at midnight all was still, no one the wiser for my absence. We are to meet again tomorrow night, but he will bring his horse, and take me over to a public house in Oldham, where there is no danger of either of us being known. I must go carefully. He does not yet know of Jack's child: nor do I know if he has a wife. There is a way to go before I may place any trust in him. He was urging me to say that I liked him as well as Jack 'for I know what you did with him'. But I put him off with laughter, telling him, 'I am a virgin now and have forgotten such things.' To be honest I think of them all the time; but he shall not have me so cheap.

Rebekah and I have been in fits over the punishments, after Saint Joanna's instruction. But their execution is another matter. This Sabbath past, Saint Joanna and I were led into Inner Sanctum and provided with the means of correction, then faced with a queue of some half-dozen sinners. Elder Moses, supervising, spoke so vividly of the everlastingness of the torments of Satan, that two of the men were reduced to tears of fright.

I do not like the work one jot. Hannah and Martha escape it, by reason of their not yet being full church members. It seems hardly fair that while I sweat and endure the visions of hell conjured up by Elder Moses, they are sitting at their ease at Southgate, with no one to watch them or tell them what to do.

When Brother Paine began to sob and cry out to God I ceased the punishment, and then Elder Moses turned on me; 'Carry out your duty, woman! Why do you stop? Do you think you have any right to determine the duration of a wrongdoer's punishment? Beware of presumption, beware of pride, for God hates these as much and more than other sins. Brother Paine! Savour the mental anguish of your regret, taste it well, it is no more than a shadow of the torments both mental and physical, awaiting those who do not truly repent. Come, Sister Leah! Help him to penitence!'

He does not scare me, Elder Moses. I am not scared of his ranting. But it is an ugly sight to see men cry. If it were me I should not repent, I should not give him that satisfaction. Besides, what are these crimes, to God? Brother Paine is only penitent since Ann Taylor has died. I am sure God neither knows nor cares what I do with John Saddler; I am sure He has greater concerns than me on His mind. The way Elder Moses looks is enough to make one's flesh crawl. My head is stuffed with demons and hell-creatures, all wearing the triumphant, vicious features of Elder Moses. I will not think of these things, they are not to be endured. 'No one escapes God's eye! He sees every sin, both acted and imagined; He sees and He remembers.' I will not be scared by this Bogey.

Saint Joanna walked back to Southgate with me. 'Sister Leah, is it not moving to see the wringing of true repentance from stubborn waywardness?'

'I do not like it, Sister Joanna.'

'You are too soft-hearted, my dear. Think of this as the admonition – or maybe the gentle tap across the palm – which a caring mother will administer to a naughty child, to deter it from real danger.'

Nothing can get me till I die. There will be time enough to repent, when I am old and ugly as Saint Joanna.

# Hannah

When Joanna comes into our room tonight she is sagging with tiredness.

'You are working too hard,' I tell her. But she shakes her head.

'I am working for God, Sister Hannah. There can be no half measures.' Her prophet is sitting cosily in his study with his Bible and his visitors, while she slaves to get the household running. She undresses and says her prayers in a whisper, and when she crawls into bed I tell her, 'You may extinguish the candle.' It is dark, I hear her turn over. I am in my seat by the window.

But after a few minutes, in which time I supposed her asleep, she says, 'Tell me what happened to your father.' The quarter moon is up tonight, its crescent covered now and then by cloud, but now and then appearing sharp as a sickle against the deep blue sky. In the gaps between the clouds there is a scattering of stars.

'I had a young man. Edward.'

'Whom he disliked?'

'No. Or at least, not at first. He is the son of one of my father's friends. We have known each other since childhood.'

'Go on, sister.'

'He was apprenticed away in Birmingham for seven years – he is a cabinet maker – and it was when he returned . . . There is nothing to tell. We liked each other.'

'You saw him often?'

'Yes. We talked, attended meetings together – '

'Church meetings?'

'No. No. Meetings in the Mechanics Institute. Political lectures – Owenite meetings.'

'And did he ask you to be his wife?'

'Well, in the end he did. But – '

'Yes, tell me.'

'He is – he was . . . He is in America now, Sister Joanna. He is gone to America to live in one of Mr Owen's new communities, founded upon principles of freedom and rationality.'

There is a silence now, I wonder whether she has fallen asleep. Or whether she knows what on earth I am talking about. Her interest in freedom is limited, I suspect, to the Second Kingdom. The sky is full of clouds now, I can see two stars, no more.

'Do you share his beliefs, Sister Hannah? Are not the Owenites against marriage? I have been told they hold their women in common.'

Why is it that the most salacious rumours about a system of beliefs travel like wildfire, while its sober truths, and the great benefits it may confer upon humanity, are ignored?

'No, Sister Joanna. Some of Mr Owen's followers have spoken out against marriage, as an institution which imprisons and degrades both parties, and which – in law – reduces the woman to no more than her husband's property. But Mr Owen himself is married. There are no licentious intentions behind their thinking – indeed, they seek to improve, morally, upon the present sorry state of society. What virtue can there be in love that is not freely exchanged, between equals?'

Joanna does not reply to this. After a while her gentle voice says, 'I am glad that Mr Owen is married. Did your father disapprove of Edward's beliefs?'

'How could he? He himself formed my views; he set me on the path that led inevitably in that direction. He urged me to imagine the day when every man – and woman – should have a voice in government. Edward's views are no more than the logical extension of his own.'

'Well then, Sister, I cannot see why . . .' Her voice is slow and sleepy.

'No. Never mind it now, Joanna. It is time you were asleep.'

'I know. But the day runs through my head . . . Tell me, do you think Thomas should be taken from Sister Leah's care at night? She is so determined for it that I do not want to distress her – but – ' It is true, the child is crying again. We listen for a while.

'Why does she want him with her at night?' I ask.

'She tells me that she herself sleeps so poorly that it will be no difficulty to tend him. But – ah, he has stopped.'

'But why should she take that responsibility upon herself?'

Joanna sounds surprised. 'Out of care for others, Sister Hannah.'

Leah does not strike me as a woman principally motivated by care for others. But Joanna may keep her kindly illusion – I have nothing to put in its place.

'Will you pray with me, Sister Hannah? I know God can help you, I am sure of it. Only kneel here beside me, and see how your heart will be eased.' Her bed creaks and rustles as she heaves herself out and kneels on the floor. After a moment I go to join her; it seems churlish not to.

\*

When we went to Huddersfield was the first time I listened to Mr Wroe preach. He speaks every week in Sanctuary (three times a day, on the Sabbath) but I never listen there. The fine sound of his voice, together with the incense, the bright candle flames and shining wood and brasses, and the after-effect of that heavenly music, put me into a trance. I think I am not the only person to feel so, I am sure half his congregation could not tell you what he says.

On that day it was different. Our journey was terrible. All seven of us crammed in William Lees' wife's carriage pulled by two white horses with uncut manes and tails, which were so much bedraggled in the mud by the time of our arrival that I doubt Samuel will ever get them clean again. We did not set off till late afternoon. Wroe and Samuel travelled ahead in a chaise, and were able to make better time due to the lightness of their vehicle. The highway was deep with mud, in which we were bogged several times and which splattered up on all sides, finding its way in through loose windows and rattling doors, till we were all quite filthy. The air in the carriage was close and foetid, and Rachel was sick through the jolting motion, which added unpleasantly to the stench.

We jolted and slithered on across the moors till darkness fell and we pulled up outside a coaching house. I have never been upon these moors in darkness, and they are a terrifying sight: an unending expanse of flat or undulating blackness, with never a light or a dwelling nor even the outline of a tree to punctuate it. I saw two shooting stars, and a greater number of constellations than I have ever imagined. The sky here hangs low and brilliant, as if in pity of the bleak place beneath.

We slept in infested beds, and got up red-eyed with scratching and sleeplessness, to take a poor breakfast of watered milk and stale oatcakes. These last could not be broken between the fingers, but cracked like dried clay when tapped against the table.

The prophet breakfasted separately and left a full hour before us, Samuel Walker having settled our accounts with the landlord. And so it was a sorry, bedraggled clutch of virgins who were delivered at last to a large, well-appointed house in Huddersfield. The servants ran about to provide us with hot water, and we made such repairs as we could to our appearances. Our travelling clothes were hopelessly soiled, but the white dresses carried in the trunk on the roof of the carriage were unharmed, only rather crushed. Mr Wroe was to preach in the market place in the afternoon, and wished us to accompany him.

No danger of falling into a trance over this; quite the reverse! As we filed out of the house of Huddersfield's most prosperous Israelite (owner of a small woollen mill, whose chimney reared up behind the mansion as an unabashed reminder of the source of its owner's wealth) into the street, I found myself horribly wide awake and aware of the world around me. The seven of us were dressed from head to foot in white, walking in twos behind Joanna. Mr Wroe followed us at a distance; behind him, members of the Huddersfield meeting. Handbills had alerted the population to our arrival, and the streets were lined with working people who stared at us as if were were a freak show from a travelling fair.

When we seven were ranged on the town hall steps, and Mr Wroe ascended to stand in a central spot between us, I did not know where to look for shame and embarrassment. The earnest local Israelites stood directly before us, distinct in their robes and uncut hair (the City Mark, they call it); but behind them lounged a growing number of smirking men and women, chatting and pointing out individuals among us to one another, as if looking at the giant and the dwarf and the wild Jamaican. I was convinced that as soon as Mr Wroe opened his mouth, bedlam would break out.

I glanced across at the others. The only faces I could see were Joanna, who was staring out at the crowd with a beatific smile, and

Martha, head drooping like an ox, too stupid to know she had been led to the slaughter. I looked up at Mr Wroe and caught his eye: he winked. Then he looked out over the muttering, hissing crowd and slowly raised his arms (the right hand clutching his iron rod) like great wings above his head. And they fell silent.

He held it a moment, lifting the silence up through the bodies and over the heads of the crowd in his raised arms, until it was full and round as an O, and then he tolled his deep voice into its centre.

'Brothers and sisters in God: I come with glad news, from the mouth of the Lord himself. This world is in its final days: we shall see it end.'

They stood silent, round-eyed, waiting for him to continue. Again he let the silence mount and swell, before beating into its climax with masterly precision, so that it seemed the boom of his voice was created out of silence by the strength of our desire to hear it.

He spoke commandingly in more simple language than he uses in Sanctuary, setting clearly before us the signs described in Revelations as indicating the imminent end of the world, and then showing how those signs are fulfilled in our own time. He directed us to look about us.

'Look at earthly signs. Look at the poverty and starvation among the working people – brought about by greed of the ungodly, and the power of their machines, machines which are the work of the devil himself.'

At this a slow groan rose from the crowd, low at first as the wind in bare branches, but gathering in force.

'Machines: machines made with the devil's cunning to steal work from the hands of our good weavers, spinners, wool-combers. Machines, valued by those who govern us at higher than a God-given human life, for the man who raises his arm to them, to protect his child from starvation, must hang. Look, brothers and sisters in Christ, look at the world around you. Our young mothers are wage slaves in the mills, while their suckling babes are left drugged and fasting from dawn till noon-time. Who can show me the animal so depraved that it will poison its own young? Is this God's will? Or that a child, of eight years old, should labour all night in the contagious heat and hellish noise, till even the blows of the brutal overseer cannot keep him awake and he stumbles into the path of the monster machine: the strap whirls him along and up, screaming in terror, and smashes his innocent body against the rafters? While his able-bodied father can find no buyer for his labour, no market for his cloth, and slumps in the ale-house for very shame. Earthly measures cannot prevail against this evil: your strikes and combinations will fail, as the wool-combers did, according to my prophecy, until every working man and woman among you is reduced to starvation. Is this God's order?'

Again the silence, against which they beat like sleepwalkers, or like moths against a window when they seek the candlelight indoors: forming amongst themselves a rising wave of whispers upon which hungry sea his voice again set sail.

'God's order has been destroyed. The devil is out and about among us, his crooked hand is evident in all things: in the disturbances of the heavens, the eclipses and shooting stars: in the weather which has brought more ruined harvests since the turn of the century than ever before in history: in the profligacy and destruction of the French wars – '

Here he was interrupted by a terrible cry from a woman in the centre of the crowd: at first I thought her injured, and there was an eddy of agitated movement around her, then a man called out, 'Here's Susan Batsby, as lost 'er two lads to Boney!' and a ripple of sympathy ran through them as they turned back to Wroe.

'The world is upside down, evil stalks abroad. Brothers and sisters, I shall not speak of the corruption at the heart of the kingdom, among those persons of high place who presume to rule us, and whose ways are more disgusting and profligate than the citizens of Sodom and Gomorrah: for you may read of that in any penny paper. Nearer to home, brothers and sisters, ghosts and shadows of horror abound, and at every table, by every fireside, contagion lurks ready to strike. Even today, as I look at you, I can tell – '

Their listening became a holding of breath, as he took his time scanning their faces. 'There are among you two disbelievers who will fall sick before tomorrow daybreak, and who will sink and die within seven days, unless they turn and open their hearts to God.'

'Who will be saved?' A woman's voice rang out, anguished.

And pat as if he had planted her there (did he? was someone made to ask that question?) he told them about the promises made

83

by God to his chosen people, the Israelites, and how it was still possible to find salvation by joining their church.

His performance made a strong impression on me; firstly because he spoke of earthly things. He has never, in Sanctuary, made any reference to the outside world, to the plight of the weavers, to politics, or to the wars; indeed, has been careful to make a division between things of this world and things of God, and to suggest that Israelites have no interest in the former. It was with genuine passion that he outlined these injustices, which are real, and terrible, and the effects of which one may see in the faces of such a crowd; half-starved, sickly, brutalized. Secondly, I was struck by his – power. To many a simple soul in that audience, his power is quite simply the power of God. He is able to bewitch and convince them, and change their lives, because God speaks through him.

This power is not – I think, upon hard reflection – is not simply the result of the *sense* of his words. It is not the rational mind that is moved. It is easy to describe injustice, to generate pity and anger. I have heard many speakers excel at it.

It must have been in his use of silence; in the combined use of his deep musical voice and silence . . . An orator's trick, to make us hunger for the word.

But if I call it a trick; still I must admire the energy and intelligence which can perform that trick. May it not have been such an energy, in the beginning, that tricked the round earth out of chaos; the first small motion of life from stillness?

*

I am tempted now to laugh at myself; to count myself as easily swayed as the ignorant crowd who came flocking forward at the end of his speech, to join the Rolls of the Saved.

I dreamed last night of Edward. Though I had not heard from him for months before father's death, yet it seems likely to me that he *will* reply, when my letter bearing that news reaches him. Then, an instant change might be made in my circumstances. Who knows but I might leave the prophet's household for America, to live in a New World, instead of daily awaiting the destruction of the Old? I might exchange hope and vigorous action, for this quiet meditation and growing sense of my own powerlessness.

Tonight, after sitting by the dark window a good long while, I knew I should not sleep. Hearing that Joanna's breathing was slow and regular, I dressed myself again and let myself out on to the landing. The house was silent, and very dark, only the rushlight from the corridor at the bottom of the stairs casting a faint illumination. Carrying my shoes, I crept down (the stairs creaking, as they always do, on the fourth step down); turned left past the kitchen and offices, and let myself out at the back door. Boney gave a low growl as I stepped into the yard, but I called his name softly, and was rewarded by the sound of his tail thumping on the ground. I sat on the doorstep and put on my shoes.

I am not sure that I had formed any clear intention of going anywhere. I walked once around the house, noting the crack of light showing between the shutters of Mr Wroe's study window, and the darkness everywhere else – and then I set out along the lane, heading for the canal. My eyes were used to the darkness now: it was dark moon, with patches of stars visible between the fast-moving clouds; a breathless, hurrying sort of night, which fuelled my own impatience and dissatisfaction. A warmish wind, smelling of freshly dug earth and spring. I thought of my father in the ground, rotting. I imagined the clean white bones starting to appear through the dark shrivelled flesh, and I prayed he was at rest. If I could believe any part of him lurked about the world – if I could believe in the closeness of his spirit, in the possibility of his ghostly voice on the wind . . . I would be glad.

The wind rushing past my face, and threshing the arms of the beeches along the lane, was an easy figure for the tearing forward motion in my head. Nothing stayed – but past and through me whirled a host of impulses, thoughts, memories, ambitions, all so fast-moving that I could focus clearly on none. I realized that I was crying, and forced myself to stop and turn away from the wind, to feel the hot tears run down my cheeks, and steady myself with that sensation. When he died I could not cry at all, my eyes were hot and dry as if filled with desert sand. Now, with the wind hurtling past my head, I felt the lovely tears gushing from my eyes, and wiped the backs of my hands against my cheeks, and licked the salty moisture from them. Luxuriating in being a child, helpless, overwhelmed by the events of my life.

When my tears stopped I felt weak and clean. I also had the

hiccups. I leant against one of the beeches, alternately holding my breath and letting go to test if they were gone, and while I stood there I noticed a darker shape outlined against the path, moving towards me.

Clearly, someone heading for Southgate. Maybe one of the elders, with some special message to the prophet? But I could see already that it was a woman. What woman would come to visit him in the middle of the night, on foot, alone? I drew further back behind my tree, pressing my knuckles into my mouth to silence the hiccups. As she drew closer there was something familiar about the way she walked – then I knew, it was Leah. I stepped forward and called her name, at which she stopped.

'It is me. Hannah. I wondered who you were.'

'Are you alone?'

'Yes.'

She came up to me, and touched my cape. 'You are well hidden in that cloak, Sister Hannah.'

'And you!' She also was wearing a long black garment – close up, it seemed to be some kind of greatcoat.

She looked up and down the path. 'So where are you off to, then?'

'Nowhere.'

She laughed. 'You do not like imprisonment either.'

We began to walk slowly back towards the house. 'Is that how you think of it?'

'Imprisonment,' she said fiercely. 'A little life laid out of us. Rows of duties. Are you content?'

'I do not plan to stay here for the rest of my life.'

'No? Where are you going?'

'Who knows? Something will happen. But you have family, Leah, there is no need for you to stay here.'

She laughed bitterly, but did not reply.

'Is that where you have been?' I asked.

'Why should I tell you? How do you plan to get out, anyway?'

'We are free to leave. He has told me that – '

'He?'

'The prophet. Mr Wroe.'

We walked in silence for a while and then she asked, 'You were talking?'

'We sometimes talk, after his reading.'

Leah stopped and stared at me. 'I never find it possible to speak to him. He always dismisses me while I am still reading.'

'He seems happy to talk,' I told her, thinking of the several occasions now on which he has engaged me in conversation.

'Really? With you?'

I smiled to myself in the dark. 'Maybe he is intimidated by your beauty.'

She considered this seriously. 'It is possible. Do you think he likes Joanna?'

'I do not think he much likes any of us. We are not here to be liked by him. He sees us as necessary trappings to his household of God: besides which, we perform a number of domestic functions more cheaply than servants.'

'You think that is all his purpose?'

'What else do you imagine?' I knew, of course, but I suddenly wondered if his behaviour toward her *was* different.

'I imagine he may want women for the same reason any other man does, from time to time.'

'Joanna says he has a wife.'

'She is dead.'

'The church could hardly approve such – '

'The church would not know.'

'Has he proposed anything of the sort to you?'

She looked at me, her face gleaming white in the darkness. 'Not yet.'

'You wish him to?' I thought she would not reply; the silence grew between us, and it was only as we approached the back door, and I was reaching out to pat Boney's excited head, that she said in a low fierce voice, 'I wish for *change*.'

As we were creeping up the stairs she laid a hand on my shoulder to stop me, and putting her mouth right next to my ear, whispered, 'Do you know where he keeps his money?'

'No. Joanna has the housekeeping.'

'There's more than that, somewhere about.' She patted my shoulder to make me go on; I noticed that she stepped over the fourth step from the top – just as I, too late remembering, put my weight on it. She has done this before.

*

The prophet himself intrudes into my thoughts increasingly. He is at the heart of this little world; his link with God the centre around which they all revolve. And yet there are contradictions.

The faith of Dinah, the faith of Joanna – or of fifty other members of their church – is simple. Absolute. It determines every action of their lives; it glosses the inexplicable, it offers future rewards for every earthly disappointment. Now I observe their prophet, it seems to me that there is more (or maybe less) to his faith, than that. Two incidents particularly have stayed in my mind, this week, and lead me to puzzle over his beliefs and intentions. He is not a fraud, I am certain of that; and yet it occurs to me that he may not be altogether so great a believer as those who follow him.

The first is straightforward enough; the sermon he preached on the Sabbath, to the text, *The Prophet is a snare to his people*. Developing the idea in a logical manner, he warned his listeners not to follow his every instruction, not to believe his every word, explaining that God has told him; 'Son of Man, I have made thee a snare unto the house of Israel, and I have forbidden any man to take counsel of thee: for thy judgement is not better than that of others, and my children must not regard thee as wiser than other men.'

I am puzzled by his choice of subject. For this church is literally a sanctuary; a construct of rules and regulations which shelter its members from the arduous world of change and choices outside. Every detail of their lives is prescribed; clothing, diet, hair, jewellery, manners, morals – even reading matter, for their rule book states they are to read nothing but the Bible (one of many injunctions I ignore; even sister Joanna owns and reads other material). The very freedom from choice of the Israelite way of life is an attraction, and it is the prophet's rules and prohibitions which have created this secure place. Yet now he tells them it is a snare, not to be trusted?

There was no reaction from the congregation – no casting off of prescribed garments, or wild snipping of beards. I wonder if they listen to him at all, or simply think to take in virtue, as a plant takes in the moisture that it needs, by standing in the rain of his words?

I raised the question with Joanna, as we worked together in the kitchen on Sunday, but her gentle faith finds no difficulty in this.

'It is God's wish that we *choose*, Sister Hannah. Not that we are led, like blind unthinking sheep, but that we choose virtue for its own sweet sake. Ever since our first mother Eve was tempted to bite the apple, we have had knowledge of good and evil. If we follow the Prophet's dictates slavishly, then we are snared and lost; but if we examine our conscience over each question and, seeing that it please Him – in the matter of dress for example, choose to lay aside worldly vanity – then we act aright.'

On the second matter I did not consult Joanna; I am still not quite sure why. After the Sabbath evening meeting, as we were waiting for the prophet to lead us on our walk back from Sanctuary, a man suddenly burst in at the side door and pushed between us. Finding the prophet, he threw himself at his feet (this in the confined space of the vestibule, where a number of the elders, besides ourselves, were crowded) and begged mercy and forgiveness. Mr Wroe pulled him to his feet and asked – almost angrily – what was the matter. The man (a factory operative, judging by his clothes) blurted out that he had this week lost his wife and oldest child, that two others of his children were sick, and that he feared it was God's judgement for his unholy way of life. Mr Wroe instructed him to pray and seek forgiveness, to come to Bible class on Tuesday night, and to attend Sanctuary at the early morning service on Sabbath next. 'God will take you into His fold, and take your troubles upon Himself. Go in peace.' But the man could not get up for sobbing his gratitude, and then Mr Wroe brushed past him and set off towards Southgate at such a pace that we had trouble keeping up, and Martha and I fell so far behind, helping Dinah, that we lost sight of the others.

When I went to read to him an hour later, he did not request a passage, but sat glaring at me in silence for some time. At last he said, 'I cannot hear the Bible tonight, Sister Hannah. How is your faith?'

'I – much the same as when we spoke before.'

'You are not converted then?'

'No.'

'D'you believe in devils, Sister Hannah?'

'No.'

'Not even when you see a case like that fellow tonight? Lost his wife, lost his children – ?'

'There are reasons, which are much easier to find out than devils, surely.'

'Such as?'

'Maybe his wife was sickly from overwork and a poor diet; maybe their house is overcrowded; perhaps the children have succumbed to illness through lack of that fresh air and exercise which are necessary to youthful strength.'

He snorted contemptuously. 'You mistake symptoms for cause. Do you think the truth of a situation may be understood by examining its external appearance?'

'Well, yes.'

'Let me show you something.' He reached into an inner pocket and held out to me a thin gold band, similar to a wedding ring. 'A type of ring worn by female followers of the church. Here. Take it.'

'I could never wear a ring in the workshop and I would feel most uncomfortable – '

'I do not wish you to wear it,' he interrupted impatiently. 'Examine it. Tell me what it is.'

I took the ring and looked at it, then bit it. The right colour, but too hard for gold. 'It is brass, maybe mixed with some other base metal.'

'Worth?'

'Maybe a shilling.'

'I have sold them to church members for a guinea apiece, and told them they are gold.'

'Why?'

'Rings of God; angels' rings. They bring great comfort to those who wear them; each one connects its wearer with the faith of the angels. Their value is inestimable – outside the sordid calculations of jewellers and bankers.'

'But – '

'But? How can you presume to know the value of such a ring to its wearer, Sister Hannah?'

'And devils? – that man tonight?'

'If he can believe it is God's will his family should die; if he can see beyond that personal tragedy to some greater and as yet unknown good which God may bring from it – '

'Is that what you believe?'

'I believe the long strand of faith must be spun out, spun out of my entrails, like a spider's thread, to make a line across every such devilish chasm – '

I waited, but I could not help myself. 'Until – ?'

He shrugged. 'Until. Who knows. I am going out for a walk, Sister Hannah. I'll bid you good-night.' He held the door open for me, and followed me out, heading on through the great hall to the front door, where I watched him speak briefly with Samuel before going out into the night.

*

When I come into our bedchamber tonight, I smile to see Joanna at my old seat by the window, staring out across the field into the gathering dusk.

'You have taken my place, sister.'

She shakes her head. She has been reading to Mr Wroe tonight. She was going to ask him –

'Has he given you permission to preach?'

'No.'

'I am sorry – '

She shakes her head again. 'Oh no, it is God's will. The women of the church are not to preach. He will decide when and how to use us; we must be ready, that is all.' She smiles her gentle smile. I want to offer her something for her disappointment.

'I have heard some excellent women speakers, in London. A woman may sometimes speak more powerfully than a man. Anna Wheeler, for example; she does not share your faith, but the passion and conviction with which she speaks carry all before her.'

Joanna is not listening. She looks out into the field again, then stands, as if to offer me the chair.

'It is all right. You can sit there if you like.'

We both stand awkwardly, she would perhaps rather be alone. I pick up my book, intending to go and read by the kitchen fire. But as I am half-out the door she says, 'Sister Hannah. Do not go.' She laughs and shrugs, as if to shake off gloomy thoughts. 'See – I will take the seat again. You may perch on the bed in my old place. Why do you not tell me . . . you never finished telling me about Edward and your father.'

'You do not want to hear that now, Joanna.'

'Indeed I do. Nothing could interest me more.' The room is chilly, after the warmth of the day.

'Shall we go down and sit by the kitchen fire?'

'Sisters Leah, Rebekah and Rachel are down there. I – ' She gives a little laugh. 'I do not like to spoil their chatter.' I pass her the blanket from her bed, and wrap my own around my shoulders. It is ridiculous to sit banished in the cold like this.

'Your father became – grew distant – because of Edward?' she prompts gently.

'I suppose so. I did not notice when it began. I . . . well, the crisis came when Edward asked me to accompany him to America.'

'Leaving your father.'

'Yes.'

'He did not want you to go?'

'It was not that simple. When I told him what Edward proposed he asked me what I wished to do. And when I asked him for his advice, he told me I must decide for myself.'

'That was fair.'

'How was it fair? Would you think me fair if you came to me for advice on a matter affecting the whole of your future life, and I told you it was none of my business and that you must decide?'

'If your view was bound to be partial, yes. What interest could your father have in your leaving him? For himself, he could only want you to stay.'

'But it is possible to put one's own desires aside, to consider what may be the best course of action for another.'

'You should have prayed. Only God can guide us, in such a choice.'

'Not only would he give me no advice, he would not even speak to me.'

'What do you mean?'

'He stopped speaking. He no longer told me what he'd read in the newspaper, who he'd seen on the street corner, the strange thought that had come to him while he was buying a cabbage. He stopped talking, all save for essential practical purposes, such as instructions concerning the workshop.'

'You asked him – '

'Of course I asked him why. Over and over again, in as many different ways as there are days in the month – angrily, gently, teasingly, pleadingly, laughingly, in tears . . . I could get nothing out of him.'

'So you decided not to go?'

'Yes. I told Edward I could not go. What else could I do? If my father was so angered – or upset – by the notion of my going – that he could no longer speak to me civilly . . . then how could I go?

She nods. 'Was Edward grieved?'

'Not for long. He is a great optimist, he sees the best in every situation. He reasoned that it would be best for him to face the hazards of the initial journey, and the construction of a home, as a single man; in that way he could put his full energies into the establishment of the community, its buildings, its supplies, its equitable government.'

'That makes sense.'

'But when he was gone . . .' The early summer evening has darkened. I hear Leah, Rebekah and Rachel coming up the stairs, talking in loud whispers, and giggling.

'How is Dinah tonight?'

'No better. Sister Wrigley has sent a bottle of her syrup of lungwort. It is the best remedy for wheezing and shortness of breath – but the poor girl can scarcely swallow it . . . God gives her great courage. I think she must have another room-mate than Sister Martha . . . I think we must make a change.'

I realize she means either me or herself. 'What about Sister Rachel? I am sure she could look after Dinah.'

'And put Sister Martha with Sister Rebekah?' It would be an unhappy combination, I can see; besides, Leah spends most evenings in their chamber.

'Why not offer Martha the little servants' room? She seems to prefer solitude.'

Joanna does not reply. At last she sighs. 'I think perhaps I should move in to Sister Dinah's room.'

'Do not make a hasty decision,' I urge her.

She nods. 'God may send me a sign.' She turns so that I see her face in profile against the deep blue window: I cannot make out her features now, only a black silhouette. 'You always avoid the end of your story, Sister Hannah. Tell me what happened when Edward left.'

'Nothing. Nothing happened. Edward left: eventually I received a letter from him telling me of his safe arrival.'

'And your father – ?'

'My father nothing. He continued the same. Not speaking, or smiling, or showing the least interest in me or affection for me. We worked together in silence; he went out without telling me where he was going or when he would be back; he did not even cook for me, unless we were actually in the workshop together.'

'But was this general? Did he speak to anyone else?'

'Oh yes; our landlady became a great confidante, all his little frets over those customers who did not pay immediately, or who were troublesome enough to request the use of more than one colour of ink, were passed over to her: and with his other friends he became exceedingly sociable and jovial, sometimes even venturing out to pass an evening in the ale house with them – which he had never done before.'

'You were excluded from this?'

I laughed. 'You do not understand, Joanna. I was excluded from his life. It was as if I had actually gone to America; he tried to behave as if I was not there. Even when he became ill: even when he lay, weak and choking in his bed, and I had to feed him like a baby – never so much as a smile or a word of – '

She kneels beside the bed to put her arms around me. 'Sister. Sister. Do not cry. Hush now. He is with God.'

I am not crying. She is warm; it is like coming near the fire after standing in the freezing rain. 'He never forgave me. Not on his deathbed, not when I asked his blessing.'

She sits up on the bed beside me, leaning against the wall. Her voice is soft as touch. 'He was not judging you, Sister Hannah. Surely you see that. He judged himself.'

'What do you mean?'

'Surely he judged himself? He loved you too well, needed you too much, to express joy at your leaving for America. He did not beg you to stay, but he could not bring himself to wish you to go. So he remained neutral. Forcing himself not to speak, not to influence you. But then when you did not go – he feared you had made the decision for his sake – and that you regretted it.'

My breath has made the space under the blanket suffocatingly hot. I poke my head out into the air. She is a black shape beside me. 'But why did he not speak – at the very least – '

'What could he have told you? That he was afraid he had pushed you into making the wrong decision? When he became

94

ill, and maybe guessed he was dying – how could he feel, knowing you would be left alone, instead of with a husband and a new life before you?'

'If he thought he was wrong, he could have said so and had done with it.'

'How, when the wrong could not be put right? When he could not love, or want you to stay at home, any less?'

And so he continued harsh, cold, rejecting every gesture of kindliness and reconciliation; because what could my blundering attempts represent, but further cause for guilt and self-reproach?

'But then he *died* . . .'

'Yes, Sister Hannah? We must all die. He had no choice in the matter. He did not die to hurt you, I am sure.'

In the darkness I hear the sounds of the house settling, the stairs creak and are silent: over near the canal an owl hoots. Joanna sits quite silent in the dark.

She is right. He did not die to hurt me.

'Sister Hannah, let us pray for his soul. He was a good man, God will reward him.'

\*

Summer. After weeks of unchanging cloud, producing either cold rain or an apparent absence of any weather at all; a day not clear, not hot, but light and with a pale grey haze in its still air, so that on leaving the house I did not see the weather as part of here and now, but as a shaft, clear back, through all those days of my life which have contained precisely this quality of summer. Holding, in their lazy curl, essence of summer smells, holding dust of roads and scent of hay, or the sudden beauty of the workshop window flung open to admit clean balmy air into the chemical interior.

This is the day of all the year I love the best. It has no drama; no romantic thunderstorms or golden sunshine. But this quiet day, when the skies are still grey and one may be deceived, on looking through a window, into thinking it just such another as the ten preceding: this quiet, unpretentious day, makes itself known to my heart and memory as clearly as if a hand had touched my own. The stillness of the air, amplifying birdsong and the rumble of coaches on the turnpike. The haze, both of the lower edges of sky, and in the rising dust of drying earth: the sweet tender green of half-opened leaves, still dwarfed by the massed browns and greys of bare twigs, bare earth: but coming, coming in an unstoppable slow growth. There is no beauty in the sky, no azure blue or fleecy white: it is mute, holding still – on a level which is connected with the ache of longing at the back of my throat. Promises. Promises. It is the sweetest thing, this day at the edge of summer, where all is promised, all is to come, and the sky stands mute, careful, grey.

If I could I would make today stand still, I would hang forever suspended on the edge of the promise – never having to move forward into the bald reality of days ahead.

When we rose at four this morning it was already dawn, the sun fresh as a lemon in a pale green-blue sky, where a couple of the brightest stars and a faint crescent moon lingered still.

Wash-day; our third together (for we wash in the week before the feast of the New Moon). And by this third attempt, we are almost into a routine. Our devotions are shortened to half an hour, then we scatter to our various tasks: Martha and I to the pump, drawing the twenty-eight buckets of water it takes to fill the copper; Joanna to Sanctuary in the carriage, to fetch the devotional linen; Rachel to strip the beds, Leah and Dinah to gather the household garments, and sort them into colours. Rebekah lights the fire beneath the copper, and brings up the day's supply of wood.

Leah is grey-faced and furious in the early morning, we all avoid her. The baby Thomas is still asleep, but I heard him crying in the night. She cares for him with a suppressed anger which suggests she finds it a duty rather than a pleasure. Whereas Rebekah and Rachel, and even Joanna, coo over him and would smother him with soft affection. Leah leaves the room immediately one of them takes him up, as if their dotingness kindled an impatience in her that propels her from their company. I cannot muster any great interest in a baby; the dog is more companionable and intelligent, and the small fragility of the child is almost repulsive to me. I will like it better larger and more robust.

The burden of wash-day lies heavy on Joanna's shoulders; a hundred small matters lurk in her memory and fret her;

'Do not forget to bring out the pail I left in the outer office the other night, where Brother Samuel's pillow slip and night-shirt are soaking, from the nose-bleed.'

'I have forgot to tell Brother Benson to send us no cream for churning this week; we cannot spare the time, his girl must do our butter for us. Rebekah and Rachel, will you walk up and tell them, before he is put to the trouble of sending the cart down?'

'There are two pair of worsted stockings needing a quick darn at the heel before washing; Sister Dinah, you might do it instead of your other work.'

'Be sure to keep the new blue overskirts away from everything else; I am dreadfully afraid of their running. Mine was only slightly damp at the hem, and it has stained my underskirt.'

'I am afraid we shall run out of starch; I was promised some of Sister Taylor and she has not sent it over. We may leave it for today but it must be fetched first thing tomorrow. Do not let me forget.'

'Sister Dinah, you are not to overtax yourself again today. You may help Sister Leah with the sorting, and after that you take a rest.'

'I would have returned those two new washtubs to the cooper for better finishing off, if he had not delivered them so shockingly late. Whoever uses them, take care you do not get splinters in your arms, for I do not think he has sanded the rims at all.'

These little anxieties occur to her through the day, and when they do she breaks off her work to see about them, and we hear her warm soft voice centring that part of the wash-house where she is. When the water comes to the boil, we take our buckets over to the copper to fill them – our washtubs take six bucketfuls. Opening and closing the tap is a difficult business, for it is stiff and becomes very hot, so must be turned with one's hand wrapped in a towel. Standing behind Rebekah and watching her wrestle to turn it off, it occurred to me that we might get the water direct from the copper into the tubs, if we worked in pairs, carrying a tub between two of us. The advantage would be less time wasted in opening and closing the tap, and hotter water too, for the bucket method allows it to cool rapidly. I tried it with Leah, and aside from being nearly overpowered by the steam, found that we could manage a three-quarters-full tub between us. So this improvement in our working methods was adopted by all. That first lungful of steam, early in the morning, on an empty stomach, brings memory of the preceding wash-day flooding through me; the hollow stomach, aching back and shoulders, sore, raw-skinned knuckles; the pitch of physical exhaustion I reach which is almost pleasurable, for I become light and giddy. Complete happiness can then be found in taking a single bite of bread and cheese.

When our tubs are full we add ashballs and put in the whites; give them a few turns with the dolly and leave them to steep while we break our fast. This is done quickly on oatcakes and cold milk; then back to the serious scrubbing business, with sleeves rolled above the elbow, leaning forward into the steaming heat and grabbing the slippery pink bar of soap, with one knuckle beneath the stiff resistant layers of cloth. The linen of our dresses, when wet, is as harsh as sacking. Leah attacks her tubfull with frenzy, putting her whole body into the motion of scrubbing. She is always finished first. Martha scrubs, but erratically; Joanna takes her tub when she is done, and examines the contents carefully, dispatching Martha to wring out Joanna's own tubfull. No one talks. The steam in the air seems to cut each one off from the others, and our eyes are kept fixed on the cloth till I see spots where there are none, or stains that move each time I blink. Most of all I hate the hems of underskirts, for that line of dirt where it has swept the ground can never be entirely removed, though one scrub till one's fingers are raw.

'You should lead us in a hymn practice as we work,' I said to Joanna. I was half in jest, but she took up the idea, so we sang our way through the next half hour's labour, and our throats – opened by the heat and the steam – never made a sweeter sound than in the echoing stone wash-house.

The water cools, a thick grey scum lies across the surface. At last, by common consent, a common, red-faced, raw-fingered exhaustion, we begin to wring out the washing, taking sheets in a long snaking line from tub to bucket, wherein they are coiled; dripping (or pouring) water down between tub and bucket to wet our skirts and feet. My bodice is already soaked by my efforts, from splashing and from sweat. I am warm, sodden, limp with fatigue. And we are only at the morning. Now we take up in pairs again the half-empty tubs, to hoist and pour their filthy contents back into the copper. The buckets of washing are added in, the bellows applied to the fire, and the whole stinking mass set to boiling up again.

While it boils we fill our tubs at the pump – again with the innovation of working in pairs. I work with Martha, who is tremendously strong but also clumsy. There is no natural rhythm in her movements, simply a forcing forwards – through – each action. Waiting her turn at the pump, Rachel sprawls out on the sunny grass.

Rebekah has gone into the house, and calls to her sister as she returns; 'Rachel! Thomas is crying, will you do him?'

'Can Dinah not see to him?'

'She is alseep.'

There is a brief silence then Leah moves off towards the house, leaving Joanna alone with the tub at the pump: Rachel has to get up to help her.

A great change has come over Rachel and Rebekah during their time here. At first they stared at everything with wondering eyes, barely replying to questions, never speaking of their own accord. Now they chatter together all day long, and find something to giggle over every other minute. They are utterly and unthinkingly obedient to all the rules, and yet are cultivating a kind of carelessness (as shown in Rachel's sprawl upon the grass, which she would never have done even a month ago), a relaxedness which was completely missing from their characters before. Their mother calls once a week to speak with them – on a Sunday morning, when we have the dishes and tidying from the Sabbath on our hands. At her knock upon the door they are transformed again into timid silent creatures. Leah spends much time with them, in the evenings; going past their door I sometimes very much wish to enter and join in their laughter. But I know it would stop if I did.

We cannot rest. Strong-armed Martha hoists our washing out of the copper with long wooden tongs, slopping it into our buckets. We heave the buckets across to tip into the fresh cold-water tubs and rinse. Martha empties the scummy slops from the copper, a bucketful at a time. We rinse, scrub, wring: those items which remain soiled are heaved back into the copper, with another load of fresh water, and boiled up with a muslin bag of white wood ashes to lift the stains. The tubs are emptied and filled again – blue is added to the final rinse. The water now is numbingly cold, and all our hands and forearms purplish red and mottled. Leah mixes the starch over the kitchen grate and brings it round to us. Helping one another we empty our final rinse water out on to the grass and wring the clothes between us taking an end each of each item and twisting until it is quite knotted up. Now at last we shake and spread them over the hedge and over the lines strung between the wash-house and the office wall. My shoulders are a hunch of pain; I stumble against Rachel and she totters, regains her balance, turns and giggles at me. I drop my sheet on to the dusty path. At this Rachel giggles harder, causing Rebekah, Leah, Joanna to all stop and turn. Each of them begins to laugh, as I gather up the sheet, trying to save it from further dirtying and only succeeding in smearing a dusty mess right down the front of my sodden dress. We are all laughing; foolishly, helplessly, uncontrollably. I am so weak I have to lean against the door to get my breath, and Rachel, clutching a wet towel to her chest, and wheezing with laughter, sinks down on to the grass. We laugh so much I think I shall never stop. Then I see Martha's plain red face turning from one to another of us. Her expressionless eyes watch each staggering move we make.

'Sister Martha!' I pull myself together and dump the dirty sheet on the ground. I approach her with my arms open, intending – I do not know – to embrace her? to somehow draw her in. But she flinches as I get close, and then she turns back into the wash-house. Rebekah begins to giggle again, and we all laugh afresh, briefly, guiltily, at Martha's rejection.

The work goes on and on, for there are still the coloureds to steep and wash; and as the whites dry, the ironing to begin. We work for two days, from dawn till past nine at night. When I think, 'I am a laundry maid,' I am no longer angry. It just makes me laugh. It is also the best sauce to cold food that I have ever found!

*

Joanna and I spent this afternoon in the kitchen bottling and making jam from fifteen pound of strawberries sent as a gift from the Israelite farmers at the Moss. We worked slowly, with the back door open to let out the heat of our fire: as I was sawing the sugar blocks into smaller pieces, and she was hulling the fruit, she raised the question of Martha. From the carefulness with which she concentrated on her strawberries, and avoided my eye, I realized that this is something that has been troubling her for a while.

'Clearly, she has been badly treated,' I said.

'Yes indeed. Badly treated, and kept in complete ignorance.'

'Are you having any success in teaching her?'

'A little. I am encouraged, at times, to think her mind capable of retaining a certain amount of information.'

'Her manners at table are improving. I think you are making good progress with her.'

'Thank you, sister. But – ' She hesitated.

'Yes?'

'Have you watched her?'

'Not closely, no.'

'I – this may sound foolish perhaps –' She gave a little laugh. 'I see her watching us. All of us – any of us – when she is in the room. She watches all the time, like a cat with a mouse.' She laughed again. 'It seems fanciful. I know, but sometimes I think –'

'Yes?' I said to encourage her, because her speech had trailed off again.

'Yes. I am sorry. It *is* a fancy, but it is so strong at times – I feel almost as if she looks on us not as sisters but as – something quite other than herself. She looks on us – almost – with dislike.'

For a moment I was tempted to laugh with her, and dismiss the thing as a fantasy. But a couple of incidents with Martha reared up so strongly in my memory, that I was forced to pause. The first concerned a goose which I had put away in the larder one evening. We had two at table, and this second one was hardly touched, only a few slices taken off the breast. Being the last to leave the kitchen later on that night, I stacked up the cakes which had been baked in the afternoon and left out to cool, to take them into the larder. As I was arranging them into a pile, I heard (through the open kitchen door) footsteps, then the latch to the larder door being lifted. Thinking to find Joanna there with a candle, I set out with my arms full of cakes; but when I got into the corridor, it was quite dark. Suddenly Martha appeared before me, clearly alerted by my footsteps. She stared at me for an instant. I have seen her look blank, as if you were nothing, but this time I am sure there was dislike in her eyes. She was still for a moment – and the only light was that which fell through the open kitchen doorway, so I could not swear to it – then she moved swiftly past me, along the corridor and away. Once I was over my shock I called to her to fetch my candle from the kitchen, but she did not hear me, and disappeared up the stairs.

I set down my cakes and fetched the candle: as I put my goods away in the larder I noticed both legs had been torn off the goose. That must have been her errand.

The second incident was altogether more strange and unpleasant. I came upon her in the garden; well, beyond the garden, because it was the other side of the hedge. I was out there looking at the peas, which I knew were not quite ready, but still we had been sent such a fine basketful from Mrs Paine that I could not help wondering whether ours might be ready soon. The heat of the mid-afternoon sunshine tempted me to stay and walk right round the kitchen garden; which does the household credit, for it is full and flourishing and will provide us with a good deal to eat throughout the late summer and autumn. If I had thought a year ago that I should have a stake in a garden, and know the crops that were growing on! I who have never known more greenery than Hampstead Heath underfoot, or what I might buy at market! But as I walked, in the soft, insect-buzzing haze of the afternoon, enjoying the touch of sunlight on my skin, I noticed something moving behind the hedge. Not, I thought, human, nor in any way menacing. What I imagined was some kind of animal, maybe a fox or a dog – and it was no more than idle curiosity that prompted me to round the hedge and look for it.

But it was Martha. She had heard me coming, and was watching for me. She had clearly been lying in the ditch, for there were bits of grass and straw stuck all over her clothes – but she was on her feet by the time I saw her. She stood stock still for a moment, then she quite slowly and deliberately lifted up her skirt, gathering it in folds in her large hands as she raised it – right up to her waist. Her private parts were completely naked. She was staring at me, did not look down, or away, even for an instant. It was as if she wished to offer me – what? a threat? a warning? – by this display of her flesh.

I could not make myself turn and move away fast enough: could not reconcile the shock and revulsion that rose in my mind, with my sense of shame at myself for feeling offended, when she probably meant no more by it than the child on the street corner who sticks out his tongue at a stranger; that she did not rightly know what she was doing.

As I told Joanna the tale I found myself softening it, to hide the fact of Martha's nakedness. Her sensitive concern will dwell for longer, and more sadly, upon the event than I did. When she had heard me out she asked me to pray with her for Sister Martha, to which I readily agreed. For I think it likely that a mightier-than-human influence is needed, to repair that grievous damage inflicted by Martha's earlier life.

# Martha

Eat. Eat. Stuff hot cold sharp sweet. Much. Cram it in. Tear
bread crust eat. Dough soft mouth filling. Yellow cheese
crumbling sour. Hard egg slippy white. Dry inside. Eat. Shove
in mouth. Chew, swallow. Is more. And more. Apple sweet-
musty. Cooked flesh, red brown. Grained, tough, teeth go go
go. Choke when swallow. Eat. More. Pale melting oh yes cram.
No not fish she say stop, the bones. They take it away. In a
round brown edge stiff, sweetness. Tarts. Eat. Stuff. Cram.
Gorge sweet is best but here is hard soft melting chewing
crumbling slipping exploding. After is bucket. Here all together
dry wet sweet sour crunching broken. Grab and stuff ah more
as much all together –

She slap out. Dodge. 'Naughty Martha. That is the oughts.
For the animals. Not for people.'

Wait. She leave it outside.

Barn belly ache and blow. Like when. Eat. Eat. Outside, guts
vomit.

Breathe. Scoop water. Breathe. Now bucket. Take in ditch. Dry
potato sweet broken tart hard bone chew.

It hot. In by fires. Fires burn in here, in here, in here.
  'Bring wood please Sister Martha.'
  'Take ashes Sister Martha.'
  Hot. Stand. Black in eyes.

'Martha. Sister Martha! Wake up!'
  Move. Take wood. Lift. Stand.
  'She is asleep again. How *can* she? With that lot in her arms?'
  Go, go. Move lift carry go in door out door. Stop lean, wall at
back. Black in.

'Martha no! Go to bed child. Look at her. Is she sick?'
  Go. Go step move. Can no – stop. And black.

Eat. Yes. Eat eat. But now. Go round. Sitting. Black.

'She's worse than she was before. It's every time she stops now.
She never even – she has not eaten her food tonight. Just sits
upright in her chair, fast asleep.'
  'It is not like a normal sleep. When you go near her she – '
  'Yes, jumps awake. She is afraid.'
  'What of?'
  'You see her eyes, her face. She thinks she will be hit. She
always wakes just as you get near enough to – '

Hot waves come up. Belly sick. Not sleep. Watch. Jump awake.
But black. Coming. It laps. Laps where standing or sitting the
hot no-air . . .
  It roof. Over all. Over all day. It roof. No sky dark sky. Barn
has roof. But high. At night go in barn. Here in day is roof low
all day. It loses air.

Hear them talk. But eyes. Gone. They will not. Hurt. Black.
  'And you are not to get up till I tell you, do you hear?'

Ah. Ah this. This. How can I? I am. I am in this.
BODY.
Wait. I tell.
I come awake. Not by the barking or shook/kicked. I come
myself up the black to top of water floating. I sway side to side
beneath the surface grey, lightening, floating knowing it nearer
up up up to pop. I bring. Body. In rays it go all down down
thighs calves ankles feet toes to my ends. In rays it go up belly
sides breasts back shoulders arms hands fingers. It go up my
neck and spread like a flower about my head. It come from
between my legs where.
'Cunt' he said. Do not think.
But now. Watch. I like still. Flat. On bed. Heavy warm
blankets spread even on top, neck to toe. Face up. No moving.
Watch.
Where it begin? I say from cunt. But no. Circling. Crossing
toes, round, touching fingers, round, brushing cheek. Coming
round. Spreading to ankles, wrists, neck the cool sheet brushing
my neck. Neck is a thousand points, this is the new. I in each I
feel. I each one softly piercingly in to I each dot of dust of me –
skin – neck – it feels in me as if. What? Rain maybe when it
come down hard and fast and the drops on skin hit and spatter
and make all the surface joint together – that there, before they
join, when all is a thousand separate hits my neck is that many.
But not hit. Shining – each one warm. Yes. This time it go
round and round. I am a backwards water circle. Ripples grow
bigger but spreading in round and round and getting higher
passing in breasts and thighs with sweetness rounding hotter
higher in and in to centre now where sucking in great hole in
water as if a stone was heaved to have made them all round
and round with sweet hot sweet in and round and in.

See? Flashing. It dance. Suddenly lift and dance. My whole
body. Springing up at all joints and most pulsing rippling in the
centre there it leap and dance for very sweetness. And when
the movement go I am light and warm as new-licked calves.

Is this what? Do they all? In new bodies. Each part is feeling.
More I lie and sleep and float, anywhere, the ripples begin.
Outside each speck of my skin touching sheet or nightdress or

more skin shines me its sweet feeling: inside the shapes of lungs breasts belly womb buttocks are rounded glowing I am alight inside and out my body dance it dance with life alone without me move a muscle and in it every movement feeling joy.

'May the Lord have pity on her. See how she twitches and jumps. More like a dog than a human being. Oh Sister Dinah, watch her legs, the way they tremble. She must be remembering . . . some nightmare . . . running away perhaps. She arches her back!'

'Best let her sleep, Sister Joanna.'

'But do you think sleep like this can be refreshing? Look, she is convulsed – panting – '

'But then she becomes calmer, see. My sister had nightmares – she used to sleepwalk – after she started on at the mill. My mother warned us never to waken her. I think there is a greater terror in the sudden wrench from dreaming – '

'It may be. We must trust in God's hidden purposes. At least she *can* sleep how: do you remember how she crouched there whimpering at first, and would not lie in the bed? I will wake her at suppertime, and you can give her some broth. No, do not come down. You are performing a great service in watching with her, Sister Dinah.'

'I could try to sew, while she sleeps, Sister Joanna. The light by the window here is good. I am sure I can learn.'

'Very well. I will send Sister Rebekah up with some hemming. Look at her face now. She seems to reach a kind of peace, after that struggle. She smiles, and her breath comes easier. Truly, His love conquers all evil.'

'Yes, Sister. You will not forget to send Rebekah?'

Ah. I stay here now. My body. Every speck ripples as I am water, shining in the light I flow. I am. This body. I fill my shape. Delight.

See this. They bring me in. All voices going around, like bees swarming moving in one but each single too. My head is filled with sound so much I can hardly move. Sanctuary, they say. It is higher than barn but built around light which flows through top, the centre. Points of orange flame dancing here here here. And people. More than I have seen. I try to

But the voices. Also noises of things with voices. Hooting crashing sprinkling spraying and sounds like gales breaking trees. I see men doing it.

'Hush, Sister Martha,' Joanna tells me. 'The musicians are playing.' I try to because the sweet smell wants to go in to my throat I try to

but so much sounding fills my head my head to bursting so many so much fill me over the top as the rounded surface of water on the bucket will swell swell then break and drop I break. Too full.

I drop.

'Help Sister Martha out, Samuel. Sister Hannah, take her other arm. Quickly now, before the prayers. I thank you.'

I read. Joanna and I sit at table. She opens the Bible. In there are little black shapes. She points to one.

'In'

'In'

'the'

'the' The next one is long, like a spattering of piss on dusty ground.

'beginning'

'beginning'

'Good, now together.'

'In the beginning.'

They give me to eat. Fresh bread, with butter. Oatcakes. Yellow
cheese. Milk. Potatoes (cooked). Meat, in a whole piece,
sometimes hot. Cabbage. Warm porridge. Gooseberries,
perserved and cooked in sweet pastry. Tea, a hot drink. They
bring food to table and when they have eaten they take some
away. At night she gives it to the dogs.

They eat like birds picking and pecking. They do not eat
everything on their plates.

Joanna teaches me. She names things. I know these words
inside, but my mouth and throat are not familiar with their
sounds. My voice is loud like barking inside my head.

There are fires in the rooms. There are clear squares in walls to
see out, which are hard to touch. They keep out rain and wind.
There are beds, one each, with white sheets and brown wool
blanket. I can sleep. There is a jug with water and a bowl for
washing with soap and a white cloth to wipe the water off.
    There are white clothes. Dinah puts her arms through holes
in the stays and pulls it over her head. She pulls the laces tight
one by one and ties it. My fingers cannot hold laces or tie them,
or the little hooks and buttons on the dress, or the boots, or fine
needles for sewing or thin paper sheets of books that must be
turned. Their neat little fingers run like spiders. Dinah fixes me
into the clothes.

Joanna brings me into a room with a fire. She takes off the
clothes and makes me sit in a tub of water. The water is hot.
She pours water over my head and cleans my hair. When it is
dry she rubs it with a brush to pull it down and with scissors
she cuts out parts that are stuck. She pulls the brush right
through it, then she puts the bonnet on me again. She says,
'When it grows long I will braid it for you.' She puts ointment
on my hands and feet, as she does it she says, 'Oh child, child,'
and her tears drop on my legs like hot rain.

There is a privvy with a seat. The shit falls far down, into water.
I can sit there alone as long as I like.

At evening we sit upstairs. I do not fall asleep. I am sitting keeping still, but I stay awake. Dinah talks to a creature I cannot see called God. She tells me talk to him. I see each thing and its colour. The floor, gold planks with round brown eyes staring up. Window clear to outside. I move my head and the tree I see waves. It moves slowly as I. Then suddenly it ripples in water, jumps to a new place. New leaves are green. New green. Green leaves. This colour must be talking to God. I cannot say. This colour is light and dark. Shining or in shadow. Inside green there is a purple. Sometimes other colours also: yellow, silver, blue. More I look more I see. When light goes colour changes, green has gone. The sun goes down sky turns grey and leaves turn black. They hide each other with blackness, but tree still jumps in the window. I see.

I touch. The blanket I touch is now soft, the top one hairy as a sow's back. I lay my face on pillow and cold linen is smooth. I hear linen stretch and crease under my ear and the feathers sigh together. My own heart booms inside. Outside Dinah's breathing shakes the air and outside that birds call and hoot. I swell, I swell, I will burst. My nostrils seize air, warm from my body sweet from fresh linen, touched by Dinah's scent of sharp clean vinegar. I can follow each of them through the house by her smell. Joanna is water but kept in the pool, deep but not fresh; water underground. Leah, fish. Dinah, edge of vinegar, hers is the best smell, clean and sour. I want to put my nose on her skin. Rachel and Rebekah are bread with the mustiness of yeast. There is something close about their smell close and for eating. Hannah is blood, metal but salty. The man is earth, the inside of earth when leaves and small animals have rotted away. Moist black earth when you cut it open with a plough.

Joanna sits at my bedside I see her then I close my eyes. Her eyes are blue with tiny blond rays in the centre. Her skin blooms white like reflected from snow. Her hair is smoothed back and hairs by her ears float in the air as she bends towards me. I hear her voice in my stomach. It strokes the inside of my stomach with its soft finger.

In the morning we get food. Then we go to the big room and Joanna makes her voice go high and low like a bird flying. They copy, open their mouths and the bird flies out. Mine does not, it makes a different sound. Joanna puts her hand on my arm, 'It is all right Martha.' I keep my mouth closed while they do their noise, my ear follows the path of their sounds which call you to follow.

Today there is no food. We go to the big room but do not make singing. Joanna looks and brushes our clothes. We go outside. Sky is grey, it is dry. Along lane, over canal, to the Sanctuary. We walk in twos with Joanna leading. Dinah leans on my arm her legs are crooked. No one speaks. We go in the big doors and sit. People come in. Joanna and the others sing, and the musicians make singing. The priest talks and they all talk to God then sing. I watch the flames on sticks, they grow taller. We stay a long time.

At the house I go to eating room. No food. Each one in her room, they are not working. I go to larder there is food, cheese on the slab, bread, preserves. No one here. I eat. I eat bread the crust is thick and mealy then cheese its moist bitterness lines my mouth. Lick preserve from fingers it is running down in sweet lumps I cannot get enough. I put these in my mouth together, Joanna comes in.

'Martha! No!'

She takes food away. She makes me sit, she wets a cloth in bucket and wipes me. She daubs at my dress where preserve glistens, she wipes it away so only pale purple spots remain. When she has rubbed and wiped she sits beside me.

'You must not eat today Sister Martha.'

The taste of cheese lasts longest, it is still in my throat. I wish I got more.

'It is a fast day. Before the feast of the New Moon. None of us must eat.'

I will get the bucket after.

'Do you understand, Martha? No one is to eat today. Today we remember our sins of the past month: we think about what we have done wrong, and ask God's forgiveness. We prepare ourselves for the new month, by purifying and cleansing.'

She stares at me. 'We will eat tomorrow, sister. On the feast day.'

She tells me to go to my room. 'Change your dress.' She says put milk on the stains. She pours some in a bowl, then she looks at me.

'Not for drinking, Martha. Not for you. To clean the dress. Yes?'

I speak for her. 'Yes.' She smiles.

I stand. There is more preserve on my sleeve. I lick it off. She looks at me. She shakes her head.

'Were you often hungry – before?'

'Hungry.'

'My poor child – does any of this make sense to you? The church, what the Prophet says?'

'In Sanctuary.'

'Yes – in Sanctuary. But the Sabbath and fast days . . .'

'No food today.'

She nods. 'Good, Sister Martha. You do understand that God loves you? He has brought us here.' Her eyebrows go in and down suddenly. 'He brought us here, to do His will. To help the Prophet. To – ' She turns away. Her voice is falling. ' – To do the laundry and turn the cheeses, to polish the candlesticks.'

The candlesticks hold flame. Take white muslin, it is soft, dip it in mixture and rub the black candlestick. Black goes on cloth and the candlestick shines silver. I see little people in its surface, and lights, sometimes the room upside-down. She is watching me, she comes back. Her hand on my arm.

'No – it is all right, I am not going to hurt you. You are glad to be here. Even though you scarcely understand it, you accept His will with a better grace than I. Come, Sister Martha. Pray with me.'

She kneels on the floor and pulls at my sleeve. I copy. She clasps her hands and looks at the ceiling.

'Oh God, forgive Thy servants. Grant us humility. Give us the patience and wisdom to do Thy will, in whatever way Thou designest. Our Father, who are in heaven – '

She looks at me. 'Close your eyes, dear Sister Martha.'

After she says, 'You could do the garden. Perhaps with Sisters Rachel and Rebekah – perhaps the three of you working together. We will see about it tomorrow.'

There are seeds in twists of paper but I do not know. I know potatoes. A man has brought a bushel of seed potatoes. They have ploughed the plot for us, all we must do is plant. I say the stones to pick, but two boys have already. We plant potatoes, peas, cabbages, turnips. A woman from the church brings plants named rhubarb, mint, rosemary, bay, thyme, sage. She fetches currant bushes and gooseberry. Joanna says this will be our food. On our table, on plates. Rachel and Rebekah call after me.

'Oh Sister Martha, slow down! Our backs are breaking. We do not have to finish it today.'

I see the earth. When I bend, I see small moist grains sticking. I see soft hard sand stone and grains of mud which are separate but can be smeared between fingers. I see –

They shout, 'Oh come *on* Martha.'

My mind is filled with the grain of earth, I cannot move.

Here's light. As I walk out the door it comes splashing in my face, wetting up my eyes. Birds go croop-cru, croop-cru. Their sound lies on air soft as grey feathers. Shining leaves, after-dark coloured. Lying on them, silver balls can never be broken. When I tilt it runs down towards me. If I touch it makes two new balls to run, and feel of wetness on my finger.

The skin. Crossed and re-crossed with lines finer than hairs. Spotted, scarred, on my palms the yellow brown callouses are coming loose. Peel off. But the skin. Red but blue. Blue but brown. Brown but yellow. On one pin-point of me the world's colours.

Mist goes up from grass. There are water drops on it. Sky wool white, moves as smoke. White sunshine makes my eyes water. In the yard black mud and cowshit. Silver water in puddles. In hoofprints. Dung is crusted over lighter brown. Still soft underneath. Open the top door, slide my fingers through to lower latch. Cow warm air coming up my nose. She hrrumphs. I take stool, bucket, sit beside her. She stamps, breathes. Put my head in her side. Warm. My ear is pressed to the roar of her innards. Take the teats and squeeze-squeeze. Warm, moving in time. White milk shoots into my brown bucket. Squeeze squirt. Squeeze squirt. It hits bottom and splatters up the sides. White drips run down. Each sight my eyes take in. I feel cow's heat. I hear her rumbling belly and her jaws chewing, chewing. I touch her leathery teats. I hear shot of milk against leather. I see pearl white drips against dark brown. Seeing hearing touching fills me up.

Cow shifts her footing. Waiting for me to finish. I clasp my hands around the other teats. Her udder hangs slacker now. Pink furry skin wrinkling like cloth. Bend my head in to her hot side. Squeeze-squirt. The milk is frothing. Pale half-bubbles cluster together; squirt – are sunk. Slide up again. Milk in the pail is moving. Under the pail, straw is yellow. Dark yellow, lined with black. But turn my head and in at the door sun has come. Mist gone up now. Clear yellow sun in a square through top byre door. Lies in a gold square on straw. In itself, in its beam, lights the air. Gold, yellow, black, silver it burns all colours as a fire. Yellow straw in the sun.

The Prophet is in the room, I am not moving. I am washing the hearth, there is sooty water trickling across the flags, I am not moving.

'Sister Martha?'

Still, I am a stone.

'I will not hurt you, child.' He moves the chair. 'Sister Joanna tells me you are doing well, you are a good worker, she is pleased with you.'

Cold stone water trickling the Prophet's voice runs along low like water. Keep very still.

'Are you afraid of me?'

' _____ '

'Sister Martha? Are you afraid of me?' He moves nearer.

'Martha – Martha! Stop it! I will not hurt you. Look here – stand up and shake your dress. Leave that, you can mop it up later. Look, I am sitting here, on the other side of the table. I am not going to touch you Martha, I am not going to hurt you. Sit down over there, just sit and listen to me. Compose yourself.'

'Are you feeling better now Sister Martha?'

'Martha, Sister Joanna tells me you can speak. Answer me.'

'Yes.'

'Good girl. Good. Can you understand me – Martha?'

'Yes.'

'Good. Now, listen. Firstly I am not going to hurt you. No one here will hurt you. Do you understand?'

'Yes.'

'Good. Now I have some news for you. Your father has been to see me. He tells me his wife – his third wife – has died. He asks if you can be returned to him.'

No no no no no no no no no. My mouth is frozen, he must hear me.

'Do you wish to return?'

'Ah – ah – ah – '

'It is all right, Sister Martha. Wait. There is plenty of time. Calm yourself.'

He looks at his fingers he looks at the great puddle of black sooty water sprawled across the flags he looks at the window when will I be able to draw breath?

'Ah. No.'

He nods. 'As I thought. Close your mouth, Martha. I have spoken with Sister Joanna and with the Elders. Sister Joanna thinks you were badly treated; indeed, I know it myself. You were dirty and scarred and exhausted. Even worse, you had been kept in brutish ignorance of the ways of God. Is this true?'

Nod.

'Since coming into my house you have been conscientious and obedient. You have partaken regularly of Christian worship and learned to raise your perceptions above those of the animals. You seem to be content; indeed, Sister Joanna tells me you have an appetite for work and for knowledge, and that she is teaching you your Bible.'

Nod. Nod.

'Therefore I am willing, with the support of the Elders, to refuse your father's request.'

'Ah – ah.'

'Wait a moment. Let me finish. It is possible he may pursue the matter in law. I do not think it likely; and indeed if he do, the signs that we can offer of your earlier maltreatment and your Christian education since you came to live among us will count hard against him. However, if he do take it to law, you may have to be returned at the end. I wish to warn you of this now, but to assure you that I will do all in my power to protect you and retain you in the Israelite community. God has brought you here for a purpose, my child.'

' ___ '

'Do you understand?'

Speak. Speak. 'Yes.'

'Good.' He gets up, his eyes on me. I must show I thank.

I go. Near enough for him to. I kneel down. He holds his hand out. I must. Touch.

'Good girl. Now go and change that wet dress.'

# Joanna

Lord, guide us and help us, as You have already done in so many things. There is peace within the household: the sense of Your purpose strengthens us in our work. Hannah is a great comfort to me, a sister and companion I thank You for. Sister Leah's skill as a needlewoman redounds to Your glory, in the gorgeous ephods and altarcloths she works upon. Sisters Rachel and Rebekah can now read Your holy word, and gain in piety as they gain in knowledge: whilst Sister Martha at last, like a dumb seed which has been sealed in a leathery shell, forces towards the light, grows in the warmth of the sun of love, and is at points at last of casting off that dark shell of brutish ignorance forever. My days are filled with Thy service, and for this I give thanks.

But times change. Everything in this world changes, and he who seeks to build secure upon it must always fail, for he builds on shifting sands. Yaakov's communications in the past week have twice reminded us that the time of the Lord is at hand.

Last night I dreamed a terrible dream. I dreamed that we stood – many of us, hundreds – in a fine peaceful valley, with lush pastures. A child was playing merrily in the brook beside me. On a sudden the hill top burst open, and molten rock, together with flames, smoke, and a shower of burning matter, rained down upon us. Each man or woman ran to save himself, but so continual and random was the hail of fiery rocks that one after another was smitten to the ground with screams of anguish. I raced toward the child, a boy of maybe two years, and stumbled along the course of the brook with him in my arms, while the flames fell in arcs around me, and my eyes hit upon face after familiar face on the ground, rigid with agony or beseeching aid to their injuries, and which I, knowing the safety of the child to be paramount, ignored – though my heart wept to see them. A fiery cinder fell upon my head and set my loose hairs alight in a sudden burst, but the mass of it was still secured in a knot at my nape, and it did not catch. The child in my arms watched the carnage around us with tears in his eyes. It seemed to me that he must bear peculiar power, for we alone were uninjured, still struggling away from the source of destruction – all around us, the ground lay thick with the bodies of my brothers and sisters.

Before I read to Yaakov, I told him my dream. When I finshed he sat in silence a while.

'Do you interpret this dream, Sister Joanna?'

'I seek understanding.'

'What is your interpretation?'

'That there will be a time – of great destruction. That many will die. This may prefigure the end of the world, when many shall be cast into the fiery pit.'

'And the child?'

'He may stand for God's redeeming love; or for the souls of the innocent, the young. He may stand for – '

He interrupted me. 'The son of God.'

'The son of God?'

'Shiloh. Carrying him, you are saved from destruction. As you protect him, he protects you. What other child has such power? Your dream is of the Second Coming, when Christ shall come among us again to judge the quick and the dead. Your dream reveals the truth of Joanna Southcott's prophecy, that He shall come again as a child – of woman born.'

'Of woman?'

'Of you. Your dream reveals that you shall be earthly mother to Shiloh.'

'But . . .' For a while I was lost to sense, the world seemed to slide into flatness and shimmer like a great spread of water. Then the dear Lord sustained me with a rational thought. 'Mother Joanna gave birth to a spiritual child. We learned then that it is not a physical child, we must look to the world beyond the merely physical.'

'Are burning rocks physical? Is the pain of hell-fire physical? Did you see physical anguish in the faces of those smitten by the molten rocks? There will be a physical child.'

119

'But Joanna Southcott's child . . .'

He watched me closely, till I could not speak. 'Where is Southcott's child?' he asked.

'It is the spirit; the spirit of prophecy, passed on among us – an ear to the voice of God – it is our link with her, and through her, God – '

'And who has that ear? Who, especially?' He spoke angrily, as if I had insulted him. I was lost for a reply.

'Who has that ear? Who is your prophet?'

'I – The Prophet. You.'

'So the spiritual child – is in me; and must be borne of you, Sister Joanna. God's will is clear, think you not?'

In the silence of the room I heard the dusk call of a woodpigeon, its voice grey and soft as the evening air outside: in the outside world, which seemed on a sudden to be both precious above all things, and lost to me.

I have moved into an inner realm of terror, and as I formerly longed for spiritual revelation, I now fight to restrain tears of nostalgic love for the world I am losing, the shape of a cottage roof against the sky, the feel of bark, the sound of carriage wheels upon the highway.

Lord, is it true? I am afraid.

Yaakov instructed me to commence the reading: Joel, Chapter III.

*Put ye in the sickle, for the harvest is ripe: come, get you down, for the press is full, the fats overflow: for their wickedness is great.*

*Multitudes, multitudes in the valley of decision: for the day of the Lord is near in the valley of decision.*

*The sun and the moon shall be darkened, and the stars shall withdraw their shining.*

*The Lord also shall roar out of Zion, and utter His voice from Jerusalem: and the heavens and the earth shall shake . . .*

As I set down the Bible he charged me not to speak of my dream to a soul. Then his anger seemed to fall away, and he smiled.

'You are a good woman, Sister Joanna. God loves you. He will make His will plain to you, He will show you His desires. Do not be afraid, for He is with you; in your dreams, in your very heart.'

Ascending the stairs to my room I could scarce place my

numbed feet upon the steps, for I could not tell whether I stepped on solid wood or gaping air.

I have prayed and I have fasted. I have sought His guidance by day and night. Is this the purpose that lay concealed, curled like a chick in the egg, behind that first request for the succour of the women? Is this truly God's plan for me? I follow the Mother, Joanna Southcott; her life prefigures mine, my name echoes hers. She, mother of the spiritual child . . . I to be mother of the physical? But Christ was of virgin birth: Mother Southcott lived and died a virgin. As I am – now – a virgin.

Yaakov argues that the times are so degenerate and spiritual forces so weakened by the continual battle, that God's angels lack the power in these late days to penetrate the pall of darkness hanging over our sin-laden earth, and that therefore the act of generation must be carnal, between man and woman. But in that carnality, the spirit will be housed – as Christ born of Mary was made flesh: and as the flesh is gateway for the spirit. I recall to mind Mother Southcott's prophecy:

> Woman brought to man the Good Fruit at the first
> And from the Woman shall the good fruit burst
> Because no fruit did ever come from man
> Though it is often grafted by his hand.

I fear I am not strong enough. I despise my own weakness, but I am afraid. I imagine the jeers of the people. I remember the streets, at the time of Mother Joanna's confinement. I remember the crude effigies, and the cruder uses to which they were put – the foulness of the people's bestial nature exposed – Lord, I shrink before such testing. And if, like Mother Joanna, I should die . . .

Yaakov recalls me to my dream, speaking of the cinder which set my loose hairs aflame for a brief moment. This is the figure, he says, of the blessed halo which shall frame my face in eternity.

Oh is it so? Can it be so?

I am driven against the rock face of uncertainty, like a creature repeatedly beaten by the waves: there is no escape, no way out through this wall of rock, except to turn and brave the raging sea, lose sight of land, and swim.

I fear that I have upset Sister Hannah with my silence. She does not complain, but there is a resentment in the set of her shoulders. She feigns deep concentration on her reading, and does not look up when I enter the room. I am imprisoned in silence: to whom can I speak or turn except Thee, O Lord? Give me a sign, for the truth.

Yaakov is a practical man, he has in this instance a clear view of the world's opinions. The child's parentage must be kept secret from all. In so far as he fathers the child, it shall be simply as the agent of the holy spirit. This is beyond the understanding of simple mortals, who will put upon it their own gross interpretations. Secondly, there may be jealousy among the other virgins, if they are grieved that it is not they who are called. For these reasons, I must not tell a soul: though the secret burns and torments me till, like Midas' wife, I long to run down to the river and whisper amongst the rustling rushes, 'My husband has asses' ears' – only louder, 'I am to mother Shiloh!'

It will be put about, then, that the child is of spiritual conception – as indeed it will be, but not in such a way as the world can understand.

I falter. I am afraid. Is this true? Or am I Satan's plaything, dizzied with his inventions so that I can no longer see the way? Now do I understand Mother Southcott's torments, her uncertainty at the origin of her Spirit voice. Dear Lord, help me along the path; if this is indeed the path You have ordained for me, let me see, and understand, and know it to be right. I pray You help me through the dark mists of doubt.

I believe the Prophet's interpretation of my dream to come from a sincere attempt to penetrate the mysteries of God's will, and to act as His servant. I cannot believe him to harbour any base or sinful motives; nor, if that were the case, could his choice possibly fall on such a plain and tormented female as myself. I believe God loves and protects His own – just as I believe He has great plans (as Southcott foretold) for the women. Must I not trust Him then? Must I not give myself up to the will of Him who holds us all in the palm of His hand, cease my struggle and my doubt, and say with grace, 'Lord, Thy will be done'?

But then such sweet dreams, such fond hopes arise, that I tremble to own them. If indeed I was with child . . . Imagine the bliss arising from such motherhood. That I should be chosen – I, among the women of the world – for this great honour. Imagine the soft child's embrace around the neck, the touch of that small hand. If I dared believe it to be true, would not the promise of these things steel me for all insults, all insinuations, all debaucheries: and would not the confirmation of God's purpose, in the swelling growth of my belly, protect me and seal me from all danger? For who could hurt the vessel of the Godhead? What man's hand could be raised against His holiness?

I overreach. Mother Southcott was injured: hurt: insulted. Christ himself in his first appearance on earth was harried and tortured to death. Why should I escape? But I believe I could welcome the thought of such approaching dangers, could I but conquer my doubt. This is my most pressing fear – the doubt about the first origin of my dream. Could it not have been placed in my thoughts as easily by Satan as by God? What evil charade may we, in all deluded innocence, enact? And how might that prejudice His cause, in the years to come, and loose countless souls through mockery and disbelief, and weaken our church and set the tongue of scandal wagging loose amongst our members?

Guide me Lord guide me, my prayer is constant, I know neither sleep nor rest.

*

I dreamed of the child again last night: his sweet face turned towards me as if in supplication. How can I reject God? How can I reject God's will? It must be done.

After I read to Yaakov I made this known. He nodded.
    'It is right. God's will shall be done. I await His instructions on how and when this thing must be accomplished.'
    This thing. As I desire salvation I hope for success in this venture, but I am most afraid. How it may be secretly arranged I cannot imagine.

Tonight Yaakov has told me God's plan. On the Sabbath, Zion Ward, a London Israelite, comes to our meeting, and will speak in Yaakov's stead. I must keep to my bed in the morning, complaining of sick headache, and not accompany the others to Sanctuary. Yaakov will absent himself from the meeting, after it has begun, giving the need for private intercourse with God as his reason. Every other soul in the place will be in Sanctuary. He will come straight to my bed. He reasons that the spirituality of the hour, and the concentrated (if unknowing) prayers of our brothers and sisters, must help us in our execution of God's will.

*

The morning of the Sabbath was dark with rain, as if the heavens wept to see what must come to pass. True enough to say I had a sick headache, for I had not slept a wink in the night past. My Sister Hannah was kindness itself, wiping my feverish face with a cool damp cloth, fetching me fresh water, before she left for Sanctuary. And then the minutes seemed long: I tried to pray, but over and over again the mechanical repetition of words broke down, before the panic in my heart. I imagined I heard his footstep on the stairs a thousand times, and each time began afresh to beg God's blessing and help to endure this trial of the flesh, and each time was lost and confounded in my prayer by hearing a new and clearer footstep. Then I began to think that he would not come; that God had perhaps given him a sign, that it was not to be.

And then he was there. I heard him lift the latch and open the door, close it, place Hannah's chair against it. I lay completely motionless, my face hidden beneath the sheet, unable to move for shame.

'Joanna! Sister Joanna! Pray with me, for God's blessing.' He fell to his knees beside the bed, raised his joined hands, and closed his eyes. The terror is my heart was lessened: God would be with us, how could He fail to respond to so much faith, to such a sacrifice? I clambered awkwardly from my bed and knelt beside Yaakov, while he prayed aloud for blessing, for a fruitful union and for the forgiveness of our sins.

When he was done he stood up and raised me to my feet, asking me kindly enough if I knew what it was we should do. I shook my head, and he asked me if I would trust him to enact God's work, and surrender myself to him entirely as to the hand of God my heavenly husband. I could not help trembling, and he laid his hands upon my arms.

'You must not be afraid, Sister Joanna. You must rejoice. The words of the earthly marriage ceremony may be repeated in our hearts here and amplified a thousand-fold: with my body, I thee worship. With our bodies, we Thee worship. Our bodies are His agents: glorious, shining, fit for angels. We step back, sister, into a time of innocence – for shame was only learnt by biting of the forbidden fruit. Before that time, nakedness was beautiful, the actions and functions of the body were, equally with the worship of the spirit, a means of extolling His praises. Forget fear, Joanna, forget shame. We will worship.'

Saying this he unfastened my nightdress so that I was indeed naked. And then he removed his own clothes, revealing to my sight such a thing as I have never before seen or imagined; an angry leaping purple rod of flesh so terrible in its aspect that I clenched my eyes shut, forcing myself to keep the tears in.

I cannot tell what followed; only that my heart is overwhelmed with grief for womankind, to know the torments of procreation that so many endure. How greatly we must have angered God, for Him to insult us by forcing us to perform these hideous and depraved actions. Man is no more than beast, and cruel indeed was He to imbue those who must endure the actions of beasts, with the sensibilities of higher things. Forgive me, my dear Lord, but I weep for my sex, and pray You earnestly to grant us Your pity, by making me the agent which might hasten the coming of Your reign of a thousand years, when all such bodily cruelty and contact shall cease. If the body is Your temple, Lord – such desecration must give grief to Your sweet heart also. As an horse would scarcely feel the pressure of my finger, yet that pressure destroys a butterfly: as surely must a fine sensibility be destroyed by the repetition of the depraved and bestial actions of procreation.

I set myself to repeat the Lord's prayer.

*Our Father, who art in heaven, hallowed be Thy name, Thy kingdom come, Thy will be done. Hallowed be Thy name Thy kingdom* Oh God –

*forgive us our trespasses as we forgive them that trespass against us for Thine is for Thine is for Thine is. Our Father who art in – our Father our Father in heaven* I bless the words although I could not say them. In time one would learn, perhaps that would be my aim if married, in time to perfect the saying of them so that no degree of physical distress could distract one from their soothing flow.

At last he ceased and the terrible implement was extracted from between my legs, causing renewed hurt. He rose from the bed and dressed himself.

'Stop crying, Joanna. It is done now. Your self-pity mocks God. Many have made greater sacrifices for His sake. Let us pray that our endeavour is crowned with success.' He fell to his knees and began to pray silently; when I moved to join him I noticed the blood, an outward and recognizable sign of my sacrifice. Unworthy as I am, I have shed blood for You, Lord.

When he stood up he told me to take the sheets down to the wash-house, and there to wash myself. 'You must be composed and ready when the others return.'

I was (forgive me Lord) so glad when he was gone, that I burst into another fit of crying. I wish I never had to see him again, God's Prophet though he be; I cannot imagine how people who do this can look one another in the eye, or behave in any degree naturally. I cannot imagine – I cannot understand –

Dear Lord, I cannot understand. Help me to a greater humility. May it please You to accept this my sacrifice, with gentle understanding, and forgiveness for my foolish and most unworthy distress.

I must turn my thoughts forward, away from this sad pain. Let me imagine; let me dare to imagine, now, the outcome. That I may feel the child quicken in my belly, and know the heat of his warm soft body, nestled against my breast like little Thomas. The tears which swell and ache in my eyes are no longer pain, but joy. I thank you, sweet Lord, for what is promised me: I shall endeavour to be worthy.

# Hannah

I have a letter of Edward. It was passed to me after service, by Samuel Walker, who was given it by my uncle. His reply to the news of my father's death; and his first letter for over a year. I had nearly given up hope of hearing from him again; the sight of it made me very agitated, with a nervous ache in my stomach.

We had to wait, as usual, till all had left Sanctuary; then make the place neat and extinguish all candles save the seven on the altar: and then walk back, in our tidy little band, led by the prophet. There was no opportunity to open the letter until I was safely in our room (and even then Joanna looked at me askance, because I was neither praying nor reading my Bible).

The outside was none too clean, the writing a little smudged; I sniffed it, imagining that I could smell the salty sea it had passed over on its way to me.

Libertatia,
New Harmony,
Indiana
September 1829

My Dear Hannah,

How many times have I begun this letter, with hope and anticipation in my heart, only to find that I must put it aside for matters of more pressing urgency, which demand my immediate attention. So much has happened here, such a deluge of joys, disasters, excitements, disappointments, that I am at a loss where to begin to tell you our news.

Let me begin at the beginning. The great triumph of the year is the completion of our own living quarters, designed along Mr Owen's parallelogram lines. As you know, since our arrival at New Harmony we have been accommodated in the old meeting house; a cramped and generally unsatisfactory arrangement. We have been clear in our own minds about the necessity of setting ourselves at a distance from those individuals who remain here from the original New Harmony settlement of 1825, for their cynical views and return to individualism are particularly damaging to the tender shoots of a new community. The land we leased from Mr Owen is two miles down river from the village of New Harmony; and on a proud day in May, little over a year after our arrival here, we moved into our own new community house, Libertatia. It is constructed of logs, with an open courtyard at the centre, and individual sleeping quarters, 2 workshops, a kitchen, washroom and dining room (which serves us also as a meeting hall, and for dancing) surrounding it. I wish you could see it Hannah, standing clean and proud in its field, and sounding – by its very size and design – the death knell of small individual families, of competition and strife. It is a physical testimony to the ideals of cooperation and rationality: all work, education, leisure and joys to be shared.

As you know, the members of our party were carefully selected so as to provide a range of those skills judged necessary for our independence, mutual comfort, and economic survival. Due to a variety of unforseen events, however, including the theft of a considerable amount of our agricultural equipment from the barn where it was stored, the results of our farming have been less successful than we hoped. We found ourselves short of foodstuffs which we had expected to be able to grow; and thus it became necessary to buy supplies from local farmers. Sadly, this reintroduced the need for cash into our lives. For myself, I can do without money forever; would that it were banished from the face of the earth! But besides foodstuffs there were a mounting number of needs, from additional cooking utensils through sewing thread and needles, to new scythes, to tea (which a couple of our number swore they could not live without, lacking, I fear, the real disregard for luxury necessary to the lives of pioneers and breakers of new moral ground). The original communitarians having made place for us only on condition that we should be self-reliant (and indeed, lacking the resources to offer us aid, for they are now no more than a collection of individual households, whose only cooperative venture is the school; their store, granary, mills, public eating house and cook house are all abandoned), we could not turn to them. And so it became necessary for us to turn to the world outside and offer our skills in the market place.

This part of the country is inhabited chiefly by excommunitarians and farmers, many of whom are living in houses built by themselves or by their parents, using the same old simple furniture their parents contrived (or even brought with them, in laden wagons, on their first journey into the New World.) How glad I am for my skill as a cabinet maker! For every household seems to have some item of furniture in need of repair, or some small corner just needing a new cupboard. I have had more employment than I can fit in with my duties to the community (as you know, I am Superintendant of Domestic Economy, besides taking my three hours a day share of that labour in which we all partake, which was building, and is now the cultivation of two further fields of vegetables for our own consumption). I am delighted to have been able to finance both the replacement of the most essential agricultural equipment, and a new stock of medicines. (Every community suffers greatly from sickness in its early years: whether it be the change in climate, the effects of communal living, or some more deep-seated and unconscious purging of the last evils of the decaying and corrupt society they have left

behind – I cannot say.) However: I threw myself into
my work with my accustomed vigour, and was
foolishly unobservant of the sense of inferiority and
distress this caused to some of my comrades. For
whilst I was happily working, and knowing that the
fruits of my labour should contribute to the good of
all in our community, others were less fortunate.
Nicholas and Benjamin, who had charge of the
outdoor part of our enterprise (the sowing and
raising of crops, and breeding of animals), found
their activities curtailed by the harsh winter weather,
and had the misfortune to lose one sow and her litter
of ten, along with a calving cow, both in the space of
a week in April. Alongside the smashing down of the
vegetable plot fencing, the consequent eating of new
shoots by deer, and a suspicion (which had no basis
in fact) that others in the community held them
responsible for these losses, they fell into a mood of
despair which led them to seek comfort in liquor.

This has caused tremendous concern and division
among us, firstly because we agreed in our
constitution to ban liquor entirely, and secondly
because Benjamin purchased it with money which he
had earned clearing land for a neighbouring farmer,
as part of our drive to raise finance for essential
supplies. He argues that the money was his to spend,
since he earned it, ignoring one of our first principles
which was that all wealth and property should be
held in common.

This distressing argument raises its head in so
many guises, dear Hannah. I am sure nothing could
have been more equitable than our starting point, at
which each put £50, or more if they had it, towards
the costs of establishing the community. How simple
our agreement was; property and produce to be held
in common, equal returns to all from our enterprise,
and only personal property such as clothing to be
individually owned. But the arguments that do blow
up – from those who now complain that returns
should be reckoned according to labour hours put in

(for some are working harder than others), to those who, having retained a degree of personal wealth which they declined to put into the community, use it to procure individual comforts and luxuries, and so create jealousy – ensure that our weekly meetings are very frequently stormy.

The women seem exceptionally dissatisfied. I wish that you were here, my dear, to influence them with your calm good sense. They seem to share a disinclination for communal cooking and laundry work, despite the obvious benefits (in terms of the saving of labour) that these provide. And although it pains me to say so – and I cannot in the least understand why – I am become the particular butt of their discontent. In one of the farms where I worked, the daughter of the house (a sweet, intelligent girl of sixteen) showed such an interest in the aims and principles of Owenism that I invited her to come and see our community for herself. She was so impressed by it (you see, my dear Hannah! Even strangers warm to the happy, purposeful equality of communitarian life: I cannot wait till I see your reaction to Libertatia!) that she asked if she might join us, which was agreed by all at one of our weekly meetings. However, her father angrily refused it – exhibiting those signs of moral timidity and lack of vision, which we recognize as the products of old world society and, in particular, family life. Within families the relations between men and women are always those of possessors and possessed: the husband owns not only his wife but also his daughters, and seems to feel he has the right to decide upon their disposal, with complete disregard for their own wishes.

March 4 1830

Receipt of your sad news urges me to take up my pen again, my dear Hannah, and reproaches me with the long passage of time since I began this letter. I am heartily sorry for your father's death. Life here has been hard also, this winter, and it is with a heavy

heart that I am forced to relate to you a number of
occurrences which can do nothing to lift your own
spirits. Firstly there was the departure from Libertatia
of four of our most hardworking and (as I thought)
most idealistic members. Alice R., who was in charge
of the dairy, and our most expert cook, apparently
formed an association with one of the old New
Harmonists, a widower, while we were staying in
their meeting hall. Benjamin, in the interests of
openness and honesty between community
members, referred to this at weekly meeting; with the
result that Alice has left us to move in with her
widower, and her husband George, the blacksmith, is
now returning to England – with many a bitter
accusation levelled at the community. The second
exodus was of two young single men who have taken
over one of the empty New Harmony houses to live
and work there on an individualist basis; they are
both skilled shoe makers, and we shall sadly miss the
income the sale of their goods brought into the
community.

However, two of the old New Harmony members,
Angus Q. and Virginia S., are come to join us, which
I am glad of, especially since Angus is disabled by the
loss of his right hand after an accident in the mill,
and might have fallen upon very hard times if we
were not able to offer him sanctuary. I am ever
thankful for that greatest of human characteristics,
the ability we share to help one another in time of
trouble. Hannah, if that is ever lost – then we are less
than animals.

I told you of the girl who wished to join us, and of
her father's disapproval; well, he came with two of
his workers, to remove her. It was an ugly scene,
dear Hannah; I grieve for the sins my sex has
perpetrated upon your own. Immediately after, I
was put into a most difficult position by Anna S.,
who accompanied us as Nicholas's wife, and has
shared his quarters ever since our arrival here. She
came to me in tears, asking if she might be allowed to

share my sleeping quarters, as Nicholas is now
frequently drunk and has ill treated her on several
occasions. He has accused her of being in love with
me; well you may judge for yourself the foolishness
of such a notion. She is with child by him (the child
is due in the summer) and her distress was very real.
At first I suggested she should have sleeping quarters
of her own (this indeed was the original rule of the
community; that each adult should have their own,
individual, sleeping quarters, thus liberating all from
that wretched legalized prostitution enforced by
marriage. However, those married couples amongst
us argued so strongly against this from the first, that
we built six double-chambers, and it is one of these
that she has shared with Nicholas). Her response to
my suggestion was that she has already used the
guest chamber to avoid him when he is in an ugly
mood, and that he has simply broken in and violated
her solitude.

'I need to be in your room, brother,' she told me (I
wish you had seen her poor face, darling Hannah,
with the tears streaming down), 'for he is afraid of
you, and will not dare to attack me if I have your
protection.'

This matter was not resolved purely between
ourselves, dear Hannah, for as you know the minds
of many can offer solutions which one individual may
not even imagine, and I do believe the spirit of
rationality grows stronger among us, when we are
together: so it was discussed at our next weekly
meeting. A strong portion of the community were in
favour of expelling Nicholas, for his anti-cooperative
tendencies, and for the violence he has shown
towards a woman. I argued against them, for I
believe that a part of our work must be to educate
and help those to whom cooperation comes less
easily; how may we hope to develop and spread our
system across the world, if we are driven to expel one
of our first and most enthusiastic members after little
more than a year of communal life? There is also the

question of his child, which will be the second to be born to our community. Decisions on childrearing were taken long ago (you will recall, my dear, you yourself were party to some of them before we left London) and all children are, of course, to be reared and cared for jointly. But if Nicholas is expelled from the community, is he to be forbidden contact with his own child? Whatever the natural justice in the case, the paternalistic law of the land is likely to remove the child from its mother and give it entirely to its father. Sensibility of this fact caused Anna to plead that he should be allowed to stay, although she refuses to budge from my room, and claims that she will never be reconciled to him.

Sadly, our community is split by this argument – one faction being resolute for his expulsion, the other equally certain that the only right course of action is for him to stay. I have spent countless evenings, over the past month, talking and arguing with him, trying to revive in him that early passion for the principles of communitarianism, and to re-awaken both his self-respect and his respect for women. This last is a particularly distressing duty, for he accuses me of stealing his wife (which as you know my dear Hannah, I have less reason than any man on earth to do, for all my free thoughts are of you).

I am exceedingly tired at present, since the continuing shortage of basic foodstuffs necessitates that I should take on as much carpentry as I possibly can. Few of our members now have skills which can be readily exchanged for hard cash. I am urging them to discuss suitable crops and planting methods with our neighbouring farmers, for I fear that if we cannot adapt more swiftly to the land and climate, we shall always be short of food.

And so, my dear Hannah, I must end this letter – not, as I hoped, with an urgent invitation for you to join me immediately, although you know my heart desires nothing more. But it would be foolishness and indeed unkindness to you, my beloved, to urge

you over here, to find my room shared by Anna (and
before this reaches you, perhaps her child), all my
waking hours filled with furniture repairs at outlying
farms, and the community in a state of poverty and
dislocation. Within a six-month, I am sure, there will
be an improvement. Nicholas must, I am sure, see
beyond his own distress, to the communial good: our
next year's crop may succeed; and once her child is
born, Anna (who is a good, sweet woman) may feel
more able to be independent and strong.

As I hope – and know – my dear Hannah, you are.
I am sorry for your father's death, but I rest confident
in the knowledge that despair cannot pull you down.
When ever I think of you, it is as a figure of hope and
joy.

And so farewell, my dear. My next letter will, I am
sure, carry more cheerful news; you know that we
plant a seedling here, whose nurture must take
precedence over our selfish individual desires and
aspirations. Once established, it will grow into a great
strong tree of liberty and equality, which shall
recommend itself, by the shining example of human
happiness it displays, to emulation by people all
around the world.

Let us never forget, the individual sacrifices we
make must be counted light, for we are indeed at the
beginning of a New moral World.

Your ever loving
Edward.

This morning I told Joanna I had to visit my aunt and uncle, which
was a lie. I have never seen them (apart from across the pews at
Sanctuary) since I came into this household. Nor do I wish to.

I walked as far as the end of their road, and then on towards
what I judged to be the centre of Ashton. Another hot day; the
dust coming up off the roads is enough to choke one, and there is a
pretty bad smell everywhere on the other side of the canal. We are
fortunate to be out in the open fields: sickness spreads quickly in

the heat, three children of Sanctuary families have died in this last week.

I long for the anonymity of my old clothes. One cannot help but be a spectacle in this dress and bonnet; in the western part of town there are a sufficient number of the Israelite community for me to pass without remark, but on the eastern side – where I have never been on foot before – people stare, especially at the bonnet, and the children call out. I proceeded with increasing discomfort, from the attention I was drawing to myself as well as from the heat.

I soon came out at a wide and surprisingly elegant road called Stamford Street. The shops and houses here are all new, and built with a pleasing conformity. Men and women in more fashionable dress than I have seen for a long while sauntered along, gazing into the shop fronts; and one dandy on a bay cob paused to stare at me through his eyeglass. Looking back to the west, the vista is completed by a fine new gothic church, which must be St Peter's – for I know Mr Wroe goes to visit the rector there. I made my way on to Old Square. Spotting the refreshing sight of greenery to my left, I turned towards it and soon found myself in St Michael's churchyard, which is bordered on the river side by a fine orchard. I sat on a big old tombstone by the wall to cool myself. To the east, the Pennine hills are very clear. Their gentle round shapes put me in mind of a huge sleeping body, or maybe an animal at rest, ignorant of – and dwarfing – the small human concerns of the town.

I have read and reread Edward's letter. My poor love; my poor lamb. I can see him, waking before dawn, setting out with his bag of tools across his shoulder, cheerful, whistling, a great sense of what he will accomplish for the good of the community before him as the sun rises; and then at evening, exhausted in body and spirit, trying to steer a right course between the arguing factions that surround him, pouring out to them his energy and love, as if those precious resources were limitless.

How generous his vision is. I ache for him, as I ache for remembered states of childhood; for a simple world, for ignorance, for innocence. The other women are angry because he remains faithful to me. And he will do, I know, even if he never sees me again. He will hold that certainty in his heart; it will sustain him. He *is* like a part of my childhood. Have I outgrown that romantic sensibility – or was I simply never endowed with it?

Edward – Edward! I am free! There is nothing for me in the certain love of a good man a continent away. The very fact that you prefer my shadow to those warm breathing solid women about you, chills me. Easily – as easily as slipping into water – I cast off, I am free.

Sitting in the long grass beneath the orchard wall, with the lacy heads of the cow parsley nodding along the ditch beside me, I conjure in my mind's eye a picture of my life, which is a small craft on a huge and lazy river. The tiny boat is borne along gently on the current. I *think* I may determine my course; that I could have gone to America, or anywhere. With my oar I make a little splashing here, a frenzy of dabbling there. The craft spins, then veers sharply to one side. But gradually, inexorably, the gentle pace of the current bears me back to mid-stream; carries me round the slow, deep bend, and into another reach of water. I still have my oar, and with a really determined spurt of paddling, I could reach the bank, at either side. I could even, for a while, fight the current and move upstream. Opportunities missed – Edward, America – are no more than any of those other dreams and years that grow thick as virgin forest upon the banks of my river. I *shall* put ashore. I shall exercise my single right to land . . . but the strength of the current, the shape of the river, the effects of the weather, the state of my vessel, a hundred factors which lie perhaps beyond my own control, will also determine that choice. It would be worse than anything to land, and stand stranded on the bank, regretting that lost and hidden country just beyond the river's next lazy loop.

Ironic to consider that I, like Edward, also live in a community. A household of seven women and two men, within the larger community of the Christian Israelites. Ironic to consider that such benefits as I enjoy within it are the result of lack of liberty and equality. That I willingly live under the sway of a tyrant, and am grateful for that irresponsibility. Certainly we are fortunate that those sexual jealousies which have divided Libertatia cannot take hold here; it is not likely we shall squabble over the Prophet's favours!

At length I walked through the graveyard and out, behind the church, on to Scotland Street. Here the houses are older, and the roadway narrow and dark; I proceeded until I came out at a junction where stands a fine old timbered building, identified by a sign as the Manor Court House. Turning westwards again, along Old Street, I passed some of the darkest, most foul-smelling alleys I have ever seen. The cramped houses stand back to back, and thick clouds of flies buzz over the filth and nuisance littering the open gutter between them. Pressing my handkerchief across my nose and mouth for fear of contagion, I moved on. I could not bring myself to walk into one of these alleys, despite a lively sense of curiosity: I had imagined, from the prosperous orderliness of our end of town, that the greater part of the population were employed in the new mills. This is clearly not true. Men and women lounged in these dark doorways, and I saw several pallid faces peering up from cellar rooms: the lethargy in their movements, and in the spindly children who sprawl in the dust outside, indicates how near they are to starvation. The gable ends are plastered with hand bills, many ripped and hanging in shreds, adding to the derelict air of the place. One that I paused to read called for a meeting and general strike of 'all the labouring classes'.

At length I came out at Dungeon Street, which is a little wider but still bordered by mean filthy dwellings. I should not be surprised to hear that there is no night soil collection at all in this part of town. A little way up the street I perceived that there are improvements afoot. The old dwellings have been cleared, and to the right stands a large new poorhouse. I saw a young woman's pale face staring out of one window. To the left is the market place, which was opened only a week or so since. (I owe this information to Leah, who told me there would be a grand celebration at the opening ceremony; it was not quite an invitation to go with her – nor can I imagine Mr Wroe would have permitted such a thing. It seemed more as if she were testing me, to see whether I had any inclination to play truant with her. At any rate, I did not go.) It is a decent sized area, with covered stalls and flagged openings, and building work still in progress (judging by the clouds of dust) at the far side. The proximity of this prosperous site to the squalor of the old dwellings is quite shocking: there are extremes of wealth and poverty in Ashton which I had not imagined. I turned back

down toward Stamford Street, passing on the way several newly
pasted handbills advertising that Mr William Cobbett would speak
at the town hall on Monday next, on the subject of 'The present
distressed state of the country and the means necessary to be
adopted to restore it to prosperity.' I came out at the bridge and
crossed the canal with relief, able to breathe deeply again.

*

I should like to go and hear Mr Cobbett speak on Monday. Father
and I once planned to hear him at the Taylors' Hall, but missed
him through some confusion as to the time. It is partly an
inclination to hear him . . . and partly, I admit, a desire to test the
extent of my liberty with Mr Wroe. There is a world outside this
house; are we permitted to mix with it, or will the purity of their
religion be soiled by such contact?

I made my request at the usual time, after a reading. It was met
for a while with silence. Then he said, 'Why do you wish to hear
Mr Cobbett?'

'Because I admire his writings. He has a clear grasp of the
wrongs done to the working people – and many a sensible,
practical remedy to suggest.'

'You see, you already know his views. You have no need to go
and hear him mouth them again.'

'By that reasoning one need never speak to any person more
than once. I have an idea of his general way of thinking, but I hope
to learn more in detail by hearing him speak – particularly I hope
to be in some way enlightened concerning the situation of the
poorer classes here in your town.'

'Why?'

I could not think of a ready answer to this.

'There is room for charitable work within our church,' he said.
'There are always poor, and sick, to visit.'

'I am not looking for charitable work.'

'What *are* you looking for, Sister Hannah?'

'I am not looking for anything.' My answer sounded perhaps
more irritable than I intended. He raised his eyebrows briefly.

'You may go to hear Mr Cobbett. But take one of the others with
you – I will not have you traipsing about the streets alone.'

I asked Leah to accompany me: she took it for granted that this was simply a request of convenience, and at the Ashton side of the bridge, asked what time she should meet me there for our return to Southgate. I had to ask her directions to the town hall, but soon realized that I know it, for it is one and the same as that fine old court house I found last week.

When I saw the crowd on the stairs to the assembly room my courage nearly failed me. My dress is so strange that everyone stares; no, it is not that, but they were all together, each with a companion, I seemed to be the only single woman present. When I have attended such meetings in the past it has been with my father, or Edward. I think I was never conscious of how much they made way for me, and protected me from the jostling of a crowd. Here people pushed in front of me, and called out to one another over my head, as if I were a child. I could not get a seat and was squeezed up against the wall where I could not properly see the speakers. After a while I calmed down sufficiently to listen to Mr Cobbett, who was describing the plight of the urban poor. He urged the unnaturalness of the manufacturing process as one of the chief causes of the ills of society, outlining a vision of rural bliss which might be obtained by each cottager having a small plot of land, a cow and some chickens, and making his family self-sufficient in home-grown foodstuffs. His audience were ill disposed to this advice, and there was a great deal of heckling from men who wanted to know, 'Why a decent living cannot be made at manufacturing, if only the masters will give us fair hours and wages?' Many others called for universal suffrage and the proper representation of the manufacturing districts in parliament. There is, I learned, no parliamentary member at all for the Manchester district.

When Mr Cobbett stepped down, a decently dressed young woman came on to the platform and begged our patience a few minutes further. This was the signal for the crowd to start pushing and shouting again: I remained pressed against the wall, and to my huge relief the hordes began to thin. Soon I was able to take a seat in an empty row and breathe deeply. A few remained near the front, and the speaker addressed herself to them, announcing the commencement this week of night-school classes run by the Ashton and Stalybridge District Cooperative Society. She urged us to sign up at the back of the hall, for reading, political economy, or natural history. Still feeling stupidly upset by the rudeness I had encountered in the crowd, I stayed in my seat while the remainder of the hall emptied. As I made my way past the table where she sat with her lists, the woman speaker looked up and smiled at me, offering me a pencil. Her smile was so childlike, so sweet and open, that I paused.

'No, thank you. I do not wish to join a class.'

'I should have guessed that you could read,' she said, with a little laugh; and at my inquiring look, pointed to my costume. 'You are a – not a Quaker, but – '

'A Christian Israelite.'

She nodded, recognizing the name, and said triumphantly, 'And therefore you know how to read the Bible!'

I found myself smiling with her. 'I am interested to hear of your cooperative group. I was a member of an Owenite group when I lived in London.'

'Did you live in London? How wonderful! Did you meet Mr Owen himself?'

And so we began to chat; she told me her name is Catherine Woollacott, that she is education secretary of the Ashton Cooperators, and that they have fifty-two members. She speaks with great eagerness and rapidity, and fired a score of questions at me concerning London Cooperators, the Owenite Labour Bazaar, how I came to be with the Israelites, and so on; questions which would have begun to seem impertinent, from any other stranger, but all of which were delivered with such charm that it was easier to laugh at her than feel offended. I must admit that hearing my own explanation for my presence among the Israelites, I wondered at it, and felt a little ashamed that I have not made more strenuous efforts towards independence.

Among other details about herself she told me she is married – 'He is called William, he and his brother have an apothecary shop on George Street, do you know it?' I asked her age. She is nineteen; but so slight and pretty and unmarked by time that she could easily pass for five years younger. She volunteered a good deal of information about the Ashton Cooperators; they formed as a trading society, a year ago, and began one weekly reading class at Christmas.

The Salford Cooperators began with a Sunday school and now have classes every night of the week, and a building of their own.

We are following on their plan. The loan of the Methodist hall has allowed today's increase in classes.'

'And is there great demand for such classes?' I asked.

She pushed the sheets of paper across the table to me. Each contained a list of names. 'For the reading there are twenty-seven, I shall have to make a waiting list. I teach the reading myself – it is the best thing I have ever done!' She was insistent that I should attend their next cooperators' meeting; 'You will be able to introduce all sorts of fresh ideas, from your London experience – you are just the sort of person we need.'

What flattery! And I am quite susceptible to it, for there is no one in Mr Wroe's household with whom I might discuss Mr Cobbett's speech or the finer points of Owenism. I noted the address and time, and promised her I would try to attend. She is an engaging girl; as I hurried to meet Leah I reflected that there is a slight resemblance between the two of them, except that Catherine's energy is sunny and open, while Leah's seems inturned and dark.

A sense of optimism has stayed with me all the week; despite the fact that when I told Joanna my news she seemed almost indifferent. She has spent every evening this week in prayer, clearly struggling over some question of faith. I am sure it is the preaching business, and it makes me angry that Mr Wroe will not allow her to do it. That it is her natural impulse, I am sure, gives it more moral justification than could any sanctioning by Mr Wroe. I have lain awake waiting for her to finish praying, so that we can talk – hoping to be taken into her confidence; but she has closed herself up and declines to answer questions, only wishing me a sound sleep and God's blessing.

Mr Wroe being away for four days, my first opportunity to speak with him came last night. He seemed preoccupied, and I think he did not take it all in. When I finished he said, 'Why do you not call me Brother Wroe?'

'Brother?' No one calls him brother.

'You always address me as Mr Wroe. I do not like it.'

'How should I address you?'

'There are a number of alternatives. I am sure you have heard the Elders address me as Yaakov, the Hebrew version of my name John. Or you could call me Prophet Wroe. Or Brother Wroe.' Mostly the other women refer to him as 'the Prophet'.

'Very well, Mr – '

'Brother.'

'Wroe. And about the meeting – ?'

'You wish to attend a meeting of the Cooperative society on Thursday evening. Do you think this is compatible with your role in this household?'

'My work here will not be affected. I will make sure no unfair burden falls upon the other women.'

He shrugged. 'In any case, it is a waste of time.'

'Mr Wroe – how can you think it a waste of time, to – '

But he interrupted me. 'Sister Hannah, I have neither the time nor the inclination for this right now. If you can attend meetings without causing any disruption to the household, and without the other six all coming to me complaining of unfairness, then you have my permission. You must make arrangements for one of their people to bring you home, however; I cannot have you wandering the streets at night, on your own. Now please leave me to my work.'

Ungracious; rude; but why should I care? I have what I desire from it.

The meeting I attended on Thursday night was impressive, both for the enthusiasm of its members, and for the efficiency with which its business was handled. Catherine met me at the door and introduced me to her husband, and to several other members. I felt almost at home, for the composition of the group is very similar to that I used to attend with Edward: most of the members are about my own age, trades people and craftsmen, though the proportion of women here is higher, and the discussion all of a practical nature. They considered where cheaper wholesale supplies of sugar might be obtained, for retail through the society, and whether the rent desired by the Methodists for use of their hall for the night classes should be recouped by making a charge for the classes, or paid out of the trading society profits. I was astonished to hear the news of other local societies, given by the secretary; profits of trading societies in Huddersfield, Oldham, Denshaw; the success of workshops in Preston and Macclesfield. I had no idea so many branches flourished in this area. Speaking to Catherine at the end, I expressed my relief at finding them so practical and active. 'In London we seemed to spend hours on matters of theory; on the finer details of communitarian living, and such thorny questions as how wealth might be equitably divided.'

'Did your group have its own community?'

'No. But a number of our members left to found a new settlement at the Owenite community in America, New Harmony.'

She nodded. 'William visited Orbiston, the Scottish community, a couple of years back. They were suffering many difficulties and divisions – and we have heard the community has broken up since then. I am not at all sure that the purpose of our society in Ashton will ever tend towards such a community.'

I asked if she still has her long waiting list for the reading class. 'What type of people are they, who come to your night classes?'

'All sorts, and all ages. Many of them work in the mills; there are more men than women, because the women cannot get away from their families at night.'

'And do they pay for their instruction? The cotton operatives receive good wages, I have heard.'

She grimaced. 'They did. But now wages are being forced down. So many labourers have flooded in from the countryside – besides all the handloom weavers and woollen workers, whose trade has fallen away almost to nothing – that the masters can pick and choose, turn away men, to employ women and children. There is a groundswell of anger even among the cotton spinners, who have for a while been thought the best paid and most privileged group. There is a rumour now that at the next lowering of wages they will strike; many have joined the union. It is the reason for so many wishing to learn to read, so that they might understand and share the grievances of operatives in other mills, pass news back and forth – '

'This reading class – '

'Are you going to offer to help me teach it?' she interrupted. 'You must! I know you would enjoy it. William, persuade her.'

Although it had been in my mind to offer, I had certainly not intended to do so that night; but once she had hold of the idea she would not let go, and worried and teased me until I did agree. 'But I do not know the first thing about teaching – '

'I will help you. Nothing could be simpler. I will meet you an hour before class, next Tuesday, to show you – and if you are in any difficulty, I shall only be in the next room with my group.'

Once she was certain I would do it, she laughed a little shame-facedly and admitted that she had an ulterior motive.

'Can you guess?' The three of us were standing by the doorway of the Crown, their meeting having been held in an upstairs room at that inn. Suddenly we heard oaths and shouting, and a man came running heavily down the street towards us, pursued by several others. They were calling and baiting him – all more or less drunk – and as he passed us, one caught up with him and grabbed him. There was so much noise and confusion I cannot tell exactly how it happened, but within a minute the two of them were facing each other in the midst of an excited circle; members of the original gang shouting and urging them on, and a rabble of children who seemed to have come out of the very walls. William took Catherine and me by the elbow and we walked away quickly. But the sound of their fight followed us an unendurable distance. They were grunting and panting for breath and swearing, all this punctuated by sudden clanging thumps which were received with moans or gasps of pain. There must have been twenty or more spectating, all screaming at the tops of their voices, and yet that vicious metallic thud was audible over and over again.

'What do they fight with?' I asked.

'Clogs,' William answered grimly. 'Their clogs are tipped with iron. They kick each other. Sometimes for a bet they will strip naked except for the clogs, and battle it out until one bloody character drops unconscious or dead.'

A burst of cheers and screams from behind indicated that the battle was finished, and we could hear voices shouting directions, over the unmistakable and wretched sounds of vomiting.

'Put him under the pump!'

'His nose is smashed!'

'The constables – quick!'

A number of them ran down the way we had come, and I was pushed violently from behind, so that I stumbled, despite William's supporting arm, and only avoided overbalancing by stepping into a great mess of steaming horse dung. William helped me to a seat on a mounting block, and after a moment all three of us were able to muster a shaky laugh. The damage was not serious, because I was wearing my old black kid boots, not the pale Israelite footwear; I sluiced them under a nearby pump and they were soon passable, though my feet were drenched.

145

I could less easily cast off a nervous dread which the whole incident impressed upon me; the sudden and extreme flare of violence made me fearful of walking to and from a night class. Catherine and William offered together to escort me home, which I accepted, and Catherine said she would ask a member of her class to walk me home on Tuesdays. The drama of her earlier announcement had been spoiled, but when I recalled her to where our conversation had broken off, she simply said, 'Oh yes. I am going to have a child. In the new year, quite early.' I could not believe it at first because of her slimness, but they both assured me it is true; and of course, a replacement teacher will be needed.

'If the numbers stay up, we shall get a temporary replacement besides – but you will have time to get to know how it all works. Teachers are paid, did you know? Four shillings per session, it is a point of principle with the Salford Cooperators and we are following their model.'

I was relieved to gain the peaceful doors of Southgate, and spent a good while that night reflecting on whether I either wish or am ready to plunge into the frightening, busy world of Ashton. But there will be no way out of here unless I make it myself. Four shillings. It will be the first money of my own I have ever earned; it must be a start towards independence.

# Leah

Thomas is far more lively and wakeful now, than he was in his first days in this house. I am not sure so much attention can be good for him. At my sister's he slept undisturbed for two to three hours in the morning; now, between Saint Joanna cooing over him and Rebekah tickling him, and the bangs and crashes of Martha's slightest movement (she has broken more dishes in a month, than most people do in a lifetime), he has become accustomed to constant entertainment.

It is Saint Joanna who irritates me most. I cannot tell what it is about her; she has no restraint, no distance. She is all sincerity. In its way it is as bad as Hannah's coldness (I do not think that one has ever even smiled at Thomas. She takes no notice). Saint Joanna will take him up and gaze into his eyes for minutes on end. 'What innocence,' she says, to any who can stand to listen, 'Is he not beautiful? How perfect is God's handiwork, look at his little eyelashes. Do you see the perfect tiny moons upon his finger-nails?'

It is all perfection and sweetness, and if he gives the slightest cry or complaint, she will take him from whoever he is with; she does not snatch him, but she takes him calmly as if he were hers. She holds out her arms instantly, as if to say, 'You know the child is only happy with me.'

She sings hymns to him, for lullabies, and I am now forced to try the same at night, if he is wakeful. He has become so accustomed to it he will seldom sleep without it.

Will he know it is me, as he grows older? Not her, with her liquid doting, or kindly sensible Rebekah? The way she takes him – the way she walks into a room and holds out her arms . . . My love must all be in quiet things, in the thorough warming of his garments inside the old oven when the fire is low; in the careful mixing of his gruel, to the exact temperature he likes; in the smoothing of his sheets, in the night-time listening to his even breaths. She has twice offered to make a different arrangement at night, so that I should not always have him with me. When I refuse, and insist on staying with him, she thinks it strange, and wonders that I will not share that part of his care. She tells me she has heard him crying at night, when I – who am in the same room as he – know he has not stirred.

The other day she said, 'I think he has taken a chill; do you hear that little cough again?'

He has no cough, not the slightest hint of one. 'He is perfectly well, Sister Joanna.'

'I am sure I have heard him cough three times this morning. We must take greater care to keep him from draughts. You may not have heard him, Sister Leah, you may have been thinking of something else.'

If he coughs, I hear him.

She instructed me to keep him fasting, the day before Feast of the New Moon, 'that God may be pleased by the sweetness of the entire household'. How can it please God, to starve a six-months child? If she sees so much innocence and holiness in Thomas, why must he be starved to atone for sins? When she went off to pray, I fed him. And then endured an evening of her exclamations: 'You see how cheerfully the child sustains hunger? Is it not a lesson for us all, if a little child, who can have no real understanding of the meaning of this day, is yet given the strength, of God, to withstand the pangs of hunger for His sweet name's sake.'

Thank heavens he did not posset, for she would undoubtedly have taken it as a miracle, the sign of food from an empty stomach.

Rebekah is easier; she too will take him up at the first cry, but she will easily put him down again. She does not try to own him. And she can hold her tongue. When I have been out at night, she takes him into her bed without comment, and I know none will hear of it in the morning.

Does the Prophet ask Saint Joanna for reports of my child? Or has he forgot his presence in the house? He says nothing to me; when I read he speaks neither before nor after, and though last night I waited as usual at the end, he took no notice, but affected to have forgot I was still there – until at last I had no choice but to leave the room in silence.

How quick the bright flare of happiness dies down! On my way back from John last night I walked right into Sister Hannah, skulking about on the path spying on me, when she should have been asleep. I doubt she will bother to report me, but I cannot afford to be so careless. Nor is John worth such risks. Once we come to the point of it, up against the wall at the back of the inn, or wrapped in his saddle blanket in a dry ditch; what will he give me for it? It may be a pleasure – but in my present predicament I must look for more durable benefits. He will not be stationed here above another month, and then it will be goodbye and thank you ma'am. He is no different to Jack. If there is any whisper against my name now, I stand to lose everything.

Everything. What have I got? Permission to keep Thomas under this roof with me. To the Prophet himself, I am still invisible; as little as dirty Martha, less than Saint Joanna. Less indeed than Hannah, who tells me that he speaks with her when she goes in to read (true, I can verify it, for she has been in there over an hour some nights. I wondered at him making her read for such a length of time). Why will he speak with her and not with me?

It is not so much the speech, anyway. Conversation will not catch him. It is looks, it is touch. I must make him look at me again.

I should consider some means of attracting his attention when I may catch him unawares. It is not possible to get into his bedchamber, because of Samuel in the dressing room. It is not allowed to go into his study, except at reading time – and since he shares a corridor with the kitchen, there is little chance of slipping in unobserved. Therefore only if one catches him in the corridor, or on the stairs, might one . . . What? What, if he is blind deaf and dumb to my presence?

Patience will be rewarded. This evening I left my door ajar, once Thomas was settled, and listened to the household going to bed. Hannah and Saint Joanna were the last of the women to ascend, closely followed by Samuel, who went into his room next the Prophet's. This left only Mr Wroe downstairs. About an hour later I heard him open and close his study door. I was wearing my nightgown, unbuttoned at the breast: throwing off the blanket I had wrapped myself in, and taking Thomas's little cup, I set out barefoot on to the landing, moving silently and judging my step so as to suddenly come out to the top of the stairs just as he was reaching the last step. He was holding his candle up before him, and a little away from himself, looking down at his feet on the stairs; even if he had looked up to see me at the top, the flame would have blinded him. It was the easiest thing in the world to brush against him and catch hold of him to save us both from tumbling down. I fell back against the wall and he, losing his balance as I intended, stumbled against me. His candle, which he kept held up above his head, dipped but did not go out, and several drips of hot wax fell direct on to my face and neck. I had not forseen this (expecting, rather, that the candle might go out and leave us in welcome darkness) and I gasped at the pain.

'Sister Leah! I did not see you. Are you hurt?'

'No – that is – your candle! I am burned.'

'Where? Let me see. I am very sorry – ' He lowered the candle and peered into my face, as I peeled off a strip of wax from my cheek.

'What are you – ?'

'I forgot Thomas's milk – I was in bed then I remembered – '

'Did you not see me coming up the stairs?' He remained very close to me; so close I could feel his hot breath upon my neck as he spoke.

'No. I – I must have been half-asleep. I have dropped the child's cup somewhere about – ' He stepped back and we both spotted the cup together, and bent to get it. As I leant forward the unbuttoned top of my nightgown fell open, revealing my breasts to anyone who might be standing a little above, and quite close to me. As he was. Slowly, I closed my hand over the child's cup, and slowly straightened up. He was watching me. Standing quite still, holding the candle to one side so it should not dazzle us. I stood and waited.

I cannot tell how long we stood there, in perfect silence; he holding his candle, I holding the little cup. I know the same thought was in both our heads. I could hear his breathing. He was watching me, his lips a little parted, his eyes steady. I watched him, watching me.

At last, by an extreme effort of will, he abruptly turned his head and moved – rather staggered – toward his bedchamber door. I hesitated, to see if he would say good-night. But he did not speak, so I started to go downstairs. When I reached the bottom I realized he may not have noticed that I came down, and so could not even consider following me. I wished I had moved before he forced himself to turn away. If I had said, 'I am going down to the kitchen for the child's milk,' he could quite easily have followed – indeed, it would have been only courteous to light my way. Of course he could do nothing, make no move, there at the top of the stairs, where any member of the household might have opened their door upon us. But down in the kitchen, with the glowing embers in the grate, and none nearby to spy on us . . .

I crouched before the last warmth of the fire, hugging my arms across my chest – glad in the certainty that he desires me, and only impatient that I had not thought quick enough to bring it to a more satisfactory stage.

*

There has been a stream of visitors to see the Prophet: three of them yesterday in fine elegant carriages. The great hall is continually thronged with people seeking an audience. My chores yesterday included sweeping and dusting his room, and polishing his table and bureau with beeswax. Examining the top drawer of his bureau, I found a small handwritten volume, which is his journal. Not knowing when he might return, my perusal was necessarily hurried; for the most part, it seems to contain instructions from God and thunderous threats concerning the end of the world. My attention was caught by this passage, though –

> In my vision I saw a most beautiful woman. Her
> breasts appeared as if suck were in them; at the ends
> they resembled a rose. Her body was small, and her
> two thighs appeared as the thickness of her body. I
> tried to reach her . . .

LEAH

Turning the page in guilty haste, I discovered this lady to be none other than 'Mother Eve', who has given suck to mankind and is now to be a bride for God. Is this in the Elders' religion? 'At the ends they resembled a rose.' How his imagination dwells on that pretty detail!

I replaced the book and lingered as long as I dared; finally, when he still did not return, I untied my rule book and dropped it behind his chair. Hearing at dinner time that he was back, I went and knocked before afternoon duties began. He called me to enter: but as ill luck would have it, two of the Elders, Tobias and Caleb, were closeted with him. I had thought he was alone. So I was forced to waste my good excuse, and have my rule book spotted and returned to me by Elder Tobias. But I kept my eyes on the Prophet during this, enough to note that he watched me every minute. He did not smile; I think he did not even speak to me, beyond a nod. But he looked, long and steady.

If I had the ordering of this house it should not be so meanly done as now. It would be possible to present a much grander face to the world, with very little extra expenditure. The employment of seven women, for example, is an entirely false economy – for although we are unpaid, yet there is the feeding, housing, warming and clothing of us to consider. There is no great domestic skill in any of the other six; I honestly believe that I alone plus a skilled cook and a good handy maid, could achieve better results. Extra help would be needed for laundry – and of course, the women would be required for church duties, singing, punishments and cleaning: but women living at the homes (and expense) of their parents or husbands could perform these tasks, since they take no more than a couple of hours a day, and the Sabbath when they would anyway be in Sanctuary.

Without this clutter of women about the place the Prophet might make more use of the elegant parts of the house: receive his visitors in the drawing room, or invite them to stay to dinner. And no one would suffer the shock and disgust of suddenly coming upon Martha snoring, or staring in a trance – or Dinah hobbling about at tasks she cannot hope to perform successfully. Nor would I have the perpetual annoyance of Saint Joanna's doting upon Thomas. I know it cannot be long now before I win the Prophet's ear: it is only that the time and space available in this household

152

are so terribly limited. I know he wants me. The question is, when will he have the courage (and when can I make the opportunity for him?) to make his move?

The minutes, the hours, the days go by. My child is growing teeth. It is past the midpoint of summer. If I had known or thought when I elected to enter this household, how miserably slowly my desires might be accomplished – I am sure I would have stayed at home. There is no late-night entertainment now, for John is gone to Devon; I have no occasion to wear my muslin dress. I dare not precisely repeat my stairs encounter with Mr Wroe, and he has not noticed any less obvious move. Three nights running now I have gone down to the kitchen after going to bed, pretending to fetch milk for Thomas, and lingered there near the fire until I heard him come out from his study. But though I left the kitchen door open, and last night began to sing a hymn when he opened his door, he did not so much as peer in – only went straight upstairs to his room.

When he preaches he seems almost to be alight. And when he looks down into the congregation then, his eye invariably seeks me out. His heat and force are like a blast from a furnace. I am not nothing to him; I know I am not, I know it.

Saint Joanna's behaviour with Thomas is more provoking than I can say. During the daytime, he is generally in the cradle in the big kitchen, and whoever is busy there looks to him when he cries. But Saint Joanna has no scruples about snatching him from his cot when he is in the deepest and most peaceful slumber. Clasping him to her bosom she recites great chunks of the Bible to the poor bewildered little creature. I bite back my angry words, but once she has disturbed him in this way he does not settle easily to sleep again, and has spent much of the past few days in fretful, sleepy mewling. She seems incapable of leaving him in peace.

Today I made it my business to stay in and about the kitchen most of the day, in order to keep her in check. She seems to live in a world of her own, less and less able to act with common sense, or to know quickly what is to be done. Each small decision sets her dithering and wondering, and casting about for omens. She will look for a sign in the smallest detail; a spilt cup of tea, the shape of a passing cloud. The other evening, when I was upstairs with

Rachel and Rebekah, Rebekah pretended to be Saint Joanna in the garden, mourning over the early dropping of unripe apples; 'Alas, and woe, it is a terrible sign, this early falling denotes a fall from grace, premature death and an early grave! It may also betoken the end of the world!' We laughed, but from what I have seen and heard of Saint Joanna today, Rebekah's mocking speech might have been in deadly earnest.

We had swept and scrubbed the floors in the offices, and were about new-sanding them. She two or three times paused to take a good long stare out of the windows.

'Is there someone coming?' I asked her (in full expectation of a band of resurrected martyrs, or the riders of the apocalypse at least).

'There are some birds,' says she.

I had not set her down for an admirer of nature. 'Are you fond of birds, Sister Joanna?'

She did not turn her face from the window. 'It is a sign.'

Glancing out, I caught sight of two dusty grey fledglings hopping about on the path. 'Of what, sister?'

She watched in silence (leaving me to the task of lining and patterning the sand, which I in any case perform more neatly and evenly than she; it is a well laid floor, more flat than ours at home, and looks well new-sanded). At length she turns back to the room and says, 'It is a sign relating to us. As the birds have made this house their home – they were reared in a nest above the wash-house door there – so have we. As they grow and try their wings, so shall we grow in faith and good works, and as they take off and fly away, so shall we gain the power and inspiration to work as God's missionaries in this world.'

'Indeed.'

'I have watched their parents feed and tend them this past week, as assiduously as God himself tends to the spiritual needs of his children. And today they are trying their wings.'

'It is a sign for us, you say.'

'For us females – the seven of us.'

'And are there seven birds?'

'I cannot be sure. I have counted no more than five, but it is no great matter, five or seven.'

We replaced the funiture and went out to join the others, who had already made a start on the chickens. We have Elder Tobias to thank for this: hearing old Buckley's wife was sick, he gives her his usual deathbed visitation, telling her to lighten her soul by relinquishing worldly goods. The upshot is, before she's cold in the ground, Old Buckley has sent his boy down to know if we will have her flock of chickens alive or dead. There are enough chickens here to keep us in eggs, and since the house is sorely lacking in pillows and bolsters it was decided we should pluck the lot for feathers and down, and prepare the flesh for the Feast of the New Moon on Wednesday. They have hung them from hooks on the wash-house outer wall, and all save Dinah are at work now plucking. Martha, as usual, stands gormless, too hamfisted for such work: and Madam Hannah is a stranger to it, I see, tugging at feathers one by one with awkward finger tips – while Rebekah and Rachel beside her take the feathers in rows between flying thumbs and index fingers, and seem to peel the flesh bare as I watch.

Joanna and I take our places among them: the air is thick with choking down and that filthy stink of chickens. They have taken off their heads to let them bleed, thus removing part of the natural amusement of plucking – for ours at home always have their necks wrung, and dangle and jiggle quite delightfully as one plucks. I remember Anne and I in hysterics one time over the resemblance to a man's you know what, and my mother scolding us 'For shame! for shame!' till she suddenly burst out herself, and laughed till we were quite afraid.

Saint Joanna is no great plucker either, I see, nor is the work one scrap to her taste. After a few minutes she leaves her post and vanishes around the corner.

'Are they flying?' I ask, on her return.

'There is one that cannot get back on the roof. I fear it has jumped too soon.'

'What does it signify if they cannot fly away?' She tugs at a handful of feathers, not sharply enough to loosen them: they break in her fingers. I hope I shall not be lumbered with the tidying of her birds.

'It may signify a failing . . . I cannot tell.'

After a while the down and dust set me sneezing violently, and I go in to check on Thomas. He is sleeping sweetly, I am glad to say. Glancing out of the window, what should I see but a cat. A big ginger creature, lying full stretched out and a dreamy look in his eyes. On the other side of the path to him sits one of Joanna's birds. After a moment the stupid bird begins to hop and flutter: the cat lies still, only the end of his tail's raised up and sways a little – just a little, side to side. Suddenly there's a clatter and scatter of noise up above, and the cat and I look up to see the parent birds on the wash-house roof, going hammer and tongs, and four fat birdlings in a row beside them, all teetering on the edge. Well the cat looks up and the cat looks down, and then he makes a move. He strolls over to the stupid feathery ball, and sits by it. And he puts out a paw – and he knocks it over. Oh the squawking and the clattering from the adult birds, and the hopping and the scuttling from little idiot on the ground. He's making such a to do now he's ruffled the cat's temper. The cat lets him get so far, and then he pounces: takes him in his mouth and gives him a good shake. Squealing and fluttering and dragging a wing the nasty little creature reels about the path, and the cat gives him a pat here – a cuff there – a playful dab on the head, buffeting him back and forth between his paws. The parents, having reached a climax of squawking, make their first big mistake.

For they fly down. They fly down and flutter above the cat's head, hoping maybe to distract him – in which they succeed, for he leaps up after them, leaving the twitching bundle of feathers (already stale, in comparison to a healthy, flying bird) on the path. However, their other four little ones, in idiotic fright at the racket, leap after the parents. Being incapable of hovering, they land fair and square in the cat's way. That cat must have thought it was raining birds. Just then Saint Joanna comes into the kitchen. I wait for her to cry out and rail against the cat, but she does not speak: only leans against the wall staring out at them, while the cat runs this way and that, administering a blow here and a cuff there, killing none yet but buffeting them into a hopping dance, while the parents clatter and shriek overhead. The cat leaps; he stalks; he prances; a most beautiful creature in action.

'Will you not save them?' I ask Joanna.

'I cannot change their destiny.' She is crying.

'They are only birds,' I tell her, for she could not be more distressed if they were infants.

When the fledglings could no longer run, but were reduced to scrabbling heaps on the path, with the poor cat obliged to toss them in the air to give himself the satisfaction of catching them again, Hannah suddenly walked out around the corner of the wash-house. The cat vanished, with one of his victims in his mouth: Hannah surveyed the scene. Then she turned back into the wash-house and returned with a bucket into which she dropped three of the four. The fourth she set on its legs and it ran a few steps before pitching on to its side. We watched her examine it, then toss it into the bucket with the others, and head for the pump. She filled the bucket and stood staring into it for a moment, then fetched herself a stick with which she poked the contents. Saint Joanna, whiter than a ghost, went upstairs. Hannah, looking up from her work, caught my eye through the window and frowned. I returned to my plucking.

'Were you watching that cat, Leah?'

'You took his sport away, Sister Hannah. And only to kill them yourself.'

'There was no need to prolong their suffering.'

She recommenced her incompetent plucking. As with the sewing, the bulk of the work falls to those of us who know how best to perform it.

Saint Joanna did not come down again till prayer time; she was still very pale.

'I have been thinking about your birds,' I told her. She did not look at me, only at her hands twisting in her lap. There is something quite pathetic about her these days, I am sure the cares of this household do her no good at all. 'There may be other interpretations,' I told her, 'for there really only were five fledglings, which can not accurately represent the seven of us. Might one not think of the cat – which after all, is the more intelligent and beautiful creature – as a sign of goodness? If he were a figure of goodness, then we might rejoice that he has destroyed the nasty sinful little birds.' I had not really thought much about it, only I did feel a little pity for the woman. Her days, and those of the others in this household, are numbered – though I shall press for Rebekah to be kept. Five to leave and two to stay; this must be the most accurate interpretation, if she will insist upon a sign.

It was my turn to read to him tonight, and I asked if it is true we shall be going on a mission to the coast.

'Yes. We will be away for two or three weeks.'

'Will you take all of us women?'

'You are looking well, Sister Leah. How is your son?'

'He is a little fretful at present. But I think he will be well enough, if only Sister Joanna give him some peace.'

'Would you be content to leave him here in the care of others, while you were away on tour?'

'In Joanna's care?'

'Sister Hannah. Sister Joanna. Sister Rebekah. I am not yet decided.'

He would come to no harm, I am sure; and if the Prophet is taking only a few members of the household with him . . .

'Yes, I am content to leave him.'

'Then I shall take you, Sister Leah. Now, I am expecting Elder Ezekiel – '

I let myself out. My hopes are up again. 'I shall take you, Sister Leah.' I pray he may take me, and not just once, but in a permanent way. Of course it will be easier on tour, to contrive some time together, outside the rigid timetables of this house, and the hordes of supplicants and visitors in the hall. And especially if he leaves some of the others behind.

*

I have seen them: Wroe and Hannah. If I had not seen with my own eyes, I would never have believed it. Which is stupidity, blind stupidity on my part. For look at the privileges she enjoys; might I not have guessed? She comes and goes at all hours, on her night-class teaching and her goody-goody errands. Her time is practically her own, for she plays no part in the religious side of our duties; where hard work is concerned she leads a charmed life. Joanna may be a poor cook, but at least she is there, in the kitchen, sweating over her latest batch of heavy, chewy dough. When has Madam Hannah rolled up her sleeves and got her hands dirty? Her skinny, ugly, bony hands; the woman is a skeleton, dwarfish and bony. What sort of man could look twice at her?

I have my answer, and it proves him mad. What appetite sucks upon a lemon, when it could have a ripe juicy peach?

She has been cunning in the extreme, affecting all along a dislike both of the church and of him: disobeying, never seeking to please – of course, this is what has singled her out to his attention.

I can still scarcely credit the events of yesterday afternoon. Their boldness stuns me. I was at work in the sewing room, with Rachel and Rebekah, sewing nightdresses for the seven of us, Saint Joanna being busy with her idiot charge Martha, and Dinah sick in bed. I knew Hannah was excused, after she had sided the dinner dishes, without rightly knowing why. The sewing-room door being ajar, I watched her pass along the corridor from the kitchen, and listened to hear her footsteps continue into the housebody. But they did not. They moved on along the corridor, and I knew I was not deceived when I caught the sound of her knocking on the Prophet's study door. The next I heard was the door closing; she was in. It was but a half-hour after dinner – mid-afternoon. It is unknown for any to be allowed into his room in the afternoon. But in went Hannah, bold as you please. After a while I made some excuse to my sewing companions and walked down the corridor past his door. It is dark and gloomy at the far end, one may lurk there and not be seen from the kitchen. Putting my ear to the wall I heard the sound of voices, his and hers, chattering away. It struck me that they may even have been arguing. I was not sure at first whether Samuel Walker was with him, but after a couple of minutes the animation of their discussion convinced me that they were alone, and I was quickly able to verify this by glancing into the housebody, where Samuel sat in his customary place by the door.

I returned to the sewing. Rebekah and Rachel were asking foolish questions about the birth of Lizzie Ogden's baby; but I had no patience with them, and snapped at them to be quiet. And in the silence that followed, broken only by the rustle of stiff callico and the small popping of needles, I heard her. That sound, unlike any other, which seems to cut the air; the short cry of a woman at the height of her pleasure. I held my breath, but it was not repeated. Rebekah and Rachel sewed on imperviously; I guess they have never heard it before, and so discount it as the cry of a gull or some such. Putting down my sewing I advanced along the corridor to his door again – but I could hear nothing. A burning desire to have my suspicion confirmed propelled me back past the sewing room, in at the office and out of the back kitchen door. If the shutters to his room were closed, that would prove it. And if they were not; then, I might see what I might see.

Turning right, I made my way over the rough ground at that side of the house. It is planned for an orchard, I have been told; but at present is no more than a lumpy, hillocky, weed-ridden mass, where the builders have stored their stone and materials. In places, parts of the former garden still survive among the weeds: against the wall before his window, a wilderness of rose bushes and stinging nettles. Some of the roses have grown so high as to nearly obscure his study window; standing on tiptoe, at a distance, I could not see in. I was afraid of being spotted from within, so drew closer to the wall. I was not overlooked from anywhere outside the house, the hummocky ground and open meadow lay at my back. So crouching down, I endeavoured to force a way through the thick growth. My dress snagged instantly on a hundred thorns. Pulling back (with ominous tearing sounds), I caught up a broken piece of planking from the ground and used it to press back the growth and force a way through. At the side of the window I paused, my back against the wall, straining for any sound from within. Nothing. Holding still the prickly branch of a rose before my face, to keep me at least partly hidden, I peered in. Once my eyes had penetrated the swimming thickness of the glass, and become accustomed to the darkness within, I realized what I was staring at; the two of them stood near to the window, with their backs to me – Hannah's back being the first thing to make itself known in the semi-darkness, by reason of its naked whiteness.

She was clutching her dress (which was unbuttoned to the waist) to her chest, while the Prophet was about the fastenings at her back.

Though I knew what I had heard – still that sight leaps before my eyes. As if they cannot take it in, cannot accept it for a true image. I am beaten aside by Hannah, by ugly, untidy, careless Hannah. I, a fool like the other doltish women, go about my virtuous household duties of an afternoon, while the Prophet in his hallowed study fucks with Hannah till she shouts aloud.

That cry of hers seems to echo in my skull. Why, and for what, is she preferred? How will she use her influence? Already she works less, chooses her own occupations more, plays the lady while we drudge. And if she is insinuated into that place in his favours, that place is closed to any other . . . Shall I be *her* serving wench? And how have I been so blind, so stupid, not to see this before? All this time I have waited, trod carefully, avoided seeking him out too obviously . . . and while I have waited and wavered, she has marched in and taken the prize.

She shall not have him without a fight. No. I have failed to appreciate her cleverness. But now I know how things stand – I shall act. She is not the only one who may attract his attention. I have enough signs already that he is not indifferent to me. It is only that she has been bolder, less afraid of seeming forward . . . She has made fewer scruples than I. I should have guessed that that was the way to success. From the first, when he showed such warm interest in who it was I visited, and if it were a lover; I should have guessed that he prefers boldness, shamelessness. Two can play at that game, Madam Hannah.

Images of that woman have been swimming before my eyes all night long; her quiet knowingness, her nasty furtive ways. What was she about, that night I met her in the lane? She affected to think it was only I who might have been out where I should not be. Where had she been? She shall be the centre of my attention from now on, for anything I can find which may discredit her.

Not only was my night made wretched by thoughts of her cunning, and the means by which she has insinuated herself into his affections: but Thomas also slept poorly. He has a little dry cough which wakes him, and when I touched him he felt feverish. I took him downstairs to the kitchen twice, to try him with sugar-water, but he continued restless all night long, and this morning he looks pale. I wish he and I were a thousand miles from this hateful place.

# Martha

There are new things at nights. I ask Dinah. 'Did you see the others?'

'When, sister?'

'In the night.'

'Where were they?'

'They were – they were here. Joanna was singing.'

'Here? In this room?'

'I – I cannot tell.'

'What happened?'

'Joanna was singing. There were candles. I was singing too.'

'I would have woken up. It must be a dream, Sister Martha.'

'A dream?'

'Yes, while you were asleep.'

Next night I see new things. Outside, and sun is shining. I am with Rebekah in the garden. We are digging up food from earth, eggs, carrots, cabbages, cheeses. All of it buried in earth. We are laughing and holding it up to show.

In the morning I ask Dinah again.

'You are dreaming, sister. You must have had dreams before?'

I cannot tell. She laughs. 'Dreams! When you are asleep – you imagine things, you see them in your head – people or places you know, or sometimes you do not. Like a story.' I watch her. 'Do you understand what I am saying? It is not real. It is in your imagination.'

There was nothing before. Only blackness at night. Now there is a new thing every night. People, sounds. And from before. Warm arms lift me. I am held. I have a mother. These are alive at night.

162

If this world is at night, that was not there before . . . There may be more.

Before I had none and now I have two, of daytime brilliance and of night-time dreams. My eyes and ears and skin are new and can perceive. If there is a world in dark sleep, there may be one behind the surface of stone. Another beneath water in the well. Another on the other side of black night sky. As my senses grow I will reach each one, as I have gained day and night. In one is my mother, I will see her fully. I have her warm milk smell.

In one maybe I am not there. If I could see into that one, that has no Martha . . .

There are new worlds. I grow to accommodate their size, as if I swallowed eggs that hatched and grew within.

Joanna teaches me the songs now. Not to sing, but to speak the words. She sings it for me, and I must say it after.

> *Saviour if of Sion's city*
> *I through grace a member am,*
> *Let the world deride or pity,*
> *I will glory in thy name:*
> *Fading is the worldling's pleasure,*
> *All his boasted pomp and show;*
> *Solid joys and lasting treasure*
> *None but Sion's children know.*

'Good, good girl. Well done, Sister Martha. You have the whole thing by heart!' She looks at me anxiously. 'Do you understand it, Martha? Can you understand these words?'

Solid joys. I understand.

Sunshine. The green. Leah comes to me in garden.

'Get in. Get in the kitchen, you.' I go. It is dark I stand next window. The fire makes smoke in my throat. Hannah sits her arms across chest she is shut in. Leah stamps her foot like a tethered horse.

'Sister Joanna says you must learn to make the oatcakes. You two. We end up doing all the cooking. So watch, and listen. DOLT!' She shouts. 'How can anyone see to cook when you are blocking all the light? Get away from the window.'

I move. The warmth furs my skin like night.

'Here.' She tugs bowl it slides fast towards. The mixture slops to the front side and dribbles down. Her hand smears quick as if not there.

'This is the batter. Hannah, are you listening? You make the batter the night before. Five pounds oatmeal and a pitcher of water – use the big one at the end here.' She taps it. From the beam are hanging three brown jugs three white-round-green bundles of rushlights kippers greygreen herbs the empty creel white onions –

'Martha! Martha!' Leah shouts. She stands by fire circling a board. A round of batter grows across it. 'Listen, you *thing*. How will you ever learn?'

Hannah watching me. She speaks quietly. 'That is a riddle board, Martha. Coat the board with dry oatmeal; pour on a ladleful from here, make it go round like that.' Leah makes a sudden tip. The round of batter flops on to a board in her other hand and flip on to the hot.

'What do you call it?' Hannah says, pointing.

'Bakestone. Make sure it is hot.' Leah speaks as if she wishes not. 'When it is brown at the edge – see?' She steps back. 'Take the peel and flick it over – ' She does it quicker than I see. Stands quiet by the hot then bends again. Scrapes it up with one movement on up over her head. It hangs limp over the creel, making steam. 'Now you.' Hannah takes the ladle, pours on to board. The mixture runs fast to edge and down her skirt.

'You will have to move quicker than that!' Leah's voice is glad. She grabs board and shows.

Hannah does not speak. She ladles a little. Tilts board once. Tries to make it drop on to stone. It does not hold together.

Leah laughs. 'Look. Hopeless. Watch.' Leah's hands move,

the board swirls. Flick. Flick. Drop. Hiss. Scrape, flop, hiss, scrape – the swinging arm, round oatcake hangs on creel.

'See how easy it is? I learned when I was six – it's the one thing any fool can do – see?' She swoops and circles, hard and bright. She does not tell me do it. I watch the round holding in not spilling. Her movement makes it hold. Alone, I will try.

Rain coming up. Storm coming up. They are making for their procession. Feast day. I say to Joanna the storm is coming.

'Oh no, Sister Martha. I think not. I think we shall have sunshine tomorrow. The Prophet has not mentioned any storms, has he Sister Hannah? On the Feast of the Transfiguration, and a double wedding, we could not have such ill luck I am sure. And all the children newly apparelled in white and gold. God's will be done my dear: but thank you for your concern. You would not wish rain to spoil our day – a sweet thought, Sister Martha.'

More than rain. A wind to uproot trees. But she does not.

In the morning. 'You must come, Sister Martha. The seven of us must head the procession, with the musicians. Come, we must walk from Sanctuary through the town. Please God, many may be swayed by the sight of our simple faith.'

'No.'

When they return the banner is ripped. Their silks are wet and splashed with mud. Their white horses with uncut manes and tails bolted and one has broke its leg.

'Brother Tobias's flute is ruined – and I know not how many of the other instruments besides.'

'All the choir robes – there is not one not in need of repair.'

'But we were lucky to come off unhurt, Sister Joanna. There are roofs and chimneys down all over Ashton. I have had two children to the door just now calling me out to Pottinger Street, where the collapse of two houses has left a mother and child still unaccounted for – and others injured. I beg you will allow Leah to accompany me.'

'Take Sister Martha. She has more strength.'

'How did you know, Martha?'

As we hurry across the drowned field. A split beech lies like a broken straw across the path.

'I know.'

They have God. I do not know that. They have more words. They have different fear. They fear what is to come.

I have, which is given since I come here – body all lengths and shapes. Sight hearing smell touch taste I have senses inrushing as pumped water does to overlow your mouth and face. I have.

I know. That place and this. Bad and good. Weather. That Dinah will die. That Rebekah is with child. That Joanna has a rotten patch, like the soft brown side a stored apple has laid on all winter. I know Leah burns, and I know the Prophet will leave.

He fucks with me in the ditch at the back. I used to eat the bucket, in that ditch. Now I do not. There is food at table for people. Only now and then that great hunger rears up. Then I have to grab stuff grab and chew in handfuls. But now I know how to get in the larder.

He does not speak to me. He puts his hands at the sides of my head, with his thumb curled up behind my ear. His hands are hot. It makes my head a flower, held. But I know what he will do. I do not want. I move back.
  'I will not hurt you.'
  Keep still.
  'Martha, I will not hurt you.'
  Keep very still.
  It hurts. My father hurt me. And then the thing inside me, coming out the bloody wriggling thing. My father picks it up with a sack and takes it away. My insides hurt so bad I cannot stand. The blood all down me. He got a bucket of water and threw over me. He told me shut your noise.
  If I do not. This man can send me back.

I get on my hands and knees and pull the skirt over. I wait. Keep still. He moves around to my head, and crouches beside me.
  'No, Martha. Not like that.'

In this new world, nothing is the same. Bad is good. My body is not for pain. At first I. But no. And he stroke me. I am afraid. Keep still. But he pet me like a dog. He brush my skin. It hot. When the base of his belly touches mine ripples begin. His

breath is fast like running. We go. On the ground we move and
then our bodies jump together like voices singing up the notes.
There is sweat and juice on our bellies, our thighs are slippery.
When he pulls away his eyes are closed. He does his clothes.
He gives me a sweetmeat from his pocket. Then he goes back
around the hedge. I wait, as he tells me. I pull down my
underskirt and dry between my legs. The cloth dries stiff, it has
a musk-watery smell. He finds me on another day, and nods.
For me to go to the ditch. Some days or nights he nods to me.
At other times not. We do not speak. Once he says, 'When is
your time, Martha? Your women's time for bleeding?'

I shake my head.

'You do not have monthly courses?'

'No.'

'Have you never – ?'

He will not make me say it into words. Do not bring it in this
light do not.

'You are crying Martha. Hush.' He touches my cheek with his
finger. I keep still. He watches me then he goes in the house.
Not in this place of sweetness. Nothing else can harm me now,
look I am free. Once I think no. The old Martha is still there, in
that life. I am a new Martha, but the old one still lives that life. I
begin to sweat. Is it true? How can I bring her here? She is that,
as the mushroom on horse-dung: the mouse in owl's beak. I am
not moving away from her.

No. Hannah says, 'You should learn the months then you can
make sense of time. January, February, March. They follow one
another, Martha, there is an order – then the number of the
year. Do you know what year it is? Eighteen hundred and
thirty. That's how many years have passed since Christ was – '

No. No. Old Martha in the dark place, new Martha in this
sweet life. She is there still I will not make it into this world
with words for them to see. Could I bring her? The old bad time
is stronger. I will not go near it I will not touch. Only the past is
to fear.

Dinah will die. She smells bad. I do not go in her room.

Joanna tells me to empty the slops from the bedrooms.

'Sister Martha! Why have you not emptied the slops from Sister Dinah's room?'

'She will be dead.'

'Martha! You must not say that.' She looks at me, I wait.

'Come upstairs with me now. Come on.' We go to Dinah's room. Dinah breathes fast and light as a small dog. Joanna wipes her wet face and neck. She gives her a spoonful of drink. I wait.

'Martha – Sister Dinah is ill – so we must help her. We must help the sick, tend them, try to ease their suffering. Christ asked us to help the sick. The love of God has healing powers. Do you understand, Martha? We must pray for her. Come here, kneel by me.'

When an animal is dead it does not move. It is finished.

# Hannah

How I dreaded that first class! The night before, what little sleep I had was dogged with dreams of not knowing what to say or how to proceed, and watching, in ghastly silence, my pupils rise one by one from their seats and contemptuously quit my presence.

My worst fears were justified when I arrived at the Methodist Hall at seven o'clock to find no sign of Catherine. I waited outside the door for a while, then knocked and went in. The building was open but perfectly empty, then after fifteen minutes two dirty-looking young men came and sat on the doorstep and began to feast upon a hunk of bread and cheese they had wrapped in a handkerchief. They did not seem surprised to see me, so I asked if they came for the classes. Yes, they had come straight from work at the foundry, and were taking their bait before class. I began to imagine she might not come, and that I would be left alone to deal incompetently with all comers. It was nearly ten minutes before eight, and the place full of people who looked at me strangely, when she appeared. A lad with her was carrying a box of books, but she did not make any excuse for her lateness, only saying I should not worry as there was plenty of time.

She divided the students into two groups; beginners, and those who already had some rudiments of the skill. The second, smaller group (twelve in all) were to be my pupils. She gave me a pile of those penny alphabets children use, and some copies of the Co-operators' magazine. They are attempting to build up a library of simple readers, but do not yet have so many as a dozen copies of any one book. She told me how I should proceed with them, and then led me to my classroom; a small bare side-room which the Methodists use for their Sunday school. It was stuffy from the heat of the day, and smelled quite strongly of sweat. I expected that the

171

majority of my pupils would be men, but I had not expected so many of them to be older than me. Standing at the front of the room with all their eyes expectantly on me, I felt as if my nightmare was coming true, and that I should never be able to force a sound from my throat. But I gripped my books, and stared down at them until the panic subsided a little – and then I managed to blurt out my name. Passing round the alphabet books, each one read or stumbled through a page aloud, repeating my corrections hesitantly. This was until we came to a thin, ill-looking youth who simply stared at his page in silence. 'Try the first word,' I urged him, and then, when there was no response, 'F – F – Fox, Fly – can you try the next word?' He continued to stare at his page in mute misery, so after a moment I passed on to the next, who read that page and the following with ease.

As they concentrated, I became calmer, and was able to look at them more steadily. Eight men and four women, all of them in working clothes. They had the pale complexions of factory operatives, and accents so strong I had some difficulty in telling whether it was their reading or their pronunciation that was at fault. After she had read, one of the women, who was older than the others, looked up at me and smiled. I passed around the magazine and we read the first article aloud together slowly. I watched the young man who had failed to read earlier, and saw that he was simply mouthing the words, a little after the others, copying them, in an attempt to seem to be able to read with them. For the final half hour I set them to work in pairs, a weaker reader with a stronger, spelling out the words together, whilst I moved from one pair to the next, guiding them over the more difficult parts. When I came to the young man, his partner was reading aloud, while the boy sat listening. I asked him if he would read a sentence for me, whereupon he burst into tears. Everyone stopped what they were doing to stare at him, and then continued their mumbled readings more loudly. God knows I am not tall, but I seemed to tower over him where he sat on the low bench. I crouched beside him. 'It does not matter if you cannot do it. I am here to teach you. There is no disgrace in it, there is no need to cry. If these words are too difficult, you may join the beginners' class.' His partner passed him his handkerchief, and he blew his nose. He would not look at me, only kept staring down at his page, and began to talk in a soft voice so that I had to bend closer to hear.

'I can read, Miss. I can read. Father taught me. I can read my Bible. Only, I cannot make out the words.' I was at a loss what to do or say, but then the woman who had smiled at me leant back from the bench in front.

'It's his eyes, love. They're not so good.' He looked up at me then; his pale blue eyes seemed clear enough.

'Can you not see?' I asked him.

'Yes. I can see,' he said defensively. 'Course I can see.' But at length, by questioning him on items close by, and a notice pinned to the far wall, I discovered that he could make out very little nearby, and only strong, clear shapes in the distance. Promising that I would find him something he would be able to make out, for next week, I left him listening to his partner and moved on to hear the others.

I had anticipated finding myself the butt of humour, and even insults, concerning my dress, my (to their ears) strange foreign accent, and my stiff nervousness; but instead they showed the greatest respect, and were indeed so quiet and timid, that I found myself desperately seeking for kindly or humorous remarks to set them at their ease. When Catherine came in to tell us it was time for the class to end, they all said goodbye and thanked me as they left, leaving me suddenly weak with relief that it had passed off so well.

Catherine and I have discussed the blue-eyed boy, Albert. His sight is clearly impaired, and, at a guess, worsening, for how could his father have taught him to read the Bible, with such vision as he has now? I have found a book of children's verse with very heavy, large print, which he reads fluently. He is not even willing to admit that his sight is poor, so much does he fear that he may become blind and unfit for work. It is a mystery to me how he can continue about his daily life and tasks at work without accident.

At the end of the second class, since Catherine appeared to have forgotten her offer, I asked Albert if he would be kind enough to walk me home; to which he readily agreed. He has shown me a number of short cuts to my journey, and now waits for me at the canal bridge before class, to guide me there as well as back. The streets are busy in the evening just now, for when the people get home from work the carts go round with water drawn from the Tame. Albert tells me most of the wells and pumps are dry, after the past month's heat. I have persuaded him to visit Catherine's husband, William, who might be able to find out what is wrong with his eyes.

Apart from Albert, the other who has shown especial friendliness is the older woman, Annie. Arriving early for class one time, she came and sat beside me and, in answer to my questions, told me about herself. She works fourteen hours a day in the carding room at Albion Mill. Her daughter is grown up, so she and her husband Peter can both come to school. I asked her if she only had the one child; no, the others she lost as babies. Her third, the only one not sickly, she lost through leaving it in the care of an old nurse, and going back to the mill. The woman gave it opium to quieten it in the day. It is a common cause of infant deaths hereabouts, she tells me – and the nurses rarely blamed; more often are the mothers condemned, for leaving their children in the care of others. 'Although if we did not work, we should starve,' she told me cheerfully enough. Her daughter and her husband live with them, and a grandchild is soon expected.

I cannot describe the poignant mixture of sadness and pride I feel, at seeing these grown working men and women tracing along the lines of their reading books with a forefinger, attempting and stumbling over words, hungry for the sense of them. When I look at the children tumbling home from the mills, as I set out to teach my class, I burn with anger to think of the ignorance in which they are kept.

*

This afternoon I went in to discuss with Mr Wroe the question whether the Israelite press might be used to run off the spinners' handbills for their meeting next week. Members of my class are full of the news of the return to Ashton of Mr John Doherty, the spinners' leader, who will address the meeting and bring news of the General Union of Spinners which he has helped to establish. They want to get handbills out before the weekend; but the printer who has worked for them in the past has been arrested for publishing unstamped newspapers. I thought of the Israelite press straight away, then dismissed it as impossible; then changed again to thinking at the very least it is worth a try with Mr Wroe. In the right mood, he would say yes – and even in the wrong mood, he might say no more than that he did not care. The Israelite press stands idle from one week's end to the next, it was last used for a pamphlet of six sermons, back in July. No one else need even know we have had the use of it.

He was, however, resistant to the idea. Loan of the press must be requested of all the elders in conference, and is not within his power; if used for political ends (and how else could I define the spinners, with their incitement to strike and civil disorder?) the press could legitimately be impounded; and so on. We were in the middle of a heated argument (which I still had some hopes of winning, as he *was* arguing, not dismissing me with that cold contempt he uses at times) when I felt a sudden sharp pain in the small of my back. It was so unexpected that I cried out. Mr Wroe leapt to his feet and asked me what was the matter. I could only think that a bee had somehow got inside my dress and stung me – but when I moved the stabbing pain came again, just as sharp as before. He examined the back of my dress. 'There is nothing here I can see – we had better look inside.' He began to unbutton my bodice, which seemed to increase the repeated stabbing pains, so that I could not hold back tears. He unbuttoned the dress to the waist and began to loosen my stays. I felt a sharper hurt as he held aside the fabric to examine my back; then he knelt down, peering inside the dress, and suddenly exclaimed, 'Here it is! I have the little rascal!' He fumbled at the waistband, and pulled out a long needle, still threaded – clearly left in when the dress was made. 'It has made you bleed,' he said, handing me the needle. 'Who is the careless seamstress?'

'I made this myself,' I was forced to confess. My relief at the pain ending was considerable, but I was beginning to feel extremely embarrassed at my situation. 'I am very sorry to be such a nuisance.' I wanted him to fasten my stays and dress again quickly – if Joanna or Samuel had come in, what might they have thought? My face began to burn, and his serious expression turned into a broad grin.

'My dear Sister Hannah! I have never seen such a blush – it is hotter than the fire. There is no need for embarrassment – I have seen a woman's back before, you know.' I turned my back so he could fasten me, and to hide my burning face. But before he did so, he seemed to gently stroke the hurt place, in the small of my back, with his fingertips. It gave me a very strange feeling. I was filled with confusion, then I realized that he was probably wiping off a few drops of blood: almost certainly, he was wiping away blood so that it would not stain my clothes. When he had finished doing me up I thanked him and left his room quickly, still feeling rather uncomfortable. I have no final answer on the press, but I think I shall leave it. The small of my back seems to retain the impression – seems unduly sensitive. No doubt the effects of the needle.

*

In late September Mr Wroe announced that he would take three of the women on a short missionary tour of Yorkshire and eastern Lancashire; the party would be away for about two weeks. Dinah by that stage was clearly in her last illness, Rachel her constant companion. When he told me he should take myself, Leah and Martha, I suggested the substitution of Sister Joanna for myself; sweet, patient Joanna, whose entire aim in life is preaching and missionary work, and who of all of us has had least escape from domestic drudgery. But – no. She was necessary at home, against the day of Dinah's death.

'Knowing our customs as she does, and being possessed of great love and faith, she will make an infinitely better guide and companion for Sister Dinah and those who watch with her than yourself.'

I was sufficiently stung by this (albeit knowing it to be true) to refuse outright to go.

'Then you may leave this household.'

I suppose he knew I would not; which was more than I myself did, for I lay awake all night considering and planning what I might do. To take a post as governess or companion now (even supposing such a thing to be available, and I knew from past experience that was unlikely) would remove me not only from a household where I feel secure, but also from my night class and my new friends among the Cooperators. If I went on his idiot tour, well that would be two weeks away from Ashton. But if I leave the household, I must leave it all for good.

I was angry at being forced to fall in with his plans; or rather, God's plans, as he so often affirms, exculpating himself from any responsibility in a transparently childish manner.

And so the packing; the arrangements to be made concerning my absence from night school; the sad farewell with Dinah, whom I honestly thought could not last till our return. We rose before dawn (when Joanna shook me I was convinced it was washday, and felt my shoulders begin to ache before I had even opened my eyes) and got into the coach without breaking our fast, baskets of provisions tucked under our feet, and a fourteen-hour or more journey to Whitby ahead of us. Wroe sat outside on the box with Samuel, which I wish I could have done. The roads were still hard and dusty after the long hot summer, and the jolting fit to shake our teeth from our jaws. A broken axle cut short our travelling day and we were forced to put up at a coaching house, a loud noisy dirty place where the chamber maid stared so insolently at our clothes that Leah slapped her face. This took her off sobbing to the landlord, who treated us three women with the greatest rudeness imaginable. Mr Wroe took refuge in his room with Samuel all evening, leaving no means possible for us to complain at our shabby treatment, and the supper served to us in our room was as dreadful as we predicted it would be: tough, dried up, wizened fowl, cooked to the texture of wood shavings, accompanied by a mess of vegetables swimming in salty gravy.

Next day we passed through some pretty countryside, coming at length to the coast, which is astonishingly lovely. All of us, I think, felt a rush of excitement on our first view of the sea. Martha had not seen it before. Leah told us she had been to St Anne's and Blackpool 'with my young man', but that 'it was not so blue there'. For myself, I had seen only the estuary at the Thames, flat and grey, bobbing with the scum and filth of the port. Here was an expanse of brilliant blue, crested with white; rocky cliffs and strips of yellow sand, and a clean salt smell that raised the spirits on the instant. They say sea air is a tonic, and I can believe it. Imagine if I could have brought my father here and let him breathe that pure clean breeze . . .

But it was December then, there would have been gales, not breezes; an angry, not a gentle sea.

Whitby is a charming town. The estuary bustles with fishing vessels, and the fishermen's houses perch on the steep sides of the valley overlooking the harbour, with the romantic arches of the old abbey crowning the skyline above them. We were dispersed among two households, none of the Whitby Israelites possessing a sufficiently grand establishment to shelter us all beneath one roof. So steep are the cobbled lanes that our coach must be left in the yard at the Angel Inn, and we made our way on foot up to our lodgings. Martha and I stayed with a Mrs Brown, a baker's wife, while the other three were at a house some ten minutes distant.

After we had changed our travelling clothes and refreshed ourselves with a good meal, Wroe held a short meeting in the Independent chapel (lent by them on special request, and about half full with Israelite members). The Whitby Israelites wish to increase their numbers and build a hall of their own, and to this end Wroe was to speak next day in the old market place, and in the small neighbouring communities of Sandsend and Robin Hood's Bay. After meeting we were free; he appointed Leah to read to him, and charged Martha and I to meet them at the chapel at ten of the clock next day.

It was a beautiful evening – the sun, now low in the sky, sending streaks of gold out across the land, with dark clefts of shadow between them. I left Martha at the door of our lodgings, telling her I would join her soon, and made my way down the steep narrow lane towards the water front. Down by the estuary it was alive and swarming with sailors, fishermen, children and girls bearing upon their heads huge baskets of those shellfish they pick from the rocks. There is a splendid pier of stone built right out into the ocean. Leaning against its wall in the evening sun were groups of the local women knitting or busy with their fingers at some larger piece of work (I showed my ignorance when I enquired of our landlady later; 'They are making the nets. Or repairing them – their menfolk's fishing nets!') Out at the end of the pier stands a half-constructed stone tower, it will be the new lighthouse. I longed to walk out along the pier, towards the golden sunshine and open sea, but the intimacy of the groups of fisher-wives held me back. I imagined their whispers and giggles as I passed. And then I found some narrow steps leading down from the place where I stood, on to the open beach at my left. There were small boats (which they call cobbles) pulled up on the sand and some men about painting or repairing them – but beyond, the sand stretched away empty and peaceful. I walked briskly past the fishermen, who paid me no attention, and on along the water line. It was a great relief to be on my own after the stifling carriage, and the busyness of the Whitby Israelites. There were a few people about, some strolling in the evening air, like myself, others digging in the sand (for shellfish? or for bait? I could not tell).

'Hannah!' My name, called in a male voice, made me stumble.

It was Mr Wroe. He came scuttling along the sand after me like a dark spider.

'Are you alone?'

'Yes.'

'You know that is forbidden. You make a mockery of decorum.'

'I could not see it would do any harm. I am sure I am safer here than in Ashton.'

'You do not have permission to wander about alone in Ashton any more than here. Wearing the apparel of the church, you drag its name into disrepute along with yourself.'

'I am not your prisoner.'

'No. Nor are you in any way aiding my work.'

I turned and carried on walking, he keeping pace beside me.

'Do you like the sea?' he asked suddenly, after several minutes pause, as if no words had passed between us. He went on to talk about the different coasts he had visited, expressing a preference for the Cornish, which he claimed was the most wild and sublime of any. There, spray from the sea leapt up a hundred feet into the air when the great Atlantic waves crashed on to the rocks – and islands with caves and grottoes stood fantastically on the sand between land and sea, inhabited only by birds and seals. Suddenly he stooped and picked up a stone, which he examined minutely, before passing it to me. It was a black square-ish shape, worn smooth on one side, but on the other revealing a delicate regular spiral pattern – similar to the shell of a large snail, or the curved frond of a fern. The spiral was ridged with parallel lines like rays – I ran my forefinger across them, they were in clear relief; all I needed was the ink, to take a fine print of them.

'Do you know what it is?'

'No.'

'An ammonite. A creature which lived and died so many thousand years ago that it has turned into the rock, but leaves the imprint of its individual form.'

'It is beautiful.'

'A speck of life – part of the abundance with which we are surrounded. How can you find it beautiful, and lack faith? Do you think it is something random, rather than part of a tremendous and detailed design?'

I looked at the perfectly proportioned circling spiral, executed more skilfully in the rock than the work of the most talented engraver's burin on a plate. 'You wish me to take this stone as proof of the existence of God.'

'Why not?'

'And sickness, starvation, viciousness; these also prove His existence?'

'Of course.'

'And the information you constantly purvey, that He is about to destroy it all – this is part of His Grand Design?'

'It is.'

'Then I am not clever enough to follow it.'

'To be sure you are not. No one is. All He asks is that you should have faith. Then He will admit you to the circle of His love.' He held out his hand for the stone.

'If the circle of His love is after death, I reject it. Why does He not love people while they are alive?'

Wroe studied the stone in his hand, then blew down his nose like a horse. 'Too many of 'em!' he said, and raising his arm above his head, flung the stone far out to sea.

'No! Why did you do that? I wanted it.'

'What for?'

'It was lovely. You could have made prints off it.'

'He did. He has printed off a world, creatures great and small, each in its proper shape and proportion. A great abundant world of living creatures, and you talk of taking a flat image on paper.'

'That is a way of valuing it.'

'You are not asked to value it. It is not a thing of value. It dies, gets pounded to grains of sand underfoot. D'you think He is such a poverty-stricken housekeeper, that He must gather and save small remains? There is abundance, endless abundance, of these shadows we call life. Only His love is of value.'

'But His love creates life. If He goes to so much trouble, surely He must value it?'

'Do you think it is trouble for Him to make a snail? Or a human being? He who has created heaven and earth in six days from chaos?'

'Why create it to destroy again?'

'To show His love.'

'By destruction?'

'To be sure. Otherwise people will value it too much. Love His creations instead of Him, the shadow instead of the substance. Marvel over the creature embedded in stone, instead of at the infinite wisdom and skill of its maker.'

'You would throw all this away.'

'Of course.'

He glanced at me, I wondered if he was entirely serious. He increased his pace and moved ahead of me, zig-zagging across the sand, stooping now and then to examine pebbles or items on the ground. When he returned to my side he was carrying four smooth stones in the palm of his hand, which he offered to me.

'I have not found another ammonite yet, but you may like these.' He dropped them into my cupped hands, and they clacked against one another.

'Stones. Shadow, not substance,' he said.

I picked up the largest of the four and held it against my cheek. It was cool, utterly smoothed by sea and sand; in colour, dark grey, with a vein of red running through it, and shaped like an egg. He watched me.

'You would keep stones.'

'Oh yes.'

'You would not exchange this world for a better?'

'I would have this one improved.'

We walked on in silence. Then he said, 'It is time to go back. It is time for my reading.'

As we came up the hill towards my lodging he moved on ahead of me. I opened the door and went up to my room, two stones clenched in each palm, cool and smooth and solid to my touch.

Next morning the most terrible smell brought me coughing from my bed. Our landlady, who seemed quite unperturbed by it, tells me it is the smoke from whale blubber. They boil it up for oil – and use the oil to make gas for street lighting, and a score of other purposes. 'It is a pity you were not here two weeks since,' she told us, 'to see the whaling fleet come in. The whole town turns out to meet them then, and the giant carcases are hacked to pieces on the beach. Tis a fine sight.' She is full of boasts of the wonders of her town. One is that their greatest whaling captain, one Willian

Scoresby, sailed 'right up the North pole'; another, that when great storms have lashed the town, whole streets of houses have vanished without trace into the sea. Not a matter of much pride to their unfortunate inhabitants, I imagine. The smell of this boiling blubber (on venturing out I could see the filthy smoke hanging in a cloud over the estuary) was quite sickening. When I appealed to Martha for her reaction, however, she affected not to notice it.

There is still something alien about Martha; she watches, she takes note. She never speaks unless she has to, although she can speak and understand pretty well now. Therefore any attempt at conversation becomes an inquisition. I offered to hear her read, so that Joanna's good efforts might not be wasted, but apart from that brief interruption, we share our room in almost complete silence. She sits more still than anyone I have seen, as if she is in a trance. What is there? Memory? Plans for the future? The simplest questions are turned away.

'Are you glad to come to Whitby, Martha?'

'Yes.' There is always a reluctant pause before the reply.

'You like it here?'

'Yes.'

'What do you like?' Silence. 'Is it the sea?'

'Yes.'

After a while, 'Do you like being in the prophet's household?'

'Yes.' Stupid question; how could she not, after her previous existence?

'Do you think – do you imagine you may leave one day?' At this she simply stares, I wonder if the notion frightens her.

'I am sure you will not have to leave. I mention it simply because I have thought of leaving – I may, in a few months' time perhaps – I cannot imagine, you know, staying in one household for the rest of my life.'

The confidence becomes embarrassing, and foolish sounding, in mid-utterance. She has no interest in this.

We held two Israelite meetings on the second day, the first, at noon, poorly attended, but the latter attracting a crowd of some forty persons. We finished with the signings round about three of the clock, and Mr Wroe dismissed us. I said I would take a walk.

'Would you like to accompany me, Martha?'

'Yes.'

My heart sank, but I reasoned with myself that the gesture had been made by offering to take her, there was no need to make attempts to be sociable, and I would walk and think as freely as if I were indeed alone. In fact, in greater freedom, for she provided that chaperone which Mr Wroe had insisted on the previous evening.

We called back at our lodgings for shawls, then set off down the steep cobbled way towards the harbour, taking the opposite direction to that I had taken last night. Although the sun was shining and the sky overhead a glorious pale blue, the streets were as dark as tunnels, so tall are the houses, and so narrow the road-ways between them. As we came down to the harbour we could see that the first fishing boats were already home; and others coming on in. A thick cloud of seagulls swooped and screamed over one boat, where two men sat on deck gutting fish. While we watched, one stood and hurled the bucket full of offal out into the water, and the gulls dived, screaming, moving together as if they were all of a piece, like a wave. Down beside the big ships at the quayside, it is like being in a forest – so tall and thick do the masts stand. We watched them raise the drawbridge to allow three more of these fine vessels into the upper reaches of the river, where they are moored at a safe distance from the roughness of the sea. Here the smell of fish is sufficient to overpower even that stench of whale blubber. Each detail is strange and compelling; the con-trivances (being repaired by a gang of shouting, joking boys) in which they capture lobsters and other creatures of the deep; the bustling queue of carts waiting for the drawbridge to be lowered; the shouts and cries of women to men busy on the boats, and the squawks of gulls wheeling overhead. There is a thrill in the very shape of the town, diving down from clifftop height to the watery estuary at its heart. What an oppression is the tame flatness of Ashton!

'Shall we visit the ruined abbey? Up there, beside the church?'

We crossed the drawbridge in a throng of eager pedestrians, and carts laden with baskets of fish. At the other side, to our right, I noticed the large Friends' Meeting House on the corner. Mrs Brown comes from a Quaker family, they are the strongest denomination in the town, she told us. We bore left, up through the market place, where stands the tollbooth; up past open doorways where the women lean, knitting; past narrow 'ghauts' through which we caught glimpses of the river – up to the abbey steps. There are a great number of these, and they are extremely steep, so much so that we were twice obliged to stop and wait for breath to carry on. Looking back then, the view was splendid – yellow late afternoon sunshine pouring down on slack-sailed boats in the harbour, on blue sea and yellow sands, and on the dry brown fields at the top of the cliffs.

The abbey is fallen into a very ruined condition – it was broken up in Henry VIII's time. The great broken arches stand, roofless against the sky, like a natural wonder blasted by storm. The ground is lumpy with fallen stones, over which grass and nettles have sprouted, reclaiming that consecrated earth for Mother Nature. Walking through what must have been the nave, I turned and was struck by the sheer beauty of two arches set against the horizon – for directly to the seaward side the land falls away, a steep drop down to the water's edge. There is a magic in the combination of stone – worked, crafted stone, soaring – and pure sky, with no intervention of earth.

I sat on a broken column and looked out through one arch, to sea. Although I was still in sunlight, I found myself shivering; the continuation of these golden sunlit days leads one into a false expectation of summery warmth. Summer is over, and winter nearly here, as the early sunset and sharp evening chill clearly indicate. I was glad to hear Martha, who had been close behind me, move on. A lady with a sketch book was positioned not too far from me, and a young couple who were clearly lovers came into view walking past the second arch.

I watched them for a little; they were holding hands, and only tearing their gaze away from one another when there was some particularly difficult patch to negotiate underfoot. Silhouetted against the pale evening sky, their joined forms also made an arch; an irregular, moving one, but still echoing the symmetrical stone shape.

I moved on from my perch, wandering aimlessly across the uneven ground, pausing now and then to take in a view. One wall remains pretty much standing, its noble windows filled with sky, vastly more beautiful than any combination of lead and glass. As I rounded its end to gain a view of the far side, I spotted a familiar figure. The black-clad, hump-backed shape of Mr Wroe, standing in a curve against a pillar, staring into the distance. He was

perhaps thirty yards away, and not facing towards me. As I stood
hesitating, thinking on balance it would be best not to greet him,
after his criticisms of the previous night, I became aware of a figure
approaching from the right – a tall, clumsily moving woman –
Martha. The pillar was between her and Mr Wroe, so she could not
have seen him; but she was moving towards him in a straight line.
I watched her gain the pillar, disappear behind it, and then stop.
Perhaps he had spoken to her. She turned and dropped on one
knee in front of him, as if she had to beg forgiveness for being
there. Rachel and Rebekah curtsey and bow their heads to him, so
did Dinah. But to drop to her knees on a grassy hillside, in full
view of other sightseers – I am surprised he does not discourage
such displays. Then as I watched, he reached forward to her and
stroked her head, caressing it around the ear, as one might pet a
favourite dog. I watched her stand, and move to lean against the
pillar beside him, three-quarters hidden from my view.

There was a sudden tightness around the exterior of my skull. I
stood there not knowing what to do, unable to suppress a feeling
of distress quite unmerited by events. Surely I should be glad if he
treats Martha with kindness? Then the tightness around my head
contracted to pain; a genuine headache, needing the touch of a
kindly hand to stroke it away.

Picking my way as fast as I could, I crossed the abbey and
started down the steps. Down from that beautiful pink-lit spot,
into the darkening valley. Let him see her home, she would not
need my companionship now.

Next morning was damp and cloudy, not raining, but with rain in
the air, and a strong breeze off the sea. I awoke soon after dawn,
and slipped out before breakfast (Martha and I, by unspoken
consent, let morning prayers fall into abeyance, when we are
lodged together). I made for the cliff path which runs along from
the lane up above our lodgings. Once I got into the open the full
force of the wind hit me. I walked at a good speed, cursing the
voluminous folds of my skirt, which every now and then took the
wind like a sail. I shall make myself some bloomers such as the
Owenite women wear, for travelling and walking and garden
work; and if Wroe dislikes them he may try a skirt himself. Him
and his stupid petticoat rules.

Even as high up as I was, the wind carried some of the salt spray to my face – a fine sharp sticky dew. I could go. I could cross the ocean, the Atlantic ocean, as thousands have done, make my own way in that great land on the other side. Once I took the first step, a whole new life would unravel and follow. In the air below me I watched the seagulls ride and glide, part carried by the wind, part carving and steering courses of their own.

Martha returned a full hour after me, last night. But I pretended to be asleep when she came in. I find myself watching her, covertly, as she seems to watch me.

*

I had two further conversations with Mr Wroe during the tour; one in Scalby, and one on our last night, in Harrogate. In Scalby, he offered me a glass of wine after I had read to him. I have noticed him taking wine with his food before, but it is the first time it has been offered to me. I took the glass and stood awkwardly with it, until he thought to offer me a seat. It was a damp, coolish evening, and there was a newly lit fire blazing in the hearth. We both watched the flames in silence – I waiting, nervously I own, for whatever he had to say to me.

'You will be able to resume your night class when we return, Sister Hannah.'

'Yes.'

'Tell me, what do you hope to achieve by this work?' His tone was mild, but there is always an air of mockery in his voice, so that I seem to become over serious – angry – in order to defend my ideas. What nonsense. What defence do they need against someone like him?

'Within your own household you have instructed that all the women should be taught to read. My teaching enables men and women to discover God's word for themselves.'

'You do not teach them to read so they can read the Bible.'

'Why not? The Bible among other things. I sincerely hope they will read their Bibles.'

'And the pamphlets of political agitators; and handbills for secret union meetings, the vituperations of the radical press, charters and petitions numbering their so-called greivances – '

'Those too.'

'Do you think they will be any happier for it?'

'I imagine they will. I imagine it must be better for people to have some means of forming an opinion on their situation in life, than for them to remain a dull ignorant mass, as easily swayed in this direction as that by the next cunning orator who stands before them.'

'So you are teaching them to think, as well as to read?'

'Teaching them to read is no more than teaching a child to speak; it opens a door on to the world.'

'But it seems to me you are very remiss, Sister Hannah, if you teach them to read without teaching them how to think. If you give them the skill without teaching them how to use it.'

'The purpose of their reading is for them to form their own opinions.'

'Take up that book.' He gestured towards the heavy Bible I had set down after my reading. 'Solomon. Song of Songs.'

I did as I was told.

'Now read to me the opening verses.'

> The Song of songs, which is Solomon's.
> Let him kiss me with the kisses of his mouth, for thy love is better than wine.
> Because of the savour of thy good ointments, thy name is as ointment poured forth, therefore do the virgins love thee.
> Draw me, we will run after –

He interrupted me. 'Chapter V, verse 2.'

> I sleep, but my heart waketh: it is the voice of my beloved that knocketh, saying, Open to me, my sister, my love, my dove, my undefiled: for my head is filled with dew, and my locks with the drops of the night.
> I have put off my coat; how shall I put it on?
> I have washed my feet; how shall I defile them?
> My beloved put in his hand by the hole of the door, and my bowels were moved for him.
> I rose up to open to my beloved: and my hands dripped with myrrh, upon the handles of the lock.
> I opened to my beloved, but my beloved had withdrawn himself, and was gone: my soul failed when he spake, I saught him, but I could not find him; I called him, but he gave me no answer –

'That will do.'

The Bible slipped from my grasp as I closed it, and slithered from my knees to the floor. He watched me pick it up and place it on the table.

'How shall this be interpreted, by a man whom you have taught to read?'

'I . . . interpretations may vary.'

'By a working man who has learned to read in your night class?'

'It would depend on whether he attended church – on whether he had any other knowledge to draw upon, to assist him in – '

'If he did not.'

'Many Bibles are annotated to explain and interpret those passages where misunderstanding may arise.'

'The cheaper ones are not.'

'Then he would believe the verses to be about love.'

'They are about love. *Many waters cannot quench love, neither can the floods drown it. If a man could give all the substance of his house for love* – They are entirely about love.'

'I know what you are trying to make me say. That an uneducated reader might read this as a description of, of – affection – between a man and a woman – whereas – '

'Affection? Not quite the word, sister. As a clear and graphic description of the act of love, surely? *Open to me, my sister, my love* – '

It was very warm in the room. I pulled my chair back from the fire.

He barely paused. ' – but I interrupted you. "Whereas"?' he questioned.

'Whereas. You know. The love of Christ for his church.'

He nodded; 'A metaphor. Concerning the great, burning love Christ bears to His bride the church on earth, and the overwhelming love and inexpressible joy the individual soul may find in God. Certainly. *I sleep, but my heart waketh*. The corrupt and slumbering church is remotely touched by the word of Christ, but makes excuses to avoid admitting His presence. *I have washed my feet, how shall I defile them*? Indeed. The hand of the beloved in the door – the true spirit of Christ touching and awakening the heart of the church, moving it to penitence and pity for its past failings. *You* do not need an interpreter, Sister Hannah. But you will allow that it is possible to read these verses and extract from them a meaning quite other than their intended one?'

I did not reply.

'And if that is the case here, that it may be so in many others? Particularly where a writer has perhaps set out deliberately to lead his innocent audience astray?'

'The alternative is brutish ignorance.'

'Brutish ignorance: or manipulated delusion based on partial knowledge. Which would you say is preferable?'

'You are too stark. Partial knowledge may lead to fuller knowledge – people are not all fools.'

'Brutish ignorance has its own defences, its own feelers – as much as any other living organism. It can tell where to turn to the sun, how to shelter from the rain, how to grasp food or deal with an enemy. Yet you seek to meddle – are you not afraid?' His tone at last was serious, the mockery fallen away like a shell.

'Afraid?'

'Yes. That you will take away those instinctive responses which have enabled the mob to survive and fight and grab what it could when the time was right – and substitute for them a hollow pretence of equality, containing no real power.'

'No, no. Your premise is that the lot of the people can never be improved. If that were so, then it would be wrong to offer them a chimera of knowledge. But it can, and will, be improved – from this low stage to the next, to the day when every hand in a mill will have as great an understanding of political power and government – and as great a say in the government's composition – as the son of a lord or a bishop.'

He laughed. 'You take into account neither human greed nor human stupidity. But most faulty of all, you ignore the system upon which our world is built, which is but as a gateway into eternity. Each individual has a span of sixty brief years. You would have to be a profligate, extravagant, deliberately blind and wanton fool, to invest energy in seeking to improve the conditions of such a span of time – in the face of eternity.'

'The addition of all those spans together makes up eternity.'

He stood up and took my empty glass from my hand. 'You are an idealist, sister.'

'And you are – ' There were words in my head, but none of them exactly right.

'Oh, I know. A charlatan. The love you bear humanity is, I am sure more worthy than mine. I am simply sorry to see you wasting your considerable talents.'

His tone was suddenly more unpleasant than I can describe. Vicious.

'What do you think I should be doing, Mr Wroe?'

'What do women do, Sister Hannah? Many marry and breed, and pour out their great love on the endless wave of new humanity disgorged by their fertility. Others serve God, bringing new souls into His fold. Others – survive. Work, eat, sleep. Martha had a life, before she came here, you know.'

Martha. 'The life of a brute. You recommend this to me.'

'Not in the least. I do not necessarily recommend any of them.'

'I know what I want to do, and when I am able to be independent – I shall leave your household and do it.' I heard my own voice, loud with defiant anger.

'I am sure you will. I shall be sorry to lose you.' His voice suddenly low, kindly, and with a rumble – a slight roughness to it that seems to catch at my own throat. Listen Hannah, this man is a performer. This man is an actor.

But when he looks at me directly I cannot tell what to think: only that I know I shall feel foolish, and angry with myself, afterwards.

*

In Harrogate, the evening before our last big meeting, he came to me where I was ironing my dress, and asked if I could sew fresh buttons on his shirt, and mend a rip in his jacket sleeve. 'Have you been in a fight?' I asked, jokingly. He did not reply, simply set down the damaged clothes, with a needle and thread he had borrowed from the woman of the house, and left me.

'Leah is a better needlewoman than I!' I called after him; does he think I am a slave?

I was sitting sewing outside the back door, using the last of the sunlight to see by, when he poked his head out the door.

'Ah! A breath of evening air. How is my jacket, Sister Hannah?'

'Nearly done.'

'Tell me – ' he stepped out of the house and walked a little way along the path, peering over the hedge to see the sheep on the other side. 'I have been thinking about these millhands – these operatives of yours, who are so keen to read.'

'Yes?'

'What do they themselves imagine will happen, once they are literate? What do they foresee?'

I shrugged. 'How can I tell the thoughts of a mass of people? I can tell you about Annie, the spinner's wife whose babies died. I can tell you about Albert, the boy who is going blind, whose father is in the union. He has given me his father's views on the future.'

'That will do.'

'Well –' Albert and I talk on our way home after class; and often end up standing staring over the side of the canal bridge, while we finish our conversation. The last time we stood there, clumps of brownish foam dotted the surface of the water, like strange flowers. These come from the dye works at Albion Mill. 'Well, he told me his father says the masters will stop at nothing now they have lowered wages twice. That they will continue to lower them, and at the same time, bring in more and more machines to do the work of men, until whole factories may be run employing no more than two or three children to piece together broken threads: that the machines will do the work of a hundred men at once.' Wroe nodded; I had to ask him to take a step back, for his shadow was falling over my needlework.

'Go on.'

'Well, then working men and women will starve; for there is no steady labour to be had in the countryside now. Farmers everywhere have taken away their workers' rights to bits of land, and even their rights to eat at the farm kitchen table. Without benefit of a share in the produce they have helped to grow, their wages are too low to live upon.'

'Come to the point. What does your friend propose?'

I could repeat Albert's words exactly; 'My father says, we are a troublesome bunch. We will not quietly wither away, like an unharvested field in winter. We will be meddlin' and meetin' and readin' newspapers, and searching after forming our own opinions. We are a dangerous crew, he says, and magistrates were wise to call up the soldiers, or what decent folk could sleep safe abed?' It was pleasant to see the wry smile he had copied from his father's face, to accompany the words.

'Meaning what?' demanded Wroe.

'Meaning that they must combine now; that they must withdraw their labour while it still has value to the masters, and obtain some rights to safeguard their future livelihood.'

'A turn-out. Their vision goes no further than that.'

'How can it? They must grasp rights one by one, hand over hand, like someone climbing up a cliff; they must grasp each tool or support which can help them to continue their climb. It will not all be achieved at one blow.'

'So the overall vision is not theirs, but that of your educated Cooperators; of your Mr Owen, with his New View of society.'

'I have said – it is not a question of an overall vision. It is a question of survival, of grasping the tools to continue to survive. No one is forcing a system upon them.'

He took the jacket off me and held it up to the light. I thought he was going to complain about my poor workmanship, but he did not; only thanked me gravely for my trouble, and disappeared back into the house.

# Joanna

It is time to celebrate our fifth festival of the New Moon together. It falls this month on Friday, and being directly before the Sabbath, makes two days for which all must be ready in advance. We will spend these two days in preparations and Thursday fasting, in Sanctuary.

I am out of step, now, with the New Moon. For as long as I can remember, my bleeding has begun as the old moon wanes, and ceased as the new crescent appears. Symbolic and accurate mirror of our lives, the heavenly signs of the time for repentance and discharging the old: for welcoming and giving thanks for the new, the Moon has always been especially our feast – the women's feast, whose bodies as regularly discharge the past and make way for new life.

I sense my distance from my sisters: already, though they do not know my state, I am removed from the innocent cycle of their days. I can envy them their careless innocence, their childlike concern in matters of the minute, in what is cooking and what has burned, and the size of the heap of dirty linen to be washed. I remember my own closeness to such concerns, before God's great intervention, and I see a sweetness in such unconscious service, the sweetness there is in the chirruping and bustle of sparrows.

The duties of the household seem to press upon me with uncommon severity, this month: I pray God may give me strength to fulfil his works and desires. Unbidden memories of that dreadful hour of my sacrifice combine with fears and excitements for the future, to make my sleep fitful. This past week I have risen from my bed near as exhausted as I fell into it, having been subject to a thousand fears and visions in the night. By day I have suffered frequent headaches; there seems to be a mistiness before my eyes, so that the threading of a needle, and reading the Holy Book, are both great difficulties. If I blink repeatedly the mist will clear, but after a few moments' concentration upon any detail, it returns. I have been obliged to ask Sisters Hannah and Leah to read to the Prophet in my stead. I do God's will, I pray (though I know myself unworthy) He will grant me His peace. The vessel which carries His son must be calm, serene, strong: I feel my own frailty only too keenly. And until the blessed nature of my service can be revealed to the others, I must maintain a semblance of my earlier vigour about the house: indeed, I fear for household order when the time comes for me to play a lesser role.

For which fear I must reprimand myself, and increase my faith in His will, who has in His hands the organization of all things.

I ascribe to my tiredness the shortness of my temper and the irritable fault I find with my sweet sisters. I pray they may forgive me wholeheartedly – if not now, then when they know the nature of my mission. My nerves seem inflamed to such a point of foolish sensitivity that my sisters in God can do no right. How little are our hearts and minds, which can at first glance see no more than our own self-interested motives and desires: may God grant us a share in His loving vision. Without His aid we are locked in self, each as small and limited as the confines of her own skull.

Yesterday I irritably – and wrongly – found fault with my sisters Rachel and Rebekah, due to my inability to take this larger view. Knowing that today and tomorrow must be devoted to culinary preparations for the feast days, and to a thorough cleansing both of this house and Sanctuary, I was most impatient that the remains of the laundry work be dispatched with haste. Our monthly wash having been performed last week, Sister Rachel and Sister Rebekah devoted Friday and Sunday to the ironing (which I thought long, failing to take account of the excellence with which they starched and got up the Sanctuary cloths and ephods). Yesterday there remained nothing but the careful stowing away of clean bed and table linens in the chests; and ephods, surplices and all religious linens in the closets in Inner Sanctuary. I despatched them in the carriage on this errand at nine in the morning, and looked to their return soon after ten. But finding them not returned by eleven, and the slops from the bedrooms not yet emptied (for I have banned poor clumsy Sister Martha from the task, after her unfortunate stumble last week – it appears impossible to cleanse the bad odour from the stair-well, though Sister Hannah and I scrubbed from top to bottom), I felt compelled to follow them to Sanctuary to urge their speedy return. The carriage had returned empty a half-hour after their departure, and Samuel informed me they had offered to walk home when their work was complete, since they would have nothing to carry. The morning was unwholesomely close, and I regretted not taking the carriage as soon as I reached the bridge, for I was covered in a flush of perspiration, and filled with a distinct sense of nausea. These, I know, are fair signs that God's will is achieved, and I embrace them with joy – but yet, at the time, I must allow I felt unwell, and could have wished for a respite from my holy state. By the time I gained Sanctuary I fear my hasty temper had risen against the girls, for interrupting my morning's work (I had been about directions for the procuring of foodstuffs for the feast day; someone had to be sent up to Clough farm with a cart in the afternoon to collect all the butter and cheeses, and to see if he had any eggs to spare. And the outer office was blocked with four barrels of sour cyder Sister Benson sent us, to make into vinegar; which needs starting this week, while the warm weather lasts – but I digress). Imagine my despair at finding both the side door and the great door locked. The girls had already left, but I had not encountered them on my way. I had not thought to bring my own keys, feeling quite certain of finding them still in the building – and so I was forced to retrace my steps without the opportunity of rest. My physical discomfort was increased by the appearance of two sadly ignorant children, who followed close on my heels, demanding (with all manner of impertinence) to know the reason for the strangeness of my dress, if I were a lady, and if I lived in 'yon house of debauchery across the canal'. May God forgive me, I lacked the patience He has vouchsafed me in the past, to turn away their wrath with gentle replies. My attempt to hurry away from them met with a worse result, for they began to run and jump about in my way, calling upon me to reply. Two gentlemen passing were kind enough to scold them and send them off. But memory of the incident troubles me greatly: did God's own son not say to us, 'Suffer the little children'? Formerly, it would have been no trouble to me to speak kindly to them, and help them into the way of God's love.

But on with my story. I paused for breath on the bridge, and chancing to glance down, was astonished to see Sisters Rachel and Rebekah, sitting on the bank opposite to the towpath, their skirts up above their knees, and their bare feet dangling in the water. They looked for all the world like two godless mill children on their Sunday holiday. I called to them and they started up instantly, scrambling into their stockings and shoes. They approached me with smiling and obedient haste – which kindness I returned by harranguing them shamefully, in such a fashion as I now cringe to remember. How little we understand, dear Lord, the moods and desires of other minds. And yet I might have paused, I might have considered: two young girls filled by nature with all the happy high spirits of that age; two young girls as innocent of knowledge of wrong behaviour as the lamb frisking in the field; two young girls who had passed the three preceding bright summer days, either in the still hallowed confines of Sanctuary, or in the closer space of the outer office, where they had toiled from morning to evensong over piles of linen and hot heavy irons – glimpsing the chance for a half-hour's harmless recreation. Does not their easy and joyful embracing of God's bounty put me to shame? Did I thank Him for the heat of sunshine, the cool glistening water, the brilliance of the grass? Am I now blind to the joy we give Him when we rejoice in His bounteous gift of the physical world?

I pray for forgiveness, both of God and of these sisters, who must witness with astonishment this accumulation of my failings.

By lunchtime today (I have spent the morning in the hot kitchen roasting lamb and beef to be served cold at the feast, and in the preparation of numerous pastries) I felt myself so unwell as to be giddy, and charging Sister Hannah and Sister Leah with the boiling of the fowls and preparation of soup, I made my unsteady way to my bedchamber. After I had lain an hour upon my bed, I raised myself up to answer the call of nature – and then made the discovery which breaks my heart to relate.

I bleed. What does it mean? I stare at the brownish stain on my undergarments, the fresh red blood at its centre. I cannot tell what

I must do, a terrible fear gripping me makes me lethargic, scarce able to move. I had not looked for this. I fear. I fear the blood spilt at this conception: I fear I may have been injured in some way. I fear –

Dear God. My fear is that You are not with me. This is my only fear.

*

I am not with child. There can be no doubt left in my mind that this is my monthly women's courses. Out of step with the pattern of my lifetime, indeed: never before have I been unclean, and so unable to enter Sanctuary, at the Feast of the New Moon. But the absence of the others gives me opportunity to mourn that great loss which I am still scarce able to believe. Like a lost child in the darkness I seek comfort, understanding, illumination. Is this a figure of my end? That I shall be erroneously heavy and heartened with hope, only to discover that I am doomed to perpetual loss? But His forgiveness and mercy are great, He could not so abandon one who has sought above all to serve Him. Can it be as it was with Joanna Southcott, that our error lay in seeking a physical child? Was He displeased with the manner of conception – with my tearful fears and lack of courage? Did my response to that first trial of strength show Him my great unworthiness?

These questions are fruitless, harmful, arrogant. I must pray for the greatest blessing, the humility to accept His will unquestioningly. Thy will be done, oh Lord, though it involve the breaking of my heart and my hopes, I count it but small loss against the love and peace that passeth all understanding, which I may obtain by the intercession of Your grace. Teach me to be a stick, a stone, a clod of earth, that will neither fear nor regret the rain that falls, the sun that scorches, the freezing blasts of winter – teach me acceptance, I pray You, that the piercing regrets and terrors in my heart may be quieted.

*Shall the thing formed say to him that formed it, Why hast thou made me thus? Hath not the potter power over the clay, of the same lump to make one vessel unto honour, and another unto dishonour?*

And if I weep – through mere human, womanish frailty – it is only for love of Thee, my Lord, and for the hopes that I held of a warm sweet babe in my arms, into whose service I might pour the overflowing pitcher of my holy love. If I weep, do not be angry with me, but know that I weep for sorrow at my own failings.

*

Sister Hannah told me yesterday that she has seen bugs on Sister Dinah's bed; this afternoon we inspected together and found that there are a quantity of them in and around the bed. The pallet itself was perhaps infested. Now the warm weather has brought them out, and they are everywhere. We moved poor Dinah into Sister Rachel's bed and Sister Hannah has flung pailfuls of water across the floor to drown any that might attempt to save themselves. Sister Martha she enlisted to carry the parts of the bed down into the yard, where they will steep in a tub. Sister Hannah sets about the room with a fine energy; she knows such bugs from her London days, she tells me, and the cracks between floorboards, in skirting boards, in all the furniture, are places they will hide. I sit beside Dinah's bed, reading the Good Book, more lost I fear than the poor wandering patient I seek to comfort, while Sister Hannah scrubs about us in a frenzy of cleanliness, and I see (or seem to see) the horrid little creatures spilling from each dark crevice in the floor, each fold in bedding and hangings. My skin crawls, darkness runs about us.

I grieve for the lost child. Sinfully, wrongly I know, but my heart is heavy and my spirits dull, I can scarce raise my head from the pillow at morning. I am afraid. When I went in tonight to read to the Prophet he did not speak to me, only pointed to the part I must read and sat at the table with his head in his hands. From Luke, the words of our Blessed Saviour himself:

*Daughters of Jerusalem, weep not for me, but weep for yourselves, and for your children. For, behold, the days are coming, in the which they shall say, 'Blessed are the barren, and the wombs that never bore, and the paps that never gave suck.' Then shall they begin to say to the mountains, 'Fall on us!' and to the hills, 'Cover us!' For if they do these things in a green tree, what shall be done in the dry?*

Lord, I seek among thy words for comfort, and am rewarded with more pain: as a woman lost in the desert seeks water, and is rewarded with ever-increasing thirst.

Does he grieve? He neither looked at me nor spoke, so when I was done I set down the Book and left him.

I am alone. God has left me: I sense His anger. My body is dull, lifeless, single. I seem to stand apart from my sisters, I see their smiles, I hear their voices, but I cannot come near them. And the sign I saw today, in the destruction of a nest of young birds – let me not speak of it, for I will weep.

I cannot tell what I must do, how to appease His anger. I am unworthy and the child is lost – but what may I do to win again His favour? I cook, I clean, I scrub, my heart dries up at the terrible repetition of tasks and days, and all about me I see figures of an approaching end so far from that I had imagined . . . How can I break out of this prison of my unworthiness? What can I offer, do, make, to prove my love? I am trapped in a small life. Dear God, I have more to give, I pray you look on me again with love, for unused I waste, I wither like a dried twig.

Oh Lord. And in the rebellion, and the distress, and the hoping, I am also wrong. For I must accept. His will be done. I am nothing but a fragment, a grain of sand in the mortar of His great construction, and have no more right to urge and press my will than the grain of sand has to announce, 'I shall not be part of this wall, in this shape, but of a different wall, where I may sit atop the highest pinnacle.' Foolish grain of sand, to think that thy position matters one jot to anyone except thy Maker, who has planned and who will bury you deep between the dungeon layers where yet you may have the joy of knowing that you offer your grain's worth of support to the great construction, that you play your part in His plan.

Help me, purge me, cleanse me of rebellion. I am afraid, Lord. I am lost. Help me into Your way again.

The greatest sin is doubt. Dear Lord, forgive me. There are many paths to the Kingdom, and in my Father's house are many mansions. I will have faith, and my faith shall be my strength and support, and shall light me through my present dark time of the soul, into whatever new pastures He shall chose for me. I thank Thee oh Lord for weeding out my pride, for humbling me. And I am grateful for Thy kindly love, and the care Thou takest to reveal it. For when I let Thy Good Book fall open upon chance tonight, Thy message of comfort blazed up from the page before me: *Can a woman forget her sucking child, that she should not have compassion on the son of her womb? Yea, they may forget, yet I will not forget thee.*

*

Dinah is gone, praise the Lord. I thank Him that her sufferings are ended. She has been ready this long time to fly to Him, and if ever a human soul was clearly destined for heaven, then she was. I imagine her joy in freedom from her poor tormented body. How true are the teachings of our church, that death is no cause for grief but rather a reason for solemn celebration, ushering as it does the soul of the departed into new and vibrant life in His presence.

But little Thomas. When I think of his sweet face, his little hands stretching out to tug at my hair or make a plaything of my cap . . . Help me to be glad, dear God. Help me to a right vision. I must not think of his soft warm skin nor his contented little chuckles.

We are to celebrate Sister Dinah's funeral on a grand scale, both because of her position as one of the Prophet's women, and because this may be our last opportunity to attract a mass of converts. The Prophet told me this himself. It is the first occasion since the loss of our hopes, on which he has drawn me into his confidence. He has been warned of God that a great affliction will be visited on our church, an affliction which will cause the falling away of many, and division between God's chosen people. He believes that the end itself will come soon after this affliction, and he wishes us to present a united, joyful face to the Lord while we may, to show our inner readiness.

Sister Dinah's procession and festival will be held on Thursday. The hearse, gaily decked with white cloths and flowers, and drawn by six white horses with uncut manes and tails, will process from here to the service at Sanctuary, and thence to the graveyard. On the populous part of the route, from Sanctuary to St Michael's, the hearse will be preceded by the Prophet and the Elders (in ceremonial robes), we six women in our white, the children of the church newly arrayed in white and gold, the musicians, playing our most popular and rousing hymns, and the choir in full voice. When the remains have been committed to earth, we shall return in procession to Southgate, singing hymns of thanksgiving, and with our banners and pennants fluttering in the breeze. Here will be spread a feast to feed the entire church membership. We shall use the housebody as the main dining area and, by use of trestle tables and benches, plan to feed fifty at a sitting. The dining room will also be in use: I had thought, as a more secluded space for the Prophet and Elders, but he pooh-poohed this foolish suggestion, reminding me that all are equal in the sight of the Lord, and that there should be no high or low tables, no special division of places or foodstuffs. He recommended me to purchase a sufficient number of plates, tankards, knives etcetera for the assembled company, saying we should have need of them in future times, when many may take shelter from the Storm of Judgement, beneath our roof. But I hit upon the happy solution of requesting a donation of a place setting from each church member attending the feast: for does not even the meanest household possess at least a spare bowl and spoon to feed a guest? What sense can there be in the church paying for such quantities of goods, when, after the apocalypse, these items (if left in individual, sinful homes) will be consumed with fire along with their owners?

The preparation of foodstuffs for such numbers has provided a challenge, but we women of the household have not been left alone to answer this. Every able-bodied woman of the church is to provide one dish. Aaron Woollacott has promised us the supplies from his deceased sister's offices, among which is a goodly quantity of potted meat and trout. And we have two boxes of fine American apples from William Lees; all the children shall have one. We do miss Sister Leah's skills in the kitchen, though. I thank Thee, Lord. I thank thee for the housewifely talents of my sisters. I thank Thee for the opportunity to celebrate Thy glory in this coming feast day. And most of all I thank Thee for the strength to endure, that Thou hast given me. I am content to wait at Thy table. I am patient and content, though I know the end will come. I do not cry with a shrill voice for a more vital part to play. Thy will be done, Lord; blessed are they who only stand and wait. You will find me, Lord, standing and waiting, waiting and standing. My Lord, I endure.

# Leah

I am less anxious over Thomas now, he seems to rally, though his cough is not yet gone. Dinah, however, is sick in earnest. I was shocked when I took her a drink last night, to see her sudden deterioration; the hollowness of her cheeks, and the dullness of her eyes. There is a smell to her sickroom which turns my stomach. Poor little Rachel sits with her most of the time, I do not know how she can stand it.

And Madam Hannah, who has been my particular study, has spent *no* time with the Prophet these past couple of days. Of that I am certain, for I have made it my business to know where she is at every minute of the day and night. She was out all afternoon yesterday (on some business about printing spinners' handbills, for members of her reading class, she told me, upon very precise enquiry) but *he* was in his room. When he has been out, she has been at home. When she read to him on Thursday evening, she was in the room no more than twenty-five minutes, during which I contrived to pass the door twice, and heard the steady flow of her reading voice.

So the situation between them may not be as serious as I feared. Who knows, what I witnessed may even have been the first occasion of their union?

At present we are all confined to the house until Ashton Wakes are over; all the mills are out. Saint Joanna says there is dangerous drunkenness and revelry in the streets. We are obliged to pray 'for those poor sinners'. I do not care – I have no stomach for the Wakes this year. Although I have had good sport there in the past.

All my thinking and reasoning of these past few days lead me to conclude that what advantage Hannah has gained over me, she has gained only by boldness; and that it is for me to seize my opportunity. I have little or nothing to lose, for how could my current situation be worsened? Only by having her for the Prophet's wife and lady of the house, and knowing myself relegated to the status of her servant for the rest of my days. But for her shamelessness, he would undoubtedly have been more aware of my subtle hints and glances; but now the time for subtlety has gone. I know he wants me. A hundred details of his behaviour, over the past months, confirm that.

The plans for this missionary tour were at last made known to all. Saint Joanna, Rachel and Rebekah stay at home, to care for Dinah and for Thomas. Rebekah will look after Thomas as well as I could myself, and besides, his cough is almost gone, he is nearly his old cheerful chubby self again. However, I could wish for companions other than Hannah and Martha.

\*

After a tedious journey in the company of these two silent, hateful women, events at last begin to play into my hands. We are in the prosperous seaside town of Whitby. Driving in on the York turnpike I saw a number of fine stately, well-proportioned houses; but we are accommodated in cramped and crooked quarters, where fishermen and the poorer sort live. We are spread over two houses; Martha and Hannah stay in one lodgings, and Samuel Walker, the Prophet and myself in another. I am to read to him this evening; he has gone out to take a walk beforehand. Samuel is out visiting his aunt who is a stalwart of the Whitby Israelites. I have ample time to prepare myself – and let the reading take as long as it will! Even if Samuel return, there is still my bedchamber free . . .

I sit waiting on my bed. A part of me is glad I have waited so long, for I sense now that I cannot fail; and to have rushed at it earlier, and spoilt my chances, would have been cause for lasting regret. When I look in the glass the face I see is radiant.

I hear his footsteps on the stairs, his deep voice responding to some query from the woman of the house. He passes my door, I hear him enter his chamber. I give him five minutes to settle himself, then I glance again at my reflection, give my cheeks a pinch, and go knock on his door. When he calls me in I pause, then walk across to his window.

'You have a fine view of the sea, here.'

'Yes,' he replies, without moving – staring in the direction of the window, where (as I know full well) all he can see is me, for I am in the way of his view.

'Did you have a pleasant walk?'

'Yes.'

'Where did you go?' I turn to look at him now, smiling. He is watching me. He can tell, I know, my intention. He is already sitting a little forward; his hands clasp the arms of his chair. I turn so that I am in profile against the light of the window. My nipples are hard against the fabric of my dress.

'I walked on the beach.'

'The sea air is very bracing.' Must I go through the charade of reading, or will he stand up and step towards me?

'The Bible is on the table, sister. Here, put this candle by your place, the light is poor.' Our hands touch as I take the candle from him. I look at him, and he cannot meet my eye. He is mine.

I sit at the table; he gives me chapter and verse and I read. All the time I am reading I can feel his eyes. He is in near-darkness, I am lit. He is watching me. He can do nothing but watch me. The reading goes on and on, he has forgotten where it should end. It does not matter, my voice is soft and beautiful, I will read forever if he wishes, nothing can stop us now.

At last he says, 'Thank you, Sister Leah.' I close the Bible, and look at him. The look in his eyes makes me blush, which girlishness I would gladly do without. If he do not move now, I must. My whole body is blushing.

'Are you in some kind of trouble, Sister Leah? Do you require my assistance?' His eyes are making holes in me. Modestly, I look down.

'You may assist me, sir, if you wish.'

'How may I assist you?'

I glance at him. His adam's apple bobs as he swallows; his hands tighten their grip on the arms of the chair.

I wait. Time is mine, I can make it take what shape I desire. He leans forward, his lips are parted. I can already feel the warmth of his breath on my throat.

Slowly, taking my time, I rise from my chair. I feel the pull of his eyes on every limb as I move, as though we move in water, with the resistance of water all around to slow our movements. Slowly, I move to the door, draw the bolt fast. Slowly, gliding, I move across the room to him; slowly, I turn around.

'By removing my dress.' My words float out, they hang like a silver bubble in the liquid air. I hear him struggle to his feet, clumsily, like a creature in a foreign element. He can do nothing but what I say. I feel his fingers fumbling at my buttons, his hot breath on the back of my neck.

Is this how it was with Hannah? No, we are more – more hot, more heavy, our bodies ripe and swollen as summer plums about to drop from the the the tree beneath their own soft, insistent purple weight. The dress is unfastened; he drops his arms to his sides. I step forward, away from him, then turn to face him. I shrug my shoulders – a small movement – and the dress slips down. As it slips I give a little twist, so that it does not stop on my hips but slides on down into a soft rustling mass around my ankles. I am naked. Naked, blue white as a pearl, soft and full and perfect. He cannot take his eyes away. Slowly, feeling behind him for its reassuring arms, he lowers himself into his chair. Staring and staring at my pearly body.

Time: minutes, days, aeons, float in and out and past us, while his great hunger stares and stares, devouring my perfection. My body becomes liquid, sweet moon-blue milk, I am dissolving, flowing . . .

'What do you desire, Sister Leah?'

'What you desire.' How long the words take to float across the water, trailing like strands of a mermaid's hair.

'I am afraid I do not understand you. You have removed your clothes. Are you unwell?'

I –

'You do not answer, Sister Leah. Be clothed, I beg you. I cannot understand you if you will not speak.'

It freezes. Water, milk. Pins me – naked – exposed – voiceless as a fish – before him. My belly lurches. I want to vomit.

'Sister Leah.'

I break. Crouch, grab my dress, drag it up. Scrabbling and stumbling towards escape.

'Sister Leah – '

'You wanted me – ' Do not let me cry.

'Indeed. Yes, indeed, for you are called of God. To serve Him through your service to His house; in your prayers, in your singing, in your daily work. In virginal chastity, Sister Leah.'

I cannot get the door open – these ownerless fingers scrabble at the latch, oh God my eyes are blind with tears do not let him see me cry –

'Be comforted my child. Pray to God for guidance. He will ease the burning temptations of the flesh.'

'Has he eased yours? Hypocrite, fornicator – I saw you – ' That voice is screaming. Let me out of this room. God. Let me out.

'My poor child. God wants you. You have no need of the desire of earthly men.'

The bolt. Here. The bolt.

I am out. I am out I am out. I fall into my room.


Do I hate him? Hate is not enough. It will never be forgotten. I will poison his life. I will break him.

\*

We were dragged across the countryside, then, in the uncomfortable, ill sprung carriage, from Whitby to Robin Hood's Bay to Scalby to Scarborough, from Beverley to Hull to York to Harrogate: along roads so hard and dusty we were at times half smothered, and rode with scarves tied across our faces to save our throats from clogging with the dust. In places the one-track roads are so deeply rutted, and the ruts so baked in by the summer's sun, that the carriage once in them cannot easily be drawn out; and so when we meet a conveyance travelling in the opposite direction, we must all dismount – even to the removing of our boxes from the roof – to give the horses a chance of success in hauling it up on to the verge.

But I watch. Every opportunity that Hannah may have with him, I know before she knows it herself. I watch her movements; I count the minutes they spend together. I observe her scrawny, stunted shape. I imagine the sight the pair of them must make, and feel inclined to laugh. With his dwarfish height, his long straggling beard, and his disfiguring hunch, he cuts a sorry enough figure clothed; unclad, he must resemble nothing so much as a troll, a bogey to frighten children. He has little enough time for her, in which I do not blame him. He always rests in solitude after we have travelled; then comes the preaching and conversions, either in some draughty half-empty Methodist hall, or outside in a market place or on a street corner, where every idle-Jack who is passing may pause to leer at us. After we have made an exhibition of ourselves with the signings and hymns, we are generally dismissed to our lodgings, but he will stay out – sometimes for hours – disputing with new converts, or laying plans with leaders of the local meeting, if one already exist.

I miss Thomas cruelly. I pray he is recovered from that cough. We should be back for the feast of the New Moon before the end of this month; I count the days.

Wroe is certainly diseased. His perceptions and desires are perverted. At Hull Hannah and I were lodged together, sharing a room, while the rest of the party were at a house across the street. From the moment we walked in to the house the husband (a tall, handsome man with a shock of blond hair) had eyes for none but me. I gave him no encouragement, beyond coolly returning his stare: but later in the evening, when his wife was chatting with her neighbour in the yard, and Hannah gone to read to the Prophet – he slipped into my room on a very slender pretext. 'What hour shall we wake you in the morning?'

I knew as clear as he why he was there: it needed no further words. After, as I was pulling down my clothes, and him still panting on the bed, his wife's voice came to me again, still rattling on beneath the window, chatting to her neighbour about the cost of keeping pigs. The man was half mad for me, and took me in the kitchen, on the table, next morning. For Hannah was in our room, and his wife in bed with a sick headache.

Who looks at Hannah? Wherever we go, men stare for me. I could have anyone. I will make him sick with regret, I will make him choke on his own poisonous hypocrisy. He is blind to the eyes that follow me everywhere, but I will make him feel it, I will make him feel the loss of me.

*

At last, bruised, weary, sick at heart, I am back at Southgate.

Beyond the presence of my darling child, I feel no joy at returning to this prison, nor shall I remain here any longer than it takes to engineer Wroe's downfall. Dreary and sombre enough to suit my spirits, the house is muffled, turned in on itself. Dinah is dying. She will be gone before the week is out.

My poor wee Thomas is not well. But not in the same case as Dinah, I thank God. Just a little unwell, just a slight cough. It is nothing too serious.

The routine starts up: the duties; scrubbing, singing, praying. A black thread leads me through this maze. I will destroy him. I will have patience. I have wasted enough of my life on him, I can afford to wait a little longer, for evidence none can deny. Evidence of his fornication with Hannah; evidence which I may take to the Elders, and so discredit him before them all.

I can wait, and watch them. I can destroy him.

I seem to be very tired. I cannot tell how it is. There seems to be almost no daylight. The winter evenings are drawing in. But they draw up so tight I could swear I have not seen the white light of day this week. Thomas is not sleeping well. It is just this tiresome little cough. Nothing to worry about, only that it wakes him. He wakes and then he is restless. I take him into my bed but straightaway he is too hot. So I hold him over my shoulder and pace up and down my room. I pace this maze. Lead a thread through. I will weave a plot to destroy that Prophet. I will weave a trap which will catch and hold him fast: pilloried, to their contempt. I give the child a sip of sugar water but he coughs, and cannot swallow. It is a weary thing, this cough, I wish it soon gone.

In the morning (is it morning? there seems to be no daylight. The clouds so low, the continual rain, there is no distinction left between day and night) Saint Joanna at my door. I have missed prayers, will I not come down to breakfast. But Thomas is so sad and tired, his night has been so wakeful. No, I thank her, I will stay with him a little, soon he will drop into a peaceful sleep. The worst of his fever is past, you may see, only look into his face.

Later she comes back (is it afternoon? It is already dark, to be sure – but was it light?), she brings me bread and cheese and tea on a tray, and a small basin of gruel for Thomas.

'Can he try a spoonful?' she asks me. There are tears running down her cheeks, this is a puzzle. I think he will not take the gruel just now. Perhaps when he has slept a little. Tears are coursing down her cheeks. I struggle to remember.

'Dinah?'

'Yes, Dinah is – is also – she suffers. I pray He may take her in the night. Oh my poor child!' She tries to stroke Thomas's head but he is hot, she will bother him with her clamour. All he needs is a little peace and quiet, a little rest. I ask her to leave, but she falls to her knees and begins to pray. How can he sleep with that noise going on? I beg her to be quiet; she lowers her voice to a whisper, while I wipe his poor hot little face with a damp cloth, and soothe him against my breast. He is cooler now, and calmer. He is nearly asleep. I motion her to be quiet, and she creeps from the room. Look, he is sleeping now.

Joanna and Hannah. The two in front of my bed. Joanna is still crying, crying again. Is it still dark? Is it always dark?

'We must make him ready, Sister Leah.' Hannah is speaking. I do not like Hannah.

'Come, he is at rest now. You can do no more for him. He is with God.'

I wonder at its being so dark.

When I slept I had nightmares. Saint Joanna sat with me, but she was praying. I was glad when she went and it was quiet. Quiet and dark. They leave food and drink beside the bed. Later they take it away, and then they bring more. Everything here is still. I am still. The shadows are still. There is a dark still shadow in his cot.

But when I look, his cot is empty.

# Hannah

Since our last conversation about my reading class, Mr Wroe has shown the keenest interest in my students, wanting to know about them by name and in detail: wanting me to relay exactly what happened in each class. He is busier than ever, engaged in endless meetings in Sanctuary: in the training of missionaries for Scotland, Spain, Eastern Europe and North America; in discussions with Jewish leaders in Manchester; in receiving God's word, of course, which keeps Samuel Walker busily writing for the greater part of every morning; in raising money toward the construction of a sanctuary for the Bradford Israelites (for at present they have no building large enough to take their numbers, and when he holds a service for them they must gather in the old cock-pit); and in the daily stream of converts and penitents, lapsed or stricken Israelites who come to him for advice, comfort, prophecy, protection. This activity alone leads him into further loss of time arguing with the elders. He has told me, half-jokingly, that he can do no right at present. 'Elders Moses and Caleb fear my laxity, Sister Hannah. They urge the expulsion of all backsliders from our church. Did you know that only 144,000 may sit with Christ during his blessed reign? All who have shown the slightest deviation from right principle must be cast out: we tarnish our own purity by clutching sinners to our bosoms. Should I cast you out, Sister Hannah? If Elder Moses knew of your beliefs, I am sure he would despatch you straight to hell.' He pokes vigorously at the fire with his iron rod, but his voice is weary. 'He would despatch us all to hell, if he could, and reign alone himself with God.'

This morning as I was walking along the gallery with my arms full of clean linen the hubbub below caused me to pause and look down. The housebody was crammed with people – all the elders of the church on seats alongside the fireplace, and the rest of the place filled with more than thirty people standing patiently or leaning against the walls. As I watched Wroe came in at the door beside the stairs. The room fell silent, immediately: he stood just inside the doorway for a moment, taking them in, then invited the elders to enter his study, where he would join them in twenty minutes. With those remaining in the room, he at first said a short prayer, then divided them into three groups, telling each a time later that day when they might return and find him at leisure. He concluded by offering his remaining ten minutes to any whose business was urgent. As the room emptied two young men drifted forward to speak with him. After some earnest conservation they thanked him and departed, and he turned into his study to join the elders. What held me there, at the side of the gallery, was his authority. He remains absolutely calm, his deep voice always even: and people trust him. What is that influence he carries about, to make people listen, to calm them, to suggest the possibility of peace and safety and comfort – no, all those are wrong – to suggest that he knows best? Why, at the sound of his voice, or the raising of his iron rod, do they fall silent?

I watch him now. I watch without that first astonished rush of enthusiasm, without that uncritical desire to also fall under his sway: but when I see him with other people I know it is not possible to deny his authority. I do not know whence it derives – whether from God, or from some inner source; and certainly it does not matter, to any great degree. What matters is that he has it, and it is not, as he has claimed (as I have claimed) a performance. If anything, he is more genuinely himself when speaking to and directing a crowd of people, than when he speaks to one person alone. For it is then he seems to waver, and become contradictory. The mockery, the continual slicing away at each blade of grass we stand on, only happens when he is one to one.

Is that true? Not entirely. I have heard him before a full congregation in Sanctuary mock and denigrate their view of the church, themselves, and himself – their Prophet – but so skilfully, with such conviction and authority that they followed every step of the way, trusting and confident that he would bring them out at solid ground again.

I have moved off my line of argument, which was simply to show that he is busy with a thousand cares – not to mention those presented by Dinah and Thomas's deaths – and yet he has the memory and attention of a keen young scholar, for he does not forget so much as the name of one of my pupils. He retains details of each of my anecdotes more clearly than I do myself, so that he has on a couple of occasions caught me out embellishing the facts.

Last night Leah was the subject of our conversation. I felt no surprise when he told me that Thomas was Leah's own son; I think we have all known that, without its ever being spoken. I was glad to be able to report that she is entirely recovered from her grief at the child's death. Sister Joanna was quite frightened by her first reaction, for she seemed to sink into a stupor and would not shift from beside his cot, nor could she be persuaded to eat or drink. Joanna herself was so clearly distressed by Thomas's death – besides bearing, as she always does, the brunt of the practical arrangements for the funeral feast – that I offered to take charge of Leah. I found her rather like a person in a trance, for though she would do nothing of her own accord, she put up no strong resistance when I took her by both hands and led her from the bedchamber, to the warmth of the drawing-room fireside. And when I repeatedly placed a cup in her hands, she did at last sip the contents. I attempted to encourage her back to some interest in life by prattling on about small matters; a mouse was found swimming in the milk-churn that morning; Elder Caleb's horse bolted with his gig last night, and a wheel is smashed. I obtained from Catherine a tonic which is very popular with their customers, and fed Leah on spoonfuls which she took quite obediently. William advised against the use of leeches, in a case like hers.

She never made any reply to what I said, but when I went out to my meeting on Thursday night, Rebekah sat with her, and when I came home I found that they had spoken together. Next day (two days after the funeral) she asked if she could move back into Rachel and Rebekah's room, and now she has taken up her normal household duties again.

I am amazed to see such a recovery within a week, for, like Joanna, I honestly thought her nearly deranged by grief. Now it seems she has quite forgotten the child, it is as if he never existed.

She seems to avoid me; indeed, she has not spoken to me directly since before his death. I can only ascribe this to her sensing that I tended her when she was at her lowest. She is maybe uncomfortable at the thought of obligation towards me. I have taken my cue and kept my distance: I certainly do not wish for any thanks from her, I am only glad to see she has recovered so fully, from a distress which might have haunted a more sensitive person for months. I admitted my astonishment to Mr Wroe, adding that I must be a poor judge of human emotions.

'Do you not think God has had a hand in this recovery?' he enquired. 'Why should you ascribe it solely to Sister Leah's own powers?'

'God does not always comfort the bereaved so efficiently,' I answered, half intending to tease him; but he replied very seriously, that both Sister Joanna and he himself have besieged God with prayers for Sister Leah's comfort.

I felt a little uneasy then, for the lightness with which I had spoken. But he suddenly smiled at me, and added, 'Or it may be that she has had a very kind companion to help her through the early days of her grief.'

The surprise of this compliment brought a blush to my cheeks. He delights in embarrassing me, for he laughed at my blushing, which made it even worse – though it was, I must admit, kindly laughter.

\*

Today: this morning. There is a light frost on the grass, a haze of blue across it. The leaves are turning, falling in yellow and red drifts beneath the apple trees. In the shelter of the wall the roses have grown very tall, their leaves are dark glossy green, they are still flowering. I can see two huge rounded blooms, ready to drop their petals at the first breath of wind; heavy, pink, bloated with their own intense smell.

Joanna comes into the kitchen where I am chopping fruit for mincemeat, amidst the sweet scents of cloves, cinnamon and lemons.

'Was that you?'
'Was what me?'
'Humming.'

I cannot remember, but she begins to sing the hymn we practised earlier, which has danced in my head all morning.

> *The house of Israel are as bones,*
> *Which have no virtue; – or as stone,*
> *They scatter'd are upon the earth,*
> *As chaff by wind is driven forth.*

She nods at me, and I join in:

> *But now the Lord His word doth give*
> *And asks if these dry bones can live;*
> *And makes His chosen servant cry,*
> *And on these bones to prophesy.*
>
> *Prophesy! Son of man, go forth!*
> *From the four winds come Holy breath!*
> *Breathe on these bones that they may live –*

I break off and laugh, because she has heard me miss my note. 'You see why I would not sing alone for Sanctuary!' Martha and I were the only two who did not.

She shakes her head, smiling. 'You are happy.' There is a note of sadness in Joanna's voice which makes her words almost an accusation. I am not sure if she is right. Happiness is not a thing I imagine being part of. When I was a child my father and I always stood outside happiness, watching the rest of the world indulging in it. Feeling, I suppose, superior; certainly, sorry for them, because we knew how blind and short-sighted they were to give themselves up to such a thing. Edward looks forward, too. There will be happiness, happiness is to come. Compared to that future happiness, the present is no more than a pale shadow.

Happiness now: I think it is a puzzle. I think it may be like the gigantic puzzle I once saw at an exhibition in Wedgwood's showroom. There were a tremendous number of pieces, 5,000 or so, depicting the flagship of the fleet, with blue seas and skies behind her, and Nelson and his men on the deck. Who can gather 5,000 pieces together? Or assemble them correctly? If the great puzzle were broken up and scattered among us all . . .

Last night Mr Wroe and I were talking a long time after I finished the reading. He told me portions of his history, of which I knew nothing before; the terrible illness which preceded his first visions, and of his search for the right church to join. Then he told me about his missionary work in Gibraltar, Spain and France, whither he and Henry Lees travelled alone, speaking no word of any language save English. I was reduced to laughter at the spectacle the two of them must have presented, to the monks, archbishops, and rabbis they sought out, with their message that all faiths must unite because the world was about to end.

'It pleases you to laugh,' he said, 'but that work was commanded by God.'

'But what were its effects? *Were* there many converts?'

'We planted a seed; an idea. Where it fell on fertile soil, it will have grown. The time is coming when I shall do missionary work again, Sister Hannah. God has called me to Australia.'

'What will happen to this household then?' I asked.

'Why on earth should you want to know that?' he mocked me. 'You will be long since departed, running your own schools for the enlightenment of the poor – or leading the working people of Ashton on marches to London, to petition for their rights. You will have no interest in us!'

This morning after breakfast, when I should have been at my housework, I went out; when I saw the frost on the grass, the clear sun pouring down to thaw it and bring it out into steaming mist, which hung over the canal like a soft white net – energy surged inside me, sending me running headlong across the untrodden silvery field. If I had stood still and silent, containing it, I think I would have exploded into a thousand pieces.

Is it happiness? Is it only me? Martha goes about in the same slow dumb dream; Leah works with frenzied efficiency, keeps to herself, or speaks only to Rebekah; Rachel seems lost since Dinah's death, is paler and frailer than before, spends all the time she can in prayer. Joanna, like Rachel, retreats into prayer, and the rest of us become irrelevant. There is a dissonance in her; grief? uncertainty? I cannot help but think of it as loss. It seems to me she buries herself deeper and deeper in that inner religious world, and cares less for any connections it may make with the world outside. During our first months here she regularly visited any members of Sanctuary who were ill, with newborn children, or elderly. Frequently there were strangers in the kitchen, filling up on bread and cheese or whatever else she had found for them. I have seen her stop in the street to follow a woman who looked distressed, in order to offer her solace in the two forms of food and spiritual guidance. At Sanctuary on a Sabbath there might be a whole row of Joanna's waifs and strays, kneeling and standing at raggedly the wrong times, joining uncertainly in at the responses, and staring at the candles and splendour with wide dazed eyes. She moved around the world with enough love to extend to all who came near her. Yet now she is narrowed, shrunken, her warmth is lost. She seems to pass people without seeing them. Beggars are never turned from the door, but they are certainly not brought there by Joanna. The kindness and concern she showed to me – But perhaps that is all I am missing. Perhaps her kindness and concern comes only in response to a need for it: where she sees suffering and grief, there she offers comfort. Has she drawn away from me simply because I am less unhappy?

Albert tells me of great plans among the cotton spinners. When they turned out last year, hunger forced them back to work, at the end, without the satisfaction of any of their demands by the masters. But since then they have joined together with other groups of spinners up and down the country, to form the Grand General Union of the Operative Spinners of Great Britain and Ireland. Now when any area turns out they may rely upon support among their fellow spinners up and down the country. Encouraged by this success, their leader is suggesting the establishment of a general union of *all* working people.

If there were such a combination, to which every working man and woman belonged, demanding universal suffrage, the rights to decent wages and education, able to back up their demands by withholding labour (what could the magistrates do, if three-quarters of the population turned out? The soldiers would never raise their weapons against them: it is the very circumstances which make another Peterloo impossible, for no one would dare to attack so vast a party) – then how might the world be changed! By those who are in it, and prepared to stand out against its crying injustices; unlike Edward and his fellow idealists, who imagine that they must hide to discover a perfect system, which they can then pass on to the poor ignorant people.

216

There is to be a great meeting in Manchester, at the new Mechanics' Hall, which will be addressed by John Doherty, and the leaders of the hatters, and the bleachers and dyers; where this idea of a General Union shall be more fully aired. At the night school on Tuesday, Catherine asked if I would go with her. William cannot leave his business, but she and I might get a ride with some of our students. I had not thought of going myself, feeling a slight awkwardness at the prospect of so large a gathering of working people. But Catherine poured scorn upon my fears. 'We have as much right as any to be there; this must be the end and aim of all educational work – for the people to combine and take back what is rightfully theirs. I would not miss it for the world. Besides, why do you set a division between yourself and them – do you not work for your daily bread?'

I admitted that I do, and she pursued her line of questioning until she discovered that Mr Wroe pays us no wages.

'You must leave! Immediately! If only there were more night classes you could teach . . . you could perhaps work in William's shop for part of the week – which I shall no longer be able to do, nearer to my confinement – and come to live over the shop. You could share the back chamber with William's mother – there would be almost no additional expense – '

I found myself confused into silence by her rapidity. As regards the union meeting, well, yes, I do work – but I am not, any more than she is, a member of the labouring classes. Nor have I ever suffered the privations, both physical and mental, which they must endure. (In last week's class Annie spoke of universal suffrage and old Adam Baker called out to know what it was. Before Annie or I could answer, he added under his breath, 'Ay, th'art an owd fool, 'tis broad as day. As we are all working folk, so mun we all suffer, 'tis universal among us.' A number of them then agreed in all seriousness, that universal suffrage shall be equal suffering for all.)

Of course I should attend the meeting with Catherine; she has a task to fulfil there which would validate our presence even if one could give any credence to my silly scruples: for she is to write a report on the meeting for next month's issue of the *Cooperator*.

As to the business of Mr Wroe, and wages, and moving to her home – I thanked her sincerely, but this is something that may be put off till another day. To begin with, she must discuss it all with

217

William and his mother – as must I with Mr Wroe. Not that there would be a great deal to discuss, if I really were leaving . . . Clearly she is right; it would be a sad foolishness for me to stay, and not have those freedoms I should have, to attend meetings and come and go as I please. Certainly, the value of my labour about the house must be greater than the food I eat – and why should I donate my services to the glory of a god I have no faith in? When I think about it, to be sure, it would be a strange choice to stay – if I had any alternative way of living.

Mr Wroe gave permission easily for me to attend the Manchester meeting. Recently he has presented no obstacles whatsoever to my requests for leave of absence. He asked who I should travel to Manchester with, and when I said with Catherine and members of my class, he expressed the hope that we would not walk; at which point we were interrupted by Elders Caleb and Tobias, come on urgent business, and so there was no further time to discuss it.

It was a fine dry day. Albert met me at the canal bridge, to take me to the inn yard where we were to begin our journey – on the back of a brewer's dray, belonging to a friend of Peter's. Peter and Annie and a couple of others were already settled in with bundles and some straw to soften the jolting, but there was no sign of Catherine. It was a quarter-hour after our agreed departure time, when a lad arrived with a message for me, from Catherine, requesting me to make notes for the *Cooperator* article, and giving tiredness and heaviness as reasons for her absence. I was thoroughly irritated with her; though the events of the day were sufficiently distracting for me to forget to tell her so. Peter fussed around me with cushions, offering to build me a more comfortable seat, and making me feel quite ill at ease. But then he and Annie and the brewer settled into an argument over the proper length of a working day, and I was left in peace to describe the scene to Albert. Albert is perfectly simple and natural, I can feel at home with him, he does not mind my accent or my strange dress. As we neared Manchester we saw a good many who *were* walking, including a deputation of the Ashton spinners, who had set out at six that morning.

I felt a momentary panic as we forced our way into the crowded hall, for Peter and Annie met up with some old friends, and stopped to speak with them, and Albert and I were forced on by pressure of the mass coming in behind us. There were many delegations carrying the banners of their trades; the Rochdale Female Operatives, the Denton Hatters, Bleachers and Dyers Federation, and so on – and all waved their banners and cried out to make a rallying point for any like them. Albert and I were pushed into a space where there was no further room to move forward, and I was very relieved when I looked back and saw Peter forcing his way through towards us. Mr Doherty took the stage and the whole crowd errupted in cheers and stamping for so long that I was nearly deafened. When at last he could make himself heard he described how the National Association for the Protection of Labour, or NAPL, as he proposes to call it, will help the working people. Local unions of all trade clubs will be members, and pay in contributions; these shall be used to support any workers who turn out over cuts in wages. This was greeted by a tremendous roar from the crowd. Their excitement, and roughness, frightened me a little, but I soon perceived there was no dangerous intent anywhere in that packed hall. The sense of power and promise conjured up by the idea of combination lifted them to the absolute heights of dizzy excitement, and the speakers' words were repeatedly drowned out by the crowd's enthusiastic roars. It was as if all that was proposed had already come true; on all sides, smiling faces, shaking hands, brotherhood and sisterhood.

Just as I began to feel less alarmed, and to enjoy the spectacle of that tremendous swell of hope in the crowd, the group in front of us were pushed back and a large heavy man staggered against me, stepping on my foot. I cried out with the pain and would have fallen, but Peter steadied me, and half dragged me through the crowd towards the nearest exit. I began to feel better as soon as the first breath of air from the open doorway reached me, and remonstrated against being taken any further. But Peter made me sit on the top step, 'to get some fresh air in you'. As soon as he had assured himself that I was comfortable, he darted back into the hall again. I eased my shoe off and examined my foot. It was very painful, and already beginning to swell. If Peter had rejoined the others, I should have the greatest difficulty in finding him in the midst of that crowd – and the idea of putting weight upon my foot was not appealing. I reckoned I had enough material for my report: in truth, little that was new was being said, only different ways of expressing that euphoria and hope for change which the sense of strength-in-numbers was giving to the whole crowd. There was no doubt that a General Union *would* be formed, nor that those present were completely in favour.

As I sat in the cool air considering these points, a gig drawing up on the road opposite caught my attention. It caught my attention because it was familiar – the driver even more than Elder Tobias' gig. For the driver was Mr Wroe. He had not seen me, but the gig was stopped by the side of the road there, as if he were waiting for someone. I could not imagine who that might be – unless myself. If he were here to meet me, it would be extraordinary, though; for he had said nothing about it, nor could he have had any reasonable expectation of finding me, amongst so great a crowd. He remained sitting on the box, so I hobbled down the steps and crossed to him.

'Ah, there you are. What have you done to your foot?' He was not at all surprised to see me.

'What are you doing here?'

'I can give you a ride home. I had to come on urgent business to see Mr Zion Ward, who is preaching in Manchester tonight.'

'Have you seen him?'

'Yes. I am done and ready to return to Ashton.'

I found it hard to believe him, for he was still in Ashton when we left. We would surely have noticed if he had overtaken us on the road?

'Where is Samuel?'

'Are you going to stand there asking questions all afternoon, or climb up and take a seat?'

'But Peter and Annie will be worried, they will be looking for me – ' I could think of no way round this difficulty for a couple of minutes. How on earth could I find them, to tell them, in such a crowd?

'Come up and sit while you think,' he urged me; and it is lucky I did, for from the height of the gig I could see the brewer's dray, standing among a group of other conveyances, on a patch of waste ground at the side of the hall. It was an easy matter to leave a message with the lad who was minding the horses.

The meeting had not yet broken up, and we set off at quite a pace. He asked me a few questions about the Grand Union, and what I expected of it – not mockingly, but in a fair and considered way. I asked after his meeting with Zion Ward, a fanatical, hell-fire preacher who spoke once at Sanctuary in the summer, and who is reputed to have announced in recent times that he is the promised Shiloh – but Mr Wroe seemed irritated by the subject. All I could get from him were some venomous remarks concerning 'Elder Moses and his party, who seek to burden the church with that maniac'.

'Will they take Zion Ward as prophet?' I asked.

'They may do as they like, but not till I am gone.'

As we approached Failsworth he expressed concern for my hurt foot, and said he would stop at the coaching house there, so I could bathe it in cold water. I said there was no need, but he ignored me. Once indoors he found a serving girl who led us upstairs to a private apartment. Mr Wroe instructed her to bring us a bowl of cold water, and some towels, and something to eat and drink. 'I have not yet broken my fast today – have you?'

'I – yes. I had some oatcakes and milk before I left the house this morning.'

He nodded. There was a feeling of awkwardness between us. We have been alone together often enough, in his study at Southgate. But there was something . . . not quite tasteful about the furnishings of the room, the pink plush settee and heavy drapes, the soft fat cushions. I sat on the edge of the settee and he brought a footstool for my hurt foot. Then the maid came with the water, and he sat down to his food, while I retired into the bedchamber to remove my stocking and soak my foot. The cold water did bring some relief, but I could not quell my sense of agitation at our situation. In what was it strange? What more natural than that Mr Wroe, on finding himself called to Manchester, should offer to bring me home? Or that, seeing I had hurt my foot, he should stop at the first inn so that I could bathe it? But the strangeness of us being in such a place together swam before me continually, and when he knocked firmly upon the bedchamber door I nearly jumped out of my skin.

'Sister Hannah? Can I come in?' I was decent; only my naked foot, protruding from beneath my long Israelite dress, dangling in the bowl of water.

'What is the matter? I mean, yes, if you wish.' I could feel myself beginning to blush, which tell-tale colouring I wish more than anything I could control. He entered the room, glanced at me, then went and stood by the window.

'Is your foot feeling better?'

'Yes – yes, thank you.'

'Will you take anything to eat?'

'I am not at all hungry, thank you.'

Another silence.

'My foot is much better. I will dry it now and we can be on our way.'

Still he did not move.

'Mr Wroe?'

'Yes, Hannah?'

He did not call me sister.

I could not think what to say next. My foot was becoming very cold, so I lifted it out of the water. He remained completely still, staring fixedly out of the window. Then I said a stupid thing, I still do not know why, except that I could not stand the continuation of that hopeless silence between us. I said, 'Why have you brought me here?'

He replied swiftly and easily, turning to me with a laugh, 'Why, to make your foot better, of course. What on earth did you imagine, Sister Hannah?' And laughing at me, he went out into the other room and down to settle with the landlord.

I could feel the blushes sweeping up and down my body in hot waves as I dried my foot and replaced my stocking and shoe. How could I say such a foolish thing? How dare he interpret it in the way he clearly had?

I felt so mortified I could not bring myself to look at him at all as he handed me up on to the gig; and I am sure he was still laughing. I found myself becoming angry, for even if what I had said were foolish – and wrong – clearly, a wrong and foolish thing to say; yet even so, is it so absurd as to be deserving of a whole hour's laughter?

*

He talks about the end now, at every meeting. His talk is whipping up what amounts to a frenzy among the faithful. In May, and in June, it was always in the future, comfortably distant. Now it may well be tomorrow noon, to hear him speak. This holds no terrors for me since it is clearly nonsense: but I do fear his certainty. When other prophets have been moved to name a particular day or time, they have, inevitably, been forced to watch their power wane as the day of judgement arrives and passes with no more attention from the heavens than a scattering of rain or a few stiff gusts of wind. If he is as close as I think to naming a day, and that day to be soon, then he is deliberately seeking to bring down the edifice of his prophecy, if not the entire church.

Last night I asked him why he speaks of it as imminent.

'Because it is.'

'You believe that?'

'Of course.'

'Do you feel yourself ready?'

'How can we ever be ready? First there is the question of souls, and prayer – we ourselves must be ready in our hearts. And then the Lost Tribes must be gathered: from both Papists and Jews, besides the rest; the Walls and Gatehouses must be complete and fortified: supplies must be laid up – can you conceive how we shall fare when the population is decimated? How we shall obtain the simplest necessities of life, food, clothing?'

'Surely God will provide?'

'He has given us brains and arms and legs so that we can provide for ourselves. Why do you think we have the ability to plan? What do you think we are doing, the Elders and I, in our daily meetings? Supply lines must be drawn up as for a war. Which indeed it is – a war between good and evil.'

'But His reign will have begun – surely the Good will already be victorious?'

He threw down the papers he was holding and looked up angrily at me. 'Why are you talking about this? You do not believe a word of it.'

It was some time after this that the most remarkable of our conversations occurred. I was walking back from Sanctuary where I had been engaged in polishing the candlesticks and other brasses; supposedly, with Leah, but she had stayed at Southgate, saying she needed to talk with Sister Joanna.

It was a cold blustery November day, and had rained earlier. Now the sky was full of low, round-bellied clouds rolling east-wards in a continuous stream. I sniffed at my fingers, which stank of the vinegar and wax I had been handling. The sudden vehemence of succeeding gusts of wind, which had at first struck shockingly cold, seemed in a short while invigorating, after the close, still, incense-ridden air of Sanctuary; and I stopped on the bridge to breathe deep. Turning to look back the way I had come, I saw Mr Wroe approaching me, also heading for Southgate. He slowed when he drew near, and we moved on together. He was having to hold his hat clamped on his head with his left hand, and looked absurd.

'Why do you not remove your hat?'

Maybe the wind blew his answer away; but I think rather that he did not reply at all. Ahead of us, I could see the beeches along the lane bending and thrashing in the wind; the last leaves stripping from them as ripe grains of oats will slide from the stems, when you tug your fingers through their grassy heads.

Suddenly he said, shouting to be heard over the wind – but it had fallen into a sudden lull, so his words were almost deafening – 'You do not believe the end of the world is near.'

It made me feel like laughing, but then I thought, where has he been? At the bedside of someone very sick, perhaps. 'I do not know. It is like one's own death: one cannot imagine it.'

He grimaced. 'How lucky you are.'

'Why?'

'I imagine it all the time. It is more real than this cold wind – than this ground beneath my feet – ' Ducking suddenly, he scraped up a handful of wet earth, scooping it in to the palm of his hand with his fingernails. Rising, he held it out to me, squeezing his fingers into a fist so that the dark mud oozed out between them. 'There is nothing else. Everything we do – every act, every speech, is pointless, in the face of that void. Our occupations are no more than distractions, toys which will be crushed and ripped away – leaving us naked, and alone.'

'But you will not be alone. Your faith – your religion – '

He looked at me; hat still clasped to head, hair and beard fluttering in the wind, eyes black and intense, and one filthy hand extended before him – he looked indeed like a visitor from God, or from some other region.

'What? My religion what?'

'Well, it must comfort you. To know you will be saved. And that you have helped – so many – ' My words were lame. I could not think why he was making me say these things – knew I was unusually late in getting a feel for whatever trap or trick he had planned for me.

'It does not help at all.'

'Why – why not?'

'Because it is a fantasy. It is no more real than the rest of the charade.'

'I do not understand you.'

'You are not listening. I said, there is nothing. Void. Nothing.'

'But afterwards. Eternity. The tribes of Israel gathered. The woman clothed with the sun – all that.'

He was shaking his head.

'What do you mean?' I said.

'No-thing.' He said the word deliberately slowly, exaggerating his enunciation by pushing his lips forward over the 'no'.

'That is ridiculous. Your whole life-work consists in going around saying there is.'

'Of course.'

I knew it was a game; when he said this I found myself laughing. 'Well then!'

'Hannah. Listen. You have your own way – do you not – of offering comfort?' I stared at him.

'To the world's distress. You have your own notions of how the lot of the working people may be improved – ' (here he left a slight, ironical pause, and added) 'by teaching them to read, for example.'

'There is no need to mock me.'

'I am not; listen, Hannah. Where is the point in labouring to achieve these things – these very difficult things – when any success you may have will be as ephemeral as that flash of sunlight on the hills just then, that the following cloud has already rolled over?'

'Are you back to this again? A *day* of misery is long enough.'

'No one is saved. No one is spared the amount of misery they can endure, in this life. And when they can endure it no more, they go out – like a candleflame.'

'Really. Then what is the purpose of your mission?'

He stopped walking. We were close to the house, I glimpsed Martha by a downstairs window, and saw her move back out of sight.

'You can provide material comforts – as one gives a crying child the tit: the vote, bread, shelter. Or you can provide spiritual comfort, mother's milk for the imagination.'

'Your religion is a mother's dug?'

He did not laugh. 'Yes. But elevated at least by the notion that it answers to the nobler and more far-reaching hungers of the imagination and soul, not the dung-heap needs of the body. It all comes to the same nothing in the end; but I would rather deal in visions of the imagination and leaps of faith, than in parsnips, or the carcases of turkeys.'

'You could not speak as you do – you could not move and convince people as you do, if you did not yourself believe – '

'There would be no point in doing it if I could not do it well.'

I turned away from his gaze, to look back towards Ashton. At that moment I think I half believed – I half hoped – to see it disintegrate before my eyes, to see his Day of Judgement really arrived.

'You are making them prepare for the day of Judgement. You have had Gatehouses built – '

'If you want people to believe a thing, it must seem certain. What is more certain than buildings?'

'You are tricking them.'

'Yes; they should count themselves fortunate. I would give a great deal, to be tricked myself.' Suddenly he took my hand. 'I am fond of you, Hannah. But . . .' There was a silence. Both our hands were sticky with sweat, despite the cold wind. I tried to keep my fingers still.

'But?'

He shrugged. 'I am finished with the Israelites in Ashton now.'

'Why?'

'I cannot – I cannot sustain it any longer. I cannot keep inventing it for them.'

'Then why . . .' I do not know what happened to my question, what I had intended to say. My thoughts were distracted by a sudden memory of Edward, and how glad I was I had not gone with him, because it would have been necessary to act as if the world were as he wished it to be: because to have seen it as it is, would have destroyed him.

'Look,' I said – not knowing, really, what at, but suddenly wanting to pour out at his feet a whole treasury of comforts: of those round stones he gave me at Whitby; of my joy at the sound of my class puzzling their way through a maze of difficult sentences; of Sanctuary music; of his own deep warm voice mocking me, and of the wave of elation that lifted all in the General Union meeting – 'look – ' And while I hesitated, reviewing their suitability as an offering, he dropped my hand and took a step back.

'That is the trouble. You cannot show me anything which will fool me, Hannah.'

A torch of pure rage flared up inside me. 'I cannot show you anything! I cannot! You yourself can see nothing! You dismiss life, because you cannot have it forever! Like a spoilt child, you throw the bauble out of the cot, because it is not given you for eternity.' I could not stop myself. Tears of anger were spouting out my eyes. 'I would not stoop to "fool" you. A woman would be mad, to set herself up as your saviour. To offer you love and companionship, while you sat in your gloomy superiority, not deigning to appreciate these treasures, because you know that at the end you must die. Your life is poisoned by your fear. I won't show you anything that will fool you – no I won't. If you cannot open your own eyes, you must remain in darkness.'

I broke away and ran for Southgate; ran until I was scarcely able to draw breath, and my lungs were on fire. Never in my life have I felt so angry as I did at that moment.

# Leah

On the night of All Souls, the spirits of all who in the coming year should die within the parish appear in bodily form at the church. My Aunt Catherine told me she watched for my Uncle Abraham, the year he was sick; though she had no need to, for it was plain in daylight that the man was dying.

I was not sure whether to go alone or take a companion. At the last I asked Rebekah, who never seems to be afraid, and we set out together at eleven, when the household was asleep.

A clear, cold night, with a moon waxing near to full, and the beginnings of a frost underfoot. I have my woollen stockings over the cotton pair, and the black greatcoat to keep me warm, but I am chilled to the marrow when we reach St Michael's. We passed a few stragglers outside the inn, but no one else to speak of. As we come into the graveyard Rebekah takes my arm, whispering that she has no fear of spirits, but is eager to avoid any mortal company which may frequent the place.

We stand clutching each other in the shadow of the wicket gate, staring at the stillness of the scene before us. The flat stone slabs are pale in the moonlight, rimed with frost. Between them shadows lie so black and deep it seems the tombs are floating on a bottomless dark sea. There is no sound. Stillness: a thousand times worse than their threatened day of Judgement, with its fire and thunder. Stillness: crosses and boxes of stone, glittering in the moonlight.

An empty cot.

The world of things stands, perfect in our absence.

I wish we might hear the muffled chink of the Resurrectionists at their digging – to know that something living stirs besides us.

Holding fast to one another, Rebekah and I creep toward the church porch. The saying goes that the spirits are visible 'at the church', and in the porch we must surely see them, going in or coming out. But the porch is blacker than a pit, both seats completely shaded – the moon standing by now almost directly overhead. So we settle ourselves on a large tombstone over to the right, out of sight of whoever might be lurking in the porch, and yet still able to keep our eyes fixed on that entrance.

The chill of the stone striking up at us makes us ache. We dare not speak, or move, for fear of disturbing whatever might come – but after a while the ache in my thighs and backside turns into a cramp which pains me so severely that I have no choice but to hobble to my feet. The sound of the night watch calling midnight comes as clearly to us, through the still air, as if he was on the next grave. I move from foot to foot on the spot, trying to ease the stabbing pains in my right thigh and clenched calf.

And as I raise my head, from looking down to what is underfoot – I see them. Not what I imagined. Not one by one, walking fast or slow, up the pathway to the church, in order of their time of death – a trickle of individuals. No – not as I imagined.

I see them suddenly, all at once, pressing in on me. Filling my entire vision, crowded five and six to a gravestone, squeezed into the dark cracks between, some towering, some dwarfed, pressing in so tight there is no room to put a pin between them – staring at me, some fearfully and some with seeming anger – the greatest crush of humanity I have ever witnessed, wedged from church-side to the end of my vision, too many to count. The front ranks are perhaps twenty paces from me, and will surely crush me with their onward movement, as stampeding cattle trample everything in their path. I turn to seize Rebekah.

'Leah? What are you – ?'

Without looking back I run, dragging her after me, stumbling over stones and into cracks of darkness on my way – on into the blackness of the church mouth. There we stand, backs against the big studded door, hearts leaping at our throats. When she has her breath, she gasps, 'What was it? What did you see?'

She saw nothing. At last we creep forward to the edge of the porch where the empty graveyard lies before us, still as ever in the moonlight.

'There is nothing there.'

'No.'

There is nothing there. Only the empty graveyard. Cold stone in the moonlight.

Absence.

And will we all die? Not ones or twos but hundreds on thousands, wave on wave, the living piling in after the dead, like grains of earth into a pit? The whole population of Ashton in this coming year? Will it be the end he prophecies?

To nothing? Leaving an empty cot?

Am only I afraid?

I never used to be afraid. In the night-time churchyard with Anne and Ruth – were we fourteen? fifteen? Come to find out who our husbands would be. Round the church thrice at midnight, scattering hempseeds.

> Hemp-seed I sow, hemp-seed I sow
> And he that must my true love be –
> Come after me and mow.

Giggling so hard breathing hurt, shivering and glancing over our shoulders at every shadow that moved, yet knowing nothing of fear.

That night the graveyard told the truth. Anne and Ruth both saw young men. And both of them are married. Me, I saw nothing, nothing behind but black emptiness. Whereat I laughed heartily and charged them with invention.

Now I laugh again. No, I am not afraid. The end is his prophecy. It has been his aim, to make me nothing.

Though this is true: though blackness comes behind to swallow me, and takes the sweetest first. Though blackness makes me nothing while the horde of them who will believe his cant go streaming up to heavenly light: yet I am. And in the here and now, before darkness swallow this last crack of light, I shall harm him. Here, in this world, I have a little power.

*

Now I move quickly, before light dies. I am quick and cunning as a rat. I will succeed. First to Saint Joanna; then to the Elders. Before Sabbath he will be stripped, exposed to the contempt of all.

Joanna is in the dining room. She is cleaning the silver. All the spoons and forks are spread across the thick unbleached swathe of linen she has put down to protect the table top. The knifebox is on the floor by her chair. She is singing to herself;

> . . . *guide us, guard us, keep us, feed us*
> *For we have no help but thee* . . .

I enter quietly and close the door.

'Oh! Sister Leah! You surprised me.'

'Sister Joanna, may I talk to you?'

She puts down her cloth and knife, and leans forward to peer at me across the table. Her eyes are not very good. I wonder how much of me she sees. 'What is it, Sister Leah? Are you in trouble?'

'Yes, Sister Joanna, I am. I have to tell you of a dreadful wrong. I – I have tried to keep it hidden, but – It is a sin in the eyes of God, it must be made known to all, and atoned for.'

Saint Joanna sits still, staring at me. I wait for her to speak. I am composed, but shortly I shall cry. She will be moved by that. She is soft-hearted.

In my room. Tears coursing down her cheeks. Is it Dinah? No. They do not understand that I still protect my child. While I live. The Prophet calls the future. Knows the unfolding story. But if I break him; God's Know-all, Mister 'Now live' and 'Now die' and 'You are nothing'; if I break him, I make my mark on time. The swallowing of my son, the swallowing of my own life, the swallowing of every dream of happiness – shall at least be registered, by the livid scar I shall make. Mister Dispenser of Futures, I have the power to blight yours. I do not grieve for Thomas. I avenge him.

'Let us pray for the Lord's help and guidance, sister.' She falls to her knees beside the table, and bows her head. Her cap is level with the table-top. When I kneel down too I cannot see her at all, only the edge of the table between us. If I bend right over and look under the table I can see her knees on the floor, it reminds me of hiding with Anne when we were children. We could sit under the table, no one would know where we were. We could just stay there. While tall people walked past, doing what has to be done. All we could see is their legs. Hidden, under the table.

'Amen.'

I hear her getting up and settling herself on to her chair again. She waits till I get up there too, then she nods to me. 'Tell me, Sister Leah.'

'The Prophet is guilty of the sin of fornication. He has made improper suggestions to me. Things not fit to be spoken of.' She does not react.

'I am ashamed to speak of it, Sister Joanna. Only I fear God's anger.'

Saint Joanna blinks. Does she *know* what is improper? Her innocence swathes her like a thick veil, she struggles to peer through it. 'What did he say?'

Say? I am not talking about what he *said*.

'What did he tell you? What reason did he give?'

I am puzzled how to answer her. What reason does she imagine may be behind fornication? Lust. What can the poor woman imagine may happen between a man and a woman? That a man gives a *reason* for what he does?

'He did not speak, Sister Joanna. Only – excuse me, the memory brings me much distress – he removed my clothes.' I take out my handkerchief and begin to cry. The memory brings me much distress.

'He removed your clothes.' She speaks in a whisper, her face is white. I am almost sorry for her now. What dark things must she learn of human behaviour, which has all been clean and good till now.

'Yes, Sister Joanna.'

'Where?'

'In his room.'

'Was it – was it on a Sabbath? During service?'

What does she imagine? 'No, sister. While we were away on the missionary tour. One evening. In Whitby.'

'And when. When he had removed your clothes. Did he – '

'Sister, I cannot bear to talk of it.'

'My poor child. My poor child. May the dear God have pity on us.' She is up from her seat and around the table; she leans over me, cradling me against her side. She is crying too, as if she knew precisely how terrible it was. After we have sobbed together a little while, I blow my nose, and say, 'There is more.'

She takes her arm from my shoulder and leans forward on the table, then lowers herself on to the chair beside me. She is trembling. 'You are sure he said nothing?' she asks, clearly confused.

'What should he have said?' I wonder.

'Nothing,' she answers quickly. 'I cannot tell. Only sometimes – an excuse might be found – '

'That he loved me? But in the eyes of God even that – '

'No, no.' Her voice is impatient. 'Tell me the rest.'

'It concerns Sister Hannah.'

'Hannah!'

'Yes. And it is for this reason I must make these terrible things known. I fear he may have – designs – upon the innocence of others among our sisters. He has – he has committed the act with Sister Hannah.'

She stares at me, her mouth a little open. I can see where the corner of her front tooth is missing, that she cracked on a plumstone in the summer. At last she says, 'The same? With Sister Hannah?'

'I know no more about it. I know it is true for I saw evidence, with my own eyes. But you must question Sister Hannah concerning the – the details, and frequency.'

'Frequency?'

'If it happened more than once. Which I suspect.'

'Oh.' She has stopped crying now. She sits limply in her chair, staring at the fan-shaped spread of silver across the linen. I cannot get her attention.

'Sister Joanna. Sister Joanna.'

'Yes.'

'I am going to tell the Elders. They will decide what is to be done.'

'Yes. Yes, you must do that. The Elders . . . they will decide.'

'Are they meeting today?'

'Today. Yes. This afternoon, in Sanctuary.'

'With the Prophet?'

She looks blankly at me. Then I see her make an effort. 'Yes. We must send a note to Elder Tobias. I will accompany you. Take heart, my poor child. The dear Lord God sees and understands all, He will lead us into His path.'

Yes.

They looked, they listened. Some with shock and distress, a couple nodding to themselves. They know it is not impossible. It has always been in some of their minds. Elder Caleb could not hide his smiles, while Moses was almost drowned in his own salivation. I have seen him at punishment.

I only glanced up at them a moment, then kept my eyes modestly downcast. Saint Joanna, sitting beside me, lent weight to my story by weeping quietly throughout. They were quickly decided upon a trial, in Sanctuary, at which each of the women is to be called to witness. We were sworn to secrecy.

'For a scandal of this nature, spreading amongst all Sanctuary members, and thence out into the world at large, can do nothing but harm to our church; makes a mockery of our faith.'

In the interests of secrecy the trial is to be held with the greatest haste, on Wednesday, the day after tomorrow. As Saint Joanna and I left Sanctuary, a bitter argument broke out between Elders Moses and Tobias, with Moses calling for open publication of the sin and the trial, and the public lancing of this boil of evil. As we left Sanctuary I could still hear his shrill voice crying, 'Lance the boil! Let all see the running pus of corruption!' Even Prophet Wroe, awaiting their pleasure within the thicker walls of Inner Sanctum, must have heard him.

*

Now, in the small dark hours of the morning, before he faces his trial, I wonder if he lies awake. I hope he sweats. I have added to the charges of improper behaviour, that he drinks too much wine. Which is almost certainly true; I have noted the number of bottles in the cellar, as to empty and full, and can testify that he alone, or with his guests, has drunk an immoderate amount. The two sins, of drunkeness and debauchery, are so insidiously linked that each lends great support to the other.

I am waiting now. There is a kind of peace. I am not afraid of tomorrow: I know how I shall look, answer, speak, cry. I know how I shall sit, at the centre of Sanctuary, with my hair braided and piled high beneath my bonnet, but for the wisps that will escape and curl lightly at either cheek; with my face pale and my eyes black (I have new belladonna, of Mother Fenton). I shall sit upright but with my white neck drooping slightly, like an injured flower. I know their sympathy cannot fail; and I shall make them envy him. They will judge him the more harshly for their own guilty warmth.

And in that moment of his judgement, when I see him thrown down from gloating contempt to lowest mud; in that moment, I shall rejoice. I, Leah Robinson, in the year before the end of the world, make of myself an obstacle to the coming dark. I am not – I will not be – nothing.

# Joanna

Dear God. Grant understanding and clarity to my poor female mind, that I may come at this aright.

Leah – Sister Leah – has told me . . . of a great sin.

Can it be true?

I dare not doubt it. Both for the bitter tears the poor child shed at the telling, and for the circumstantial evidence she brought to bear upon her tale.

The Prophet has sinned. He has taken advantage of her youth, and her beauty, for the gratification of base desires. She tells me that Sister Hannah also . . .

Dear God. How can such poor frail creatures as ourselves hope to be instrumental in the achievement of Thy grand designs?

Have pity upon Sister Leah. Have pity.

I cannot gather my tumultuous thoughts into any sort of order. The effects of these revelations upon the church . . . Our future in the Prophet's household . . . The Prophet's own future . . . circle sickeningly in my head, each question leading only to further questions.

Mr Wroe has sinned. Entrusted by God with a sacred mission – with Mother Southcott's sacred mission – he has abused that trust. The man in him, the male part (in appearance, close to that guise favoured by Satan himself at the Fall – a serpent) has betrayed all the higher, spiritual trust, repaying God's favour with the behaviour of a beast.

How great, how far reaching his sin, must be a matter for the Elders to determine. Sister Leah, in the extremity of her distress, believes his sinful intent was first revealed at the very inception of this household, in his request for seven virgins. I have reflected on this throughout the night, praying to God continually for insight into the affliction He has seen fit to visit upon His people. I cannot believe that that initial request was a sinful one: any more than I can believe the Prophet to be simply an agent of Satan. Too often, I have seen the evidence of his God-given power. And did not God himself speak to my heart also, on the day of that first request? I knew I should be chosen, I recognized God's will. No, I believe the temptation and the urge to sin have grown throughout the weeks of Mr Wroe's proximity to the beauty of Sister Leah; not that this makes his sin any the less.

I thank the Lord he has never offered a similar insult to my virtue. I thank God I have been spared such an ordeal.

The question remains, how best to protect the name of our church from the slurs the making public of such behaviour will bring? Our household cannot continue, for the virtue of every woman under the Prophet's roof will fall into question. Dear Lord, help me to divine Thy will, Thy plan, in this. Shall we be returned to our former homes? How might I best then serve Thee? The lesson we must learn is plain already; humility. Even the Prophet – chosen and favoured by God above all others – is susceptible to temptation, and to sin. All human flesh is frail. How vigilant we must each be, constantly on our guard against the wiles of the Serpent. I pray for Sister Leah; I fear for her soul. For must not her sin be judged equal to his?

Now we are gathered in Sanctuary. The trial begins. I thank God that, by staying up till the middle of last night, we were able to complete our preparations. For there were foodstuffs for two days to be made ready – both for the Elders and us women. Now I pray that He will clear my head of petty matters; that He will help us all to honesty, and that these distressing charges may be speedily cleared.

I am called to the stand. May He help me to answer and give evidence in accordance with His divine wishes. Dear Lord, Thy will be done.

# Hannah

The Ashton spinners have turned out! My reading class are full of the news; the masters have reduced wages to 3s 9d per thousand hanks, and the whole of the spinners, together with the other hands, have left their employment. The silk weavers have also turned out, and there is tremendous optimism that with the support of the NAPL the spinners can resist the reduction.

Albert tells me that fifty-two factories in Ashton, Dukinfield, Stalybridge and Mossley are already standing idle; and that the spinners are meeting and marching together to any that are still working, to force them to turn out. 'We shall not see a repeat of last year's defeat – this time we are set to win!'

He described to me the tremendous number of operatives (near on ten thousand, he reckons) who marched to Mr Howard's mill in Hyde, bearing tricolour flags and huge signs reading 'BREAD OR BLOOD': how they were assembled by the sound of a bugle, and how orderly they marched (some, he says, are armed, for there are soldiers stationed at many points nearby).

There is a great sense of excitement and danger in the streets, which were thronging with people still when we set out on our way home after class. William came to meet Catherine, and I was glad of Peter and Annie's company, besides that of Albert, for he is only a boy. Annie tells me that this latest reduction is absolutely the last straw, for the wages will not feed a family. But she fears that hunger may force them back sooner rather than later, 'for half a loaf is better than no bread'. Peter is confident that the NAPL will help them, from their funds, but they are also discussing ways of advertising their grievance and so winning support from other parts of the populace. A group of them are to meet tonight to draw up a letter to the *Manchester Guardian*, setting out their case.

I told Annie (rather shame-facedly, for it seems little enough) that I should be able to put together a basket of foodstuffs from the table and pantry at Southgate each night – which she welcomes; Albert and his younger brother are to come and fetch it.

*

Now everything changes. Now our household stands poised on the brink of self-destruction. Leah's accusations are transparent, conjured out of thin air by her own insistence that life should conform to her imaginings. But she may be believed by the elders; and it seems to me that that is what Mr Wroe wants. He has finished with this little world here, and now his prophecy will fulfil itself. He will supervise (indeed, become the cause of) the destruction of all that he has so painstakingly created.

We women must all appear before the elders; we must all submit to their prying questions. Joanna tells me that Leah has lodged other accusations, concerning myself and the prophet. How ironical.

I cannot entirely suppress a desire to fight. Why should he have it all his own way? Why should all that has been good, and hopeful, be blotted out by the dark ink of Leah's accusations? This household has nurtured . . . has helped to . . . Look at Rachel, and Rebekah! And Dinah was happy, before she died. Take Martha. Even if she is a little strange; yet in comparison to what she was! She was a brutalized slave, and now she can sit at table, speak, understand, recite her prayers, even read a little. It may be Joanna's work, but it is Wroe who made that possible. To be sure, any person inspired by common human decency might have done the same, but nevertheless, it was he who did it. At the very least the elders can be reminded of this, by way of contrast to the black picture Leah will present to them. I am sure Martha may be persuaded to tell her past. How could she desire the collapse of this household?

I am still angry. But as fire burns, so it purifies. If I admit there is a wound, then I may be allowed to cauterize it, knowing that at least it will then heal clean.

Joanna is against me. Tonight in our room I sit in the old place by the window; she will not even sit while I talk, but pretends to busy herself with tidying and undressing and shifting objects about.

'Joanna, we must talk.'

'What about, Sister Hannah?'

'You know Leah is lying. You know these things are not true.'

'Sister Hannah, she accuses the Prophet of things not fit to be spoken. I am not one of the Elders. I do not sit in judgement.'

'But her accusations are unfounded. Concerning myself, for example. There has never been anything improper in my relations with the Prophet.'

She raises her head from the heap of clothes she is arranging, and looks at me. Her eyes are dull – distant, as if my words scarcely reach her.

'Joanna – listen. It is not *true*. Surely you know better than to take the words of a giddy girl like Leah, against the Prophet, a man of God. You more than any of us, have invested so much in his mission – '

She remains still, staring, for another little while, then she slowly shakes her head. 'I cannot tell, Sister Hannah. One may fear one's own motives; one must subject every impulse to scrutiny. The devil is cunning, and he is at large among us.' She lapses into silence again.

I get up from my chair and lean on the bed beside her, trying to get her to pay closer attention to me; it is as if she is behind a wall. 'Joanna, your impulses have always been good and true. You have had courage, and faith, you have created this household as much – more, than him, because it has been built on your willing labour and love. Joanna – why let a girl's spiteful jealousy destroy it?'

She smiles wanly, but I am glad at least to see a sign of the old Joanna in her eyes. 'It is in the hands of God, Sister Hannah. We are no more than His servants. What purposes must work themselves out, I will not begin to guess. There is a wrong here somewhere, and God is displeased. I cannot answer it; the salvation of my own soul must be my study now, I will neither sit in judgement upon others, nor seek to prove their innocence.'

'But you cannot simply sit back and watch . . .'

Slowly, she nods. Then a small frown, creasing the skin of her broad clear brow. 'Sister Hannah. You cannot change this. It is done. You must learn . . . you must learn to accept His will. Come, pray with me.'

I cannot. I cannot reach her; I will not pray with her; and I shall accept nothing. For myself I could leave tomorrow (and shall, as soon as the trial is over, no matter what the outcome. William has added his voice to Catherine's offer of accommodation, and I may scrape together enough to live upon, through my teaching and through helping in their druggist's). I have a world to move on to, and would rather hurl myself off a cliff into a dark abyss, than offer it up to Mr Wroe's greedy despair. My decision to contradict Leah's accusations is based solely upon a desire to see justice done.

*

Sanctuary has become a court room. The twelve elders of the tribes sit as jury, in the choir stalls; we, the witnesses, are ranged on the front two pews, and interested members of the church packed in behind us. Mr Wroe, black hat on his head, rod in hand, sits on a lone chair to the left of the pulpit.

Tobias is leader of the jury, and after a prayer, leads the proceedings by reading out the charges.

'That John Wroe, also known as the Prophet, Yaakov, did abuse his position in the church of the Christian Israelites, by lustful and licentious living. That he frequently drank wine and strong spirits, and that he adulterously suggested, and performed, acts not fit to be mentioned, with two of the females of his household.'

Wroe stares up at the organ pipes behind our heads. He has adopted the estranged, passive face of a victim, withdrawing his great power and magnetism as a snail draws head and horns into its shell. Till we see such a man before us as may indeed have stooped to lust and licentiousness, been unable to govern the small greeds of the body, and thus lost a great spiritual mission.

We are called to give evidence in order of seniority, Joanna first.

. 'Let us take the charges in order. It is alleged that Mr Wroe indulged – over-indulged – in wine. Have you seen any evidence to support this accusation?'

'Yes. I have seen him drinking. After his Bible reading in the evening, I have seen him drink a full bottle of wine.'

'Alone?'

'In my company. But I did not drink.'

'It was not offered to you?'

'I never drink wine. The Prophet knows this, and so he did not offer.'

'Did he become drunk? Lose control of his faculties in any way?'

Pause. 'No.'

'Would you say he drank to excess?'

'He habitually drained a full bottle in the evening after his reading.'

Did he drink a full bottle each evening? I remember the first time he offered me wine – I had not noticed its presence before that night. But it is impossible that Joanna should tell a lie.

'And now to the second charge. Has the Prophet ever behaved in a licentious way towards you in person?'

Joanna crimsons at the very thought, as do a couple of the elders. It is less easy to imagine than that a dish of plain milk could set the table afire. No, he has never behaved in such a way.

'Have you ever had any reason to suspect the Prophet of impure intentions either toward yourself or any of your sisters?'

'No.' Each of his questions is followed by a calm and negative reply. Up until,

'Has the Prophet ever appeared before you in a state of undress?'

This meets with silence.

'Sister Joanna. Has the Prophet ever appeared before you in a state of undress?'

Still no reply. One by one we look up at her: her red flush has drained to a yellowish-grey. The colour of an old person's teeth.

'Sister Joanna. I must remind you you are on your oath before God to tell the truth. Pray answer the question, sister.'

'Yes.' Spoken so softly he must ask her to repeat it: then digested with a gasp of amazement that runs around Sanctuary like a flame. Tobias bends to confer in a whisper with the other elders.

'In what place did the Prophet appear in a state of undress, sister?'

Joanna is looking straight out ahead of her, her grey face is puckered with a puzzled little frown. 'My bedchamber.'

'Your bedchamber?'

'The room I share with Sister Hannah.'

So profound is the silence, that it seems it could suck in Sanctuary's thick walls and make the building collapse. A few heads turn to peer at me.

'Was Sister Hannah present at this time?'

'No.'

'You were alone?'

'Yes.'

'Please tell us what happened.'

Sister Joanna's smooth forehead is ruckled and ridged, like Albert's when he is labouring to read. She turns her head this way and that, seeking escape. 'I cannot.'

'Sister, you can and will. We are here in God's house to discover the truth of a number of serious allegations. As God loves the truth, and hates lies, it is our sacred duty to discover the truth; to aid the repentance of those who have sinned, and to cleanse this impurity from our church.'

'But this was not a sin.'

'Then you need have no fear in telling us of it, Sister Joanna. Praise be to God.'

'I – it was on account of my dream.'

'Your dream, sister.'

'Yes.'

'Tell us your dream.'

Again she twists her head, and wrings her hands in her lap. I see her look to the back of Wroe's head for assistance; she cannot see his face from where she is sitting, and he does not turn to look at her. But when she begins to speak, her voice is no longer agitated; it is as calm, and melodiously dove-like as it has ever been. 'If it is God's will,' she says. 'This great trial of my strength was sent by Him and if it is His will I should reveal it, then – ' Here she momentarily closes her eyes and lapses into silence.

'Sister Joanna,' Tobias reminds her.

Turning to face the elders, she begins to relate a dream, in which she rescued a boy child from a scene of devastation. Her role of protector to the child afforded a mysterious protection to herself. The child inspired extraordinary love and care, while all around them fell wounded and dying. She told the Prophet her dream, and he gave her the interpretation; 'That she was to mother a second Christ child, to save the world; this child should be fathered on her by the Prophet.'

One of the elders, I cannot see whom, begins to choke, and has to be patted and given water before he can get his breath. Joanna falls silent.

'Did you agree with the Prophet's interpretation?'

'I did. At first I was unsure, but I prayed and sought God's guidance. The dream was certainly a message from God, and I could find no other interpretation.'

'Why did you not seek advice from the Elders, since there was such a difficult question of morality in the case?'

'I do not know.'

'So what did you do?'

'We – at an agreed time – we did as God desired.'

'Be precise, Sister Joanna.'

'We performed the act of procreation.'

Tobias as incredulous – and as incapable of concealing it – as the rest of us. 'You and the Prophet?'

She inclines her head, once.

'Are you sure of this, Sister Joanna?'

'I am sure.'

There is a silence, then whispering between several of the elders. I glance at Leah's stunned face, and at the others. Rachel is quietly weeping; Rebekah, her face set grimly, clasps her by the arm. Joanna must be mistaken. She is innocent of what 'the act' is. Tobias and the elders think like me.

'Sister Joanna: for the sake of clarity, I am afraid we must ask a few details . . . When did this – act – take place?'

'In the summer. July.'

'At what time?'

'The Sabbath. During service.'

The strained credulity of the gathered people snaps under the burden of this detail. The elders shake their heads; a ripple of disbelief runs around the building.

'You are overwrought, Sister Joanna. You are – this cannot be possible.'

But she does not look overwrought. Her face is as still and pale as dead ash in the morning grate.

'May I question her?' It is Elder Moses. He paces up and down a few times before he starts questioning Joanna, with the air of a man sharpening a knife. 'These events took place in July, Sister Joanna?'

She nods.

'It is now almost December: and even now you only admitted them as a result of close questioning under oath.' It is not a question, and she does not reply.

'Is this true?' he bullies.

'Yes.'

'Why have you attempted to conceal these facts from the eye of the church?'

'Because – I thought it possible the Prophet's behaviour could be misinterpreted. I did not wish to bring any scandal to the church.' She hesitates then quotes softly, almost to herself, *'The Lord seeth not as man seeth; for man looketh on the outward appearance, but the Lord looketh on the heart.'*

'Is your pride so great that you think it is within your power to make or mar the name of our church?'

'I hope not. No.'

'You speak of misinterpreting the Prophet's behaviour. Have you considered the interpretations that may be made of *your* part in this adultery?'

She blanches at the word. But she continues steady. 'I acted in good faith, as my Lord and Master knows.'

'Sister Leah has told us she makes her allegations against the Prophet in the hopes of protecting her sisters in God from his debaucheries. If you had felt a similar sisterly care, you could have brought your story to the Elders four months ago.'

'But the Prophet was not debauched or sinful . . .' Her voice is faltering.

'Sister Joanna, your wilful blindness is an embarrassment, in a woman of your years.' (Tobias here attempts to interrupt him. It is hard to believe anyone is speaking to Joanna in this way.) Moses continues remorselessly. 'It is perhaps necessary to spell out to you, without the protection afforded by your self-justifications, what you have done. You, an unmarried female, whose life is supposedly devoted to the service of God, have committed fornication – secretly – with a married man, during the hallowed time of a Sabbath service. Do not imagine that all the penance in the world could clear your own name; for what can be more foul, in a woman, than impurity?'

245

Joanna begins to sob.

'That you have attempted to justify your wickedness with concealing lies, with prattle of dreams and interpretations, makes it even more unspeakable in the sight of God: for you have taken His holy name in vain, as a cloak for your own base lusts. Even at the very best your actions are motivated by sinful pride, for what makes you think that you, of all the women on earth, are most fit to bear God's son?'

Joanna shakes her head as she cries; a gout of snot drops from her nostril and she wipes it quickly on the back of her gloved hand.

'Complacent as a beast wallowing in its own filth, you have hugged your sin to your heart, nor admitted it to be a sin: and that it is indeed a sin, is most conclusively proved by the absence of that result for which you *say* you hoped. There is no child. You are barren. I call upon all members of the church to join with me in condemning Sister Joanna for a sinner of the blackest dye. Let us condemn her so that she can turn to the Lord with a truly contrite heart – for her suffering here is as nothing, to the eternal suffering He has made ready for the souls of such as she.'

Moses' call to condemnation meets with a baffled silence; he is drawing breath to continue when Elder Tobias pulls him back.

'It is enough,' I hear him begin – but the rest is lost in the hubbub that breaks out around the room. Joanna, slumped on her chair, is weeping, oblivious to all. The sight of her wrings my heart. I leave my seat to go to her side. I hear Tobias say to Moses, ' – and even if it were true, it is not she who is standing trial – '

'May I take her out?' I ask. Tobias nods; and after some persuasion I get her to her feet and lead her, stumbling like a blind old woman, to the door. My poor Joanna. My poor, sweet, innocent, hurt sister Joanna.

But this thing happened. I believe her now. He planned and executed it: she, in fear and trembling, but in utter conviction that it was the will of God, played her part. This thing happened.

Her aunt joins us as I struggle with her down the aisle.

'She must come home with me. Bring her home to my house, pray, do not take her back there.' Of course. Of course she will not come back to Southgate. I help her up into the carriage, and her aunt climbs up beside her.

246

'Joanna. Dear Sister Joanna. I will – may I come and talk with you? Tonight?' She is incapable of response, and her aunt wishes me gone. I kiss her poor wet cheek and climb down; they rattle away around the corner.

Joanna. Mr Wroe. Mr Wroe. Joanna. He did this.

Soon everyone begins to crowd out of Sanctuary. The elders are to come back to Southgate for dinner, before the trial continues. Mr Wroe is to remain in Inner Sanctum, watched over by Tobias and William Lees. Rebekah, Rachel, Leah and I are handed into his carriage. We are all silent until the horses start to move.

Then Leah: 'She is crazed. No one could believe that tale.'

Rebekah shakes her head. 'It is as if – I wonder if she dreamed the whole thing. But Moses – they should not have let Moses – '

Rachel is still crying, and sniffles through her tears, 'It was very cruel. I cannot think how they let him behave so. If he is set to question me I shall not answer at all. I never saw such hatefulness.'

'Do you think it possible?' Leah asks me directly, now.

'Yes.'

She stares at me curiously for a moment. 'Well I do not. Why should he go to such lengths of deception – for a woman like Joanna? It is a part of her own mystical invention. She has lost sight of what is real.'

'There was no harm in it, till Moses started,' adds Rebekah. 'No one believed it, we all know it is impossible. But now look how he has upset her – for a dream!'

Maybe Mr Wroe believed the dream, I tell myself. I do not think it likely.

Rachel and Rebekah's father comes to Southgate while we are dining. He asks to speak with the elders, and when he has done so he comes in to the kitchen.

'Rachel, Rebekah, you are to pack your things. You will come home with me, after the session this afternoon.' They stare at him in appalled silence; it is Leah who asks him, 'Why?'

'Why? I am surprised that you, above all people, would need to ask. Are you not the one who has brought this depravity to light? My daughters will not stay a night longer under this fiend's roof –

nor would I advise any of you to. The contamination of his sins with that woman are set like a black mark on all who have been blind enough to follow him.'

There are others, then, who believe Joanna's story. I am not alone.

Rachel and Rebekah do as they are told. Leah follows them upstairs, and when she comes down again, she also brings a bundle of clothes.

'I shall go back to my parents,' she tells me, and throws a contemptuous look at myself and Martha. 'I wish you two joy of him!'

Joanna is not in Sanctuary in the afternoon. Otherwise, we are as in the morning. But there is a different feeling in the air. A fear; the foul taste in our mouths of the spectacle of Joanna's humiliation; a fear of hearing more. I am called to the stand. Not by Moses, but by Tobias. His questions follow the pattern he used with Joanna, only I am able to answer every one in the negative. I am not angry. I am not afraid. I am – blank. What I had prepared to say in his defence is dried up in my mouth. I have nothing to say, my questioning is quickly done.

Next Martha. She also answers 'no' to every question; rather too quickly after it has been asked, like a child with the responses.

'Has he ever made any improper suggestions?'

'No.'

'Have you ever seen him in a state of undress?'

'No.'

She will be done even more quickly than I. But when he asks if she has anything to add, she replies, 'Yes.'

The history I asked her for. When I wanted him to be defended. In her flat, expressionless voice, with no more emotion on her face than any of us have ever seen there – a mask, with moving lips – she tells her early life.

Ironically, it has the effect I desired. The silence in Sanctuary, which was of fear and a species of horror, is now pitying; Mr Wroe, her saviour, is looked upon with grateful relief. When she is done a few are weeping; others fall to their knees to thank God for His goodness. It is a fine note on which to end our afternoon.

Martha and I travel back in silence. Only two of us now. No one has told me whether Mr Wroe will return to Southgate tonight. In the kitchen I prepare the customary basket of food for Albert's family, and for Annie's.

Joanna and Mr Wroe. Mr Wroe and Joanna. Still a fact, lodged like a lump of food in my gullet; it winds me, but I can neither choke it up to taste, nor swallow it down to digest it.

Nor can I go and speak to Joanna tonight. A lethargic weariness has dropped on to my limbs, I can scarcely move. What could I say to her? I am sorry, Joanna? Why did you not talk to me? Was my friendship so worthless?

I make up two platefuls of the remain of the elders' dinner, and set them out on the kitchen table, then I go to call Martha to her supper.

She is not in her room. The house is dark; I have not bothered to make a light anywhere save the kitchen and corridor. Mr Wroe is not here, the houseplace stands bare and empty as if it were midnight instead of six o'clock. In the dining room the fire is out. I make a round of the rooms, guarding my candle from the fierce draughts; she is not indoors. In the kitchen the burning peat smells like smokey bacon, suddenly memory imprints itself upon my vision, and the template of past loss fits so exactly upon the present (ironic that it should be bacon, peat – the latter unknown in my previous existence, the former unknown in my present) that I cannot move. I cannot continue this pretence of volition, control. We are no more than toys. And I am alone in this great house. This is the change a day has made.

When I open the back door I can see her light in the wash-house. And when I draw near I can see her, inside. She has a bundle of implements on the stone slab, and is binding them around and around with a length of rope. Garden tools; spade, dibber, scythe, shears. One of the washtubs is filled with an iron cooking pot, a ladle and spoon, a coil of rope, and a sack whose base bulges around its contents. After a minute she senses my presence and looks up. She does not stop her work.

'What are you doing, Martha?' I know she has heard me, but she does not reply. 'Martha, I have been thinking. You need not fear leaving this household. I will speak to Tobias; one of the elders shall find a place for you, as a maid. You will not be returned to your father, I promise you.'

She pulls the rope tight, knots it, and stops still looking at me.

'Do you understand, Martha? You can go to someone else who will be kind to you. What are you doing with these goods?'

'I am going. I will take these. To grow food and to cook.'

'Martha? But where – where are you going?'

'I do not tell you, Miss Hannah.'

'But where will you live?'

She pulls her bundles together into a closer pile.

'Martha – you cannot just – '

She lifts the bundle of tools, hoisting it over her shoulder, testing the weight. The rope holds them fast.

'Now? Martha, are you going now?'

She nods. 'I come back tomorrow for the rest. And for the chickens.'

Before I can reply she has moved past me, through the doorway, and out into the darkness.

'Martha! Martha!' Her shape is already lost in the blackness. She moves as surely as a cat.

It is cold, standing here by the wash-house. After a while, I go back into the empty house.

# Martha

My first life is dark. A stone. Rain falls, wind blows, sun heats. It endures, knowing nothing.

Hannah says, 'Tell me now, Martha. Tell the elders about it. You had to work very hard – you were so tired. Tell them what you did.'

When I look at it it tells me nothing, it has no language.

The old Martha sits in my belly like a stone. If she could be. If I could be. Delivered of her. I should travel the lighter for it.

It was before this, and its length of time was greater. Its place was my father's farm, but that was not known – the fact that it had limits in space, was not known. The place and time were not for choice, any more than a boulder on the moor can say I will move.

It is dark, speechless. This life is its opposite. All that this life is, it was not. This life is hot sweet bright smooth gold. Has water fruit skin eyes breath dreams singing voices the flight of birds. All these were absent.

I who was a stone am now tree and bird, I who was blind am sighted. I am a living woman.

If I could pull that dumb weight from my entrails and heave it on to the table before them. Let them try, one by one, to lift it. Let them see its dull black, let them feel it's harder and colder than wet slate. Delivered of it I would rise through the air like a bubble through water. Hitting heaven I would make stars.

But how can I get it out? What wise woman knows the delivery of a great black stone? They would cry, 'Witchcraft, the devil's work!' to see me brought to bed of a stone. There are no powerful herbs, no potions no prayers no conjunctions of the moon and stars, no spells which might deliver it out of me. I have never seen a devil. I know there is blackness but nothing lives in it. Not a devil if he walked and talked like a man. There'd be no harm in him, I reckon.

I was a stone. He gave me life.

There are no words in the dark. If I reach back from lightness to put words on the dark, I illumine it also. Where words light it, it is safer and more knowable than it was. If I cover it all in words like ivy growing and forcing its tendrils into the small cracks – I would gain a purchase to move on further across it. If I could force back into that stone-darkness a light from this time, language to speak the old bad life, would that be delivery?

Words forced in will not show the truth of it. Because the truth of it is wordlessness. If I describe it, then it is no longer it which I am describing. It may be like: but only as like as a broken mass of weathered ivy-covered pebbles is to a bare black stone. The truth is a black stone it cannot speak.

I knew nothing. I named nothing. To name it now, I invent.

Invent the night. Blackness, cold. The barn. The heap of sacking where I lie, unconscious. Not sleeping, because now I know sleep has dreams, and layers. Sleep has levels and glimmerings. I lie unconscious. Invent the bark that makes me awake. The dog barks when my father puts out food. I crawl out of my den, open the barn door. There is coldness, snow. I go across the yard. I have clothes. I have an old dress bound around at middle and arms with strips of sacking. When he give me to the prophet he put me a dress of hers and clogs. I never had shoes before that day, it near broke my neck. My feet had shoes of skin.

I cross the yard. My bowl of food is by the door, on the ground. If I do not come quick he lets the dogs have it. I crouch down to eat with my hands and mouth. I wonder why, now with words to wonder, I did not carry it back to barn and sit on milking stool to eat. Too much effort. Crouching here I know just – food, eat. Eat, food. Push food in mouth, swallow. What is it? I do not know.

Maybe burned potatoes, stale bread. Scraps from their table. Cold porridge. Push it in mouth, chew, swallow. I push it all in, I lick the plate. I pick up the bucket, I go back across yard to the well. My hands on icy rope. I let the well bucket drop. As it hits water for a moment I stand upright and sleep – for the length of time it takes the bucket to float filling in water. I come awake as it's full, heavying. I start to pull on the rope. It comes up swinging, slopping. I pour water into my bucket and heave it across the yard. I pour it into her barrel. I do this six times. On the last journey I cup my hands in the bucket and drink.

I return to barn. The cows are inside, it is winter. I milk the cows and take milk to dairy. They fill three pails. I pour it in churn. I pour cream off yesterday's churn into butter churn. I churn butter. I turn and turn, I am machine. On the slab I shape the butter. It is freezing, my job is easy. In summer it melts and slithers, I have to draw up new water and sluice the slab.

When the butter is done and pails scoured with sand I turn the cheeses. Up on the ledge they are dead weight, I have to take in a breath and heave on it, held. I do not think this. Turn one, two, three, four, five, six, seven. They are bigger than my head. Then I take milk and butter to the house. He takes it off me on the step and tells me my day's work. Stone-gathering. Before spring planting. As I stand still for a moment to be told, I sleep. I return to barn, hook a basket over each shoulder, set out on to lane. Darkness may be lifting. Invent dawn. I do not notice it. I know where I must go so my feet rise and fall on the frozen rutted ground. I am not thinking. I see nothing. At the field I start at the lane end, working across and back. Stoop, pick, drop; stoop, pick, drop. If the stone is small I can pick another in same hand. Stoop, pick pick, drop. If the stone is large I need two hands to raise it. The baskets fill. Every time I reach the wall end I empty them, making a pile. Repairing the wall comes later.

It is not interesting to tell. Because I see nothing, feel nothing. Invent pain. Invent an ache which lies across my shoulders and sends stabbing knives down my back. Invent sore, bleeding fingers. Invent a weariness which swims up with the ground to meet me each time I stoop, and recedes sickeningly as the fall is prevented and I remain upright. I can invent these things but I do not think I knew them. The rope handles of the baskets of stones

cut into my shoulders but I do not know it. So these are
inventions. Just words laid across the black rock like autumn
leaves, unattached, shifting with each wind.

When field is finished I go back along the path to the farm with
my baskets. I hang them in barn. Pick up shovel. Out to the turnip
field. I know it is next thing to do. Invent a reason – daylight has
brought a slight thaw, the surface of ground is now slippery with
a sheen of mud, softening. It will be easier to dig. I do not know
this. But I go now, to dig. Thrust shovel blade into ground. Stand,
heave. Beneath the surface ground is rock hard. I chip and hack
them out, tearing with fingers at the frozen soil and frozen turnip,
until I have filled my bucket. The cows feed. I do not eat turnip. I
have lied – I have some knowledge. Like knowing to go for my
morning feed before he lets the dogs have it. Although I am near
to starving I know raw turnip gives belly ache. I know also the
cold will keep him indoors today. Unless I anger him I am safe.
    Daylight is going now, maybe gone. Invent darkness again.
When I have given cows their turnip I milk them again. Take milk
to house this time. He gets it off me at door, sets down my plate. I
crouch and eat. I carry water for the cows, the horse. He feeds pig
himself. He thinks I would steal its food. He is right. He tells me
to clean its pen before I sleep. I take shovel and bucket again. He
has left a rushlight burning in the pen and pig is standing against
the wall staring at me and the light. I raise shovel, sink it into the
liquid mass which buries my feet. It feels soft. Invent a stench. It
runs off shovel. Scoop raise slop, scoop raise slop. I do it and do
it. Pig shifts round against the wall away from me. Each time the
bucket is full I carry it out to kitchen garden. I stumble in the dark
but I do not notice. I must not stop or fall because I would freeze
where I lay. Knowing what to avoid. Seeking survival. When the
pen is cleared I fetch armloads of straw from barn. Litter it down.
Kill the light. Return to barn. The ground is hard with frost again,
I do not look up or down, to see frozen mud or stars. I shut barn
door and go to my lair. I fall into it and am unconscious. One day
is over.

Each day of this life, my new life, is different. In the old life days
were the same, endlessly. Now I know sun shines, rain falls, mist
hangs in air. These things may indeed have happened, changing

from day to day, but I was not able to know it. My senses could not tell. Even to tell me discomfort – in August too hot, with husks of barley prickling and scratching through the sweaty layers of my rags, my whole skin red and itching from sun and dust and husks. In February soaked to the bones by a small cold driving drizzle which never stops for long enough for my rags to dry, rubbing stiffly against the sores in my armpits and at the backs of my knees where skin is broken and bleeding, each time I move. I do not feel these things. There is no difference. There is only movement (work) and being still (unconscious). I know *he* is dangerous, I avoid him – but unthinkingly, as I would walk round rather than into a fire. No more than that. I did not know . . . I did not know it was suffering.

Only the present gives me that knowledge.

Nor did I know (did I? No. I had no memory. I had no mastery over time.) I did not know there is past and future. I only knew the same. This new world has shown me time and dreams. Through their illumination I am able to discover specks of a life beyond – before – the drudgery.

The first is my mother's shoulder and arms. I am lying down. The space over me is darkened by a presence which bends low. A large hand scoops under my head and another against the small of my back. I am lifted into a warmth of body big solid firm dark and pressed against and encircled by it.

I try to arch my neck back and glimpse her face. But I have not yet managed to do this.

The second is the day he – my brother – died. The horse reared up – I did not look. My stepmother shouted his name and screamed 'Get your father! Get your father!' I ran – this is the vision – running running running across the endless field to where my father stands I gasp and point and he starts to run hard. I cannot keep up with him I watch him running fast further and further back to the house. No. No. I am stopping. Running after him then stopping. I do not want to run back now. Because I am afraid.

What I see (I do not see my brother. I cannot find him) is the loss and terror. Here was lost – the thing which does not come back.

In my earliest life I had some part of what is now. Touch taste
sight time. These things belong to many lives, I understand. I
may uncover more. As I have uncovered my warm mother's
arms. But my brother. I do not know what I had when I had
him. What the this was I lost. I only find standing in the field,
and pure terror before me like the ground falling away.

Perhaps I will come at him one day in the dreams. Perhaps I
will regrow it as I have regrown vision, hearing, all the others. I
know there are things belonging to the other women which are
not part of mine. I am outside something. I watch sisters Rachel
and Rebekah. Or sometimes Hannah and Joanna. When they do
not notice me sometimes, if they are talking. Suddenly they
laugh together. Or one reaches across and pats the other's
hand. I blunder at it. A thing which means each is not guarding
her own self against all. I cannot tell. If it was mine. If it will
come again. Who can tell?

What I have is riches and more to uncover. Hannah does not
know, nor anyone. I have buried stores of food on the edge of
the woods beyond the second field in three diggings. Besides
food I have candles tinder box blankets knife shovel pan bucket
and axe. Before the end I shall take more. In the woods or if I
decide so, up on the edge of the moors behind Stalybridge. I
shall make my shelter where no one knows. There are ruined
cottages, there are stones and timbers to be had by anyone who
has the strength.

I shall have my world in freedom. No set times and tasks, no
questions no rules. No start now and stop now Sister Martha. I
shall have the world to stare at, to hear, to feel against my skin.
To scent on the wind and taste in my mouth. I shall have days
of light and nights of stars to watch in. Until I strain through
that membrane which at present encases and deadens the
further reaches of my senses. I have worlds, and worlds to
discover.

# Hannah

Joanna, and Mr Wroe. All night. Mr Wroe, and Joanna.

I must have slept at last, for now when I wake it is getting light, it must be after eight o'clock. I dress myself hastily; it is bitter cold, but there is not the time to light the kitchen fire. They will be ready to start in Sanctuary at nine, and I do not know if Tobias is sending the carriage for me or if I must walk. This question is answered as I pull on my boots, for I hear the horses approaching down the lane. Leah, Rachel and Rebekah are inside.

'He has been sent round to fetch us all,' Rebekah tells me, and then asks after Martha. When I tell them she is gone and I do not know where, there is no surprise.

And so the second day of Mr Wroe's trial. Leah's accusations are clear and precise; an immodest suggestion during her reading one night, an attempt to unfasten her clothes on another occasion, and lastly a rape in his room during our stay in Whitby. They have the ring of truth, to my ears. I dare say he did these things. Why, they are nothing, after his treatment of Joanna.

Tobias conducts all the questions himself; clearly Moses will not be unleashed again. He presses her for particular detail of time and place for each event, and these are noted by the other elders. She claims also to have seen me with the Prophet, 'in a state of undress' one afternoon in October. She was looking through his study window. This allegation baffles me completely until I force my memory back, along the winding lanes of those sudden ups and downs of happiness and despair, back to the afternoon I am still embarrassed to recall, when he helped me with the needle in my dress. 'Sister Hannah, do you think I have never seen a woman's back before?'

Rebekah and Rachel are questioned next, and both answer negatively to all questions (although Rachel at one stage breaks down into a flood of nervous tears and cannot speak at all. This despite Tobias' gentle patience in questioning; Moses would not have got a word of sense out of her). Her testimony is interrupted by the sounds of a disturbance outside Sanctuary. She falls silent, and we listen to the muffled roar of thousands of voices, chanting in unison. Of course – it is the spinners. Albert told me of this, that on two days this week they would march through Ashton, to rally in the market place and hear speeches. They need to keep up their courage, for a few are already talking of starvation, and of returning to work. I strain to make out the words of their chant. 'Oor . . . up . . . ing – oor . . . up . . . ing – ' I know it. 'Four and tuppence or swing'; the lowest wage they will accept; and which the masters have refused them. The sound of their voices warms me. I wish I were outside there with them, part of their warm comradeship and struggle; instead of in this strange white dome, where an inhuman man is being dissected alive.

The sound moves around us and then on, a great wave breaking and rolling past our tiny island. Sanctuary walls are thick; it is the first time I have ever heard sound from outside penetrate them.

At last, Mr Wroe is called. He stands like a hanged man, head below the outline of his hump, staring at the ground. He does not so much as glance at Tobias, or his accuser. He denies all knowledge of Joanna's dream, and every one of Leah's charges.

His denials are delivered in a completely flat tone. It would appear he has no interest in the outcome of this trial. I am called back to answer Leah's charges, which I simply deny. It is not worth explaining the needle in my dress to them. After some uncertainty about procedure we are told to leave, for the elders to consider their verdict.

William Lees' coachman is there to take us to our respective places; I decline a ride and elect to walk back to Southgate alone. It is cold but dry, with a scent of snow in the air. I consider whether I shall remove to Catherine's tonight or tomorrow. I should take a leaf from Martha's book, and clear out the offices and stores. Our housewifely skills have made enough jams, preserves and pickles, salted beans and hillocks of potatoes, to last a fair-sized establishment through the winter. I must speak with Peter, get him to send his friend the brewer round with his dray, and load it up to distribute among the spinners. This is not stealing; after all, it is the produce of the women's labour.

And so I cross the canal and walk down the lane, beneath the bare silvery trees, to Southgate.

Mr Wroe.

Mr Wroe. Joanna.

He knows what she is; a stranger in the street knows at five minutes' acquaintance, what she is. Simple, open, bound to God. The most hardened, callous villain in the world would not try to impose upon her. Who, in her life, has ever thought it necessary to trick her or lie to her? Any more than you would seek to deceive a child.

But he has. What satisfaction did it give him?

You walk on hot coals, my dear Hannah. He has had all seven of us in view, picked over us . . . no doubt Leah's story is true. Rachel and Rebekah are pretty girls.

Why should I imagine, why cherish the delusion . . .

Self-contempt twists the thought, for where have you led me now; into *envy*? Envy for poor exploited insulted *ravished* Joanna? Or for Leah?

No. It is offensive to imagine I am jealous of it, there is no need for me to wallow in that indignity. I am sorry – for him, and for them; but heartily glad to have escaped such a cruel violence.

He has not been cruel to me. He has been kind. One does not cancel out the other. It is possible to imagine a mind which contains contraries: in which the most deep-seated desires are locked in conflict. My father, for example, who both wished to keep me, and wished me to be free. As my poor Joanna helped me to see, the effect of these contradictions rubbing together daily, nightly, was to produce a poison of paralysing power.

And Mr Wroe? Why not pursue a vicious lust, which he knew must be universally condemned (pursuing it for that reason? desiring to sully purity, without knowing that himself, drawn irresistibly to spoil the whitest flower)? It will all end in death, no matter what he does. The form of the sin is ingenious, for it mocks the very God he invents daily for his followers. Or else is a part of it; did he make himself believe this dream? Yes – surely – for much of the time, he must believe the Voice he hears, whose commands he reports to the church. If a man take one part of his mind and give that part authority over all his other thoughts and instincts (and how else could he be convincing?); makes it King to the rest, which should be equal – then he will commit the same atrocities as any despot upon his people. So he seduced Joanna. In the name of religion; knowing? or not knowing? what he was doing.

But then imagine, in conflict with this . . . need: the growth of a more human sentiment, an affection, a companionship (can I call it affection? Yes. There was an affection between us). If he is to recognize it – if he is to imagine reaching out a human hand to grasp another, equal hand; then he must fall into a true vision of his earlier behaviour. The lust for Joanna becomes obscene. How is it possible to take a course of action which reveals your earlier actions to have been wrong; defines them, even, as evil? What could he do? but stand paralysed between the two sides of his nature – until the anger at powerlessness that gripped him made him decide to smash up this little world.

You can understand God flooding the earth. What a mess, all the details awry – nothing working quite to plan. What could be better than washing it away to start again? What could be worse than having to tinker at each individual mistake in an attempt to – by a little adjustment here, a little adjustment there – get it functioning in a semi-satisfactory way? Sending messengers, like workmen to repair a leaky roof, who botched and patched – all those prophets and saints – but could not quite get it sorted out, could not get to the root of the problem . . .

Of course the Israelites need the end of the world to come. Mr Wroe does, above all. So much imperfection and contradiction, there is no putting it right. It must be demolished. And in the New World that follows, they themselves will be saved; which is to say they will become single in intent, contraries will be removed. Wroe's instincts will agree with his lusts which will agree with the desires of his rational mind and higher spirit, and be sanctioned by his conscience. All will be made simple. The crooked path shall be made straight.

In another, new, world.

Which is death. The removal of contraries is death.

As he told me. That their heaven, or world's end, will be nothing. Cannot be, anymore than a living animal can be divided into a measure of so much solid matter (bones, skin) and so much fluid (blood, juices) without actually destroying the thing it is (a living creature) and being left with components which no longer have any meaning whatsoever.

Where have I come out? On a mountain, with a view? Or into thick, obscuring mist? Have I justified his crimes? My head aches, my eyes are red and sore. I have not moved an inch. Over and over again, I fabricate explanations; tell myself stories in the hope of illumination. And come no closer to understanding. As if I painstakingly laid a line of straws across the black and windy depths of the night sky, and hoped to use them for a bridge, to cross from one star to another.

*

Expectations of a verdict brought many people to Sanctuary for the first service of the Sabbath, on Friday evening. But Tobias announced that this would be delivered tomorrow morning. Mr Wroe was not present. As the familiar hymns and prayers washed over me, and as my spirits were eased by the still-strange beauty of the music, I considered whether I shall continue to attend Israelite service, when I am no longer of the household. I rather think I shall.

I instructed Lees' coachman to set me down at Catherine's house, after the service. I had the conveyance all to myself, for both Leah and Rachel and Rebekah were accompanied by their own families. Catherine has been expecting me for the past two days (the elders would be grieved to hear how fast and wide rumour of the scandal has spread). She was at table with William and his mother (who has a withered arm); all three of them urged me to move in immediately, and so I was shown to a crooked, low-ceilinged upstairs chamber, where they have already put a pallet on the floor for me, beside the mother's bed. 'William has the promise of a bedstead off a good customer of his,' the mother told me proudly; but there is no reason why I should not fetch my bed from Southgate, who needs it there? They made me a supper with food from their own plates, though I told them I was not hungry. For a while I was almost overcome by my sense of their kindness in taking me in. But when I attempted to express this, William hushed Catherine (who will talk, like the rapids of a river, and almost as unstoppable) and told me quite simply that they are happy to have me. That for himself, he will go about his work and daily business the easier for knowing that I am near Catherine 'and able to exert your steadying influence upon her', and that by reason of my help in the house and the shop, and by taking over Catherine's educational responsibilities with the cooperators, when she is unable to fulfil that role, I shall contribute at least as much to their well-being as they will to mine. 'And that is what is most desirable; that both parties shall benefit equally.'

It was kind of him to speak so honestly, for it did make me feel easier (that is, less indebted). And I can already see, from the hasty and at times bad-tempered way in which Catherine treats her mother-in-law (a slow, inoffensive old thing), that she is in need of a companion who will stand up to her, and guide her away from some of those impetuous decisions she is prone to making. She seems to grasp ideas so quickly and lightly that I tell myself I am dull-witted; and yet, many a time, she lacks the stamina to bring them out to their logical conclusions. And so I do see a partnership, rather as if the tortoise and the hare were to combine their talents, where each of us may strengthen and help the other.

They wanted to know all the news of the trial, and this I exchanged with them, for news of the spinners' progress. The magistrates have posted notices against their marches and assemblies in the market place, calling it a threat to public peace. The word is that if they persist, the military may be called in to break them up. There is division among the strikers, between those who wish to abandon the assemblies, and those who are intent on gathering more weapons and plan to defend themselves if any attack is made. Many of their families are desperate now, for it is their second week without wages; and though the NAPL have called for a universal strike of all those spinners who receive under 4s 2d, the Scottish and Irish spinners will not leave their work – and indeed, nearer to home, there are some who continue to work for less. Without that general support promised of the NAPL, I fear greatly for the outcome.

I fell asleep that night with the sound of the spinners' marching feet and chanting voices outside Sanctuary, ringing in my head; and woke three times in a sweat of anxiety over the loss of something which, if I could have recalled it, would have been saved. But I could not tell what it was.

The morning service. Sanctuary is packed, and each of the doors guarded by a church member, to prevent the entrance of outsiders – who mill about excitedly in the road, clamouring for a view of 'the demon Prophet'. Mr Wroe is standing in his accustomed place, hat on his head, rod in his hand; exactly as he has been at every service I can remember. Joanna still absent. I must go and see her today, I pray she may have found some comfort in her aunt's company, and her old familiar surroundings. I sit alone on the virgins' pew, for Leah, Rebekah and Rachel are with their parents. The musicians strike up, we all rise for the hymn.

> Christ's second coming is at hand
> In might and pow'r twill be
> For Christ will renovate the land
> And set the captive free.
>
> Then wars on earth shall be no more
> And tears He'll wipe away
> The lame, the blind, infirm and poor
> Will bless that happy day.
>
> For paradise will be restor'd –

I cannot sing, I think my throat will crack for dryness. The priest leads us in a prayer for guidance in a time of trouble. There is a rustle amongst the congregation, as dead leaves stir and are lifted by a small wind, before the first real blast of the storm. Tobias rises to speak.

'We, the Elders of the twelve tribes of the Church of the Christian Israelites, in the city of the New Jerusalem, hitherto

known as Ashton-under-Lyne, having deliberated among ourselves under the guardianship and benevolent influence of our
Heavenly Father, hereby deliver our verdict on the charges laid
against Mr John Wroe, Prophet of our church.

'To the first charge, of immoderate drinking, not guilty.

'To the second charge, of fornication, not guilty.'

A moment's silence, in which all are held frozen. Wroe comes to
life. He steps forward and raises his arms. 'Brothers and sisters – '

'Will you listen to this man?' screams a woman's voice.

'Devil! Imposter!'

'Get him out!'

'Down – down – get him down!'

Cries burst out on all sides. Wroe stands quite still, arms half-
raised in his habitual crowd-quietening gesture, like a great bird
poised for flight above us. If he speaks, if he cares to raise his arms
to their full height, and demand their silence – he may yet calm
them. But he does not; and seeing he does not, their rage
increases. Those below begin screaming and urging those in the
gallery to grab him and hold him fast. All around me the
congregation are shouting out, calling, stamping, crying – some
begin to throw objects. Their hymnbooks, their hats. There is a
rush toward the front; Tobias and the elders are submerged in a
crowd. Above all the shouts, one piercing cry rings repeatedly,
insistently, like a machine which cannot be stopped – 'Guilty!
Guilty! Guilty!' Leah is fighting her way along the pew, eyes fixed
on him – as I look up to follow her line of vision I see him duck out
of the way of a hurled missile, and run along the back of the
gallery. 'Get him! Get Wroe!' Now the whole mob is focused on his
movement. There is a surge towards the gallery stairs, which are
swiftly blocked by the crowd. One enterprising fellow jumps on to
the top of a pew beneath the gallery balcony, and makes a leap for
the railing. Grasping one of the balcony supports, he hauls
himself up till he can poke his feet through the balcony rails – and
then he is up and over the railing, to a cheer from the crowd. They
form a chain, helping to haul one another up, and scatter across
the balcony. 'Where is he?'

'Get Wroe!'

'He is gone!' Angry cries and shouts now, their fury becomes destructive, they begin to rip hangings – tear the altar cloth down; haul open the door of Inner Sanctum and fling out the books and papers they find there.

'Where is he?'

'Where is that devil?'

I have stayed – as well as I can – on my seat: pushed once to my knees by the crush of people forcing past me, but now in quiet isolation amongst a half-dozen empty pews. There is a fight beside the alter table, men pushing and shouting, among whom I recognize a number of the elders, but not Wroe.

'He is got away!'

'Get him!' The shouts and cries are down towards the main door now; people are pushing and shoving to get out. Gradually, Sanctuary empties. Here and there people still sit, in ones or twos, like myself – waiting the return of peace.

I watch the Elders Tobias and Joseph, helped by William Lees, eject Elder Moses, who is fighting like a cornered pig.

At last it is quiet. The floor is littered with books, torn papers, scattered garments. The altar table lies bare – its cloth sprawled across the floor, the candelabra bent and twisted beside it, its lights extinguished.

Tobias, a livid red mark on one side of his face, raises his hands to us. We stand; a motley collection of some twenty people.

'Brothers and sisters. Let us ask God's forgiveness. For this desecration. Have mercy, Oh Father – have pity on us.'

One by one we leave the building. I stop to ask Tobias.

'Yes, he is safe.' He smiles wryly. 'A miraculous escape. There is a secret way out.'

'Where will he go?'

'To Huddersfield, in the first instance, I imagine. He would not be wise to return to Ashton.'

'You found him innocent.'

Tobias hesitates, looking around Sanctuary, as if appraising the cost of the damage. 'Yes.'

I returned to Catherine's; thence to Peter and Annie's, where the aid of the brewer's dray was enlisted for removing supplies from Southgate (still standing empty, when we arrived there in the early evening. I had half expected to find the place plundered).

And on to my final call of the day – Joanna. Her aunt opened the door to me herself, and seemed glad to see me. 'She is in the drawing room, my dear. She is still very much distressed. I hope you may be able to comfort her.'

Joanna was sitting alone, before a large fire. There was no other light in the room, but what the fire provided was enough to show me how puffy, blotched and ill she looked. Her eyes were no more than slits, and her lips bitten raw. She greeted me without surprise, and made no comment or reaction when I told her of the day's events.

'I am sorry you could not turn to me, Joanna. I wish I had been able to help you.'

She shook her head. 'Those evils were necessary. It is His plan. It was necessary for that man's wickedness to be revealed, for the next stage of His plan. I am glad to have been of service; happy the servant who is called.' I took her hand, and clasped it between mine. It was cold, her flesh dense and moist.

'Joanna – what is this plan?'

'You will help me, Sister Hannah, I know. All the women are called. We are to form a women's church; where none but women may preach, none but women may sing, none but women may make the laws. Our church is to be founded on the writings of Mother Southcott. As God previously loved and upheld men, so He now turns to women – *we* are His beloved, for men are raddled with sin. He has revealed this to me, Hannah, through my sufferings, which have been a trial of purification.'

I sat with her for upwards of an hour, making several attempts to guide the conversation on to other topics; but she continued regardless.

'Men have glorified His name only as a means to their own aggrandizement; men have built up churches to establish power on earth for themselves. Sister Hannah, you know this. Men, taking the government of nations upon their shoulders, have neither helped the poor nor healed the sick nor fed the hungry nor brought the little children into the ways of God. Their greed has grown as it has been fed; the world's goodness is stuffed into their ravening maw, as into the gaping mouth of hell itself, and still they are not satisfied.'

'Sister Joanna, be calm. He is cast out; the church members have cast out Mr Wroe.'

'In the first part of history were women despised, and blamed for loss of Eden. Thou cursed woman, dear God, promising that she should travail and bring forth children in pain. And we have suffered; generation upon generation of women have suffered, bringing forth children, serving men. Until at last the great balance tips in our favour; the sins of men outweigh ours by as much as a thousand times.'

'Come, Joanna, it is over now. Let us think of the future. We have our freedom now, you and I – shall we take a walk tomorrow, if the sun shines?'

'We women have no need of a prophet, in whose hands corrupting power may be concentrated. God will speak openly to the hearts of all the women in the church. Our task is to prepare the world for Judgement, Sister Hannah. All the old prophecies are true, it needed only this final reversal to bring women into the full light of His love again, before the start of His thousand-year reign of bliss!'

When I left I kissed her and she urged me earnestly to come again the next day – which I promised I would. In the hall I consulted with her aunt, who has called the doctor twice, and is ensuring that she eats regularly, 'though it seems impossible for her to sleep, poor soul'. I pray that Time may do its work, to heal up the savage wound that Mr Wroe has made.

*

Now the start of a New Year gives many signs that optimism shall be rewarded. Catherine is delivered of a healthy baby boy. I am working five days a week in their shop at present, earning my keep and making many plans. So successful have the night classes proved that we (that is, the Ashton Cooperators) are considering the establishment of a day school, for young children, to be run along Owenite lines. I have just read Mr Robert Dale Owen's book describing the schools at his father's factory in New Lanark. There is a suggestion that two from Ashton should travel up to Scotland to visit the school and learn the key to its success, and I hope that I shall be one of the two. I am convinced that this is the way forward; through education – through encouraging and fostering communial care and love. Not by the present defective and tiresome system of book learning, but by new methods of instruction founded in nature, in singing and dancing and through the gentle encouragement and satisfaction of natural curiosity. If (as in New Lanark) children may be kept out of the mills till they are ten, and sent to our school . . . We are likely to face opposition from their parents, who rely upon their wages, but by persuasion and example at the end I am sure they must come to see the benefits. There is now an Ashton Factory Reform Committee, founded by a crippled ex-operative named George Downes; he is pressing for shorter working hours for children, which would leave some daylight hours for schooling. As Mr Mudie says, truly the school is the steam engine of the moral world. For once a child learns that his happiness is dependent upon the common happiness of all; then dissension and strife must disappear.

I have broken off my connection with the Israelites, for Zion Ward is now adopted as their prophet. He claims to be the Shiloh himself, and spouts fire and brimstone upon the congregation every Sabbath. Elder Moses is his bully boy. When I spoke with Tobias he was less downcast than I expected; he tells me Zion Ward has a greater prize than Ashton on his mind, and will soon be off to London to win a great following there. Then the Ashton Israelites may settle back into a calmer state, 'and those of us who have seen the truth', he said, 'will hold the reigns of the church in quiet peace, until our Prophet Wroe returns'.

Mr Wroe . . . Yesterday I heard his voice in the shop. The low, close, sound of his voice, just on the edge of hearing. I looked up from the account book through a sudden blur of heat, expecting to see him on the other side of the counter. But Mr Wroe is departed on a mission to Australia. So I was told by Elder Tobias. I do not think much about him.

The church is shrunken from its former size and state, for many left as a result of the scandal. The former Israelite draper, on Stamford Street, told me that on the afternoon of Mr Wroe's escape no sound could be heard in that quarter of town, for the stropping of razors and snipping and shaving of beards.

Of my former sisters in God, I see Joanna most frequently. It is still a struggle to overcome that sickening sense of – regret? guilt? I do not know what to call it – which rises in me at the sight of her; at the sense of my own failings as her sister and her friend. She seems to have put all that behind her, and works tirelessly for her Church of the Women, in which I wish her every success, for I am sure she will make as good a preacher as any man. Rebekah, they say, is to marry Samuel Walker, by whom she is with child. Surprising news, for I never guessed at any friendship between them.

The spinners continue their strike and many hold great hopes of success. But fear of armed conflict grows daily; on January 1st the Fourth Foot paraded through Ashton and were taunted by 2,000 spinners. And at the end of that week Thomas Ashton, a mill-owner's son, was murdered – shot, they say, by one of the spinners. I cannot guess what the outcome will be, but they remain firm in their cause. More generally, I see every reason to feel optimistic concerning the aspirations of the working people. Mr Owen tours the country now, speaking to vast crowds of supporters in the Union movement. In May there will be a National Cooperative Congress in Manchester, to which will be invited delegates from trades unions and labour exchanges around the country, besides those from cooperative trading societies. A wealth of issues unite us; universal suffrage, the taxes on knowledge, factory reform, poor wages and unemployment. And when we *are* united, as (I believe) a people can never have been before; why then, the world will be ours. And that spirit of communial help and sharing which proves (as poor Edward wrote) so difficult among our generation, will be simplicity itself, to children educated along the right principles.

We stand, I truly believe, at the dawn of a New Age, in which human happiness shall increase a thousandfold, through its own agencies and exertions. There is a hymn which was printed in the last issue of the *Cooperator*, whose words summarize those sentiments of hope which I am coming to share:

> *Mankind shall turn from competition's strife*
> *To share the blessings of communial life.*
> *Justice shall triumph – leagued oppression fail –*
> *And Universal Happiness prevail!*

# Joanna

The foundation of a new church is paramount. Night and day I am beset by intimations of the end – it is close now. As my Lord has seen fit to punish me with physical and public humiliations, so through erosion of my happiness and self-interest I have come to a state where the grosser delusions fall from my eyes, and the inner truth becomes clear to my vision. I do not sleep, for at night the silence and darkness bring me closer in knowledge to His awful power, to the dread void that existed before His miraculous touch, and to the aching emptiness that must succeed, for those who cannot be saved. For what are these stories of hell fire, eternal punishment and the ingenious tortures of lesser devils, in comparison with the absence – the loss of hope – which must be attendant on knowing your exclusion from His presence is eternal?

The lid of my consciousness has become thinner, thanks to my trials. I now begin to see beyond my former daily perceptions, of a closed material world. Gleams and flashes come to me: the close sense of great movement in the world just beyond our own, the sense of His Presence and Intention hovering, focused, above us – almost, I may say, like a cloud. Yes, like a cloud, which gathers slowly and thickens, blotting out the light of the sun with its intention, with the moist deposit for earth that it contains.

*Drop down dew, heavens, from above, and let the clouds rain down righteousness; let the earth be opened, and a Saviour spring to life.*

\*

The time is now. Praise Him, praise Him.

Though we quake and quail and scarce know how to embrace a joy of such piercing and rapturous proportions – the time is now. He has breathed the germs of the end into our air, and none can escape. Throughout the streets of Ashton, people drop where they stand. Travellers' reports show the contagion to be working with a similar effect in cities as far afield as Liverpool and Birmingham. They are calling it the Cholera: they may call it what they will, it is the agency of His plan. It is the rapid end of this sad, sinful, masculine world: it is the cleansing away of the old life, before His glorious new Dawn.

The town is transformed overnight; shops and streets stand empty. All avoid crowds, for they say the contagion there spreads more rapidly. They are so ignorant of God's designs that instead of rejoicing and welcoming the dissolution of the flesh which must precede the liberation of the spirit and the advent of the Second Kingdom, they attempt to hide. But the contagion finds them out; the disease that cures us of this life, it finds them all, it is borne on every wind, it sparkles in the air of every breath we take. Praise God, our atmosphere is so imbued with it there can be no successful avoidance.

As I walked down Old Street this afternoon I saw a man approaching from the opposite direction, walking most unsteadily. While he was yet some distance from me he staggered against the wall, vomiting, leant there for a moment, then slipped to the ground. Advancing to assist him I discovered him to be in the last stages of the disease (which moves with such miraculous rapidity that many are dead within the first day of infection, and some indeed within an hour or two!) I knelt to rejoice with him at the passing of those last dreadful moments of mortal pain, and to remind him to keep his eyes fixed on that Promised Land so soon to open its gates to him. Before I had finished a cart came into view, already heaped with a number of bodies groaning, choking and calling out in whispering tones of the most acute distress – bound for the cholera hospital. The driver and his assistant jumped down and dragged my poor fellow to the cart – one holding him upright while the other removed his watch and a couple of guineas from his pocket, kindly explaining to me that such valuables were often mislaid at the cholera hospital, and he therefore took them into safekeeping.

'Are you going to the hospital now?'

'Where else would we be going with this lot, lady?'

They made no objection to my climbing on to the back of the cart. I am reminded of God's care in every detail, for the cholera hospital – the building where the souls of so many were and are to be released into the New Life – is none other than our Eastern Gatehouse, Samuel Lees' old home. Thus Prophecy begins to be fulfilled.

Within doors lay score upon score of the sick and dying, many (indeed, most of them) oblivious of their own good fortune and coming glory, but maybe sensing dumbly, like animals, their own unworthiness. In cracked and whispering voices they cried perpetually for water:

'I thirst . . .'

'Drink – '

'Give me water!'

'Thirst . . . thirst . . .'

I have no need of Prophet or interpreter to tell me that this all-consuming, terrible thirst with which they burn, is the passionate thirst for the refreshing streams of His forgiving love; that their parched souls cry out for the gentle and cleansing dew of His sweet absolution; that life itself is the fiery fever from which they struggle to escape, into the cool balm of His paradisical New Kingdom. I fetched a jug of water from the pump and took one of the pewter tankards from Samuel Lees' dresser. Where he is gone I do not know, but there was no one in the building to attend to the needs of these poor creatures, whose bodies expelled putrid liquids from every orifice, and whose limbs seem to twitch and dance of themselves, in frenzied and violent attacks. I began to administer water, saying a brief prayer to each as I stopped, to give sorely needed refreshment to their desperate spirits. For is it not written. *God shall wipe away all tears from their eyes; and there shall be no more death, neither sorrow, nor crying, neither shall there be any more pain, for the former things are passed away.* Though the air was foul and the distress of many pitiable, yet I could scarcely suppress a song of joy, so happy was I to see His promised day arrive at last – and in my lifetime!

*

How long I have laboured here, bearing His message of forgiving love to all, I cannot tell. The floors are full; they heap new arrivals at the door, until the men can come to clear away the dead. So many – and so many – truly His ways are mysterious, and wonderful. He has fallen upon His people like the Reaper upon the corn.

My own strength is flagging. Twice now searing pains in my belly have halted my progress. There seems to be – a thickness in the air – an odd glowing softness hanging about the flame of the lamp on the wall. I cannot tell. The ventilation is so poor – the heat in here is so extreme – modesty forbids that I remove any further layers of clothing but I am so drenched with perspiration I cannot –

Dear God. Oh my dear God.

I burn. Lord – Master – I burn with thirst. I cannot – the cup drops from my grasp – I find I must kneel here – beside this poor lifeless woman – I can not move.

Oh Christ. My sweet Lord Jesus have mercy and pity.
I thirst.
Water.
Oh I thirst, my throat is on fire.

I am lying here. My face against her shoulder. Is it me that is coughing? There is a slow bitter liquid trickling from my lips across my cheek. Dear God I bless You. I bless this day, I praise His name. He calls us to the New Kingdom. The end of the world is here.

Oh sweet Lord. The transforming pain. Melt, melt this stubborn body in the crucible of Thy love.

Dear Lord. Its last act of worship – my body dances. Glory glory glory – each limb – Oh God – leaps – to His glory – to His glory – I dance. I come, oh Lord. I come to Thee.

# Historical Note

Readers who are interested in the historical background might like to know more about the real John Wroe. He was born in Bradford, son of a woolcomber, in 1782. He is described by contemporaries as small, dark and hunchbacked. Before he became religious, he married and fathered three children. During an illness in 1819 he had visions which instructed him to join the Jewish faith; while attempting to do this he attended the Bradford Southcottian church led by George Turner, and became a member of this instead. Turner had taken over the northern leadership after the death of Joanna Southcott in 1814. At that time the Southcottians had about 100,000 members, mainly in Joanna's native Devon, in London, and in the northern industrial towns. Joanna (like Wesley) hoped to remain within the fold of the Anglican church, but when she failed to persuade the bishops of the truth of her calling, she determined that the Southcottian church should become a rallying point for all denominations.

Wroe seems to have been responsible for coining the name Christian Israelites, although there were prophets before him (notably William Brothers) who suggested that the lost tribes of Israel were to be found in Britain. The task of the Christian Israelite church was to gather together the scattered tribes of Israel, in readiness for the end of the world, which was imminently expected. Church membership was open to all who agreed to obey Mosaic law and efforts were made to teach Hebrew to all church members, since this would be the common language in Heaven.

Before settling in Ashton, Wroe travelled to Italy, Gibraltar, Spain, France and Austria, in a personal attempt to reconcile the Jewish and Roman Catholic churches. He was accepted as Prophet

by the Ashton congregation in 1822, and it was revealed to him
that Ashton was to be the New Jerusalem. The Sanctuary was built
in 1825, at a cost of £9,500; a sumptuously furnished building with
the star of Judah over the door. It later became the Star Cinema.
Four gatehouses were built, one of which was used in the 1830s as
the Ashton cholera hospital. It is currently in use as a pub.

Church members seem to have been mainly artisans and trades-
people, with a few wealthy millowners and landowners, and a
small proportion of labourers. Their strange clothes and beards,
and their beautiful music, were the main characteristics noticed by
outsiders. Wroe conducted public baptisms in the river Medlock,
and was publicly circumcised. Many of his contemporaries
thought him a complete fraud ('He is the personification of
ignorance and vulgarity . . . a most vile and immoral character,
wholly ignorant of Joanna Southcott's writings and mission' wrote
one W. B. Harrison) while others were convinced he was a
genuine prophet. He made a number of strikingly accurate
prophecies about mechanical inventions and politics – of which
the following is my favourite:
   'Mr Wroe preached to a large congregation in a field . . . and
said *A light shall break forth out of this place where I stand, which shall
enlighten the whole town, with a light also to enlighten the Gentiles*. The
prophecy was fulfilled in a practical manner by the erection of the
Ashton Gasworks in the very field.'

He also predicted a 'grievous plague' in Ashton, to follow his
banishment – and the cholera arrived on cue. His journals and
sermons were published by the Christian Israelite Press, and can
be read in Tameside Local Studies Library.

Wroe asked for seven virgins in 1830 and these were provided by
church members. After he had been on a missionary tour with the
women, two of them charged him with 'indecency and things not
fit to be spoken'. There was a trial, at which he was acquitted, but
this was followed by a riot in Sanctuary, from which Wroe barely
escaped with his life. He returned to Ashton the following Easter
to take away the Israelite printing press on a wagon drawn by four
black horses. Most of his career after this was passed in missionary
tours to America (he had a following in California) and Australia

(where the Christian Israelite church still survives). He died in Melbourne in 1863 on his fourth Australian tour. On his visits back to England he supervised the building of a mansion, Melbourne House, near Wakefield, paid for by his Australian supporters. Wroe's descendants lived in Melbourne House until 1956; since then it has been used as an old people's home.

His successor, Zion Ward, became a crowd-pulling preacher in London, attracting large audiences to the Rotunda, where he declared himself to be the second Christ, and advocated Free Love. He was imprisoned for blasphemy in the 1840s.

Although I have used the outer circumstances of Wroe's life as a framework, I have invented his character. I intend no disrespect either to the memory of the real man, or to his present-day followers.

Of the seven virgins given to Mr Wroe, there is no record at all – which made it possible for me to write about them.

Because I didn't know what material I was looking for until I found it, I have meandered through a lot of books about the early nineteenth century. Any historical errors are my own; for what I have got right, for inspiration and for insight, I owe a particular debt to the following:

E. P. Thompson, *The Making of the English Working Class*

J. F. C. Harrison, *The Second Coming: Popular Millenarianism 1780–1850*, and *Robert Owen and the Owenites in Britain and America*

Barbara Taylor, *Eve and the New Jerusalem; Socialism and Feminism in the Nineteenth Century*

Caroline Davidson, *A Woman's Work is Never Done: A History of Housework in the British Isles 1650–1950*

Helena Whitbread (ed.), *I Know My Own Heart: The Diaries of Anne Lister 1791–1840*

Samuel Bamford, *Passages in the Life of a Radical*

and to Tameside Local Studies Library.

Thanks to the Society of Authors for their grant from the K. Blundell Trust. And thanks to Mike Harris for much useful criticism.

J.R.

# Faber International Fiction

All these books are available at your bookshop or newsagent, or can be ordered direct from the publishers. Just tick the titles you want and fill in the form below or submit a separate order.

**Faber & Faber Limited, Cash Sales Department, PO Box 11, Falmouth, Cornwall TR10 9EN. Fax Number: 0326 77240**

UK customers including B.F.P.O.: please send a cheque or postal order (no currency) and allow £1.00 for postage and packing for the first book plus 50p for the second book plus 30p for each additional book up to a maximum charge of £3.00.
Overseas customers including Eire: please allow £2.00 for postage and packing for the first book, £1.00 for the second book and 50p for each additional book.

NAME (Block Letters) ................................................................................
SIGNATURE ................................................................................................
ADDRESS ....................................................................................................
....................................................................................................................

☐ I enclose my remittance for ..................................................................
☐ I wish to pay by Access/Visa Card –

Number ☐☐☐☐☐☐☐☐☐☐☐☐☐☐☐☐☐☐

Expiry date ................................................